Doubles

By the same author

Fiction
Fatima's Scarf
Dr Orwell and Mr Blair
The Women's Hour
Veronica or the Two Nations
News from Nowhere
The K-Factor
The Occupation
The Decline of the West
Comrade Jacob
At Fever Pitch

Non-Fiction
Isaac and Isaiah. The Covert Punishment of a Cold War Heretic
Marechera and the Colonel
Politics and the Novel During the Cold War
The Dancer Defects. The Struggle for Cultural Supremacy during the Cold War
Joseph Losey. A Revenge on Life
Sixty-Eight. The Year of the Barricades
The Fellow-Travellers. Intellectual Friends of Communism
The Great Fear. The Anti-Communist Purge Under Truman and Eisenhower
Collisions. Essays & Reviews
Cuba, Yes?
The Fellow-Travellers. A Postscript to the Enlightenment
The Illusion. An Essay on Politics, Theatre and the Novel
Frantz Fanon
The Left in Europe since 1789
Essential Writings of Karl Marx
Communism and the French Intellectuals

David Caute

Doubles

a novel

Totterdown Books

Copyright © David Caute 2016

First published in Great Britain in 2016
by Totterdown Books
41 Westcroft Square
London W6 OTA

A CIP catalogue record for this book is available from the British Library.

ISBN 978-0-9530407-3-5

Printed and bound in Great Britain by imprintdigital, Devon, EX5 5HY

Distributed by Central Books, 99 Wallis Road, London E9 5LN
Tel: 0845 458 9911
orders@centralbooks.com

For Ed

Acknowledgements

My gratitude extends in several directions. First, to family and friends whose comments on the novel in draft proved to be acute and fertile: to my wife Martha, my son Edward, and my friends Nicolas Tredell and Nicole Boireau (who brought a rigorous native eye to my French). My thanks to Glenda Pattenden, who copy-edited the typescript, undertook the design, and gave invaluable support throughout the production process. My friend Nikolai Tolstoy pointed the way to the generously granted Russian-language expertise of Maria Gavrilova at the Azbuka Foundation, London.

1

How innocent of cruel reality I was in 1952, when this chronicle begins, exhausting myself at school reading through the night by the light of an illicit torch. And reading what? The forbidden classics of Marxism, as rigorously banned as *Lady Chatterley's Lover* but available dirt-cheap from Collet's bookshop in Charing Cross Road. Stalin's works I devoured if only because he, unlike Marx, Engels and the great Lenin, was still alive, still wisely guiding the socialist sixth of the world to ever-greater social achievements – universal education, universal health-care, universal equality, the atomic bomb and something I did not quite understand, 'abortion in case of urgent medical necessity'. These cheap editions poured from Moscow's Foreign Languages Publishing House, printed in smudged type on coarse paper, entirely captivating.

Over there in Moscow they were about to celebrate Comrade Stalin's seventy-third birthday – his last, as it turned out, his death for me at sixteen a cause of desolation. The Cold War was at that juncture a glacier incapable of movement except for the menacing floe of war in Korea. I did not believe that the subjugated nations of Eastern Europe were by now corralled in chains. Capitalist lies! I did not believe that murderous show-trials in the 'People's Democracies' paraded innocent defendants accused of treachery and treason. They went to the gallows but to me they were not innocent. I did not believe that Stalin presided over an empire of darkness, nor did I believe that no prominent Jew was safe within his vast dominion.

No. All that was the rhetoric of the infamous Churchill's 'Iron Curtain', so fondly echoed by my idiot schoolfellows, the ones who had no better use for illicit torches than *Paris By Night*. In my mind America's countervailing empire of light was in the grip of hysteria, rampant economic expansion and the messianic fever of the 'American Century'. Britain abjectly tagged along, despatching to Korea conscripts of whom I, my chin bleeding from the first shaves, could soon be one.

But I must here begin in Moscow, 1992, forty years after I discarded these illusions. (How and why is none of your business.) A professor from England wearing his habitual tweed jacket – didn't he bring a change of outer garments from London? – and a new pair of spectacles to counter dwindling sight, was to be found in the Pushkin Museum of Fine Art conversing with the Deputy Director. Vasily Mishkin[†] looked younger than his years, fashionably dressed with a lingering hint of the bohemian *stilyagi* and never far from a smoke. Call him an affable bureaucrat, occasionally a source of rare information if he judged he could get away with it.

We were discussing Soviet attitudes to Western art, to modernism, the Soviet era having dramatically toppled into its huge grave. I had no premonition where this conversation was to lead – that is to say back to an extraordinary, hitherto unknown, event of forty years earlier when I was reading the works of Stalin by torchlight.

I put it gently to Mishkin: 'Soviet curators like yourself have no regard for modern American art, is that the case?'

'Soviet?' Mishkin smiled, re-crossed his smart trousers, and blew smoke.

'Yes and no. To tell you the truth, we genuinely find little of value in American painting. Not since Benton perhaps, Ben Shahn perhaps...'

'Is a black square by Malevich intrinsically different from one by Rothko?'

'Well, when it comes down to it, we regard the American "innovators" as mere imitators. And I personally find among our gifted Russian Constructivists of the Kazimir Malevich era no precursors of Lichtenstein's vulgar populism or Warhol's dead

---

† Mishkin is a pseudonym

2

array of soup cans. The essential difference is the disappearance of the human being in contemporary American modernism.'

'But Soviet curators used to bring the same charge against the cubism of Picasso and Braque. Now they're kosher – although the average museum visitor still argues with his wife about where to find the man in Picasso's *Man with a Guitar*.'

Mishkin nodded. 'True.' He smiled. 'And where is the guitar?'

He knew that I was currently working on an essay about Picasso's politics in the 1950s, the era of the peace dove which I had boldly pinned above my bed at school. (It didn't last long.)

'An interesting project, highly contentious of course. Are you interested in Picasso's women?'

'Which one?'

'Did you know that he had an affair with a Soviet woman?'

'In Paris?'

'It started in Paris.'

'She was an artist?'

'No, no. A curator who began her career here at the Pushkin – as it turned out a difficult career which might interest you. A very beautiful woman in her day, I'm told. Is there such a thing as an utterly innocent femme fatale? If so, Olga Lepinskaya was it.'[†]

'How did she form a relationship with Picasso?'

'That I am not at liberty to say.'

'No *glasnost'* today?'

What had brought me to the Pushkin Museum, and to Vasily Mishkin – my sixth visit to Moscow as a professional historian– was not only *glasnost'* but intense curiosity about the dramatic change in official Soviet positions on modernist art during the final years of Communist power. I had no expectation of a discovery as unlikely as the one about to unfold in these pages – a clandestine visit by Picasso and Charles Chaplin to celebrate Stalin's seventy-third birthday. After all, no halfway sane historian sets out to discover why (say) El Greco and Christopher

---

† Lepinskaya is a pseudonym, Olga is not.

Marlowe were summoned to Muscovy in 1583, at the invitation of Ivan the Terrible, to celebrate what was to prove to be that dreaded Tsar's final birthday. Imagine presenting that as the subject for your doctoral thesis! You would have to call in Daumier to record your Supervisor's twisted expression as he enquired after your sources and your sanity. By nightfall you would surely be tucked up in the Warneford, an Oxford hospital crammed with the proposers of adventurous doctoral theses. (I have more than once been admitted to its friendly beds set in a garden landscape after reading insane attacks by charlatans like Professor Abe Kahnleiter on the accuracy and integrity of my published work. But no more about Kahnleiter...yet.)

My interest in the recent acrobatics of Soviet official attitudes to modernist art had first been awakened when visiting the Paris-Moscou exposition held at the controversially designed new Pompidou Centre in 1979. The long-suppressed Soviet avant-garde of the revolutionary era was suddenly – it seemed a miracle – on full display, although the exhibition catalogue essays by Soviet curators (our friend Mishkin included) yielded no hint, not a whisper, that the great artists Tatlin, Chagall, Malevich, Goncharova, Kandinsky, Lissitzky, Rodchenko and Popova had either been forced into exile, or removed from Soviet galleries, or compelled to adapt their gifts to mass production. Something was afoot in Soviet museums, a kind of hesitant Resurrection. But why, how?

I came back to Moscow in pursuit of the veteran curators who had discreetly masterminded Soviet participation in a series of prestigious international exhibitions designed to promote the silenced Russian avant-garde artists locked out of sight for many years in air-conditioned museum vaults. The names and work of the forbidden painters had vanished into the huge black hole of the Soviet universe, but now they were paraded in Western Europe and indeed Moscow as the inspirational pathfinders of artistic innovation previously condemned as 'formalistic', 'abstract', 'anti-human', 'bourgeois', 'decadent'. Focusing always on the vital Russian connection, these collaborative exhibitions had extended their embrace from pre-1914 Paris to Weimar Germany and pre-fascist Vienna – although post-1945 American art remained off-limits. Pollock, de Kooning, Rothko, Warhol, Lichtenstein, the innovators so admired by the Russian dissidents of the Brezhnev era, the Moscow artists whose street exhibitions were smashed by municipal bulldozers – they remained beyond the pale. The gradual Soviet retreat from this cultural apartheid interested me, likewise the post-Stalin Soviet cultural strategy of wooing 'Old Europe' away from the USA.

Seated opposite the affable Mishkin in the Pushkin Museum, I repeated my taunt. 'No *glasnost'* today?' Who was Olga Lepinskaya?

He sighed, lightly dusting ash from the lapels of an elegant suit which might have been bought off the peg in Carnaby Street during the Beatles era – except that Mishkin's waistline had filled out as an ascending member of the nomenklatura. He wanted to be helpful, to be 'post-Soviet'.

'Strictly between ourselves, Lepinskaya was Picasso's close companion while he was in Moscow.'

A hesitant patina of April snow was struggling to disbelieve in the dawning spring on the imposing windows of the famous Pushkin Museum. Studying Mishkin's barely suppressed smile, I had cause again to wonder whether Russian curators were now driven to invent fairy stories by their resentment of the unseemly influx of Western scholars and journalists scrambling for open archives while waving wads of dollars.

'Vasily, you know perfectly well that Picasso never visited the Soviet Union.'

'No? If you tell me so, professor. I have probably said too much. We under this roof all still live in the shadow of history and here in Russia there are always two histories, sometimes several. Olga Lepinskaya is the most hidden of histories – perhaps the most dangerous kind.'

'Then I should meet her.'

He lit another cigarette from a packet of filter-tipped Pall Mall then relented a little. We had known each other, on and off, for many years.

'Of course you should meet her. But they say she is notoriously difficult to reach, an ageing recluse fiercely jealous of her privacy – and her secret. I'm told she regards Westerners as parasites.'

'How do I find her?'

He opened his hands in a display of innocence. 'Even I do not have her address.'

'Who does?'

'Why not enquire of our mutual friend Svetlana Tairova? But please do not mention that I suggested it. I like my job.'

~

So Picasso had an affair with a Soviet woman, a curator at the Pushkin Museum? A tall story, would you agree? About the geo-politics of the mid-century there was an abundance of available evidence – except for the sealed Soviet archives. We were already in the age of the mass media – indeed the historian was confronted by a surfeit of information. We may revere the paintings of the seventeenth-century artist Johannes Vermeer, but the basic facts of his life are shrouded in the smoke of burnt-out attics and the waters of flooded cellars: how many paintings did he finish and what happened to them? Who was the girl with a pearl earring – was she Vermeer's housemaid, his mistress, perhaps both? We can only speculate; but when we jump forward to the twentieth century we find that the identity of pretty well every female figure rendered by Pablo Picasso is known to us, likewise the where and when. Even his numerous whimsical sketches, the work of five minutes on a table napkin, are now catalogued by museum curators and art dealers informed by electronic scanners that circle the globe meticulously ensuring that knowledge is money.

So we can be sure that we know everything about Picasso's women worth knowing. But would you care to gamble on that? These pages will reveal how I discovered one major event in the life of Picasso which has hitherto eluded the biographers and historians. It was an intensely political chapter not a casual affair with a new mistress by the seaside at Golfe-Juan. (That this concealed episode did in fact carry a sexual dimension should not surprise any student of the Minotaur's rampant libido.) We shall presently understand why and how knowledge of this happening has been suppressed to the present day – and why this clandestine event also embraced another figure of world renown, Charlie Chaplin, perhaps even better known to millions of devotees than Picasso.

I lost no time in contacting Svetlana Tairova, while not mentioning Mishkin. Svetlana after all was my best friend (I perhaps too rapidly assumed) among Moscow's senior art curators. Now retired, she had once worked at the Pushkin Museum and was what might be described as a 'character' – bohemian, extrovert, outspoken, joyfully indiscreet, a jewel with an uncomfortably prominent nose. She was as ugly as Lotte Lenya and no less attractive, or would once have been. Yet she too was well versed in boundaries of discretion, of survival.

'Tell me, Svetlana, do you happen to know someone by the name of Olga Lepinskaya?'

Svetlana chain-smoked *papirosi*. 'Does Vasily Mishkin say I know her?' (She got it in one.)

'He did mention your name.'

'John, beware, you are entering a minefield. Frankly, I think you should speak to Dominika Nikolaevna.[†] She's the boss among us. None of us can open the wrong side of our mouths without her say-so.'

I knew the name: Nikolaevna was the veteran curator of avant-garde art at the Tretyakov Museum and by reputation hostile to Westerners.

'But last week you described her to me as a neo-Stalinist.'

Svetlana slapped her wrist, sending bracelets jangling. 'A slip of

---

† Tairova and Nikolaevna are pseudonyms

the tongue. Nikolaevna is the eye of the needle which might, just conceivably, lead you to Olga Lepinskaya.'

Svetlana then warned me not to mention her name when and if Nikolaevna agreed to see me (she might not).

Nikolaevna did indeed refuse to receive me, that is to say her secretary told me fairly curtly that she was 'in a meeting' and in any case did not have time to hobnob with unknown strangers. I left my card along with my extension number at the Hotel Rossiya. To my surprise I received a friendly telephone call from Nikolaevna herself the next morning. Yes of course she would be delighted to give me half an hour. Did I perhaps wish to discuss evolving Soviet attitudes to modernist art? (she said 'Soviet', couldn't help herself). I did? Excellent! Decades of misunderstanding and 'Berlin Walls' needed to be dismantled.

I took the metro to the Tretyakov and was warmly received with vodka as well as tea along with the inevitable cigarettes. (I don't smoke.) I found this high-coiffeured lady to be elegant, charming and, on crucial points of art history, subtly evasive. I began counting the lies but, of course, said nothing. But when I brought the conversation round to Picasso's reputation in the Soviet Union, Madame Nikolaevna lifted her finely tended eyebrows and refilled my glass:

'There is more to that story than you can possibly know.'

But surely it was accepted that Picasso had never visited Russia?

Nikolaevna nodded, studying me intently. 'Well accepted,' she affirmed.

Picasso was half-expected in Moscow (I went on) when he was granted an exhibition in 1956 but 'events in Hungary' (I chose my words) had intervened.

Nikolaevna came down on this like a guillotine. 'It was nothing to do "events in Hungary".'

I waited while she twisted a magnificent ring from ancient Rus on the third finger of her left hand. (She was known to be married to a dissident theatre director only now emerging from disgrace.)

My dilemma was obvious – I had no choice but to toss, come what may, the name of Olga Lepinskaya on her desk. Nikolaevna froze.

'I regret that I do not have an address for Madame Lepinskaya since she went into retirement. No one is granted access to her.'

At this juncture Nikolaevna took a telephone call, swivelling her chair away from me towards a high window – the snow had given up – as she spoke and, mainly, listened. The call concluded.

'My apologies, Professor. Well, I think we can help you. Forgive me, but we have been uncertain about your...orientation, your background. A colleague informs me that you have worked for the *New Statesman* in London. We don't entirely approve of the *New Statesman* of course but (she smiled) what do we entirely approve of in your domain? I gather you have a reliable body of published work. Our French friends think well of you.'

I said I wouldn't particularly want to be 'reliable'.

Nikolaevna accorded me a further scrutiny. 'It was Svetlana Tairova who just called me. Svetlana is a close friend of Lepinskaya's, it goes back I don't know how many years. She can give you the number to call. She now has my permission. Everything is permitted here in Moscow except what is not permitted. But take my advice, Monsieur, and proceed circumspectly. If Madame Lepinskaya consents to receive you, you will have to draw upon all your resources of tact and understanding.'

Rising from her chair to terminate the interview, Nikolaevna looked me over again, no doubt in search of such qualities.

Later that day I took the metro to Svetlana's apartment. Greeted warmly, as usual, I protested that she had sworn me not to mention her name to Nikolaevna!

'One can never be too careful if Russia is one's mother, John. I must warn you that Olga never gives interviews. She will say no.' Another *papirosa* smouldered.

'How old is this lady?'

'Well, perhaps touching seventy, almost my age. You would never guess. History and personal affliction have eaten into her soul but her face still lays claim to the 1950s when she resembled a Madonna by Raphael.'

Svetlana emitted a curious grimace. 'Or so they have told Olga. She is vain enough to believe them.'

The tone of this remark surprised me. Svetlana then explained that Olga Lepinskaya had once been a young curator at the Pushkin Museum before the time of the great Director, Irina Antonova.

'Some believe that Antonova would not have hired Olga.'

Why? No reply. I found these little cuts odd, but I was failing to see what I was hearing. Many months were to pass before I did.

'Who was Madame Lepinskaya's Director at that time, then?'

'I can barely mention his name, but if I must, the ineffable Vladimir Kemenev.'

'I'm familiar with his attacks on Picasso and modernism.'

She laughed from a rasping chest like a diesel-driven tractor. 'But you survived the experience.'

One could imagine Svetlana at home among the bohemia of the Weimar Republic, rubbing shoulders with Kathë Kollwitz and George Grosz; indeed, as she had told me, her Jewish mother had fled from the Nazis, survived internment in a French camp, and ended up marrying a Soviet prisoner of war. Svetlana was proud to be only half-Russian because, as she put it, 'Those of pure blood do the devil's work in every country.' Her Moscow flat was covered in artefacts from every corner of the globe. Now, downing her third whisky and over the frontier, she was visited by a false smile:

'Olga will undoubtedly try out her charms on you. I don't believe she can yet boast of an English conquest.'

Her husband Mitya chuckled: 'There's always a first time.' Mitya was the Soviet 'prisoner of war', a stout figure invariably at her side, usually a silent but amused observer, habitually slumped alongside his belly in an armchair all his own, steadily smoking Camels (one could barely see across their sitting room).

Mitya was a retired architect who had been, he confided, the designer of 'the ugliest apartment blocks in Kiev'.

'Quite an achievement I can tell you. I wanted to bring something of Gropius and Le Corbusier to the job but the city planners showed me the budget and told me to forget it. I forgot it. I'm still here.'

Mitya was always there, my arrival evidently an entertainment. According to Svetlana, he had once been an 'unregenerate cosmopolitan' (a crime in Stalin's time), and Mitya nodded, happy with the description. 'Just another Jew,' he added. Sometimes their son Yuri looked in, he also an architect, fluent in English like Mitya, and by repute rather more successful. The reader will discover the part played by Svetlana, Mitya and Yuri in the story about to unfold.

As I took my leave Svetlana scribbled a telephone number and address on the back of a cigarette packet – an address in a Moscow suburb I shall never forget.

'Wait until I have spoken to Olga. She's not good at surprises. And brush up your French because frankly, John, when you speak Russian you sound like an Oxford quad.'

'A what?'

Mitya guffawed from his armchair. 'Walking on the grass forbidden.' He and Svetlana had undertaken an architectural tour of England the previous summer, he being rebuked by an Oxford college porter for straying on to the sacrosanct grass while taking photographs in All Souls' north quadrangle.

'Arrested by Hawksmoor!' Mitya bellowed as I took my leave. I had heard it before.

By evening, Svetlana had left a message at the Rossiya to call her back. Madame Lepinskaya would receive me at 10 a.m. the following morning. I was not to arrive a minute late or a minute early. 'Moscow time,' Svetlana added sardonically.

2

Our story begins on a Monday in September 1952. A few minutes before 9 a.m. Olga Maksimovna Lepinskaya emerges from the Kropotkinskaya metro station and walks swiftly up Volkhonka. She is 1.68 metres tall, say 5ft 6ins, well above the average of 1.60 metres for Russian women born like her in 1924 – and we shall see in due course why her height becomes vitally important for reasons she could never have anticipated. She wears a silk scarf over blonde hair and Italian crocodile shoes, heels not too high, not too obviously foreign. As she passes the old woman selling *Pravda* and *Literaturnaya gazeta* she recalls her favourite comedian, Arkady Raikin: 'If you want today's news, come back tomorrow.' Invariably a few turning male heads mark her swift trajectory through the morning crowd, though such displays of interest are frowned on by Moscow's solid phalanxes of dour middle-aged widows, short, square women who like to block pavements by linking arms. Carrying a large leather portfolio of the sort that accommodates prints and artworks unfolded, a gift from 'Uncle' Ilya Ehrenburg, Olga mounts the broad steps of her place of work, passing between the classical statues guarding the inner staircase of the *Gosudarstvennyi muzei izobrazitel'nykh iskusstv imeni A.S. Pushkina* – the Pushkin State Museum of Fine Arts. Reaching the cloakroom – no top clothes are permitted in the office – she shakes out her golden hair then walks briskly to the curators' open-plan office and her own desk. She is twenty-eight years old, in the prime of her beauty although shy with men and still a virgin, still unaware that this is to be for her a fateful day which will govern the rest of her life – no turning back. On Olga Lepinskaya's desk, top of the pile, is a message from her Director, Vladimir Kemenev. It is a summons, urgent, come without delay Olga Maksimovna.

Olga shares an office in the museum basement with a dozen

highly trained art experts, but few as young as she. Her friend Pyotr Davidov's[†] chair remains empty as usual. She knows how eagerly he uses first light to paint in his attic studio in Cheremushki, as the autumn days shorten, just as she knows how her colleagues keenly observe, out of veiled eyes, her frankly dangerous relationship with this delinquent of the Pushkin's staff – ill-considered if not downright dangerous for a candidate Party member with brilliant prospects. A few have tried to warn her that Pyotr's attitude towards Director Kemenev barely falls short of open disrespect. Take for example the short lecture Pyotr was recently allowed to deliver to selected curators on Van Gogh, Munch and the German expressionists. Pyotr had turned up, long haired and wearing jeans beneath a three-toned shirt worthy of the new breed of street-corner *stilyagi*. He then strode back and forth, talking fearlessly about revising the entire Soviet canon on modernism. Director Kemenev sat rigid in the back row.

'Our problem in the Soviet galleries,' Curator Davidov announced, 'is that we display only what we approve of, and are obliged to approve of what we display. When the director of London's Victoria and Albert Museum unpacked crates sent from France after the war, he found works Picasso and Matisse he loathed – but he nevertheless included those paintings in his exhibition.[‡] Was he wrong to do so? We of course condemn such eclecticism as "bourgeois lack of principle". But we are wrong to do so and I will now demonstrate why –'

But here Pyotr Davidov was cut short. The curators sat frozen while Director Kemenev stalked from the room. Without exchanging words or even glances, they then meekly filed out and back to their desks. Olga remained behind while Pyotr stood rigid at the lectern, a St Sebastian shot by an arrow.

'They are performing Gorky's *Mother* at the Mali this evening,'

[†] Davidov is a pseudonym
[‡] Leigh Ashton's disparaging comments about three or four Picassos are found in a memorandum, 30 November 1945, to 'the Minister' (unnamed). See Victoria & Albert Theatre Museum, RP/1945/576, `1945-6, VX, 1945.003.

she smiled up at him. 'Want to join me?'

Olga and Pyotr are habitually to be found sharing a table in the canteen. At the close of work calculating eyes observe them vanishing together into the Kropotkinskaya metro. Of course this is reported – probably half the curators are informers for the MVD – to refuse is to become a suspect. The curators daily expect Davidov to be wiped from the official list of Pushkin staff like a speck of dirt from a clean windscreen – but Director Kemenev is a cautious man. Can he have caught wind of some unimaginable change in the Party line?

Olga promptly answers his summons, her Italian heels clicking on the Italian marble slabs, the heels being another gift from old 'Uncle' Ilya Ehrenburg, a distant relative of her mother and recently returned from his latest privileged trip abroad, a *kulturkampf* against American cultural penetration in Italy – one glorious dinner after another (Olga gathers) as the guest of Visconti, Rossellini, de Sica, Rossi, Moravia, not forgetting the big-breasted heroines of the Po Valley rice fields, film stars like Anna Magnani and Silvana Mangano, ladies who don't object to a distinguished Soviet writer's straying paw. Olga thinks perhaps they do.

Unlike Ehrenburg, Comrade Director Kemenev travels very little, doesn't want to. His large desk is neat and tidy, an antique said to have once belonged to Catherine the Great's chief minister, Potemkin, he who erected entire film-set villages so that the Empress could take comfort in the prosperity of her subjects during her *tours d'horizon*. The Director's desk now displays little beyond the routine statuettes of Lenin and Stalin. Since the lean Kemenev is standing erect in his invariable double-breasted suit, Olga is not invited to sit. He shoots his cuffs.

'I have news for you, Comrade Olga Maksimovna.'

Olga listens, first baffled, then alarmed by the news that Kemenev and Ehrenburg have decided that she must travel to France without delay. Her mission has been authorised 'at the highest level'. The urgent aim is to bring Pablo Picasso to Moscow 'at the earliest opportunity'. Such is the Director's total submission to bureaucratic formulas that any of his staff, his subordinates, find it hard to credit that he is also an art historian and critic of some distinction who occasionally strays, the vodka bottle close to hand, into originality.

Only once has Olga travelled beyond the borders of the Soviet Union, a privileged study tour of the Louvre under the alert eye of an MVD minder. When the minder suddenly took off with a tart in the Tuileries Gardens, Olga broke away from her group and rapidly headed for the forbidden collection of contemporary art in the Jeu de Paume, the highlight of her visit – but omitted from her report to Kemenev. Yet she was expected to catalogue the banned works of Picasso, Matisse and the expressionists held in the Pushkin's cellars, to monitor their condition and elucidate their provenance, technique, style and influence. What official idiocy would not allow her was the subversive experience of viewing similar pictures put on open display to the public by a bourgeois regime. After her return from France she was de-briefed three times by the security organs, their best question being 'Did you at any time succumb to the false charms of decadent bourgeois formalism?' She said yes but 'our lofty Soviet ideology and the guidance of our Party were ever in my thoughts and prevailed.'

Her interrogator winked: 'You mean you had a good time in Paris. So did I.'

Allowing himself a further drip of vodka, Kemenev now embarks on a not uncharacteristic retreat about sending her to France 'without delay'. If the Pushkin Museum is to greet *le grand* Maître Picasso with an exhibition of his early work hitherto kept in cellars and not publicly listed – well, Comrade Curator Lepinskaya's contribution will be indispensable since she is the Museum's expert in modern French art.

'So obviously you cannot go – yet.'

Her hands clutch at errant strands of her long hair. 'I do not think I am fitted for this task, Comrade Director.'

'Now come, Olga Maksimovna. You do your Soviet duty as the Party commands. You were a Young Pioneer, yes? Later a Komsomol, am I right? And now a candidate member of the Party – chosen from a field of two hundred – and our acknowledged expert on the work of Pablo Picasso.'

'Oh, Comrade Director, I am out of my depth. Surely you yourself should carry the invitation to Paris...someone of your seniority and eminence....'

Kemenev chuckles, a rare moment of mirth observed dourly by Gerasimov's twin plaster statuettes of Lenin and Stalin.

'Olga Maksimovna, that man Picasso hates me, and with good reason. I have always regarded his output as the epitome of anti-human bourgeois decadence. I have published several prominent articles to the detriment of Picasso. And further' – he pauses. 'And further, whatever mirror you and I choose to look in, which is of us is more likely to overcome the old man's legendary fear of flying?'

'Flying you say?'

'To Moscow.'

'Comrade Director, I too have been implicated in preparing your negative appraisals of Picasso – may I say your diatribes. He knows we have kept his early work from the Soviet public. His temper is legendary. He would toss me into the bull ring at Arles.'

'Yes, Olga Maksimovna, if you're lucky. But this is a vain old man anxious to please his comrades in the French Party. They in turn believe that a Picasso retrospective held in Moscow could reduce American cultural penetration of France by fifty per cent. Your "Uncle Ilya" agrees. It is through Ehrenburg that we have received a green light from Casanova, Aragon, Triolet and other French comrades close to Picasso. It can be done – if we want it to be done.'

'Do I gather that you yourself are in favour of this démarche, Comrade Director?'

'That's no longer an issue. A decision has been made' – Kemenev gestures up at the sedately rioting nymphs adorning the ceiling. 'Picasso can be brought to Moscow if we offer him a full-scale public exhibition of our holdings, pre-1914.'

'Then why send me to France?'

'You will take with you a lavish portfolio of what we can display of his early work. You are the curator who knows the collection better than anyone. You speak excellent French and some Spanish – Comrade Picasso can lapse into Catalan when the mood takes him. If he discovers some pleasure in your company, that will do no harm. Comrade Elsa Triolet will be your chaperone.'

'May I think about this?'

'Of course. Talk to your mother and give me your answer tomorrow. As you know, you and she are able to share an apartment in Moscow only because of your loyal work for our Museum. Don't forget that you carry an eternal stigma – your father was arrested as an enemy of the people.'

'My father was never an enemy of the people. He gave his whole life, as a scientist, to the Soviet cause. Will that be all for today, Comrade Director?'

'Olga, let me repeat this: I have been instructed "on highest authority" to send you – you personally – to France to hook Big Poisson Pablo Picasso.'

'"Hook"?'

'You leave for Paris as soon as the required documents and visa come through from our Foreign Ministry and the French Embassy. Meanwhile, you and I have work to do.'

∼

Only one month had elapsed since the staging of the Nineteenth Congress of the Communist Party, 5 to 14 October 1952. This was the first Party Congress convened since the war, in itself a commentary on Stalin's escalating autocracy. It was at this gathering that Stalin made his last public speech. He also requested to be relieved of his duties in the Party secretariat because of his age, but the delegates, horribly aware how deviously the scorpion's mind worked, sweatingly declined to find him anything other than what he had been for twenty-five years – indispensable. On their feet, their clapping could not be stopped, none dared to be the first.

Stalin continued to launch brutal attacks on Western policies while calling for peace and detente through the Moscow-sponsored Stockholm Peace Movement. Ilya Ehrenburg had drafted the 1950 Appeal, Picasso was among the signatories. Having authorised North Korea's military attack on the South, Moscow led the world in alleging American use of germ warfare and in promoting Pablo Picasso's celebrated Dove of Peace, an olive branch tenaciously held by the beak. But Picasso was only one of many celebrated Western fellow-travellers – writers, philosophers, painters, actors, scientists, historians – cultivated by Moscow. Clearly it would have been a symbolic victory if Picasso and Chaplin had travelled to Moscow to join in the celebrations preceding Stalin's seventy-third birthday on 21 December 1952 – but no record of any such visitation was to appear in the Soviet or foreign press throughout the remaining half-century. Why?

∽

As a junior curator specialising in the Pushkin Museum's suppressed collection, 'The Paris School, 1870-1950', Olga Lepinskaya has been in daily communion with masterpieces never shown to the public since the Revolution. She rarely fails to steal a few moments with Picasso's early works – the so-called blue and pink periods. She and Pyotr Davidov agree that fifty years ago Pablo Picasso was painting real human beings with genuine tenderness. Here one finds a little acrobat girl balancing on a ball, performing shyly before the muscular hulk of an inert figure – the older brother? – who is seated on a flat block of stone, with fields and gentle hills in the background, a grazing horse, a small peasant family in the distance, mother and children. Utterly beguiling, but then –

'But then what happened, Pyotr? Such tenderness can scarcely be compared with the aggressive ugliness of what followed, the hideous *Demoiselles d'Avignon*, prostitutes rendered inhuman by the artist's sudden invention of cubist surgery, crudely imported African masks – and, frankly, dismemberment.'

Pyotr shrugs: 'Even close friends like Braque and Derain walked away from that canvas, shocked, appalled. No wonder the nations slaughtered themselves soon after Picasso produced *Les Demoiselles d'Avignon*. But I like it – a masterpiece.'

'For me, Picasso embodies the male violence of his native Spain. And he harbours a rather infantile desire to be both the bull and the matador.'

Olga has one night to convey her decision to Kemenev. Pyotr is waiting for her at the entrance to the Kropotkinskaya metro. He takes her arm tenderly.

'Something has happened, Ochka, I can tell. You look shattered.'

She avoids discussing Kemenev's proposal in the metro. They take the Sokolnicheskaya line, alighting at Okhotny Ryad, then walk up to the cobbles of Red Square, paradoxically one of the safest places (she wrongly believes) in the city. As she discloses her dilemma she can feel his arm stiffen.

'You can't agree to it, Ochka! Say no.'

'I thought you of all people might welcome a reversal of State policy,' she says without conviction.

'If it were genuine. This is a charade, a public relations stunt. Kemenev and his bosses are utterly cynical. Once they get Picasso on Soviet soil they'll put his paintings up on the wall, show them to our apparatchiks, the nomenklatura – and somehow never get round to admitting the Soviet public.'

'You are always so sure about everything, Pyotr. I bet you instructed your mother which breast to feed you.'

'But she always knew I was right. Did Van Gogh ever approach a canvas in a state of uncertainty? Did Dostoyevsky lack an ego? No, my Ochka is not to be sent like a prostitute to seduce Picasso.'

She trembles with indignation, the more so that Pyotr echoes her own thoughts.

'I must go home and talk to Mama. If I say no to Kemenev we could lose our tiny accommodation. He hinted as much.'

'He's bluffing. He bluffs in the bath. That swine needs you.'

Opposite the history museum they turn round and walk back towards St Basil's Cathedral, falling silent whenever strangers drift too close. The MVD are inexorable presences in their lives – what did he say to you, what did she say about him?

'Listen, my Ochka, tell Kemenev I'll go to France in place of you.'

'You! They would never let you out of the USSR. The moment your feet touched French soil you would demand political asylum.'

He is angry now. 'Then go! You have the click-click high heels to turn heads and make men dream of where your legs may come together. Kemenev is sending you to pleasure the great Picasso, a notorious lecher. And you know it, Ochka.'

Now she is crying. 'Pyotr, my good father was executed as an "enemy of the people". Only Uncle Ilya Ehrenburg's support keeps me in my job.'

'And the noble "Uncle Ilya" is prepared to lift his paw from your thigh long enough to despatch you into Picasso's paw like a bunch of carnations.'

'You are utterly beastly, Pyotr. You grant me no honour.'

'But I do. That, my Ochka, is what it's all about – your honour.'

～

Olga and her mother occupy two rooms in a communal apartment. These 'rooms' are in reality just spaces divided by improvised cardboard walls as soundproof as a migrant birds' nesting ground. Good, carefully chosen furnishing and hanging fabrics from the Brussels school, all lent to them by Ehrenburg, partly make up for the lack of space and privacy, the communal lavatory with its morning queue of tenants not on speaking terms, the mean resentments and petty thefts of cooking oil and sugar by neighbours who can smell 'old gentry' in the Lepinskaya women. Ekaterina is now fifty but could be mistaken, at a passing glance, for sixty-five, the skin beneath her eyes creased by suffering and nicotine. Her treasured author, never on open display in the apartment, is Franz Kafka. Her inner commitments and true moral universe belong to the past, the time when regular visitors to her parents' house in Leningrad included the poets Blok and Mayakovsky, the maverick Gorky and the painter Repin. Ekaterina had lost her job as an editor in the Children's Literary section (Detizdat) of the State Publishing House after it was shut down during one of the Leningrad purges. A new wave of repression hit the city after the assassination of Kirov but the terror of terrors did not strike until 1937-38. Only then did they take away Ekaterina's husband, Olga's father, the physicist Maksim P. Lepinsky. In no sense a political man and never a Party member, he was arrested in August 1937 without charge or explanation. Olga heard from her mother how she, then thirteen, did not fully wake up when her father took her in his arms and hugged her for the last time. Then he went down the stairs stepping lightly and quickly between the soldiers and turning around as he went and smiling so that his wife and daughter should not be afraid.

Ekaterina Petrovna Lepinskaya had embarked on her long and futile vigil, joining the all-night queues of desperate women throughout an icy winter, snaking round the Winter Palace beside the frozen Neva. On Shpalernaya Street you found a little wooden window. When the shutter opened you must immediately shout the name of the arrested man: 'Lepinsky, Maksim Petrovich!' She held out some money. From somewhere above her a deep voice boomed, 'Gone!' and a man whose face was too high for the visitor to see used his elbow and stomach to thrust her hand with the money away. She went to the Prosecutor's Office at Liteyny Prospekt. There you could spend freezing nights on the steps, swaddled in six layers of clothing, finally to be told that to find out what decision had been made in the case of Lepinsky, Maksim Petrovich, you must take a train to Moscow.

'Report to the Military Prosecutor's Office.'

Ekaterina took the overnight Red Arrow, bitten by fleas in the baggage-and-mail wagon. On arrival she was of course kept waiting in another long queue. Finally she was granted ten seconds of their time:

'Lepinsky, Maksim Petrovich? Ten years without right of correspondence and confiscation of property.'

It was a standard formula. Ekaterina knew what such a sentence might mean for herself as the wife – arrest and exile – but she did not yet comprehend what 'ten years without right of correspondence' really signified – death. She remained unaware for years that leading Soviet scientists had bravely joined efforts to secure Lepinsky's release – among them S.I. Vavilov, A.F. Ioffe, and I.E. Tamm. None had dared write to tell her.

Now, in the time of the Cold War, Ekaterina lives for and through her beautiful, clever, loyal daughter.

'Mama, should I go to France? If I don't we may be thrown into the street.'

Ekaterina lies down on her cot, turns her lined face to the wall, to the Brussels tapestry, and closes her eyes. 'You must follow your conscience, Ochka darling. Kafka saw it coming. He foresaw everything.'

≈

Tuesday, 9 a.m. Not so many male heads are turned today by Olga's passage from the Kropotkinskaya metro station to the Pushkin. Something huddled and anxious has invaded her 168 centimetres; she has retreated into drab flat heels, the kind of shoes, so Arkady Raikin's famous joke goes, whose soles get worn out while queuing to buy them.

By 9.15 Olga has delivered her answer to the Director. Kemenev offers her a wintry smile and a thimble of vodka.

'Too early for me, Comrade Director.'

'I'm glad about your decision. I expect your mother gave you wise counsel. Ehrenburg will be delighted. The Party will take note of your fidelity.'

She thinks: and what happens if the whole Picasso project is suddenly reversed – like the projected Delacroix exhibition. By eleven she is calmly inducting the staff of the West European Section as Picasso's early paintings are brought up from the vaults for expert appraisal, cleaning and, where necessary, reframing on stretchers. Kemenev has plans to bring in art students as tour guides for the magnificent Picasso Exhibition. They too must be inducted, trained how to answer questions from the public. You can never be too careful with the public, Kemenev warns.

Before lunch she finds herself summoned back to Kemenev's office. A half-empty bottle sits on his desk. He is staring into space, his pale, gaunt features filmed in sweat, his narrow Slavic eyes half closed. As usual she is not invited to sit.

'Gerasimov was on the phone. He is against the whole project. He reminded me that scientific socialism is not an acrobat – it doesn't stand on its head.'

She waits. Aleksandr Mikhailovich Gerasimov is the President of the USSR Academy of Arts. He has painted or sculpted Stalin too often to count.

'Since then I have spoken to Ehrenburg who has spoken to Gerasimov who has spoken to Malenkov.'

She waits. Malenkov is widely regarded as Stalin's successor.

'I had a call from Fadeyev. He said he had spoken to Aragon in Paris.'

She waits. Aleksandr Fadeyev is Secretary of the Writers' Union.

'Comrade Beria came on the line. Of course it wasn't Beria himself – his secretary. He said he'd heard we were equivocating and vacillating – he even mentioned sabotage.'

Olga is gazing at her shoes. After Stalin, Beria is the most powerful man in Russia, presiding over the vast empire of the Ministry of the Interior, the MVD.

'Are you listening, Olga Maksimovna?'

'I am listening, Comrade Director.'

'Ehrenburg rang to inform me that the English comedian

Chaplin has also been invited to accompany Picasso to congratulate Comrade Stalin on his 73rd birthday.'

'I see.'

'What do you see?'

'I see that you have drunk half a bottle of vodka in the course of the morning, Comrade Director.'

'Actually a bottle and a half. There is nothing in *Das Kapital* to forbid it. Don't feign innocence, Olga Maksimovna. Given your widespread contacts among the so-called "liberal intelligentsia", you must know what is going on.'

A faint lifting movement of Olga's shoulders in their lambswool cardigan is all he gets. She is familiar with Kemenev as prosecutor, she can feel his paranoia rising.

'Has it occurred to you that your "distant relative", Ilya Ehrenburg, whose private collection of modernist art may rival our own, is a Jew?'

'Yes, Ilya Grigorevich is a Jew.'

'Then you, too.'

'Actually, not – I don't have a family tree to hand.'

'Ehrenburg is the kind of trout who surfaces only when the flies lie thick upon the water. Why did he propose you for this mission to France?'

'I think you yourself explained my suitability yesterday. I'd be delighted if you changed your mind.'

'There are others operating within the liberal ring.' (He utters 'liberal' like 'libertine'.) 'You must know young Yuri Lyubimov, director of the Vachtangov theatre?'

'I have enjoyed his productions, I remember Gorky's *Philistines* and Miller's *All My Sons* – but I don't know him personally.'

'They say Lyubimov is to produce Bertolt Brecht's dangerous play *Galileo* at the Vachtangov...well, perhaps next year. They may bring Brecht and his wife Weigel to Moscow – on instructions from Dymschits.'

'Who is that?

'He runs our cultural commissariat in Soviet Berlin. Another

Jew. Probably a Cosmopolitan conspirator playing Ehrenburg's game.'

'This is all beyond me.'

'I am not so sure about that, Olga Maksimovna. You must have contacts within Sergei Eisenstein's circle, the famous "liberals" conspiring to bring Chaplin here.'

'I thought Eisenstein was dead. I read his obituary three or four years ago.'

'He was. He is and he isn't. The dead awaken.'

'I have no flair for riddles, Comrade Director, and I have no such contacts.'

'I am advised that you have a friend called Nina Bolsharova who works for Mosfilm and who believes – according to my reliable sources – that the Soviet public should have been shown Part II of Eisenstein's film *Ivan Grozny*.'

'I have met her once or twice. She is not a friend. I didn't take to her.'

'Did she not confide to you that she is being sent to London to bring Chaplin to Moscow just as you... Need I continue?'

'I know nothing about that.'

'Olga, let us sleep on this. Say nothing to anyone. You are not to make contact with your friend the *stilyagi* Davidov. You and he were observed conversing in Red Square last night. He is an agent of the Americans, of Uoll Strit† – objectively speaking. That connection must discontinue. Understood?'

She does not deign to answer – and is not sure what her answer would be.

---

† Wall Street

3

~

A ll this I was to discover forty years later when I set out for
my first meeting with the elusive Madame Lepinskaya, a
lady now sixty-eight years old.

A strict instruction not to arrive late or early at an address you
know only from the street map means, must in Moscow mean,
setting out early then cooling your heels round the corner while
your nerves played up. Fortunately the weather could have been
worse. So on a frosted Friday I found myself approaching a large
apartment block at ul. Sivashskaya 12, kv. 10, Moscow 113149.[†]
One must head south, alighting from the metro at Nakhimovskii
Prospekt, a station of the Serpukhovsko-Timiryazevskaya line –
'Look out for Nagornaya, the previous stop,' Svetlana had
warned. The journey took half an hour from the Rossiya.
Following negotiations with an elderly female concierge doubtless
retired from the KGB but not lacking new masters,[‡] I was finally
permitted to press the doorbell of number 12. Eventually an
elderly woman's uncertain voice came through the black hole of
a decrepit intercom. As advised by Svetlana, I spoke my first words
of self-introduction in French. At the top of the bleak, heavily
stained stairs I had to wait again while scrutinized through (I
assumed) a spy-hole: what she saw was a middle-aged academic
in spectacles, greying hair cut shorter than usual, wearing a quiet
tie and carrying a briefcase.

Now the door had opened just four or five inches, on a chain.

'Dobryi den, bonjour, Madame Lepinskaya. I hope you were
expecting me.'

She released the chain, the door opened – yes! I was gazing at

---

[†] The street number and apartment (kv.) number have of course been altered.
[‡] In post-Communist Russia, KGB functions are performed by the Foreign
Intelligence Service (SVR), the Federal Security Service (FSB), and the Federal
Protective Service (FSO).

a face worthy in its youth of a Madonna by Raphael.

'You are the Englishman,' she said, not quite stepping back to let me in. 'How do you pronounce your name? It looks to me French.'

'My grandfather was from Charente.'

'I have never been there,' she said, leading the way into an ill-lit narrow corridor whose numerous paintings were shrouded in shadow. 'I know Paris of course, and the South, but not the Atlantic coast.'

Now she offered her hand, but reluctantly. It was quickly withdrawn, almost at the first touch.

'Actually, Madame, Charente lies inland of Charente-Maritime. My grandfather was a barber's apprentice in Angoulême, a *friseur*.' (As usual, when nervous, I utter gratuitous remarks.) We were now in her small sitting room amid more pictures crowded on the wall, faintly reminiscent of those old Academy rooms set up for a final vernissage. Wearing a tight-fitting terracotta polka-dot silk dress, extremely pleasing to the eye, the figure beneath still admirable, she wore make-up at the mouth and round the eyes, but modulated to the quieter sound of her years. Her fair hair, displaying some grey at the roots, was brushed up and bound in a chignon – and that is how I shall always remember the beautiful Olga Lepinskaya.

'Yes,' she said, indicating one of two chairs, 'I have seen photographs of Angoulême, a beautiful hilltop town with a great medieval cathedral.'

I remained standing because she did. 'Yes, Madame, quite beautiful.' 'Shall we continue in French?' she suggested. 'I used to speak English quite adequately, indeed Mrs Chaplin once congratulated me on it when she thought better of hitting me in the face. But now I have forgotten most of it.' She smiled at last. 'So why are you not a Frenchman?'

'My grandfather settled on the south coast of England in search of work.'

'Did he prosper, your grandfather? Was it he or your father

who could afford to send you to Oxford? Very expensive, *n'est-ce pas? Très* "exclusive", is that the English word?'

'They gave me a scholarship.' I might like this woman.

'And then you wrote a book about the French Communist intellectuals? I have been reading the French translation, sent to me by Svetlana. Please sit down. I cannot offer you a choice of chairs, I have kept only two in this room since I found myself living alone and moved into a smaller apartment. This chair is good for my back, though frankly nothing is.'

I sat myself in the other, my briefcase at my feet, and said something inane about back pains being the scourge of the world. This she passed over.

'Of course,' she said, 'I read with close attention the passages devoted to Picasso in your book.' She sighed but perhaps more wearily than happily. 'No one has properly understood Picasso, have they?'

'Possibly because there were so many Picassos.'

'Yes I know what you mean but there was only one, *vraiment*.'

'Where did you first meet him, Madame?'

'In Paris. In September-October 1952.'

'When was he in Moscow?'

'We are talking about late November and early December of the same year.'

I strove not to betray my excitement. Either this lady was riding the back of a gigantic lie or this was the *coup de recherche* to make my detractors (there was no shortage) weep.

'Madame, I confess that I am baffled. There is no recorded trace of any visit by Picasso at any time to the Soviet Union. Not in the Press, not in the biographies.'

She took this with serenity. 'No one is better informed than I. *Vous péchez, Monsieur*.'

But was she saying *vous péchez* (you are wrong, you transgress, you offend, you fail) – or *vous pêchez* (you are on a fishing expedition, Monsieur), an adjustment of the accent easier to read than to hear? But she now courteously provided dark tea and biscuits, then brought out an album of black-and-white photographs from a locked console lacquered in the Ming style. What she showed me were perhaps a dozen high-quality pictures, beautifully set up, of a young woman indisputably herself half-smiling gently in the company of a man exactly resembling Pablo Picasso at the age of seventy-one. I noticed the word Kodak on each print, so the photographer was not ostensibly Russian, but I knew that Stalin's Moscow specialised in doubles and impersonators, many of them out-of-work actors from the Moscow Art Theatre, the Mali or the Vachtangov. I was always conscious that Mishkin, Nikolaevna, Svetlana (and even Lepinskaya herself) may have been in cahoots to set me up for an elaborate hoax whose purpose I could only guess – though discrediting the Western scholars and sleuths currently flooding into the Moscow archives with their all-conquering demands would be the most obvious.

Several of the photographs suggested Picasso's antique studio in the rue des Grands Augustins but others had deliberately included distinctive Moscow settings like Red Square, St Basil's Cathedral, the entrance to the Pushkin Museum, and Sokol'niki Park (where a soaring monument to Soviet space flights would some ten years later be raised). Most of these photographs had been focused to include only Picasso and Olga Lepinskaya, though you could sense other persons in the vicinity. Several prints embraced a wider group in which I found figures I recognised, notably Louis Aragon and Elsa Triolet, both of whom I had long ago interviewed in the course of other research.

'Who was the photographer, Madame?'

'They are all by Dora Maar.'

I registered astonishment, incredulity. 'In 1952 Dora Maar had not been with Picasso for six years.'

'They are all by Dora Maar, which is why she appears in none of them. She would never for a moment yield up her camera so that she could be included in the group.' Madame Lepinskaya seemed to be on the verge of explaining this but fell silent and reached to take back the photographs. Unabashed she carefully counted them, putting down a marker for our relationship, before replacing them in the Ming-style console. I was not unaware that the Kodak inscriptions could have been expertly faked here in Moscow.

So we sat. I postponed the questions pressing in my head, sensing that she would prefer to retain control of her own narrative.

'I know why you have come here to see me, Monsieur. You did not make the long journey for nothing. Will you pledge to me that you will never repeat a word of what I tell you or show you to anyone anywhere?' It was a touching imprecation but an alarming one.

'Madame, I am a writer. That is why I'm here.'

Oddly, she seemed calmly to accept this as my assent to her stipulation, though I'm not to this day sure why. Madame Lepinskaya certainly seemed to be in full command of her faculties but, well, in 1993 she was approaching seventy, a time when the mind may reconstitute language to echo its own desires.

She smiled as if about to cut a wedding cake. 'When and where shall we begin?' She half-rose as if making a decision. 'Shall I tell you? Please follow me, I have something to show you.' She led me to her very small bedroom (9 square metres was my calculation). Most of the room was filled by a bed whose coverlet was brocaded in satin. You had to squeeze past the bed to bring your gaze close to the portrait, done in oils and surely resembling this face of hers in its youth, a portrait which clearly echoed the 'Small Cowper' Madonna by Raphael – the fair skin and hair (but without the faintest golden halo surrounding the head as in the Raphael) – and there the Madonna sits on a simple wooden bench in a meadow, her slightly downcast expression wistful, holding the large, naked baby boy, large in the Renaissance style, under his buttock while his hands clasp her neck, he looking back over his shoulder with the most ethereal of smiles. But in the portrait now before me Raphael's distant Italian church in the far background has been replaced by the multiple onion domes of St. Basil's Cathedral – an icon without the customary gilt! Yes, in its own way a Madonna by Raphael by Pablo Picasso. Yes, surely it conveyed this woman in her youth forty years ago. So search in vain the catalogues raisonnés and the websites to find this version of the 'Small Cowper' with the onion domes of St Basil's in the background.

Of course the familiar signature could have been forged by anyone.

Picasso's signature has been faked more times than that of any other artist. Russia has not been short of skilled practitioners, mainly 'dissident' artists denied a livelihood. Madame Lepinskaya was monitoring my expression and, no doubt, my thoughts.

And why the child? Where did he come from? I drew breath and asked her.

She sighed. 'My friends think Pablo was anticipating events – a prophecy displayed. You can see the original Raphael in the National Gallery in Washington – though of course I can't. Have you had the good fortune to view it?'

'I have.'

'Do you recognise the connection with my portrait?'

'Yes, but the church in the background here is St Basil's.'

'You are observant, Monsieur. Perhaps you had a training in the fine arts at the Slade or, since you are French, at the Beaux-Arts in Paris?'

'Nothing like that, Madame. The little I know about painting, and it is very little, is self-taught.'

'But you are from Oxford!'

'Perhaps oddly to your ear, that's a place where you learn that you must find out for yourself whatever you want to know. Tell me, Madame, did you sit for this oil portrait or did Picasso...?'

'Did he do it from memory? Is that what you ask?' I searched her still-beautiful features and found the ghost of a smile forty, or four hundred, years old. 'Of course I sat for it, at his behest. For Picasso much of the pleasure resided in the sitting. Of course there was no baby!'

(Reader, you will need to remember that claim, 'Of course I sat for it'.)

'Was it done here in Moscow?'

'He did some preliminary sketches at his studio in the rue des Grands Augustins, the resultant portrait in oils a little later at his apartment in the *ulitsa* Gorky.'

Reluctantly I tore myself away from the portrait as she led me back into the sitting room, a slender arm superfluously indicating my chair. I could sense how anxious she was to remain in control. Quite soon afterwards – too soon – this elderly lady showed signs of fatigue, for which I apologised, and I departed in a state of exhilaration. She had promised to receive me again, I had passed the test. Perhaps.

4

Curator Olga Lepinskaya surveys her class. She is wearing a Jaeger-style twinset in ochre, with a pleated skirt in Scottish tartan, both brought by Uncle Ilya after his visit to a freezing Sheffield on behalf of the Peace Movement. She looks a treat.

'Although I should not say so myself, Monsieur. But the significance of my appearance cannot be evaded. If I had looked like one of Platkov's broad-beamed peasant girls bringing in the harvest, none of this would have happened.'

'Bien entendu, Madame.'

'Colleagues,' she begins, 'we need to understand the extraordinary versatility of Picasso's output. This great artist has produced some 2,000 *objets d'art* as a ceramicist. His work as a graphic artist comes in a variety of forms: drawing, etching, line engraving, lithography. He displays a fine line, now flexible, now sharp, and a palette ranging from soft monochromes to sharp contrasting colours.'

Today she will not meet Pyotr in the cafeteria. Either he, who paints under the name of Sobaka,[†] which means Dog, is keeping his distance or is too busy preparing his six permitted canvases for an imminent exhibition of 'alternative art'. The authorities have given it a green light – which flickers. Instead she is joined in the cafeteria by a fellow-curator, a specialist in Cranach, Bosch and Dürer, who never offers any pretence about his zeal as an informer

'What has Director Kemenev been saying to you today? Was he nervous? Uncertain? And Davidov, has he tried to persuade you not to visit the comrades in France? And your good mother, does she remain bitter about your father's death? Who visits her? Who does she talk to when she goes shopping? Does she tell

---

† The real rude name under which he painted has been changed.

anyone that her husband was not guilty of anything? Does she keep his photograph by her bedside? Does she put thoughts of revenge in your head?'

They pursue this rigmarole month after month, blind dogs haunted by the stench of the purges. Soon she may be required to report to this same man on Picasso and his decadent entourage: Does he swim in the nude? Does he copulate in the sea? Have the French coastguards mistaken his erect member for the periscope of a Soviet submarine?

In the physical preparation of the Picasso exhibition Olga is supported by gallant assistants astonished and excited by what is suddenly coming up from the cellars, yet she feels depressed and increasingly tired through lack of sleep and, above all, by having to deal with Kemenev throughout the working day. Discussions with him about the content of the catalogue go round in circles and never seem to be resolved.

'More generally, Olga Maksimovna, we could fasten firmly on to recent political trends in the USA.'

He struggles to clear his head and when he gropes for the bottle she dares to place a restraining hand on the sleeve of his double-breasted suit.

'Enough, Comrade Director.'

'Yes, of course, of course.' Abruptly he leans forward, brimming with lucidity as if the drinking was playacting. 'Take care to point out – now listen carefully Olga, you have never been good at politics – that the plutocrats who control the more enlightened American collections, the various modernist trends, have recently found themselves under fire from philistines in the American Congress and reactionary pressure groups like the American Legion. Yes, good, good! We are getting there, Olga. These cultural gangsters like Congressman Dondero have been claiming that every "ism" in modern art – constructivism, futurism, impressionism, cubism, surrealism – can be exposed as part of a gigantic global plot to deliver American civilization into the hands of the wicked Bolsheviks. So –' Kemenev hesitates, reaches for the bottle, doesn't. 'So! Ha! By staging a Picasso exhibition here we are hammering the philistine witch-hunters in the American Congress! Perfect! We kill two bones with one stone! Yes?'

'I think you mean two birds, Vladimir Petrovich. Killing a bone with a stone may be beyond us. Could we put the vodka in the cupboard?'

'If you say so, Olga.' He watches trembling as she puts it away.

'Of course such an approach is not without its problems,' Olga points out. 'Won't Congressman Dondero jump all over the place shouting "I told you so! Picasso and all the 'isms' are running to their true spiritual home, Moscow"? Don't you agree, Comrade Director?'

Kemenev's brow darken, his triumph ebbs, his unsteady hands flail through the menacing pile of print on his desk, any or all of which could mean (or not) midnight feet on the stairs of his comfortable Party apartment in the *ulitsa* Kirov (*or wherever the Kemenev family live, Madame Lepinskaya never told me*).

'But we score heavily against Uoll Strit,' she consoles him, placing on his desk her revised entry for the forthcoming edition of the *Soviet Encyclopaedia*.

'You read it to me, Olga. Really I am suffering from this sty in my right eye. The doctors are negligent. Can you see it?'

'No.'

'You are beautiful, Ochka, a model for Russian womanhood, you will hook Big Poisson Picasso.'

His black Bakelite telephone rings. He grabs it, fumbles: 'Yes, Kemenev here.' As he listens to a voice whose harsh bark Olga can hear, his face falls into its separate parts, even Picasso would have been nonplussed to capture the disintegration. She fears he is going to collapse under his desk, observed by Lenin and Stalin.

'It was Khrushchev. Is he number five or four now? He is against. He threatened to have my testicles in aspic, apparently a Ukrainian delicacy.'

'So it's off?'

'Yes! No! I'm surprised at you, Olga, to ask me such a question.'

These nights she cannot sleep. Pyotr no longer waits for her at the entrance to the Kropotkinskaya metro. Only in her troubled dreams does he offer his arm, striding long-legged beside her in his flapping black coat, a forbidden novel by Dostoyevsky under the other arm. She can hear him, small-boned and saturnine, arguing the case for the German expressionists, the Brücke group in Berlin and Blaue Reiter in Munich. He laughs caustically: had not Hitler himself more than once designated 1910 as the moment of degeneration into modernism? She glimpses Pyotr striding through the sedate, shadowy suburbs of Wilhelmine Berlin toward the Brücke Museum, in resolute pursuit of Kirchner, Heckel and Schmidt-Rottluff. But where is Van Gogh? Dead, gone.

Next morning, after an early visit to the doctor for medication to boost her energy, she finds waiting on her desk an editorial from the art journal, *Iskustvo*, along with Kemenev's command: 'Read'. Her handbag at her feet, her shoes off, she curls her legs beneath her and reads. After a few lines she begins to sweat and her feet hit the floor.

The lead editorial calls for relentless Bolshevik struggle against disguised Zionist cosmopolitan elements which have infiltrated this journal, *Iskustvo*, in order to falsely attack *Guernica* as 'monstrous' and 'pathological'. Worse, *Iskustvo* has unforgivably denigrated Picasso's work in general as 'morbid', 'repulsive', and designed 'to make an aesthetic apology for capitalism.' The editorial castigates Vladimir Kemenev's erroneous lambasting of Picasso for tearing human beings to pieces, and for creating the empty geometric forms promoted by the imperialist camp preparing for war. Such slanders must now be repudiated.

Olga straightens up and adjusts the tortoiseshell comb fastening her hair (which she hasn't washed for a week, such is the struggle with other tenants to gain possession of the single bathroom serving the whole tenement). Someone powerful is warning Kemenev to abandon his hesitations and commit the

Museum whole-heartedly to the Picasso exhibition. The placing of the editorial in the pages of a specialist art magazine does not deceive Olga: it could have appeared in *Pravda*. The Director's predictable summons follows at mid-morning. She finds Kemenev surprisingly calm, almost serene, behind his desk.

'Well, Olga Maksimovna, how did you interpret it?'

'Vladimir Petrovich, my commiserations. It seems so unfair that they should lambast you in person.'

'Yes but who is "they"?'

'I have no idea, Comrade Director.'

'I had a call from Beria. Well, his assistant. Well, an underling. Well, to be frank, I wrote the polemic myself after I heard from Beria. The editor of *Iskustvo* was waiting for my copy. It's the green light. I hear from sources who cannot be identified that Khrushchev is our enemy – and will soon be eating his own balls – in aspic.'

'So we go ahead with the exhibition?'

'What? Yes of course. Probably. Never jump to conclusions, Olga Maksimovna'.

Madame Lepinskaya looked as exhausted as the young woman she was describing, such was her empathy. 'Enough of that,' she said.

'Does this bring us to the ill-fated Fortochka exhibition?'

'You know about that?'

'I found an oblique reference to it in the archives.'†

'You did! Where?'

〜

NEW FACES NEW VOICES. MOSCOW ALTERNATIVE ARTISTS.

This banner has been boldly draped across the entrance to an old theatre off *ulitsa* Arbat, a small building now fallen into chronic disrepair and constantly threatened with closure by the authorities. It is called the Fortochka, (a specifically Russian small window which opens to let in air on summer nights). Productions at the Fortochka had mainly been the work of actors from the

---

† RGANI. Fond 5.op.36, ed.kh 111

nearby Vachtangov Company, run by the young Yuri Lyubimov, the most adventurous of Soviet theatre directors. A few of his 'too adventurous' productions were staged in the comparative obscurity of the Fortochka. Pyotr Davidov contributed scene paintings in the *surovyi stil'*, the 'severe style', and did so free of charge. Most of the Fortochka productions were foreign plays of the kind seen only in avant-garde little theatres off the beaten track in London and New York. The joke among the players was that 'off-Broadway' meant in Moscow 'off-limits'. The Fortochka's 'little window' was particularly open to the new 'theatre of the absurd' and perhaps the most notable production was of Samuel Beckett's *Waiting for Godot*, if only because the Fortochka production actually preceded by a few months the première in Paris on 5 January 1953 in the Théâtre de Babylone. (Put this down to Lyubimov's contacts in France and his friendship with the actor-director Roger Blin.) The Fortochka prided itself on laying on the best American jazz despite the ferocious clamp-down on saxophonists, trumpeters, bassoonists and drummers under Stalin. Neighbours complained, the militia came, doors were sealed until the authorities dropped their guard and the next production nervously surfaced. All of this greatly excited Pyotr Davidov and it was through his friends at the Fortochka that the plan emerged to use the theatre for an exhibition of dissident art, which was also conceived in the absurdist style as the best answer to the sterile classicism of official Soviet art, the only kind allowed. Some of those taking part like Oskar Rabin had been influenced by impressionism and cubism, others were keen observers of the American scene, notably the emerging movement known as 'abstract expressionism', not least the work of Jackson Pollock and Willem de Kooning (whom Pyotr Davidov admired intensely). The plan for a dissident exhibition is said to have filtered up to Lyubimov himself, who apparently said 'Nothing to do with me but why not?'

Olga is on her way down *ulitsa* Arbat to the Fortochka, which she has visited more than once out of loyalty to Pyotr if not to his version of the 'severe style', which strikes her as insulting to a Soviet spectator – like a blow to the face. She wears dark glasses, a scarf round her head – even to be seen here is a risk for an established museum curator but she cannot let Pyotr down, not least because he may be putting at risk his coveted job at the Pushkin. She has told him that the unlicensed display would almost certainly be closed down before it could open, but her warnings only excite derision.

'Square!' he says, 'you are square, my Ochka.' He uses the American word and accent.

'Oh, and what does that mean?'

'Hipsters and beatniks, man.'

'Must you address me as "man", Pyotr?'

'It comes from the square representing a four-beat rhythm as shown by a conductor's hands. Yeah. All the squares go home!'

She finds that buying an entrance ticket is voluntary, a contribution to 'keeping dissident artists alive'. People are drifting in, young students and intellectuals on the whole, many of whom sidle past the voluntary contribution bucket but she donates her ten roubles. The scene outside the Fortochka is lazily tranquil, nothing abnormal, no sign of what Pyotr calls 'the mounted cavalry'. But as soon as she steps inside she finds a gathering of journalists in the lobby, smoking, bored, not much interested in the paintings. She is warmly greeted by an artist who recognises her as Pyotr's partner – but no sign of Pyotr.

'You will find your friend inside the hall,' Pavel says, then smiles: 'The Sobaka is barking at anyone who will listen.'

'You have a lot of journalists here today, Pavel.'

He nods. 'It's not the paintings they have come to see. Clearly we are to receive visitors.'

Her heart sinks. Something awful is about to happen. Recognising her, one or two of the journalists from cultural magazines turn their lenses on her. She dodges out of their sight – everything can be incriminating.

The pictures in the theatre lobby extend into the main hall

where the seats have been removed. She stops to look at a prominently hung painting by the veteran Robert Falk who (she remembers) had taken part in the Jack of Diamonds avant-garde exhibition of 1910, but who later withdrew to Paris. Soon she reaches canvases by the 'severe school'. Here she sees Pyotr-Sobaka wearing his most flamboyant outfit, hair long and straggling, sandals not shoes, finger tips browned by nicotine, with the palor (she fears) of consumption. Gesturing passionately, he is engaged in animated discussion with a few amused members of the public. Six of his canvases are on display, Olga knows them all. She replaces her dark glasses and hangs back shyly.

Then suddenly pandemonium, an inrush into the hall of bulky suits following a senior member of the Party praesidium, the short, flamboyant, potato-face Nikita Khrushchev, chief of the Moscow Party. The exhibition room is suddenly alight with flash bulbs. She recognises some of the dignitaries arrayed behind Khrushchev, most obviously the diehard Aleksandr Gerasimov, president of the USSR Academy of Arts and chairman of the *Orgkomitet* of the Union of Soviet Artists. Yes, and Vladimir. A. Serov. And Kemenev himself. They march in like acolytes, Olga remembers that it is Serov who had painted *Lenin Proclaiming Power*, with Stalin mistakenly shown in the background, but later airbrushed him out, replacing him with a smudged nobody. The reporters crowd in.

Khrushchev is steaming with energy and bile. He pauses before Falk's *Nude in an Armchair.* 'I would say this is not a painting it's just a dog's mess,' he loudly declares, then rambles on about a friend who was given a picture of a lemon as a wedding present. 'Just a mess of yellow lines which looked as if some child had done its business on the canvas.'

The entourage moves on. Khrushchev hectors the accompanying journalists – 'Pictures painted by jackasses aren't worth two kopeks.' They scribble on the crude lined paper of Soviet shorthand notebooks. A film of sweat on his forehead and swelling cheeks, the Ukrainian boss of the Moscow Party, a member of the Praesidium, of Stalin's chosen Ten, is now scowling at a landscape by Pyotr's 'severe style' hero and paragon, Yuri Kalinikov. Here the thick, rudely applied patina depicts a group of political prisoners engaged in forced labour, breaking boulders and shovelling them into a mule cart while two half-asleep guards smoke cigarettes. The rough, rock-strewn landscape lies at an angle; Khrushchev keeps tilting his head in jocular mockery of the painting's perspective.

'We are not going to take these lifeless blotches with us into Communism,' he tells Gerasimov, Serov, Kemenev and the world. He turns to the artist, Kalinikov: 'Our art should arouse us to perform great deeds. Do you think that stuff like this is going to carry us into Communism?'

Olga can read Kalinikov's answer from his expression: I hope not.

Khrushchev trundles on plus entourage. He has reached Sobaka's canvases. Olga watches as Pyotr offers his hand, which is accepted but immediately accompanied by a tirade

'Sobaka, you call yourself? Dog? What's your real name? We should take your pants down and drop you in a clump of nettles until you recognise your mistakes. Are you a pederast or a normal man?'

'I am an artist,' Pyotr replies. 'A true artist is never "normal".' (Olga's heart is hammering.)

'Ha! Tell that to Rembrandt. They say you like to associate with foreigners – Americans.'

Pyotr does not retreat. 'May I explain our philosophy, Comrade Khrushchev?'

'Philosophy you call it? We have donkeys who can do better with their tails. In the West they are showing finger-paintings done by monkeys. We can give you a one-way donkey ticket.' Khrushchev turns to his aides. 'Find out which of these "artists" hold teaching posts. Find out which of them occupy comfortable jobs in our great galleries and museums. Take appropriate measures.'

Khrushchev marches towards the exit. He has seen enough. Desperately alarmed, Olga sees Pyotr scrambling after the chieftain, struggling to thread himself through the throng, desperate to explain that emotions are alien to the classicism of severe art. Anyone who knows Picasso's silhouette of Don Quixote and Sancho Panza, black ink on white paper, will understand. So will anyone who has been allowed to see Kazimir Malevich's static figures of Russian peasants. In each and every case of the severe style it is the viewer who must provide the emotion. This (Pyotr is raving for the benefit of the general public pressing round him) is the equivalent of Brecht's *Verfremdungseffekt* in the theatre. This 'Alienation Effect' is the key to the severe style's quest for an art which will force spectators to form their own judgments.

Of course Pyotr's choking manifesto is heard only in fragments as he struggles with the scrum. Olga's ear knows it all. But now in her acute alarm for Pyotr she feels her period coming on ahead of time, as tends to happen when she is struck by anxiety – fortunately she carries a spare sanitary towel in her bag but she must find the toilet, it's bound to be closed, out of order, in an old, delapidated building with a mouldering fabric.

Meanwhile, the general public has fallen back from the Severe canvases as if anxious to avoid contamination. Olga notices among the journalists a tall figure who had once visited Pyotr's run-down studio in Cheremushki and bought a painting at the asking price. This is Harrison Salisbury of the *New York Times*, virtually the only American correspondent granted a work permit apart from four veterans attached to the news agencies, AP, UP and Reuters. As Khrushchev's group departs, Kemenev still in poker-faced attendance, Olga sees the American journalist fall into conversation with Pyotr. Should she join them? – no, her premature period rapidly carries her away.

Two days before she is due to fly to France, Pyotr has not been sighted at his desk in the Museum. He owns no telephone so she makes her way after work through the puddles and scavenging stray dogs, tucking her hands in her sleeves, to his attic studio in Cheremushki. He does not answer her call, does not come to the door, the place is empty, they have taken him. The following morning she confronts Kemenev and throws him on the defensive:

'I know nothing, Comrade. I was merely informed by the Organs that administrative measures had been taken... and that Davidov has ceased to be a member of my staff.' Her gaze is unforgiving. He dare not offend her. He must get her on the Ilyushin to Prague, to Paris. 'Believe me, Olga Maksimovna, I had no part in this.'

'I was at the Fortochka on Saturday, Comrade Director.'

'I know. I have eyes in the back of my head. You heard what Khrushchev said. I'm told he is now Number 3 – or maybe four. I am merely a powerless functionary, Olga.' He reaches for the vodka bottle. 'Perhaps I should mention one other thing.'

'Perhaps you should.'

'Olga, some people insist on making trouble for themselves. I don't mean Davidov-Sobaka's obscene paintings, although they are filthy enough. When your double-headed friend left the Fortochka with his canvases, he was seen in the company of the notorious anti-Soviet journalist Harrison Salisbury. They drove straight to the American Embassy and stayed an hour. Davidov went in carrying six of his paintings and emerged with none. Did you know that? Such treachery cannot be forgiven. His arrest followed as night follows day.'

With aching heart she stares at the twin statuettes of Lenin and Stalin. Should she demand Pyotr's release on pain of refusing to travel to France? Had he been so incensed by Khrushchev's bluster that he allowed himself to commit the ultimate sin – can he really have entered the American Embassy?

5

~

Kemenev is sufficiently anxious that he personally drives his underling out from the Museum to Sheremetyevo in his Zil. He will not leave the airport until he can see her Ilyushin rising into the grey clouds.

'Do you have the following, Olga Maksimovna: Passport? Foreign currency in dollars and French francs? Bank of Moscow travellers' cheques? Our dossier of the early Picasso paintings from the Morozov and Shchukin collection? Our draft catalogue of the exhibition in the French language? Two or three gift photographs of yourself?'

'Yes.'

'You must bring back something nice for your mother, Olga Maksimovna. Have they given you enough foreign currency?'

'Yes.'

'Don't forget my promise of a Black Sea holiday for you and your mother.'

'Thank you. My mother was very excited when she heard about it.'

'Good! Aragon and Triolet will buy you some nice clothes before you meet Picasso. You must look your best.'

'Yes.'

'We are sending Picasso the most beautiful young woman in Moscow, but with the tag "Return to Sender".'

Olga remains silent.

'Shall I tell you something you should know, Olga Maksimovna? I mean the woman situation over there. In Paris. Our Embassy sources report that Picasso is back with the "weeping woman" herself.'

'Dora Maar, you mean? She and Picasso parted company six years ago.'

'But she is back in favour. More reactionary than ever, not only a Christian but also a believer. Our Embassy in Paris sent a comrade to watch her apartment in the rue de Savoie. She was seen emerging in the company of Picasso and entering his limousine.'

'That is surely no concern of mine.'

'Oh but it most certainly is! Sometimes your naivety worries me, Olga. You cannot make your moves unless you know the pieces currently on the board.'

'Picasso lives with his companion, the mother of his recent children, at Vallauris.'

'Gilot? We think he may have parted company with her. I have even heard the absurd rumour that it is she who has parted company with him.' Kemenev laughs drily, both hands fastened on the steering wheel. 'With Picasso nothing is ever permanent. Perhaps Maar, the original "weeping woman" of the famous portraits, is currently weeping no more. And Maar is an avowed enemy of Soviet socialism. She is not only surrounded by surrealists, she lays orchids at the feet of the Virgin. Worse, far worse, she listens to Chagall, who has given an interview on Radio Monaco mocking Picasso as a naïve *compagnon de route*, a fellow-traveller: "Moscow wants the man not his paintings," laughed Chagall.'

'I do not think I am the right person for this mission, Comrade Director. Won't you please think again?'

'You are the only person for this mission, Olga. Take comfort that Picasso admires Comrade Stalin. After all, it was the Soviet Union, not the Western appeasers, who came to the aid of the Spanish Republic against the onslaughts of Hitler, the Condor Legion, and Mussolini's fascist bandits.'

'True,' she whispers.

He leans towards her, his voice muted. 'Strictly between ourselves, Olga Maksimovna, we have contrived to plant a small device in Maar's apartment in the rue de Savoie. We have heard her in conversation with Picasso. We have heard her denigrate Comrade Stalin in words I cannot repeat, so shameful. We have heard her warn Picasso about competing factions in Moscow, diehards and liberals, generals and party secretaries, all engaged in Levantine manoeuvres, jockeying for position, as the Generalissimo sinks into terminal decline – *lui*, Him, the world's spiritual governor.'

'Please drive carefully, Comrade Director, you are all over the road, motorists are blasting you with their horns.'

Picasso, says Kemenev, invariably takes pleasure in provoking Maar. '"Stalin," he laughed in her face, "now there's a man I admire. It's a big country, Russia, one sixth of the earth. One man, even a genius, cannot see in every direction. Not all the time. If Stalin knew half of what goes on in Russia's museums, he'd put it right, bang, just like that."'

Olga, too, almost smiles but sharing a joke with Kemenev is like sharing a lamb with a wolf.

'And never forget, Olga, how the Americans have reviled Picasso. That is a weapon you must deploy. According to our sources, his FBI file is now bulging: his portrait of the Rosenberg martyrs, his open support for the Hollywood Ten, his cable to a Madison Square Garden rally in honour of Spanish Republicans hounded by the witch-hunt sweeping the USA: "Fight today or you will have an American Guardia Civil tomorrow," he declared. When Picasso applied for an American visa, the US Ambassador to France cabled the State Department advising that it be granted to maintain America's international image.'

'But it wasn't granted, Vladimir Petrovich.'

'All the better for us.'

Olga cannot help reflect that *Guernica* now hangs in New York's Museum of Modern Art, the cultural showpiece of the Rockefeller family currently competing with the Whitneys and Guggenheims for the Medici mantle. Picasso is known to want its home to be the Prado in Madrid – when Franco has been overthrown.

'Olga, on every occasion you will accept the advice of Louis Aragon. He and Elsa Triolet are dedicated to bringing Picasso to

Moscow in honour of the birthday of Iosif Vissarionovich, the Georgian cobbler's son born Dzhugashvili. May it not be his last birthday, may none be his last.'

'Amen.'

'You must regard Louis Aragon as the fountainhead of French Communist literature. I suppose you have familiarised yourself with his numerous praise-poems in honour of Comrade Stalin?'

'I've read a few.'

'Then recite.'

'Must I?'

'Recite.'

'*Et Staline pour nous est présent pour demain*
Et Staline dissipe aujourd'hui le malheur...'

'But that's Paul Éluard not Aragon! You will bring about my death, Olga.'

'*Forgive me for asking, Madame, but do you remember these exchanges word-for-word?*'

'*For me it was a very vivid time. I was still young, my mind was retentive. I can hear Kemenev as if yesterday. I need only think of him and he begins to speak. Then I can hear myself.*'

After boarding the plane and finally shot of Kemenev, Olga relieves her feet of her tight shoes and recalls a dinner described to her by *Pravda*'s Paris correspondent, Mikhail Koltsov, an admirer who never failed to approach her during his visits to Moscow. He had been invited to attend a dinner held in the elite restaurant of St Paul de Vence. Aragon and his wife Elsa Triolet had laboured to assure a sceptical Picasso that his art was due, at long last, to be acclaimed in Moscow. But Picasso had not forgiven Aragon for obediently reprinting a poisonous, two-thousand-word diatribe by Vladimir Kemenev. According to rumour (said Koltsov), a furious Picasso had told Aragon that he had six faces which was why he, Picasso, had never accorded him the honour of anything beyond a cursory sketch on a table napkin. 'After all,' he said, 'it's the artist's privilege to add extra faces and what can you do if the fellow has six already.'

'Well, I composed the diatribe at Kemenev's behest,' Olga told Mikhail Koltsov.

'I bet you didn't sleep at night.'

'Oh I did. Basically, I have always agreed with Kemenev about Picasso.'

'I have to admit to you, Monsieur, that it was what I genuinely thought before I flew to France.'

'What changed your mind, Madame?'

'We shall see.' Madame Lepinskaya reached to adjust the broad tortoiseshell comb which fastened her lustrous, swept-back hair.

Now, at the restaurant table in St Paul de Vence, Mikhail Koltsov listened as Prince Louis proudly read out his latest 'confidential bulletin from Paris' to the reigning boyars of the Soviet Writers' Union. He described Jean-Paul Sartre as a fashionable petty-bourgeois who had slanderously written in *France Observateur* about 'the nausea of the Soviet boa constrictor, unable to keep down or vomit up the enormous Picasso'.

Olga laughed. 'Not bad.'

'"Comrades," continued Aragon, "the renegade Malraux has mocked us in similar terms. We must now strive by all available means to reverse these vile calumnies based on past misunderstandings in our ranks."'

'Of course I was destined to spend time in Aragon's company, always courteous but I never could like him. I can imagine his starched table napkin drawn fastidiously across his mouth, as if wiping away these provokatsia *by Sartre and Malraux.*

Madame Lepinskaya glanced shyly in my direction, as if abashed to have 'imagined' anything. I told her that Koltsov's was an excellent verbal portrait of Aragon. She asked whether I had ever met Aragon. Yes, I had, in 1962, while writing my study of Communist Intellectuals in France.

Picasso (Koltsov told her) continued to grumble genially as the plates were carried away, course after splendid course. 'Ha! Didn't they call me a surrealist, a "dog like Dalí," in their Great Soviet Encyclopaedia?'[†]

'All this will be rectified,' Aragon promised. 'A new edition will be launched to coincide with your visit to Moscow.' He extracted an unfolded envelope of photographs from an inner pocket and presented it to Picasso. 'It's for you, dear Pablo, please take a look, high-quality colour.' Aragon was smiling appreciatively: 'Her name is Olga Lepinskaya. She will be the principal curator for your exhibition at the Pushkin Museum. She is already composing the catalogue and she has been commissioned to re-write your entry in the Encyclopaedia.

Picasso snorted like a bull. 'Pah! Then she works for that shit Kemenev. And she's too young.'

'Her expertise is the Paris School, pre-1917,' Elsa Triolet assured him.

'Hm.'

'You learned all this is from your Pravda *man, Madame?'*

'Yes, Mikhail Koltsov, son of Mikhail Koltsov, Pravda's *correspondent in Spain during the civil war'*

'But then executed after he came home?'

'I believe so.'

'So you and your friend had both lost fathers in the same purge?'

'It was a bond but only a tacit one. We never discussed it.'

Then (Koltsov told her) the French bourgeois press got wind of this posh Red dinner in St Paul de Vence – but not of the Napoleonic Masterplan to capture Moscow by putting old Picasso on Aeroflot. What came out was that the Party had paid for the entire restaurant bill including three fine wines. The PCF's cultural commissar, Laurent Casanova, pleaded in *l'Humanité* that all the wines were French and that none of the guests had drunk American Coca-Cola. When Picasso's long-suffering secretary, Jaime Sabartés, read him the sardonic commentaries in *Le Figaro* and *France-Soir*, Picasso was reported to have

---

† On Picasso see *Bol'shaia sovetskaia entsiklopediia*, 2nd edition, volume 33 (1955), p. 28; 3rd edition, volume 19 (1974), p. 527 Regarding *Guernica*, the Russian word *panno* is translated 'mural' in the American edition (1978), p. 525, but *Guernica* is not a mural. When I made this point to Lepinskaya she agreed, adding that American translators were 'notoriously ignorant'.

bellowed: 'Tell Chagall I am going to Moscow.'

Having concluded with some degree of self-satisfaction his long report of the dinner he had attended in St Paul de Vence, Mikhail Koltsov invited Olga to come back to his apartment. He always did. 'My time in Moscow is so short,' he pressed her. She always refused.

Madame Lepinskaya told me all this calmly but she was not calm. She was back in the prologue to the adventure which was to change, perhaps ruin, her life.

The young Olga Lepinskaya well knows that she is about to encounter a morose hypochondriac, though remarkable for his stamina in the studio, who complains most mornings that it is not worth getting out of bed because he is a dying man callously neglected by his wife (whom he summons with a bellow) and by his negligent doctors, not forgetting all those mistresses and children hiding under his bed while plotting to inherit his fortune. 'I bet they hope I will die during the flight to Moscow, ridding them of an embarrassment. No, I won't go!' Why should he? By staying put where he feels at home, close to the shores of the Mediterranean, or in the cavernous studios of the rue des Grands Augustins in Paris, he accrues prestige, adulation and wealth unavailable to any other contemporary artist. And he is free to work, his sole sustaining passion.

Yet he is a Communist! He had flamboyantly joined the French Party in 1944, after the Liberation of Paris, when the PCF's prestige was rising to a peak of a million members, and eight years later he remains loyal, the jewel in the Party's cultural crown. Picasso has designed the famous dove whose wings carry the Peace Movement's message across the world, from Paris to Peking. Fronting the Peace Movement is a cosmopolitan Soviet man of letters, a personal friend of Picasso, the wily old fox Ilya Ehrenburg, who has already sent him a message, 'Come to Moscow, Pablo! Now is the moment.' Free to travel to Paris (sometimes, it depends on Stalin's mood of the moment, which defines all lesser moments), Ehrenburg has introduced the great

Picasso on platform after platform amidst anti-American rhetoric and uplifting applause (to which the painter is not averse, encircled by so many admiring friends, he an icon for *les lendemains qui chantent*, the singing tomorrows). If the old Jew Ehrenburg assures him that *le tout Moscou* awaits him with open arms, well, you have to listen. But he hates cold weather. When Picasso finally consented to be led to a Peace Congress in Sheffield, to denounce the 'Marshallization' of Europe, he almost died of hypothermia and didn't find anything he could eat for two days.

'It's a mystery how the English take their clothes off long enough to procreate,' he reported to the comrades.

Picasso is tempted to accept. Julius and Ethel Rosenberg, humble East Side Jews, have been condemned to death in New York on a charge of atomic espionage, a crime of which they are totally innocent (the Party is determined to insist on that). A touching sketch of the martyred couple by Picasso has duly appeared in *l'Humanité*.

Even so, Olga knows what she is up against. She would have to tame and shepherd an artist of legendary rages, a Catalan-Spaniard, a matador of the Mediterranean, a lover of bullfights, a willing tormentor of the women who adored him. A Soviet girl might well tremble at those photographs showing him naked from the waist-up, the half-smile poised to disappear when his mind turned to the relentless Soviet denigration of his work, the art of four decades, even extending to his masterpiece, the huge canvas condemning the fascist bombing of civilians during the Spanish Civil War: *Guernica*.

Olga shudders at the prospect.

Madame Lepinskaya broke off, exhausted. 'Monsieur, there we will have to leave it for today. I had not anticipated how sapping this business of exact recall across forty years could be. I am no longer young and must rest now. Perhaps we could meet again before your departure.'

'Madame, is it possible to fix a date here and now?'

'I shall need time to think over what I have told you. If I feel up to a

further meeting I shall call you.'

This was late in 1992. As if in compensation Madame Lepinskaya disclosed, rather reluctantly and with obvious inhibition, that a former colleague of hers – 'Not exactly a colleague but involved with Chaplin' – lived in London. Olga found a recent letter from this woman, which she firmly declined to let me read but allowed me to take down the name, address and telephone number: Lady Nina Stears, aka Nina Bolsharova. The address was Cheyne Walk in Chelsea, I knew it a bit.

Olga did not contact me to offer a further meeting. Frustrated again, I did dare once to telephone her and beg for an account of her trip to Paris and her meeting with Picasso, but she rather crossly explained that she must first look up her diaries and did I not appreciate how long ago it all was? I flew home.

6

~

It was the summer of 1993, a warm day, the clouds over the
Thames as fluffy and idyllically lonely as the poet's. I had been
trying to arrange a meeting with Lady Stears for some weeks and
I set out for Chelsea without much conviction that she would keep
the appointment she had at last granted. 'We have Centre Court
seats at Wimbledon for the afternoon,' she had warned in perfect
Queen's English over the telephone, 'so come early.' Normally her
forbidding diary involved uncancellable venues further afield,
Paris, New York or the Getty Museum, but today an afternoon at
the Centre Court threatened to curtail my visit. I set out from
Ravenscourt Park shortly after eight, taking the District Line to
Sloane Square, then walked down to the river, passing Wren's
Royal Hospital. Cheyne Walk runs parallel to the river, a terrace
of attractive residences built in the early eighteenth century to
overlook the Thames and later fronted by the Embankment.

But if one has an eye for architecture, by no means all of them
could be counted as the Georgian originals, though these as usual
carried the exquisitely symmetrical, flat-fronted façades missing
from their Victorian successors with their boasting bay windows
and fussy conceits. The Georgian brick was a mellow blend of
darkening yellow and brown, whereas the Victorians built in a
harsh red brick whose superior quality of duration defied,
perhaps unfortunately, the passage of time. The original houses
which most pleased my eye extended from No. 14 to No. 28,
although 2 to 6 are equally estimable. All of them are in sight of
the beautiful suspension bridge named after Albert, Prince
Consort to Victoria, and begun in 1870 some nine years after his
death. The art deco brutalism of Battersea Power Station lurks
out of sight further down river.

Happily, Lady Stears's residence stood within the original
Georgian cluster behind a magnificent, high wrought-iron gate

topped by a little golden dolphin. The intercom bell is on the street. If admitted, you walk up a patio path, passing potted plants and mounting seven steps, $1 - 1 - 5$, to the front door. The Georgian façade shows four storeys plus a basement. The bricks are a pleasing medley of red, yellow and brown. A wrought-iron balcony runs beneath the first-floor windows, which are often shuttered from the inside. The architect of this terrace chose curved tops for his windows, which carry eight panes of glass (and which I like less than the strictly rectangular windows of the period). One is also struck by the exquisite sundial inlaid between the first and second floors, flanked by a centred bas-relief showing two men in profile facing one another. Henry James's house at No. 21 is fronted by a huge wisteria, no doubt an ally to his coveted privacy but perhaps planted more recently.

Now I am going to admit, however shaming, that I had already prowled Cheyne Walk and its environs even before I got her firm invitation. I had vainly hoped to catch a glimpse of the occupants leaving or entering, Lady Stears herself being the prime target. About her I had developed a curiosity whose intensity is difficult to convey unless one parades the word 'obsession'. Naturally, all this snooping carries its dangers: one must take care not to linger too long lest, when the day comes, one is greeted with 'Oh, you're the man we see loitering outside, scribbling in a notebook'. A bad start. So keep moving while looking and 'scribble' while standing outside a different house further along. It's not a bad idea to make a show of examining the high trees which shield the houses, since nature lovers are generally excused their annoying attentions.

I knew that Nina, now Lady Stears, had become wealthy and lived accordingly; her telephone (this was pre-email) was ex-directory and invariably answered by a male assistant with a threateningly Russian accent: 'Uoo U? Vot U vont? She beezy t'day. Coll agin.' The answer device, when activated, was scarcely more welcoming: 'Yes? Leave message.' Each of these Cheyne Walk residences was already worth millions, although not so many millions as a decade later during the obscene property boom of the post-millennium. I arrived with a new notebook in my briefcase and a small Sony tape recorder in a specially sewn inner pocket. When it was activated you had to move as close as you could, or decorum permitted, to the interviewee – you also had to keep very still because Sony enjoyed nothing so much as the rustling of the jacket cloth which blitzed words spoken from any distance, particularly the voices of women.

After some hesitation, I had worn a tie. It might be a mistake, not at all in accord with what I guessed to be Lady Stears's Getty-hunting milieu, not Beaubourg. I approached the house in a nervous condition because so much was at stake – here at last was someone who could confirm and validate the bizarre story Madame Lepinskaya had begun to tell me in Moscow. Fifty-six years old and feeling it, on that warm early morning I could have been mistaken for a young boy setting out for a new school reputed for its bullying. I expected to be granted a hard time and little time. Lady Stears had made it clear that without her friend Olga's intercession on my behalf, it would have been no time. (Evidently she was more of a 'friend' to Olga than Olga was to her.)

I had always vaguely assumed that 'Cheyne' was derived from the French word for an oak tree, but my meticulous preparations for the encounter revealed that, as usual, it was down to the original landlord, Lord Cheyne (perhaps oak trees were among his ancestors). A little research revealed a dazzling list of former residents of Cheyne Walk.†

The present narrator's only social visit to Cheyne Walk had been in the 1970s after his publisher George Weidenfeld moved

---

† Thomas Attwood, a pupil of Mozart and organist of the St Paul's Cathedral and later the Chapel Royal headed the list. Elizabeth Gaskell was born at No. 93. J.M.W. Turner died at No. 119. George Eliot spent the last weeks of her life at No. 4. Henry James had settled at No. 21. Dante Gabriel Rossetti lived at No. 16, where he was banned from keeping peacocks due to the noise. James Clark Maxwell caused consternation by using his iron railings to conduct two electro-magnetic experiments. Algernon Charles Swinburne lived at No. 16, David Lloyd George at No. 10, Ralph Vaughan Williams at No. 13. Erskine Childers lived at No. 20 while writing *The Riddle of the Sands*. Not forgetting Hilaire Belloc, Sylvia Pankhurst, Laurence Olivier, Diana Mitford, Mick Jagger, the multimillionaires John Sainsbury and John Paul Getty II.

there as Lord Weidenfeld of Chelsea. – about whom a no doubt apocryphal story may amuse. Visiting the Frankfurt Book Fair, George Weidenfeld encountered his émigré rival André Deutsch, who mildly complained that George had been poaching young Caute from the Deutsch list.

'Now come, André,' George boomed, 'two Jews must not quarrel during Yom Kippur.'

Small and dapper, Deutsch looked puzzled but unsure – neither publisher was exactly an observant Jew. Neither was likely to shove, barge and bully the stewards on an El Al flight because his allotted seat was next to a woman's. Of course it wasn't Yom Kippur at all. This was early October and Yom Kippur had been and gone in September. It was simply Frankfurt. It was simply George who, when he apocryphally stepped out onto the balcony of St Peter's as the Pope's Easter guest, caused an old Ukrainian peasant woman in the massed crowd below to mutter, 'Who's that up on the balcony with George?'

So here I was, now in late middle age and no longer 'promising', again approaching Cheyne Walk and, for the present project, by design nobody's author. And what was this working-class Soviet girl from Volgograd, Comrade Nina Bolsharova, doing here? One was bound to assume that the clue resided in the two marriages she had made since her defection when in her forties: first as Mrs Marcus Epstein, more recently as Lady Stears, now all of sixty-four years old and (I guessed in advance) with the peppery, peremptory manner adopted by pretty women frustrated by the loss of youth. (I safely assumed she had been pretty because selected by Mosfilm to seduce Charles Chaplin in the Savoy Hotel, London.) On the dot of nine I rang the front-gate bell and waited for a response through the intercom. That familiar wrought-iron gate swung open, I climbed the seven steps and waited while the front door failed to respond. What kind of muscular butler or minder would after thorough scrutiny admit me? Was I to be confronted by Uoo U? I waited. A grand house never reveals any sound from within.

The figure who opened the door brought with him the body-language of one prepared to chase away Saladin's army, plus a gargoyle face distinctively Russian, a sleek head boasting the immaculate, windproof haircut of the hour, his torso straining against a gangsterish black suit of the sort you find lounging against vast limousines outside Moscow's big hotels.

'Leddie Shteerrs? Foll-ow.'

I followed this Ivan up the elegant Adams-style staircase, passing a huge, gilded mirror which caused me to avert my gaze from my reflection. Lady Stears was waiting as we reached the first floor, always the drawing room in a Georgian house, her hand outstretched, an affable smile, two emeralds and a ruby paying court to a brilliant diamond on a smooth, slender neck which could not properly belong to a woman of sixty-four. She addressed me in the perfect English and crystalline accent of RADA film stars of the 1940s and 1950s, the Vivien Leighs, Joan Greenwoods and Claire Blooms.

'I am so glad to meet you at last, Professor. Our ships have always passed in the night.' She led the way into the drawing room. Ivan had disappeared, replaced by a maid in a white cap and pinafore, only her hemline separating her from *Mansfield Park*.

'Now do please choose the chair that suits a distinguished historian. And do you drink tea or coffee?'

'Coffee, please.'

I was struggling not to look at the vast panoply of paintings wallpapering the high-ceilinged room, shoulder to shoulder and nose-to-tail. As a guest one should look only at one's hostess, not her furniture, until the moment of release arrives. I take this to be the difference between a guest and a visitor to a National Trust mansion. Nina was attended by two King Charles spaniels reluctant to come to rest. I saw at a glance that Lady Stears's impressive collection were invariably of the modern movement – Russian constructivists, German expressionists, French cubists and fauves, the New York school, a Pollock, a Lichtenstein, a

Warhol, plus a miniature Bacon and the hairy genitals of a Freud jostling for attention.

Lady Stears was monitoring my gaze. 'You like?' (She sounded Russian only when she chose to, perhaps luring me into 'I like'.)

No, she did not remotely look sixty-four and I guessed that the full ingenuities of modern surgery had been devoted to keeping her down to forty-plus. Not an ounce of surplus weight threatened her flamboyant Centre Court dress. While waiting for the pinafore-maid to return with the coffee, we spent a few sparring moments reflecting on why we should be in the same room. Nina regretted that she had not read any of my books (a delightful smile: 'I prefer one-page synopses') but she knew people who had heard from others that they (my books) were 'highly respected'. Of course she also knew my publisher, her near-neighbour 'George', who, or a friend of whom, had encouraged her to receive me. She had also heard from her esteemed colleague Olga in Moskow (sometimes 'Moscau'), who had recommended me as 'serious' and 'full of understanding' about those distant, dark days when Stalin was still Stalin. (In fact the art curators considered themselves a clear cut above Mosfilm employees who might be captivating the cameras one minute and sweeping the studio floor the next.) I did wonder why Nina should know Olga and whether the connection fed back to *Operatsiya Dvoinik* forty years ago. Olga had offered a hint: 'Chaplin'.

The Centre Court *fest* loomed, so I lost no time in asking Lady Stears the lead question: how could a visit by Picasso and Chaplin to Moscow in 1952 have escaped the attention of the world's press, not to mention historians and biographers – everyone?

Lady Stears fondled the lucky spaniel. 'Well, I assume that's what you've come to find out. But we won't get through all that in a short morning, I'm sure you know what the traffic to Wimbledon is apt to be like on semi-final day.'

I bent with the wind – was she a sports fan?

'Oh, I don't go to watch the tennis. It's the people, and meeting them in the Members' marquee over champagne and strawberries. One finds clients there. Some play truant from the Royal Box between matches – even between sets.'

I reached into an inner pocket to quell an itch under my arm, activating the little Sony. I then produced a notebook and asked whether I had her permission to use it.

'Does Olga allow it?'

'Sometimes yes, other times no – she's very shy.'

Nina shrugged delicate shoulders. 'Why not? London is not Moscau.'

7

Charlie Chaplin is currently preoccupied by the international release of his new film, *Limelight*. Up at six, he is immediately immersed in telegrams, international telephone calls, the projected box-office figures both sides of the Atlantic. Still brimming with projects under his well-groomed sheen of white hair, Chaplin has brought his current family – his young wife Oona and their four small children – from California by the Santa Fe Chief and on from New York by Cunard liner. 'The world premiere of *Limelight* is scheduled for London in October, simultaneous in New York. Chaplin is advised by his lawyer to lie low because a former employee has brought suit against United Artists, Chaplin's studio, and a process server might come in search of him to thrust the summons into his hand. He remains below decks as the *Queen Elizabeth* shudders from the Cunard pier on West 49th Street.

But the Chaplins are no sooner out in the Atlantic than news comes through that U.S. Attorney General James P. McGranery, a fiercely devout Catholic, has issued a statement dated 19 September 1952:

'There have been public charges that Chaplin was a member of the Communist Party, grave moral charges, and the making of statements that would indicate a leering, sneering attitude toward a country whose hospitality has enriched him. No harm can come from a fair hearing, and if he can meet the standard of our laws, he will be readmitted.'

Chaplin walks the deck of the *Queen Elizabeth*, the world's largest passenger liner. The weather is clement, the mid-ocean waves seem to be decorously greeting him, though unexpected gusts of wind force you to hold on to your hat. Oona often walks beside him, her arm through his, her own hat tied round the chin by a lovely chiffon scarf. Sometimes the couple talk, sometimes they are busy returning the greetings of the passengers who recognise the famous Chaplin, sometimes they smile when others on the first-class promenade deck throw a doubting glance then huddle in whispered consultation: can it really be...? Of course he's no longer young...isn't she the fourth wife..? Did you hear that...? They say he's in real trouble this time... Of course he's an escape artist like Houdini... Chaplin himself gazes at the swell of the sea so magnificently ignorant of human affairs, and gradually comes to terms with the Attorney General's vile statement – his life has changed for ever. Chaplin is a cocky little Cockney fighter who loved to watch Joe Louis in the ring, but he may never set foot in America again. After forty-one years he has in effect been expelled from the country in which his fortune still resides. 'You will have to go back and get it,' he tells Oona, who says, 'I will, Charlie, count on it.' Gripping the rails, watching the swaying sea dancing with the sky until the two are one, he asks whether she is prepared to live permanently in exile. She is. Charlie is her life. Her brilliant husband is now a refugee hounded by the Legionnaires and witch-hunters.

The four children are romping below decks in the care of two nannies.

Chaplin is always news. He bustles back into active mode when he sees a swarm of reporters boarding the ship at Cherbourg. He is never at his best when talking to the press but thinks he is. 'I am not political,' he tells them. 'I have never been political... I don't want to create a revolution. I only want to make some more films. I shall probably be in pictures till I drop dead.' He is also reported as saying: 'Today is not the day of great artists. Today is the day of politicians. People are only too willing to make issues about anything...'

Asked about his citizenship, he retorts: 'Super-patriotism leads to Hitlerism. I assume that in a democracy one can have a private opinion.'

Disembarking at Southampton, waving his homburg to the sightseers, then on to Waterloo Station and outright adulation,

Charlie hasn't visited his native London for twenty-one years. Now he takes up residence with his family in the Savoy. Barely an hour passes before he is staging a press conference in his penthouse suite overlooking the Thames. The place is packed out and blindingly lit for the American television cameras. One obscure figure in attendance is the accredited correspondent of the Soviet film magazine *Kino*, a dowdy woman in a fawn alpaca coat and shoes obviously bought cheap, wearing spectacles and a woolly little black beret. She has positioned herself next to the film correspondent of the *Daily Worker* but asks no questions, just scribbles diligently. No one notices her. The name on her accreditation and in her passport is Elena Nabokova. Her real name is Nina Bolsharova. She is studying Mrs Oona Chaplin closely, like a biologist bent over a microscope. Twenty-seven years of age, with dark hair and prominent dark brows, elfin-like, always devotedly at Chaplin's side, sometimes patiently pursuing her embroidery while attentively listening to Charlie's every word, liable to flash a toothy, effulgent smile, happy to laugh, liable to describe herself as 'shanty Irish' if pressed, capable of a 'what the fuck' or 'a fucking bore' in private and off the record, and showing early signs of the drink habit that runs to and from her illustrious father. Oona Chaplin is beautiful and widely liked. Nina monitors her expression, her smile, her clothes, her make-up, the characteristic movements of her hands. What Nina needs now is the voice, its pitch, its timbre, its accent. That's what interests the film correspondent of *Kino*, that's her job. Bolsharova is a qualified double, probably the most able among women, trained in the studios of Mosfilm and the cellars of the MVD.

Chaplin begins with a bad joke: 'Yes, most of the gold stored in Fort Knox came not from Morgan, Rockefeller or Ford, but from a little tramp down on his luck.'

No one laughs.

As the session progresses Nina reckons that Chaplin is far too anxious to rebut the charges against him – the when, where and how of his persecution by the FBI and the US Immigration

Commissioner. Was there a law (he asks rhetorically) against supporting the National Council for American-Soviet Friendship, the Artists' Front to Win the War, the Screen Actors Guild? Was he not legally entitled to befriend the longshoremen's leader, Harry Bridges, an alleged Communist? Or to have dinner with the Red composer Hanns Eisler?'

Nina observes that Oona is smiling brightly and nodding enthusiastically at every word – can she really fail to recognise that his derisive tone succeeds only in provoking resentment, even antipathy? Nina has never been to America but she is in love with Hollywood and knows why the demagogues like Senator Joseph McCarthy can create the illusion that these very rich, spoiled movie stars are secret Commies engaged in vile subversion of everything held sacred by Middle America. The aim – as she has been taught in Moscow – is to demonize the progressives who want to continue the New Deal, the work of Roosevelt, the shrinking minority who aspire to live in peace with the Soviet Union.

Chaplin continues to defend his record: 'Commissioner Boyd asked me: "Have you ever made any donations to the Communist Party?" I told him never. They started asking me about Communism as a way of life. Frankly, I don't know anything about the Communist way of life, but I must say this, I don't see why we can't have peace with Russia. I frankly believe the press is trying to start a war with Russia, and I wholeheartedly disapprove of it.'

Nina wonders what he's really like, this infinitely famous Chaplin now sixty-three but full of vim and, on the evidence, highly, irrepressibly sexed – one reason why the MVD has chosen her for this assignment, for *Operatsiya Dvoinik*, she a gifted double fluent in English and exactly the same height, weight and build as Mrs Chaplin. It's the woman's voice that remains Nina's worry. That and the geography of her pubic hair.

The reporters are still coming for him: 'Why didn't you ever become an American citizen despite living in this country for forty years?'

Another takes this up: 'Mr Chaplin, we who landed on those beaches in France resent your not being a citizen of this country.'

(Nina notes that Americans here in England are always in America.)

Chaplin hits back: 'You're not the only guy who landed on those beaches. My two sons were also in Patton's army, right up in the front line.'

The questions are now shooting at Chaplin, volleys of them. He admits that when *The Great Dictator* was threatened by violent pickets, he sought protection from Harry Bridges and his waterfront men. 'Maybe I prefer England where an actor may have dinner with a trade unionist without suffering government harassment.'

The Hearst *Journal-American* asks whether Chaplin believes such freedoms exist in Soviet Russia.

'The Hearst press will never be happy with me.'

'Charlie, do you have plans to attend some kind of fellow-travelling junket in Moscow?'

'None at all.'

'Can you confirm the Reds will stop at nothing to get you over there?'

Nina's brow furrows a fraction: where did they pick up that idea? Has *Operatsiya Dvoinik* been betrayed?' Anxiously she scans the faces around her. Her MVD controllers have shown her press photographs of Charles and Oona Chaplin in the audience at a rally for the pro-Soviet Henry Wallace during the 1948 presidential campaign.

'The Russians may threaten me with Siberia if I don't come,' Chaplin quips. 'But no one has issued an invitation. I haven't spoken to a Russian since I landed in England.'

'The war in Korea, with American boys dying, doesn't that make a difference?'

'What we need is peace. If the President of the United States or the Prime Minister of England sent me to Korea to negotiate peace, I would go. As a matter of fact I can disclose that I carry in my pocket an invitation from Prime Minister Churchill to visit 10 Downing Street and renew our old friendship. If he invites me to carry proposals to Premier Stalin for ending the war in Korea, I shall accept gladly.'

'Charlie, are you engaged in US tax avoidance?' He denies it (he has had to pay over a million-dollar deposit as the price of a re-entry permit to the USA).

'What do you have to say about Charles Skouras's decision to ban *Limelight* from his movie theatres? Loew's have done the same. Independent exhibitors and local-chain owners are pulling out across America. Don't you have only yourself to blame?'

'No, I blame the Catholic Legionnaires who are picketing the theatres. Maybe no one ever told them about the First Amendment to the Constitution.'

'Have you ever committed adultery?'

'An FBI agent visited our home uninvited and asked that question. I said no – and did he recommend it?'

Nina observes Oona laughing along with everyone else and of course the reporters are all looking in her direction. The laughter only intensifies when a notorious reporter from the Hearst press angrily shouts, 'How about cutting the jokes, Chaplin!'

Chaplin smiles, for a moment he is happy. 'Why is it that for forty years the world has been crowding into my movies in order to tickle its ribs – but as soon as you people catch me outside the theatre you start yelling, "Don't try and be funny, Charlie"?'

More laughter. Oona's expression seems to say both, 'That one never fails' and 'I never heard that one before.' Nina watches her intently.

The Hearst Press weighs in again: 'Get to the point, Mr Chaplin. Are you a running dog of Stalin's dictatorship – yes or no?'

'I never heard of it,' Chaplin snaps back foolishly. Even the faithful Oona looks disconcerted. Nina tries (following the Stanislavsky method of the Moscow Art Theatre) to penetrate the

American woman's inner state of mind. The Mosfilm sound archive has not been able to find a single recording of Oona O'Neill Chaplin's voice. She had been New York debutante of the year in 1942 when only sixteen or seventeen, she had decided to live it up and frequented the Stork Club, she had gone out with an obscure writer called J.D. Salinger and wanted to be an actress, they say her father the playwright Eugene O'Neill had told a friend that 1942 was a year for becoming a Red Cross nurse or an airplane factory worker, not a glamour girl, a floozie, God deliver me from my children, as O'Neill's own father used to remark. Oona rejected an offer from Vassar College, took part in a summer-stock production of *Pal Joey* in New York, then went to Hollywood for modelling and one screen test for 'The Girl from Leningrad' (but she could not think of any Leningrad lines to speak while the camera turned). She met Chaplin and fell for him, undeterred by his ongoing sex scandals – Joan Barry claiming paternity and all that headline stuff. But Oona never made a film, her voice never travelled to Mosfilm in Moscow. Nina could ventriloquize the different American accents. She assumed Oona must be East Coast but maybe with the sharper cadences of New York. Maybe after the press conference the dowdy *Kino* correspondent could push in with a thick Russian accent, 'Mrs Chaplin, how doss your children liking London?', stuff like that. Take care to measure your height against hers, probably identical, it's the eye level that counts, she's certainly as tall as Chaplin, wears low heels, they say he doesn't tolerate women taller than his own 5ft 4ins. Is this vain genius going to like me? – it could be uphill if he doesn't.

The first English voice is heard from the press corps (*The Times* of London): 'Mr Chaplin, would you tell us why and how you have been become the victim of a medieval witch-hunt?'

Relieved, Chaplin smiles affably: 'Gladly – don't I remember you from Eton?'

Oona is the first to laugh gaily (Nina can get that laugh in one but she doesn't get the Eton joke).

The Savoy press conference finally turns in Chaplin's favour when he is asked what his American wife makes of the adultery allegations.

'Oona has promised not to bring a paternity suit against me.' *Huge laughter. Chaplin triumphant.*

When it ends, the room thick with the smoke of cigarettes and cigars, ash on the Savoy's carpet, the American reporters scanning their notebooks for the killer lines, Nina Bolsharova heads for Mrs Chaplin, priming her Russian accent, her words thick with praise and sympathy, we in the Soviet Union so much admire Mr Chaplin, he our idol, and how doss your children liking London?

Oona responds warmly though her bright eyes keep swivelling. 'Oh they love London, the beautiful parks and so much history.' Nina hopes that Mr and Mrs Chaplin will one day visit Moskau.

'Every Soviet citizen will embrace world's greatest actor'. Oona says that would be 'just great'. Yes, she and Oona are the same height, eyes level, Oona chats for a moment about *Limelight* and Nina's ear gets it, exactly: upper-crust East Coast, cultivated and preppy Park Avenue debutante. This Soviet woman never loses track of a voice once she has heard it and could overthrow the entire capitalist system if it were just a matter of imitating female voices.

'Please tell me, Mrs Chaplin, which of your husband's many films is your favourite?'

'Always the one he's just finished. Right now, *Limelight*.'

'But apart from that?'

'Apart from that, all of them.' She flashes a smile then offers to confide a story especially for Nina's Moscow magazine.

'But you won't believe it because nobody does.'

'Please tell. I will believe.'

'When I was a deb in New York, a famous man took me out, read my palm, and prophesied that I would meet Charlie Chaplin and marry him. The famous man was Orson Welles.'

Next morning the Chaplins are out on the town, touring

Covent Garden vegetable market, a perambulation for old times. Nina and a scattering of reporters follow. Chaplin is shyly greeted by the cockney porters: 'Good to see yer, Guv'nor'. Accompanying him (for snappy promotion) is the young English star of *Limelight*, Claire Bloom, currently Juliet at the Old Vic and tactfully wearing flat heels (Nina notices). Pressing closer to Bloom, Nina hears the tinkling RADA accent of an English actress for the first time outside of a Mosfilm studio. Fame! Intoxicating! This plain little man carried with him an aura, a magnetic field, a compulsion to be adored.

Comes the night of the première of *Limelight*, 23 October, an expectant throng gathered for the charity show outside the Leicester Square cinema bathed in klieg lights. Charlie steps out of the limousine, Oona emerges in a chic white satin gown, wow, both smiling and waving to the crowds before progressing inside to take up position in the receiving line to be presented to Princess Margaret. Nina is again accredited and observes keenly – the Princess sounds super-RADA as she intones 'How do you do? Aym delayted to meet yew.' The Chaplins bow and curtsy with panache, the smiling Princess is delayted to meet Claire Bloom tew.

The glitter of the grand occasion both erodes Nina's cynicism and reinforces it – the antics of the bourgeois world. Yet Hollywood is her dream and Chaplin is Hollywood. You see both a plain, dumpy little ageing man and then, when the crowds press in on him, cheering and smiling and blowing kisses, you remember that Chaplin is the great transformer: put him in front of a camera with a script all his own and the metamorphosis is nothing short of miraculous – the entire world laughs. Nina's whole being was dedicated to the worship of performance. Charisma? Does Chaplin wear it like a shimmering halo? She has never before seen a Western publicity relations exercise at full throttle. You are bound to feel the isolation and estrangement of Russia continually congratulating itself and its puppets decked out in male gold braid and wide military hats. Here in the West you sense the prominence of woman, of the feminine, Oona in particular – Chaplin would not be complete without her.

But Nina must rely on the English newspapers for a description of the dinner given for Chaplin at the Mansion House by the Lord Mayor, Charlie raising a cheer from the white ties and silk gowns by describing England as 'my country'. But, as *The Times* sardonically points out next morning, 'Mr Chaplin is not inclined to settle for the draconian taxes enjoyed by the rich who choose residence status in this country'.

Through the Soviet Embassy Nina keeps contact with the Western press. The British papers report how the Chaplins were presented to the Queen and the Duke of Edinburgh on 3 November at the Royal Variety Performance at the Palladium after taking tea in Fortnum and Mason's. From Paris, *l'Humanité* is blowing kisses and urging 'Charlot' to accept 'the warm embrace of the World Peace Movement, a fatal blow to the high priests of the Cold War.' A message to her ('Elena Nabokova') from the MVD confirms that the French Communists have been kept in ignorance about *Operatsiya Dvoinik* – understood, Comrade?

'*Da, Tovarichsh, ponyatno*', *Vy pravi* – understood, you're right.'

Nina has already invented Oona's comment when she finally learns of the invitation to Moscow: 'Why does Mr Stalin insist on having his birthday in December? Is that friendly, Charlie?' Nina also imagines Oona fending off the press. Reporter: 'Do you plan to accompany your husband to Soviet Russia, Mrs Chaplin?' Oona: 'I don't have anyone else in mind at the moment. But you never know.'

Of course Nina does not pass back these imagined exchanges to the comrades in Moscow – for Beria's men it is an unspoken point of honour that only men make jokes.

8

While the Chaplins are in Paris for the première of *Limelight*, they are no less royally received than in London by the ruling republican establishment – dinner with President Auriol, a Légion d'honneur for Charlot, a grand visit to the Opéra, as well as an event widely discussed in Paris: a first meeting with Pablo Picasso. Louis Aragon arranges a dinner (no wives) to which Jean-Paul Sartre is invited (despite having outraged the Communists by his boa-constrictor remark in *Le Nouvel Observateur*). Aragon is the only one present who speaks both French and English, so the convergence of all these geniuses leaves Chaplin somewhat adrift, smiling and nodding instead of speaking. The one positive thing that emerges is an invitation to visit Picasso's studio in the rue des Grands Augustins, happily accepted by Chaplin on behalf of himself and Oona who (he conveys to Picasso through Aragon) is 'a great fan of yours', which eventually emerges as 'Mrs Chaplin adores your '*Femme à l'éventail* – *Lady with a Fan*', a painting by Picasso from 1905.

Nina has little difficulty in wangling her admission to Picasso's studios. The Communist journalists are there in force and we are not short of their published accounts of this celebratory gathering of the great and good. Aragon again occupies centre stage as translator, eloquently explaining to the Chaplins that Pablo admires Charlie's films – notably the rapid, deft way Monsieur Verdoux flips through the pages of a telephone directory in search of new female victims, and the way he counts their money after disposing of them.

'After seeing the film,' Aragon tells the Chaplins, 'Pablo then tried to count his own money equally fast. As a result he made more and more mistakes and there were more re-counts.'

'Doesn't he know about banks?' Oona asks.

Elsa Triolet intervenes: 'Pablo has always carried around with him an old red-leather trunk from Hermès in which he keeps five or six million francs. He calls it "cigarette money".'

'Should he be smoking so much?' Oona asks – though Triolet herself is shrouded in Balkan Sobranie smoke.

Chaplin beams genially: 'As Henry Ford once remarked to me, a man who knows how much he's worth isn't worth much. For the record, I almost bought Pablo's *Guernica* for my film *The Great Dictator.* You remember the scene where Adenoid Hynkel kicks a paper globe around? *Guernica* was to have been glimpsed – for a split second – in the dictator's grandiose office.' Chaplin sighs contentedly: 'The asking price was prohibitive.' Chaplin opens his hands in resignation, offering his famous wistful smile, impervious to his guests' horror. Picasso himself cannot follow a word. Aragon leads Chaplin aside with the gravitas of a prelate murmuring an opinion in the Roman curia:

'May I advise you not to repeat this story to Pablo.'

'Repeat it? He's here.'

'But mercifully he didn't understand.'

Oona asks Triolet about Picasso's current marital status.

'Pablo currently lives like a monk,' Triolet replies.

'Frocked or unfrocked?' Chaplin quips.

'Believe me, his work is everything.' Triolet says.

In fact, Aragon and Triolet have also impressed the need for tact on Picasso after taking him to see *Limelight*. 'I don't care for that maudlin, sentimentalizing side of Charlot,' he has confided on leaving the cinema. 'That's for shop girls. When Charlot starts reaching for the heartstrings maybe he impresses Chagall but it doesn't go down with Picasso. It's hand-me-down threadbare romanticism and it's just bad literature.'

Nina picks up this anecdote from *l'Humanité*'s man charged with the duty of accompanying a rather dour and dowdy correspondent from *Kino* who speaks bad French. And now seeing Picasso and Chaplin together, the two prized comrades coveted by her controllers, Nina feels exhilaration, the doorstep to triumph, but then anxiety when you remember that they are not twins, each ego must be seduced and captivated separately – and as far as she knows the woman from the Pushkin Museum, Lepinskaya, has not yet set out from Moscow in quest of Picasso.

'Comrade Triolet,' *l'Humanité*'s man further confides to his Soviet colleague, 'says she has detected in Picasso the virile male's fight against the ageing process, the loss of potency. She told Laurent Casanova, the Party's cultural chief, that when Pablo saw *Limelight*, he was incensed by the ageing clown sacrificing himself sexually and turning over his beloved ballerina Claire Bloom to a younger man – played by his own son, Sidney Chaplin! Pablo has no regard for his own son Paulo whom he employs as a part-time chauffeur and handyman. Pablo told Comrade Elsa he'd rather let a beautiful young woman die, any day, than see her happy with someone else.'

'But that cannot be reported to the Soviet public,' Nina says severely. 'We have high standards of morality.'

'Certainly not, Comrade, just between ourselves.' The man from *l'Humanité* becomes even more indiscreet. 'Actually, it is my own opinion that now Picasso has set eyes on Madame Oona he must realise that Chaplin is by no means the clown of *Limelight*. In the film old Chaplin gives up young Bloom but in real life Chaplin fully possesses young Oona – who bears a striking physical resemblance to Claire Bloom and even doubled for her in the film. Pablo will regard this as a challenge!'

'What does "doubled" mean?' Nina asks solemnly.

'It means an understudy seen only at a discreet distance from the camera.'

Nina assumes the pose of Garbo in *Ninotchka*: 'We do not allow doubles in Soviet cinema.'

More guests and not-guests are arriving, comrades and hangers-on crowding in to witness this historic convergence of two geniuses of short stature, expanding girth, incredible fame, and legendary wealth. The Chaplins merely peck at the culinary delicacies offered, Oona smiling serenely while saying no thanks are these ones snails? The room falls absolutely silent when

Picasso grabs Aragon and instructs him to pass some profound thoughts to Charlot. Aragon rises to the mission:

'*Mon cher* Charlot, Pablo is saying that mime is the exact equivalent of the gesture in painting by which we transmit directly a state of mind – no description, no analysis, no words.'

Chaplin affably nods his agreement, not having understood a word. The princely Aragon settles for a second, truncated version:

'Mime, Charlot, is you. No words. *Le geste, c'est tout.*'

But 'mime' comes out as 'meem' and Chaplin looks puzzled. Politely he lifts a hat he is not wearing, wriggles his eyebrows and twiddles an invisible moustache. He then performs the dance with the rolls from the new year's eve sequence in *The Gold Rush*. Huge applause. Oona is delighted. Holding a bottle of wine more or less her own, she now stands back-to-back with Chaplin, bends her knees, and giggles.

'See? Charlie's taller.'

'*Moi aussi!* I try!' roars Picasso, aflame. He is an inch shorter than Chaplin.

Oona obliges him, and by no means coyly, again bending at the knee, while playfully butting his bottom with her own.

'Pablo may be a monk but definitely unfrocked,' Chaplin tells Aragon, who reluctantly translates at Picasso's insistence. '"Unfrock" en anglais, ça veut dire "déshabiller".'

Picasso smiles broadly. 'He means he wants me and his wife to undress? Why not? Tell Charlot I wouldn't want to insult him by giving the impression that I don't desire his wife. Tell him only a very wealthy friend is worth cuckolding.'

Only now does Nina notice a woman standing entirely alone at the back of the studio, rather handsome, perhaps in her mid-forties, her face and dark hair somehow familiar, a long ivory cigarette holder jutting from her teeth at a rigid angle above a chin more pronounced than most women would want. But why is she familiar? Nina approaches the woman and introduces herself. The woman barely turns her gaze and says not a word. Nina retreats.

'*Ty znaesh*' who she is?' Nina asks *l'Humanité*.

'*C'est Madame Dora Maar* – perhaps you know Picasso's "weeping woman" portraits?'

'*Bozhe moi!* But why is she standing there alone?'

The question is overheard by Louis Aragon, who takes the Soviet comrade 'Elena' from *Kino* aside and smoothly explains why Dora Maar's reinstatement is, '*entre nous, provisoire*. She is no longer the *châtelaine d'auparavnt*'. And then Aragon amuses himself by explaining to Nina the quality that both Pablo and Charlot hold in common apart from genius.

'Both had a son by an early marriage, Paulo and Sydney, both boys taller than their fathers, both cursed as the offspring of their rejected mothers, both berated by their fathers with scorn and sarcasm.'

Elsa Triolet has joined them. 'One hears that Sydney Chaplin received the customary treatment on the set of *Limelight*. Charlot and Pablo are *au fond* cruel and sadistic men towards anyone they no longer need. Particularly women. Poor Dora stands there not knowing from one moment to the next whether she is needed. The Weeping Woman has become The Waiting Woman.'

Aragon nods in assent. 'So tell me, comrade from *Kino*, what do you make of the very young Madame Oona?'

'Is she a good mother to her four children?' Triolet wants to know. 'One hears that she dotes on Charlot, never out of his sight. The joke in Paris is that if all the Chaplins were placed on a sinking ship with only one lifeboat, the cry from Oona would be "Charlie first".'

The regal couple turn away as if pulled by a single string, Nina not having spoken a word.

9

I soon detected a difference between Olga's narrative of those distant events and Nina's. Both diligently recalled what had befallen them, the roles they had been assigned, but whereas Olga was drawn deeper inside her young self, re-living every moment and liable to fall silent or weep under the weight of recall, Nina's acute memory was more detached, more sardonic, and much more concerned with her disguises and 'doubling', an exercise in theatre performance.

We were in the late months of 1993.

'Okay, since you ask. *Operatsiya Dvoinik*, yes, was a super-secret, MVD-led operation. *Sovershenno sekretno.* Ministry of Internal Affairs under Lavrentiy Beria. All the more secret because the top Party bosses were sharply divided over such an enterprise which might fail disastrously.

'Ideologically risky?'

'Call it the liberals versus the old guard. Comrade Beria was the prime manipulator, with Ilya Ehrenburg moving the chess pieces behind the scenes, that wily old Jew...'

'He being close to Picasso's friends and desperate to secure a success for himself while Stalin's final pogrom was in full swing?'

'Just so.'

'You don't care for Jews?'

'Who does?'

'And you count Beria as a "liberal"?'

'You might not.'

'And Stalin himself?'

'Stalin knew nothing.... But Stalin had a knack of suddenly waking up and spreading his breakfast table with severed heads. Even Beria was swallowing tranquillisers. He had enemies. In the end they executed him but I am running ahead of myself.'

'And the French Communists were kept in the dark?'

'Of necessity. Party journalists in Paris thought I had come to see *Limelight* and report on American hostility to Charlie. Only Aragon and his wife Elsa Triolet among the Party's leading intellectuals knew the real mission.'

'What about the Soviet press?'

'No problem. They were told to say nothing. The editors of *Pravda* and *Izvestiia* fingered their necks every morning while shaving. Correspondents for our art and culture organs were more excitable and had to be invited in for special lessons in silence which involved deprivation of food and sleep for forty-eight hours.' She laughed teasingly. 'Or so your Western Kremlinologists would have us believe.'

'Consequently the Soviet journalists rapidly discovered that they had never heard of Picasso and Chaplin?'

'Correct.' Lady Stears uttered this quite solemnly, as if awed by memory.

I asked her about Beria, head of the NKVD-MVD since 1939, successor to Yagoda (executed) and Yezhov (executed). How close had she been allowed to come to Beria?

Lady Stears sighed a little and gave thought to my question. 'Not close. Beria was a Georgian like Stalin. Pince-nez spectacles, liked telling jokes. I found his eyes fiercely intelligent but unreliable. He looked through you and you weren't sure what he found the other side. But charming to women. I couldn't disguise from him my interest in Hollywood, which amused him. He once called me his Mary Pickford – but only once.'

'Did he ever discuss politics with you?'

'Meaning?'

'Did he mention what Malenkov thought, or Molotov, or Khrushchev, or Voroshilov?'

'Never. They didn't exist.'

'Or Stalin?'

'No one ever spoke of Stalin unless quoting from his Works. To do so was blasphemy.'

'How did the Ministry of Culture brief the Moscow

correspondents of the foreign Communist press – *l'Humanité*, the *Daily Worker, Unità, Neues Deutschland*?'

'I don't know, I wasn't involved, but I imagine the East German journalists were no problem, they belonged to us and half-regarded themselves as still prisoners of war. If told to clean out the latrines they would make an excellent job of it.'

'But the French and Italian Communists, wouldn't they get excited if Pablo Picasso suddenly turned up at the Pushkin Museum or Charlie Chaplin emerged smiling from the studios of Mosfilm?'

'The Communist foreign correspondent comrades were invited to a briefing in the Lubyanka. You only had to step into those white-tiled corridors, and hear your shoes on the iron grilles...'

'To become a changed man?'

'The foreign scum? Yes – for ever, Professor.' She laughed.

I took note of Lady Stears's capacity to be both cynical and playful, yet at the flash of an eyelid a Stalinist apparatchik, her xenophobia still on full throttle.

'And if all went well, according to plan, the press would suddenly be given the green light, big headlines, Moscow Radio at full stretch?'

'If all went well.'

10

The Chaplins have returned to the Savoy from the festivities in Paris and Rome. Nina Bolsharova makes her move on 17 November as soon as BOAC confirm that Oona's flight had taken off for Shannon. The Soviet Embassy's informant on the Savoy hotel desk passes the message that Mrs Chaplin and her expensive bags are heading for America, where (as Nina knows) her urgent mission is to retrieve the Chaplin Crown Jewels before the fortune is frozen or impounded. What Nina cannot know is how long Oona will be gone. (In the event, it was ten days.)

It is evening, time for lights-out in the children's rooms, and Chaplin sits brooding in the Savoy suite while his kids try to lure him into bedtime stories and the antics they have grown up on. Sensing his despondency, his inclination to dismiss the children impatiently, the faithful nanny McKenzie, known as Kay Kay, is trying to coax them into bed. The telephone rings. He snatches at it, hoping it is Oona (10 a.m. over there at 1085 Summit Drive on the West Coast), anxious for news about the house, the banks, the securities...but not particularly about the faithful servants now facing dismissal. He hopes she won't be too sentimental, too generous.

But it is not Oona. The Savoy reception desk advises Mr Chaplin that a lady in the lobby is desirous of seeing him. No, she does not have an appointment. She says she is a Soviet journalist who has attended his press conferences in London and Paris.

'Not the dowdy woman in spectacles? Tell her to make an appointment with my secretary. Tell her I'm tired.'

'Well, sir, I wouldn't say that description fits at all. Extremely elegantly dressed and... In fact she somewhat resembles Mrs Chaplin....forgive me.'

'Nonsense. Probably another goddam impostor claiming paternity.'

'A moment, sir, while I speak to her again.' The receiver dangles in Chaplin's hand, the children are shouting for him, Michael the loudest, possessed by one of his demonic rages. Chaplin broods: why does Oona want ever more children?

Reception is on the line again. 'Sir, Madame Bolsharova has shown me accreditation by Mosfilm and by the Soviet Embassy. She wants to discuss an imminent premiere of *Limelight* in Moscow.'

'She's not the dowdy woman from *Kino?*'

'Definitely not, sir.'

'Send her up.'

What he sees is indeed by no means the dowdy woman in thick spectacles but almost a replica of Oona, beautifully attired and wearing the latest Parisian version of the New Look, padded shoulders, a full bosom, the jacket pinched at the waist, a pencil skirt down to mid-calf. He sees a vermilion hat like an upturned bell perched above delicately coiffured black hair done à la mode, the eyelashes long and by no means real, the lips matching the hat and very real. He notices that the heels of the calfskin shoes are not too elevated. Can it be Claire Bloom playing a prank? No, this woman is not innocent like Claire, not Juliet on the balcony. He has made a lunch date with la belle Claire while Oona is away...

He extends his hand, feels a delicate pressure beneath her chamois leather gloves. And such perfume!

'Maestro Chaplin, thank you for receiving me, I shall not take up your precious time. I come on behalf of the Union of Soviet Socialist People's Republics. Generalissimo Stalin has personally instructed me to visit you.'

Chaplin is puzzled. She is clearly saying Russian-type things, very severe, he is reminded of Garbo's sublime performance in *Ninotchka*, yet he could be listening to...to Oona!

'Are you Russian?' he asks shrewdly.

'Definitely. You wish to inspect my passport, Maestro?'

'Anyone can forge a passport.' (He's no fool.) 'And you say you have been sent by Stalin? Stalin himself! Well, I haven't heard from him recently.' (Or ever.)

The woman smiles sympathetically and – can he be mistaken? – conspiratorially. 'I believe Prime Minister Churchill has been in touch with Comrade Stalin following your recent meeting in 10 Downing Street,' she says silkily. 'They are of course old wartime colleagues and such bonds do not wither.'

'They want me to wind up in the war in Korea. Won't you sit down?'

'Thank you, Maestro.'

Chaplin indicates a chair and tries not to watch as she arranges her legs.

'I also bring you a personal message from your old friend, People's Artist Sergei Eisenstein.'

'Sergei? I knew him well in Hollywood. A great man, he always cheated at tennis.' Chaplin sighs. 'He died before his time.'

'Happily this was a false report in the bourgeois press. The Hearst press and its syndicated *doyenne* Louella Parsons even claimed he committed suicide, such infamy. He is currently working on necessary revisions to *Ivan Grozny*, part II. I work with him at Mosfilm and can assure you that our greatest Soviet director is very much alive.'

'Well, I'd take some convincing.'

Nanny Kay Kay McKenzie comes in from the adjoining bedrooms, takes a quick look, a seasoned navigator scanning the weather, brows fractionally lifted, then sweeps out, starched skirt rustling, back to the clamouring children. By now trips round London have run out of steam, they're missing their friends, they need a proper home not room service. McKenzie has overheard Mrs Chaplin urging Mr Chaplin to rent 'one of those cute little mews houses near Harrods' but he keeps brooding over a large pile of reports of his press conferences, some air-freighted from America.

McKenzie wishes he would say goodnight to the children, wobbling on the edge of a cliff while the bear (also Charlie on all-fours) doggedly pursues him, tongue lolling hungrily, Geraldine watching sceptically but glad he's there. Sometimes Michael upsets the act by insisting on playing the bear, roaring on his hind legs, because only he understands about bears and needs to command his father's attention (in fact everyone's). When Victoria begins to hide her face under the pillow, her dad leans over tenderly and quotes A.A. Milne: 'Isn't it funny/how a bear likes honey'.

'I believe Mrs Chaplin is in America?' Nina is saying. 'I'm sure the journey will be very arduous for her – in the face of so much reactionary hostility.'

He shrugs, and listens. This glamorous Soviet woman seems to be offering him not only a showing of *Limelight* but a full Chaplin film festival in Moscow plus a grand house once belonging to a nobleman of the Romanov era, Count Tolstoy. Plus political asylum and Soviet citizenship thrown in for good measure. Sometimes this woman's voice veers from Oona's to an uncanny replication of RADA, of Claire Bloom. This deepens his suspicions. The Hearst papers may be setting him up, stage-managing another sex scandal. But he feels tired, uncertain, and brimming with unspent lust. He must make a stand or a one-night stand, unclear which.

'Are you aware that *Modern Times* and *The Great Dictator* have never been released to the Soviet public? Sergei Eisenstein himself told me.'

'That is why he is so anxious to make amends, Maestro. The time, he feels, is now right to show your great masterpieces in their original versions.' She recrosses her legs with a swish. 'Maestro Eisenstein has spoken to Stalin. I have with me a personal letter from him.' She offers Chaplin an envelope.

'Is this in Cyril?'

'In Cyrillic? No.'

The message is short, in English and he recognises the handwriting: 'Dear Old Friend Charlie, come now to Moscow for *Limelight* première and a season of your great films. Big reception promised. Do not delay, the right time is now. All the asylum seekers are currently travelling in the opposite direction. What a blow to the Americans, don't you agree? Affectionately, Sergei Eisenstein.'

'*The Hearst press would have rejoiced,*' I broke in. '*Hedda Hopper would have yelled* "What did I tell you!" *in* Variety *and* The Hollywood Reporter.'

Yes, yes, but Charlie could not think very straight. He was traumatised. His world of forty years had been cruelly snatched away like a street mugging. His fortune might be frozen even if he stayed in London because, you know, their banks were hand in glove with the Americans.'

Chaplin sighs. 'Well, you must excuse me, I have to put the children to sleep now. They will be out with their nanny tomorrow morning so why don't you come back at ten thirty? To finalise the deal.'

'The cleaning staff will not interrupt us?'

For a moment he looks confused, uncertain where he is or who she is. The woman presents him with a gift 'from the Soviet people', a book beautifully wrapped in shiny red paper adorned with yellow hammer-and-sickles. He accepts it, bemused – he is no longer young.

'It is known as the *Kniga*,' she explains sweetly. 'That means "book", our Soviet *Book of Tasty and Healthy Food*. It has run through a dozen editions with eight million copies in print. Here is the new edition for 1952, brown cover this time.'

'But it's printed in Russian,' he sighs. 'How did you call the alphabet a moment ago...Cyril?'

'Cyrillic.' She glows, her eyes luminously reflecting the aphrodisiac power of genius. 'But you can enjoy the pictures in the *Kniga* and when I see you tomorrow at 10.30 a.m. I can translate the captions. Bye.'

She is gone. Who is she?

Before extinguishing the light and extending his short, ageing body down the half-empty king-size bed, its sheets in crisp Irish linen embroidered with the Savoy crest, Chaplin takes a few moments to leaf through the gift that the Soviet woman has left behind.

He falls asleep, not knowing what he does not know, the brown-bound *Kniga* at rest on Oona's pillow.

Nina has gone back to her precious, once-in-a-lifetime hotel bathroom where she spends most of her time making up faces and identities in front of the mirror. When she returns to the Savoy next morning, Madame Bolsharova will not inform the maestro that due to Moscow's perennial meat shortages (not mentioned in the *Kniga*), she herself normally relies on vegetarian *kotleti* made from cabbage or beets, although she has little time for shopping or cooking on a single gas burner and prefers the canteen at Mosfilm. Occasionally she buys the ubiquitous 'Chatka' cans, mayo-drenched salad of crab, potatoes, cucumbers and tinned peas. What she will translate for him from the introduction to the *Kniga* is the advice to Soviet citizens that the working masses under capitalism are shockingly malnourished and often condemned to starvation.

'Don't you agree, Maestro?'

She is wearing a new outfit, a different perfume, heels designed to tower over him, and he feels no interest in food, or starvation. She has calculated that although he doesn't like to be in the presence of taller women, and is prepared to lose his temper about it – he really does. Does want. Does want to have a glamorous woman bearing down on him and coaxing him to autograph her thigh.

'And the cleaning staff didn't disturb you, Lady Stears?'

'Chaplin had given instructions to the House Manager.'

'And the children didn't burst in causing interruptus*?'*

'Causing what? Chaplin had told Kay-Kay and the junior nanny to take them to the London Zoo, a special treat. I think the McKenzie woman, they called her Kay-Kay, very nice, very practical, understood the situation. I could tell that she didn't like to leave me and Charlie together but Charlie was not a good father while Oona was away and

if my presence consoled him, lessened his bad temper with the children... Frankly, it wasn't difficult until Oona returned several days later.'

'Wasn't he afraid of more damaging publicity?'

'Yes when he remembered to be afraid. He told me in the Savoy that maybe his reputation as an immoralist with women had done him more harm in America than the politics. Of course I was very sympathetic to that. He told me he had never been unfaithful to Oona in ten years of marriage. Of course I was very sympathetic to that, too. He told me he had an abhorrence of condoms and I was sympathetic. My main worry, frankly, was pubic hair. I'd had no sightings of Oona's and in any case it's always hard to replicate unless you yourself have more rather than less. I needn't have worried.'

'What did you feel? In bed with the great Chaplin.'

Lady Stears gave me the look I deserved, but then Nina burst through: 'He couldn't be too premature for me. All my life I have put up with the repulsive embrace of old men either spurting prematurely or unable to come.'

11

Back in Moscow, Madame Lepinskaya never enquired after Nina or my visits to Cheyne Walk. By late 1993, more than a year after our first meeting, she had become sufficiently relaxed to throw teasing remarks at me – I would say 'unbuttoned' but this was a lady whose appearance was never other than meticulous; her loose, blue-and-black denim trouser suit worn in a style suggesting an artist's smock was as attractive to the eye as her tight-fitting terracotta polka-dot silk dress. Perhaps these changes of costume reflected shifts of mood. It is interesting how the passage of time, even when not shared time, brings people closer even when they do not see each other for months on end. But absent time is indeed shared time. I suspect that a kind of friendship results from mutual congratulation on having defied mortality – 'You again! Well, we're both still alive!' Madame Lepinskaya was no longer reluctant to display pleasure at my arrival, allowing herself the kind of rudeness which comes with intimacy:

'Of course one cannot expect someone as blinkered as yourself to understand our situation in those days...' Or: 'I hope you have not brought your prejudices with you, Professor.' But then she would yield a smile and resume her narrative – then suddenly stall. One waited. Elegant, serene and outwardly composed, her cosmetics applied with perfect discretion, she was nevertheless struggling to control her emotions as memories of the terror closed in on her. Stalin's yellow slit eyes were always at her window.

More than once I pressed her to explain why this remarkable event she was describing so meticulously remained undisclosed to the world forty years later.

'Because, Monsieur, Russia today can always become Russia in 1952.'

'But the Soviet Union is no more. The Communist Party has gone.'

'The Communist Party does not think so.'

But I suspected that the history and demise of the Soviet Union really had very little to do with her marathon of reticence. On each visit I began to notice more about her sitting room, although nothing changed: her mantelpiece (over an electric fire with artificial glowing coals) carried portraits of her father, her mother and her one living sister, but no one else. Had she been childless? Had she never married? What had she meant by 'when I found myself living alone'? After all, the majority of women of grandmotherly age in every country and culture tend to mention their children and grandchildren at an early stage of a friendship (though that was by no means the right word for a relationship always precarious however cordial).

One constant source of tension was my notebook. Madame Lepinskaya would allow me to record some of her remarks but not others. Her fear of my active pen came and went then came again. When I had first produced a notebook she had reacted with an angry gesture of horror, a swatting, as if threatened by a wasp. She chided me: 'Anyone can read what you write down. In this country nothing in your baggage or even on your person will pass unseen. Rest assured of that, Monsieur, we are not in Charente.' Of course she was naïve about this because I have a good memory and obviously wrote everything down as soon as I returned to the Rossiya. In view of Lepinskaya's unpredictable and seemingly irrational pleas of 'no notes about that!', I took to activating my miniature Sony tape recorder, poised in the lining pocket of my jacket, a trusted veteran of other campaigns, eager as a faithful askari to perform loyally. The little reels turned silently until – the awkward moment – they registered a full stomach by a terminal click. One could not reload unless natural causes took Madame Lepinskaya away from the sitting room (which they never did – she never left me alone).

She was invariably insistent about the rectitude of the Russian point of view, scornful of Western critics even though her own values and judgments often replicated theirs. For example, she was not reluctant to accuse Western museum curators of 'misusing Wall Street funding'. I asked what she meant.

'By making politics out of our difficulties.'

Her choice of the word 'difficulties' struck me as a colossal euphemism, an almost pathetic evasion of the reality. Had not Nazi apologists spoken of the 'Jewish problem' in Hitler's Germany? – but perhaps that was unfair.

More than once I reminded her that if you relied on the recognised authorities, the biographies and critical works, newspapers and magazines, you found absolutely no mention of a visit to the Soviet Union by Picasso – not at any time. Madame Lepinskaya invariably assumed that this line of thought implied that she had concocted the whole story.

'Why should I waste my time feeding you a tissue of lies, Monsieur?'

'Madame, I did not say that! That thought has never crossed my mind.' (Though it had, quite frequently.)

Occasionally I fell into the trap of arguing with her. It is common knowledge, I said, that the Kremlin in 1952 resembled a medieval court of sweating barons manoeuvring to seize the succession to a tyrant who had enjoyed unchallenged power since or even before the death of Lenin in 1924. Thirty years of One Man. Among the sweatiest barons, choking on their own trepidation, were the editors of *Pravda* (the Party), *Izvestiia* (the Government), and *Literaturnaya gazeta* (*Pravda*'s regular politico-cultural paper). The Soviet Press did not act 'responsibly' (her word), its only thought was what He, this tyrant, would think or decide if one yellow slit-eye remained open.

Listening to this, Madame Lepinskaya shook her head and reached to adjust the comb that pinned her chignon, one of her little giveaway habits when she and I were not in harmony.

'Stalin did much for Russia,' she said. 'I would never have had my education but for Stalin. The electric power which lit our houses was his work. Our country would have been subjugated by the German fascists but for Stalin – and I would probably not have been here, talking to you. Of course he had many faults of personality...'

As if to atone for what I obviously regarded as a defence of the indefensible, Madame Lepinskaya rose to her feet: 'Shall I tell you something? On the first day I met Picasso in Paris, he did a table napkin sketch of me, though the style of that line drawing was *tout à fait* different from the portrait I showed you. Please follow.'

We returned to the small bedroom, the 9 by 9. I gazed again at the oil portrait above her bed but she had in mind a different offering, something extracted tenderly from a very small leather case and carefully wrapped in tissue paper.

'I think you deserve to see this since you are appreciative of fine art. I'm afraid I cannot allow you to handle it, Monsieur, it's too fragile. Here you see a mark from Pablo's thumb, he had been eating moules with his fingers. Actually this napkin sketch was stolen from my suitcase before I left Paris but later returned to me in Moscow – that's quite a story.'

I studied it. So familiar!

'You can find this sketch repeated in the lithograph Pablo did in 1964, *Grande Maternité*. Do you know it?'

'Yes, I have a mere reproduction at home – but I have never seen your Paris napkin.'

Now she proudly produced the lithograph from the same drawer. It was signed at the upper left, the napkin at the bottom. In the lithograph a flurry of blue and black lines provided background to the young mother's head, in the napkin just a few pencil lines served an identical function. In both the image rested on an expanse of white on which a single black line captured the mother and the baby suckling her breast.

'Another baby!' I exclaimed.

She laughed. 'Yes, Pablo evidently knew already that was my destiny – though I didn't. But can you detect the element of Raphael in this napkin line-drawing?'

'No.'

'You should look at Raphael's *La Fornarina*, the "baker's daughter", naked from the waist up. She was Margherita Luti, a model and mistress to whom Raphael was passionately attached, or so they say. In 1968 Pablo executed a partly pornographic series on the theme of the painter's desire for *La Fornarina*. Picasso shows us the young Raphael's imprecations to the Pope to allow his mistress to live with him – otherwise he could not paint. "*Le Pape est assis*," Picasso wrote on his illustration in case anyone should wonder who the little man in the high hat was – Picasso remained a Communist and wanted the head of the Catholic Church to be seen as a pathetic voyeur to Raphael's fornication.'

'When did you discover the similarity, Madame?'

'Well! I could hardly discover it until Picasso produced *La Fornarina*, and then of course such things take years to reach Russia. In fact my nephew Yuri Tairov came across it on an American website.'

We returned to the sitting room, she bidding me go first – she was leaving nothing to chance.

'You mentioned your "nephew" Yuri, Madame? Is Madame Svetlana your sister?'

'She's a cousin, it's just a manner of speaking. I'm afraid my relations with Svetlana have not been easy but I'm very fond of Yuri, he was once my son's closest friend.'

We sat down. She had never previously mentioned her son.

'Madame, can you please now describe your visit to France in 1952?'

'*Oui, d'accord*.' She hesitated. 'Monsieur, before I bring my memory to bear on that, I have something less than pleasant to ask you.' She reached to adjust her chignon, a characteristic gesture when nervous. 'I have never asked you about your life in Moscow. Obviously you have friends here, and perhaps some enemies too.'

I waited for more.

'Svetlana talks to Mitya who talks – he has admitted as much to me – to your friend and translator, a Monsieur Sergei Panov. Monsieur Panov talks to your research assistant Madame Galina Plesitskaya and also to a certain American professor whose name escapes me.'

'Kahnleiter?'

'So you are aware of the situation? Perhaps you are acquainted with Monsieur Panov's daughter, little Alisa?' I stared, bemused. 'Mitya tells me that you have compromised yourself with the girl. From now on they can blackmail you at will.'

'They?'

Embarrassed, trapped between anger and contrition, Madame Lepinskaya almost took my hand but didn't. 'Monsieur, before I convey my experiences in France, which lie close to my heart, I must ask you to explain the life you lead in Moscow.'

I told her about one tenth of it.

The bulk of my working time in Moscow was spent in the company of my research assistant Galina Evgenyeva Plesitskaya, whom I remember with respect and affection, though our ultimate falling-out is something I would rather forget. We were working on a large project which came to fruition at a later date[†] long after Galina and I had parted company.

In her mid-forties, a single mother who lived with her teenage son in an apartment I was not invited to visit, about her failed marriage Galina did not speak. Among her precious qualities was complete mastery of the English language. She was level-headed and even-tempered, never late for an appointment, conscientious and loyal. She knew the Moscow archives back to front and was on cordial terms with the majority of librarians and archivists. She took a keen interest in my work but only from what I would call a technical point of view, that is to say how best and fastest I could find what I was in search of. The historical perspective underpinning my books did not in the least interest her and as far

---

[†] *The Dancer Defects. The Struggle for Cultural Supremacy During the Cold War*, Oxford, 2003

as I know she had never read even a chapter of any work I had published. The often acrimonious debates among historians of the Cold War were of no concern to her compared with the necessities of earning a living. Galina was becoming at this juncture increasingly involved in the conference industry. For foreign scholars, not least the Americans, skilled bilingual or multilingual native Russians were at a premium.

In the early days of post-Soviet rule, the Yeltsin era, impoverished Russian academics found a way of earning foreign currency by setting up a series of international conferences in Moscow. The fees charged ranged from $200 to $400 plus board and lodging. A moving spirit in conference-gestation was my Russian translator Sergei Panov, always at work on but never quite completing a Russian version of my book *The Fellow Travellers*. Occasionally he managed to rope me in as 'keynote speaker', but in the face of opposition from a group of well-funded American academics who had arrived in Moscow to devour the newly opened archives and spread the gospel of the 'New Revisionists' working under the leadership of Harvard Professor Abraham (Abe) Kahnleiter, an operator with very long-standing CIA connections who came and went and took a keen interest in what I was overtly doing and what I was covertly doing.

Most of the former Soviet librarians, archivists and museum curators whom I encountered were by no means what we call 'dissidents', although a few (hard to tell) nurtured sentiments of regret, sometimes of personal guilt, about having been assigned to service the cultural crimes of the Stalin and Brezhnev years. No, my helpers had in the main been regular, loyal Soviet citizens most of whom regarded the end of Communist rule during the fraught months of 1989-91 with mixed feelings and prevarications:

'I will enquire, Monsieur, come back next week.'

For a foreign visitor lodged in the Rossiya Hotel at fifty US dollars a day, 'next week' was a long time. You often waited through snow-bound days of silence while counting your diminishing dollars (no one, encountering a Western visitor, was interested in roubles, least of all the highly organized prostitutes who patrolled the single-men corridors of the vast Rossiya's fourth floor under the informed gaze of the female concierge, the *dezhurnaia*, supposedly the guardian of the guests' peace and security).

I paid Galina Plesitskaya one hundred US dollars per diem, but that operated only during the two months of each year when, on average, I was in Russia. Where else could be found so efficient yet so devotedly compliant a native Russian assistant? A woman of neat build, brown hair discreetly tinted and cut shortish to display a wide variety of earrings (from her new lover, *biznesmen* Nicky?), Galina taught English classes in the early evening. She was the answer to my failing sight and, let's face it, my far from perfect mastery of the language. On we toiled, she and I: only-so-many application slips permitted at any one time, a statutory wait of four working days after application, no photocopying, and later in the day, after Galina had gone home, a bleak sub-meal in the fourth-floor cafeteria of the Rossiya, followed invariably by hammering on one's door by *gyerlss* working in pairs and offering diamond-shaped blue pills, 'genuine imported Erection'.

Where did Galina and I head for during the working day?

The Pushkin State Museum of Fine Art (*Gosudarstvennyi muzei izobraztiel'nykh iskusstv imeni A.S. Pushkina*)

The Russian State Film Archive, Belye Stolby (*Gosfil'mofond Rossii*)

The Russian State Archive of Literature and Art (*Rossiĭskiĭ gosudarstvennyi arkhiv literatury i iskusstva, RGALI*)

The Centre for Storage of Contemporary Documents (*Tsentr Khraneniia sovremennoi dokumentatsii (TsKhSD)*, which holds the archive of the Central Committee of the Communist Party (TsK KPSS, Soviet era) and which was taken over in 1991 by a special commission of the Presidential administration of the new Russian Federation.

What the researcher was normally required to pinpoint was

the *Fond* (archive), *Opis* (list or schedule), and *ed.kh.*, (item of storage). I could no longer read the hazy Cyrillic typescripts available in RGANI and other archives on ancient, hand-wound microfilm machines. A detached vitreous in my good eye, with an intruding membrane between the vitreous and the retina, was causing oedema and furring the passage of light from the lens to the retina. Outcome of operation would be uncertain.

'Fifty-fifty in your case,' an ophthalmologist at London's Western Eye Hospital had advised me. 'It might be worth trying.'

In the archives Galina and I worked together from adjoining chairs in a surprisingly effective system. She would read through the index of documents, I made the selection. When the chosen documents finally crept under the door like shy moles, I scanned them through magnifying lenses for yes or no, and if yes Galina read the document aloud rapidly in her low, modulated but utterly clear voice, until I said stop and began taking notes. The guardians of the RGANI reading room, alternating pairs of immaculately laundered matrons, explained that this or that document could not be released for scrutiny because not yet 'declassified, *rassekrecheno*' or, pending further decisions of the special commission, the requested document remained only 'partially declassified' with 'limited access'. I was required to state in writing the reason for use: '*Dlia kakoi tseli ispol'zovan dokument*'. The recommended response was the non-committal 'browsing, *prosmotr*'. Sign here.[†]

I rode the back of Galina's eyes, sensible, level-headed Galina – one noticed a faint drying and wrinkling of the skin round her pretty mouth. Solicitous about my ocular infirmities, she didn't overdo it; didn't take my elbow when we crossed busy streets; didn't murmur warnings about icy patches on the pavements. No mothering, thank God. I always bought her lunch, her main meal

---

[†]   This archive was known after 1999 as the Russian State Archive of Recent History *(Rossilskii gosudarstvennyi arkhiv noveishei istorii, RGANI).* Here by 2002 about 30 per cent of the material had been declassified, while other documents were 'partially declassified' with 'limited access' *(ogranichennoe ispol'zovanie').*

of the day. During these meals she could not conceal from me that Professor Abe Kahnleiter was offering her work, here and now, as interpreter/translator. Harvard's marauding lion, author of *Myths and Lies of American Communism*, had also interrogated her about a 'secret project' I had undertaken concerning an 'old lady'.

'I told him that you had never mentioned any such project to me.' Her eyes were fastened on mine, she had been waiting for the right moment. My gaze must have dropped.

'Galina, I am not allowed to speak of it.'

'Of course.' She found it hard to conceal her disappointment but her dignity and innate reserve inspired respect. Her weekends were strictly her own and earmarked for her tiny dacha or for her new-standing 'boyfriend' (as she called him) Nicky, whose commercial ventures remained obscure to me, though apparently 'big-time'.

I knew that if I just once let the cat out of the Lepinskaya bag, then Galina would eagerly offer to accompany me as interpreter to Madame Lepinskaya – but no. Madame Olga and I communicated more happily in French, indeed our mutual use of a third language kept our relationship in 'neutral'. I also feared that the elderly lady would be scared stiff by the sudden intrusion of Galina, a Russian woman of a younger generation brandishing a notebook. With Galina in the room (there were only two chairs), my precious, intimate status as outsider, foreigner and (perhaps) admirer would surely be lost, destroyed. No!

I had to ask myself: who would these honoured Western guests, Picasso and Chaplin, be likely to have met while in Moscow? Which distinguished Soviet painters would receive Picasso at the Academy? Which eminent film directors and actors would welcome Chaplin at Dom Kino? To compile such lists was not so difficult and the pursuit began, the very occasional jewel surfacing as a reward for hours of frustration leafing through flaking yellowing cuttings in dusty boxes marked 'classified, *klassifikatsiya*', crammed with lugubrious bulletins about state prizes, 'fraternal' trips to the People's Democracies, 'progressive' international festivals. It was far from clear who might have issued the invitations to these illustrious foreign guests, Picasso and Chaplin, and who in the Stalin hierarchy would have covertly resisted or sought to sabotage the visit. One did not find that kind of information in *Pravda, Izvestiia,* or *Literaturnaya gazeta.* In vain one searched *Novyi mir,* with its densely printed, book-length articles. However, proceed to the journals *Kino* (Cinema) and *Iskustvo* (Art) – and you might begin to pick up between the lines faint traces and muddy tracks. You also smelled fear: November 1952 was a time of Byzantine intrigue obscured by the obfuscations of Soviet cultural officials who lived in terror of their own shadows – and their shadows' shadows.

At no time did I yield a hint to Galina of what I was looking for. Every archival request was presented to her in disguised form: 'cultural controversies of the early Fifties' or 'Soviet commentaries on Picasso and Chaplin.' But she was a very shrewd woman.

~

As for Abe Kahnleiter, well: myself an alumnus of Harvard, I could not help half-liking this powerful manipulator of careers and reputations whom I encountered in libraries. Occasionally we shared a coffee break – he was what one might call genial bad company for half an hour. He moved around Moscow in a wheelchair tended by a clean-cut young Ivy Leaguer who never said a word but carried, one felt, a revolver under his Brooks Brothers jacket. Not for the first time the CIA and the universities had entered an unholy alliance. Kahnleiter's new Combined Academic Press had now established an office in the Metropole Hotel, no less, poised to dig the Soviet dirt. Somehow being fellow-Westerners in Moscow brought together even enemies. Abe recalled a story told by his friend the conservative American historian Richard Pipes. At the height of the Cold War Pipes had come across his ideological foe E.H. Carr working in the Lenin Library. Feeling that foreigners should display cordiality if not exactly solidarity in the bleak environment of Soviet Moscow,

Pipes had paused at Carr's desk to greet him, but had received only a curt nod before Carr bent back to his reading.

'You wouldn't do that, John.' Abe said, producing his mischievous twinkle, always to hand.

I gleaned that Svetlana and her architect Mitya Tairov, both retired and with time on their hands, were chattering: the word had run through the circle of museum curators and art experts – the English historian has struck lucky. What is she telling him and does he incline to believe her? Kahnleiter wanted to know the identity of my 'old lady' and where she lived. He was receiving tip-offs from my translator Sergei Panov, an old friend of Mitya Tairov, who fed hints (but not names and addresses) to Sergei, who duly passed them on either to Kahnleiter or his minions in the Metropole. It gradually became apparent to me that the dates of my appointments to meet Madame Lepinskaya were being leaked – and by who else than her cousin and old friend Svetlana?

One morning heading eagerly for a precious but too rare meeting with Madame Lepinskaya, I had sensed I was being followed as soon as I set out from the Rossiya. The suspect was an unknown male, neatly dressed and (I thought) Ivy League – certainly not Russian. He followed me down into the metro, waited until I boarded a train, then entered the same carriage. He disembarked when I alighted at Nakhimovskii Prospekt, following as I began my five-minute walk to Madame Lepinskaya. I halted and addressed him in English. 'Are you following me on behalf of Kahnleiter?' He froze, muttered 'Not understand,' in an accent meant to be Russian but unmistakably Ivy League, and hurried on ahead of me to demonstrate his innocence. Academic life in the Kahnleiter era was not without its excitements.

Sergei and Zuzanna Panov (she a Polish academic) regularly invited me to share their Sunday lunch. Sometimes their beguiling daughter Alisa, an MSU student who also attended Galina's English evening course, would be present. I half-enjoyed my pre-Sunday lunch outings with Sergei although they were always a bit of a tussle. One could anticipate the disappointment, the hurt seeping up within the steppe-potato features covered in stubble, when one attempted to resist another visit to ancient churches, icons of the Andrei Rublev era, and other proofs of the incomparable heritage of ancient Rus. If I had my way we would head for the art nouveau residence occupied by Gorky after he'd made his peace with Stalin's regime, the Ryabushinsky Mansion. Or we would be reading the plaques attached to architect Yofin's apartment houses where leading Bolsheviks and Red Army generals had taken up privileged residence. Or I would conduct a grumbling Sergei to the statues bizarrely scattered around the ugly new Tretyakov Gallery, some still honouring Stalin or Voroshilov, others depicting their victims of the Gulag. In Russia the unknown political prisoner is always in the plural. I could hear Sergei's complaints in advance, he hungry and footsore, as I rubbed our noses in recent history:

'What to understand here? Terrible time, nothing good. Some animals always more equal than rest. George Orwell.'

'Than others.'

But some Sundays he had his way and there we were, ambling from church to bloody church, icon to bloody icon, he stopping off for coffees and smokes, a warm, shaggy dog oblivious to what his wife feels or what I feel.

'Isn't Zuzanna expecting us at three, Sergei?'

'*Ekh da*, yes, yes, I must be telling her we running late.'

So then my friend Sergei-Oblomov wasted more time searching for a hotel willing to offer us a telephone to call Zuzanna – mobile phones were not yet. He walked slowly, frequently stopping dead to lean on his stick and pursue (or not) some tangential line of thought. He finally located a hotel up a side-street, glared and glowered at the receiver, dithered for coins in his pocket, started to dial, coughed smokily, decided it was too late to say we're late, walked out aimlessly and started up where he had left off fifteen minutes ago about Andrei Rublev, icon painter and monk. At about four o'clock we would arrive for the lunch cooked by Zuzanna and Alisa two hours earlier.

The beautiful Alisa's project, it became apparent, was to obtain a visa to work in England and to graduate in Business Studies – Alisa, who had once presented flowers to Mrs Thatcher when Gorbachev invited her to Moscow, intended to become 'chief executive of a Global'.

'Then I enrolling in college of Business Studies and I becoming chief executive of Global and very wealthy celebrity. In Russia you having to be singer for celebrity. True celebrity is product of Western free market, nowhere else. Agree?'

'A lot of people are becoming fabulously rich here in Russia.'

'All of them older generation former nomenklatura, factory manager, Party boss. No way in for girl.'

Alisa believed that Mrs Thatcher had been overthrown by 'jealous men', and chided me when I expressed acute dislike for that great lady. 'You silly professor not knowing where bread buttering.' Alisa's preferred method of obtaining a visa to study in England, it became apparent, was to induce the middle-aged historian from London to lose his head – which entered the realm of the feasible when it emerged that after attending Galina's 5.00 p.m. English classes Alisa was among the *gyerrls* patrolling the corridors of the single-men fourth floor of the Rossiya. I was unaware of this until late one evening she knocked on my door, alone and not accompanied by the usual 'take your choice'. Heavily made-up, perched on stilettos and wearing what she was wearing, she was almost unrecognisable until she took a heavily scented step towards me, false eyelashes fluttering, and whispered softly, 'Daddy sent me. I having important something to tell you. I come in, yes?'

'No, Alisa, but we can sit in the cafeteria.'

To cut quite a long story short, it transpired that her father Sergei had been offered a tempting sum of money by Kahnleiter if he could discover which 'old lady' I was secretly visiting, where she lived, and what it was all about. Alisa's mother Zuzanna had insisted that Sergei must do no such thing since I was a friend who had accommodated Sergei when he was first allowed to visit

London with the onset of Gorbachev's *glasnost'*. I remembered that visit as interminable, our dining room table littered with empty beer bottles, Sergei's English unsteadily deteriorating the longer he spent in England and the longer he spent (following hectic and often ill-judged shopping sprees in Oxford Street) trying to describe to my wife and me the significance in Russian culture of Goncharov's character Oblomov (with whom it was possible to compare Sergei himself, forever talking about his ongoing work as my translator but never exactly doing it – forever in his dressing gown).

So Alisa and I sat in the cafeteria, battered by loud muzak, while lonely Korean businessmen cast wistful glances at her and searching oriental appraisals of me. She always wanted to help her father (I gathered) and was anxious that I should appreciate my friend's predicament because he was increasingly indebted to Kahnleiter who was (a) subsidising Sergei's unreadable political science journal (b) hiring Sergei as a 'raconteur' during all these upcoming conferences. (I already knew what Alisa did not mention, that I was to be exposed, alongside certain named American historians, as a masked fellow-traveller of Soviet Communism. According to Kahnleiter, leading spirit of the 'Revisionist' school, all my work as a historian in Moscow, including my secret assignations with this 'old lady', was dedicated to exculpation of previous Soviet crimes and misdemeanours.) Alisa anxiously explained that her poor father could not win the full confidence of Kahnleiter's Combined Academic Press, and the remuneration it entailed, unless he came up with the goods on the 'old lady'. A further carrot held out to donkey Sergei was to be the well-paid translator of Kahnleiter's masterpiece *Myths and Lies of American Communism*.

I already knew that parallel pressures were being applied to Galina. She regarded Alisa as a talented but lazy pupil horribly inclined to use the gerund instead of the indicative ('Daddy respecting you'), neglecting verb tenses ('I not meet Professor Kahnleiter'), and habitually omitting the definite and indefinite articles ('Professor organizing big conference') – all of which vexed the perfectionist Galina and would have become apparent to the reader had I quoted verbatim Alisa's passionate *plaidoirie* in the cafeteria of the Rossiya. But what most vexed Galina, I was beginning to understand, was the ambitious Alisa's double life.

'She may try to snare you, John. Generations of foreign businessmen and academics have been led astray then subjected to blackmail here in Moscow.'

I think this was the first time that Galina had ever said anything that irritated me. I found her remark presumptuous, an encroachment on my dignity. I was tempted to come back at her: 'Yet consider, dear Galina, all infatuations are foolish, that's half the fun, the reckless adventure, the forfeiture of one's dignity, the unforeseeable consequences, irresistible.'

So now Alisa walked me back along that bleak corridor to my door and sweetly offered 'you silly professor not knowing where bread buttering' the forfeiture of his dignity, half-producing from her handbag the standard diamond-shaped blue pill and condoms.

'My dear Alisa, thank you but your parents are my friends.'

'They happy if you happy.'

'You mean they know you come here?'

'Not exact.'

'I'm sorry, but I cannot disclose who the "old lady" is or where she lives because she has sworn me to secrecy. But frankly, most of what she says can be discounted as fantasy.'

Alisa did not believe me. 'What this fantasy? You please telling me true about fantasy and I giving you Business Class up and down – on the house.'

'Who is the house, Alisa?'

'*Biznesmen* Nicky. He running single men fourth floor here. He telling Galina he needing girls.'

'Galina!'

'All pretty girls nice legs in her English classes. She needing money bad and doing anything for *biznesmen* Nicky.'

'Alisa, who sent you to me – your father, or Galina, or Kahnleiter?'

She shook her long auburn hair as if I was incapable of believing there was any good in the world, just as I was blind to Mrs Thatcher's virtues.

'Alisa sending Alisa.'

It was after this encounter that I rented a bank safe deposit and began to make a habit of sending my 'Lepinskaya' notes and covert tape recordings to London by Американ экспресс. I even suffered a twinge of nostalgia for the somnambulant quadrangles of Оксфорд.

~

Hearing some of this – that one, selective tenth – Madame Lepinskaya decided to apologise for the false gossip fed to her by Svetlana and Mitya.

'Mitya was here only yesterday. I felt that he and Svetlana no longer like you, Monsieur. I don't know why, do you?'

'You are closer to Madame Svetlana than I. It may be the case that she and her husband have too much idle time on their hands.'

'Yes, Monsieur, I may have been deliberately misled. Then I owe you an apology.' Madame Lepinskaya offered me her reluctant hand. 'So shall I now recall my journey to France in 1952?'

'I would be grateful.'

But why had Svetlana so taken against me? I knew one of the reasons as one knows a stomach ache. I had only to recall an evening at the Tairov's with their son Yuri also in attendance, a man I would judge to be about forty, following in his father's path as an architect but reportedly far more successful. I noticed that he drank quite a few vodkas during the evening and he was beginning to fill out beyond his height. I found him amiable and interesting although never intrusive on his parents' passion for talking and reminiscing. Obviously Yuri was fond of them.

Svetlana was talking freely about the old regime. She lit yet another cigarette. 'You may not know this, but I served as a research assistant to Dominika Nikolaevna on the Paris-Moscou project, and not without friction. She had been in charge of what is called "storage" at the time: that meant in effect that she knew better than anyone what was held in the vaults of Soviet museums – what it would be "good policy" to bring into the light of day, and what wouldn't be at all good.'

'You and she didn't agree?'

'She called me a "gangster" because I stubbornly insisted that she should release into view Kandinsky's painting, "No. 7".' Svetlana drew deeply on her cigarette as if it was her last. Then I made my fatal mistake.

'I do find that amazing to hear,' I said, 'yet I suppose Madame Nikolaevna was typical of a breed of shilly-shallying curators and bureaucrats, who had lost touch with their own values.'

I noticed that Mitya's eyebrows were up. 'Are you implying cowardice?' he asked.

I ploughed on towards the cliffs. 'It would have been cowardice if they could remember what they once believed in. There had been a moment of freedom for the art schools after the war when impressionism was much in vogue.'

'But don't forget Kemenev,' Svetlana said angrily. 'Don't forget Gerasimov and Serov, they were typical Stalinists. They loathed modernism. During the Brezhnev era the Party's clamp-down on the dissidents was fierce. Curators like Dominika Nikolaevna lived on a knife-edge. So did I.'

'Well,' I persisted, 'a whole corpus of Soviet curators and art historians collaborated to produce inexcusable commentaries for a series of international exhibitions.'

'What was "inexcusable"?' Svetlana asked quite fiercely. I could see that both she and Mitya were becoming incandescent (Yuri looked neutral) but I pressed on.

'What was inexcusable about the printed catalogues and the wall captions for the new international exhibitions was the astonishing failure to mention that the works on display had been suppressed and hidden in cellars for years.'

Svetlana lit another cigarette with hands visibly shaking. 'And what would have happened to us curators if we had attempted to come clean?'

I shrugged (perhaps). 'I believe the regime would have retreated if you had joined forces to take a stand. Never compromise with censorship.'

'How can you know,' Mitya asked, 'if you live in a country where there is none?'

I could now be in no doubt that my hosts had taken huge offence. The atmosphere remained frigid until I thanked them and said goodnight. Neither Svetlana nor Mitya offered me their hand, a vast rebuke in Russia. Yuri politely saw me out onto the street.

'You certainly spoke your mind,' he said. 'And maybe I agree with your point of view, though it's easy enough to be critical of our parents' generation.'

I conceded that I should have kept my thoughts to myself. 'But you know, Yuri, your mother and father always speak freely, sometimes heretically, it can be seductive.'

He stood with his feet apart and his hands in his pockets, his gaze swivelling in search of a taxi. Speaking in fluent English, he said: 'But it all depends who is saying it. That's the lesson I have learned. If you are of the wrong generation, or the wrong nationality, a "bloody foreigner". They naturally become defensive and are quick to take offence.'

A taxi appeared down in the street and he stepped out to hail it.

'But I have to warn you,' he added affably, 'that if my mother Svetlana is quick to take offence, she is slow to forgive. I have never known her abandon the pleasure of making an enemy.' He waved as the taxi took me away to the Rossiya. I could not have guessed how Yuri would later re-enter the story.

12

The large leather portfolio carrying reproductions and lantern slides of the Pushkin Museum's early Picasso collection presents a problem of transportation. Kemenev will not allow it to travel by diplomatic bag, the obvious solution, because who knows who is currently Number One and Number Three in the Soviet Foreign Office and its Embassy in France? They say Molotov is on the way out although he was seen in good spirits at the Bolshoi's *Eugene Onegin* so where are you?

'I fear espionage or counter-espionage – or both. What do you think, Olga?'

'I can carry it by hand, Comrade Director.'

'Out of the question. You arrive at Sheremetyevo's check point for departures– then what? *They* have been waiting for you. You reach Prague – and who is calling the tune there? Some simpleton who has put his money on Khrushchev. You arrive at Orly – just imagine the *douaniers* triumphantly falling upon your portfolio. Where do you spend the night? – not between clean sheets, eh. Did you know that France is currently undergoing a campaign of anti-Communist terror?'

'Thanks for telling me.'

Whatever the risks she will take the portfolio as hand baggage, she must never lose sight of it. Olga's journey to Paris involves an Aeroflot Ilyushin II-12 flight to Prague/Rusyne, a stopover, then a CSA Czechoslovak Airlines flight to Paris. These are propeller-driven planes and Olga suffers a headache from the protracted engine noise. Arriving in Prague, she is greeted by not one but two Russian-speaking Czech officials from the Ministry of Culture, who usher the Soviet comrade through Customs and Internal Security, then anxiously attend her hours of waiting in Transfer. Both are familiar with France and solicitously warn the beautiful Soviet comrade that Frenchmen are not to be trusted, are shamelessly predatory, while the metro is infested by Arab pickpockets from the Maghreb – never respond to any approach by a stranger, and what is her mission? They gaze questioningly at her leather portfolio.

'To visit the Louvre,' she routinely replies.

Reaching Orly, she finds herself in enemy territory. Not far down the road notable Communists languish in detention. Here every Soviet passport holder is a potential spy. Her passport and visa are scrutinised by Immigration officials in neat round caps, the blue kepis (which she somehow associates with the Fall of France and capitulation to the Nazis). They deliberate among themselves – she hears one of them remark that he has never seen such a Soviet 'stunner', *une bombe*. The inevitable outcome is a version of Gallic gallantry involving a meticulous search of her packed underwear. The one selected to interrogate her could have borrowed his seductive smile from Gérard Philipe.

'And what will you be doing in *la belle France*, Mademoiselle?'

'I shall be advancing my studies in the Louvre and the Orangerie, Monsieur. I am a curator at the Pushkin Museum.'

'Nothing more adventurous? Where and with who will you be residing?'

'*Chez Monsieur et Madame Louis Aragon.*'

'*L'adresse s'il vous plaît.*'

Reluctantly she surrenders it.

'Is that the Communist agitator Aragon?'

'If I understand you correctly, he is a leading French writer and his wife has won the Prix Goncourt.'

'Who are your Soviet contacts or friends currently in France?.'

'Only one. I expect to be met at the exit by Mikhail Koltsov, Paris correspondent of *Pravda*.'

'Why is he meeting you?'

'He is a friend, Monsieur.'

'Which French artists held in the Orangerie interest you?'

'The Impressionists, Monsieur.'

'Do you intend to make contact with Picasso?'

Her heart lurches. She knows she may be followed by plainclothes men and dare not risk a denial.

'Well, I believe that Monsieur Aragon and Madame Triolet might take me to see his studio. However, we do not approve of Picasso in the Soviet Union.'

'But he is a Communist.'

'I meant his work, his paintings, his Cubism. Of course we love his peace dove.'

'So you will not be conspiring to overthrow the French State while our guest?'

She drags up a smile. 'Of course, Monsieur, as you can see I carry *le couteau entre les dents* – the knife between the teeth.' This phrase carries a resonance. He smiles back. 'You are free to go. *Bon séjour, Mademoiselle.*'

Her man from *Pravda*, Mikhail Koltsov, is waiting for her at the Arrivals gate. She is glad to see him – both their fathers were innocent victims of the Yezhov purge of 1938. Koltsov takes her bags (but the Picasso portfolio she will not relinquish) and leads her to a chauffeur-driven Embassy car. However, he stops to brief her before they step inside.

'Aragon and Triolet wanted to meet your plane, Olga Maksimovna, but I think it better that I orientate you first. I have fixed up a meeting for you with our Ambassador, Pavel Pavlovich Pavlov. Call that an insurance policy in volatile times. In principle the Aragons alone know of your mission but the French comrades chatter like parrots in a cage and absolute discretion is imperative.' Koltsov glances around. 'Ambassador Pavlov is a Stalinist blockhead so tell him that Kemenev has sent you to inspect the Impressionists in the Orangerie.'

Now on the road, seated in the back with Koltsov, she notices that he and the Embassy's Soviet driver exchange virtually no conversation.

'The current crackdown on the PCF here is severe,' he tells her. 'The Ministry of Information are now censoring most of my despatches. But of course *Pravda* picks up news of the latest arrests in France from AP, UP and Reuters, no problem. Did you have trouble at Immigration?'

'They asked me if I intended to meet Picasso.'

Koltsov studies her intently. 'What do they know? Has there been a leak?'

'I've no idea. Is Picasso safe from arrest?'

'In this country you do not arrest Sartre or Picasso.'

He points out some of the city landmarks to her before they reach the smart boulevard Lannes in the 16th arrondissement, the embassy gates opening at their approach, no formalities, though she notices an array of gendarmes and several *camions* stationed outside. The cultural attaché, Comrade Brodsky, obviously taken aback by her beauty, solemnly urges her to 'take care'. When she is led into the grand office of Ambassador Pavel Pavlovich Pavlov, he rises with difficulty from behind his desk, shakes her hand and conveys to her that Madame Pavlova would be happy to receive Mademoiselle Lepinskaya 'whenever your busy schedule allows, Comrade.' He then informs Koltsov that Jacques Duclos has been re-arrested, more CGT riots anticipated like those in May.

As they leave the Embassy Koltsov murmurs that the report about the arrest of Jacques Duclos is wrong. 'Pavlov believes everything his underlings tell him.' More important, where does she want to get some sleep? 'I can see you are tired, Ochka. My apartment has a spare room. But I must warn that your rest may be disturbed by the constant shout of my telephone. *Pravda*'s Foreign Editor calls three or four times a day and the French comrades always have news of "the worse the better" variety.'

'But the Aragons are expecting me. We ought not to offend them.'

'Beware travel fatigue. It's difficult to think straight when you haven't slept for twenty-four hours. Aragon and Triolet should be confronted with a clear headed Ochka.'

'Confronted, you say? Are they not our friends?'

'Too much so and distinctly overbearing. You will quickly find that you have to stand up to them. They have no children and quest for substitutes.'

'It's up to you, Mikhail. I'm in your hands.' She wonders whether he is planning to make love to her, she has always fended him off when he is in Moscow, and the prospect does not displease her, he is the first man in her twenty-eight years about whom she has ever felt like that. Pyotr's unpredictable, passionate advances in his attic studio in Cheremushki she has resisted – if Pyotr does not know who he is, man or boy, how can he know who she is? Paris is the place to lose one's virginity, after all. But then the darker thought intrudes even as she wards it off: will Picasso expect her to be a virgin?

They pick up Mikhail's little Renault from a side street. It carries a regular French registration plate but she notices that he takes a good look underneath it before opening the doors. She asks why.

'Action française. They've reverted to terrorism on the back of the war in Indo-China.'

Threading through the Left Bank – she has never seen such traffic, never heard so many car horns sounded simultaneously – Koltsov tells her that he has heard on the grapevine that Picasso has given Aragon and Triolet the slip and headed back to Vallauris, the small town between Antibes and Nice where he has his regular consort and two children.

'You mean he has returned to his companion of six years, Madame Gilot?'

'Aragon and Triolet think he's still in Paris with his *ancienne maîtresse*, Dora Maar. So we, *Ol obyazatel'nom poryadkega*, must head south tomorrow.'

'But we can't do that! The Aragons will be mortally offended! They are the principal contacts for Dyadya Ilya Ehrenburg and for Kemenev.'

Koltsov shrugs. 'The problem is that Picasso will not allow the Aragons near him in Vallauris. He sees himself in a show-down with Françoise about their future and about the children.'

'Then he's hardly likely to welcome us!'

'It doesn't follow. Frankly, Ochka, please don't be offended, I can't bear to say this but the odious Kemenev was right. And Lavrentiy Beria too.'

'Please don't look me over like that, Mikhail. I'm not a dummy in a shop window.'

He takes her hand. 'You are designed by a computer to hook big poisson Pablo.'

'What is a computer?'

'It's something they are developing in cybernetics.'

'Tell them not to develop it. And I think you are quite wrong about sidestepping the Aragons. They are the essential conduits for Picasso's journey to Moscow. It is their advice he will heed. I must without fail visit them tomorrow, *v obyazatel'nom poryadke.* And I will take my suitcase.'

Koltsov sighs. *'Comme tu veux.'*

She softens to his apartment in the bohemian rue St André des Arts, on the Left Bank, small, warm and cluttered with piles of newspapers, including the London *Times* and the *New York Times.* She feels she should be reading *l'Humanité* and *Le Monde,* but soon she is stretched out in a deep sleep in Mikhail's untidy bed, large enough (she notices before her eyes close) to accommodate two. When she awakes some hours later she finds that Mikhail has gone, leaving a note held in place by a spare key to the flat. 'I had hoped to take you out to dinner and then perhaps pursue our relationship, which makes me so very happy, my dearest Ochka, but I have been called away to cover a new CGT strike in Lille. You may have to take a taxi in the morning to the Aragons.'

She reads it again then cries. Perhaps she is still overtired but she is haunted by guilt about having done so little to help Pyotr, wasted and bullied in one of the MVD's cruel, hateful cells while she lies comfortably stretched out in Paris, disappointed not to be making love to another man.

⁓

The Aragons' apartment, like its two occupants, is stunningly elegant, the walls parading Picasso, Matisse, Léger, Malevich and Rodchenko. She sees a bust of Triolet's late brother-in-law, Mayakovsky. Although they have received photographs of Olga from Kemenev, the smartly dressed couple look her over shamelessly, like a Dior catwalk model, Triolet even pinching her cheek and suggesting a touch more rouge. Can these people really be, she wonders, *au fond* Communists? Well, not so different from Uncle Ilya.

'We were expecting you yesterday,' Triolet says, not disguising her irritation. 'We stayed in all day.' She loses no time in mentioning that the couple had come especially back to Paris from their new great estate, the Moulin de Villeneuve in Saint-Arnoult-en-Yvelines. 'Six hectares of countryside allow us to write, you should understand. But of course Louis has his duties here in Paris as editor of *Ce Soir*.'

Olga apologises profusely and half-explains about Koltsov.

'Well, you should at least have called us by telephone. Don't you understand that Soviet citizens may encounter misfortunes here in Paris – not least a woman of your appearance.'

Smoothing his silver hair, Aragon discloses to Olga that Picasso seems to have slipped away to Vallauris, to La Galloise. 'The situation is grave,' he adds gravely. '*Le coeur, c'est le sabotage permanent.*'

Triolet tells Olga with ill-concealed glee that Dora Maar is tearing her hair out about Pablo's abrupt departure, her Indian summer guillotined – but she, Triolet, is in no doubt that Pablo will quarrel with Françoise and soon return to Paris.

'But in a black mood,' Aragon adds, turning to Olga. 'Elsa telephoned La Galloise yesterday but Françoise said Pablo was refusing to come to the phone.'

'So you spent the night with Koltsov?' Triolet addresses Olga drily. 'Well, at least you're off to a good start.'

Olga absorbs this in silence. 'I have brought my portfolio, Madame, and my suitcase in case you should be kind enough to accommodate me.'

'*Vous êtes bienvenue, Olga,*' Aragon lays a hand on her arm. 'From now on we shall not let you out of our sight.'

Olga remembers Mikhail's remark about no children.

The phone rings. Triolet takes it, snatching the receiver. It's Koltsov returned from Lille. Triolet begins to rebuke him for his irresponsible conduct yesterday but evidently he isn't having it and asks to speak to Olga. Triolet accedes reluctantly, a frown extending down her long face. (Koltsov has remarked to Olga that the older Elsa Triolet gets, and she's now about to celebrate her fifty-eighth birthday, the more Russian she looks – but on inspection Olga does not agree.)

Olga takes the phone. Koltsov proposes that he collect her immediately and drive her south to Vallauris. 'We can't afford to hang about in Paris listening to their chattering intrigues.'

'Well, please give me a moment, Mikhail.' Holding the receiver, Olga conveys the proposition to Aragon and Triolet.

'Mikhail is quite mad!' Triolet explodes. 'Isn't he quite mad, Louis?'

The tall Louis Aragon ponders, again smoothly smoothing his smooth hair. He takes the receiver from Olga. 'That would be premature, Mikhail. Only as a last resort.'

Olga cannot hear Mikhail's reply. Aragon replaces the receiver. 'Mikhail is always impetuous,' he tells Olga. 'He is ever proud Roland galloping from Ghent to Aix. Do you know Robert Browning's poetry?'

She doesn't. He doesn't expect her to.

Having settled Olga into a bedroom given over to Matisse's cut-outs, the couple insist on taking Olga to Lanvin (patronised by Triolet herself) for new outfits, money evidently no problem, everything on account. During a brief conducted tour of Paris, they visit Les Deux Magots to gaze at the table Picasso expects to be kept vacant for him but is actually occupied by a huge American backpacker with cameras and telescopic lenses suspended from a beefy neck. On from there they head for Picasso's studio at 7 rue des Grands Augustins, in the sixth arrondissement, lying south of the Seine opposite the Île de la Cité. Originally a seventeenth-century townhouse (Aragon is explaining), it was reputedly once occupied by Balzac.

'I believe our great Balzac is widely admired in the Soviet Union,' Aragon says. 'Fadeyev told me that *Les Illusions perdues* has been printed in millions.'

Olga nods obediently. 'I must read it, Monsieur.'

'Comrade Olga, you must not address me as "Monsieur"... though of course I understand why you do.'

'*Comment alors, Monsieur?*

Aragon turns to Triolet; 'What do you think, Elsa? How about "Monsieur Louis" and "Madame Elsa"?'

Olga being happy with that, it is rapidly agreed, though she thinks it could make her sound like the two well-established domestics in their service. Aragon discreetly hopes that Olga will read his epic novel, *Les Communistes*. 'All dialectical dilemmas and historical contradictions,' he confides, 'are resolved in its pages – but perhaps too many volumes for you to carry on the plane.'

'Send it to her by the Soviet diplomatic bag,' Triolet suggests. 'We can throw in your love poems, *Les Yeux d'Elsa.*'

They reach the studio where Picasso has lived and painted since 1942. Behind a large iron gate a cobbled courtyard nestles in the shadows. The stairway and door are tucked into a corner. After his routine delay, Picasso's long-serving Catalan secretary Jaime Sabartés reluctantly admits them; he knows this powerful pair are not to be refused, ever, even when his master has issued strict orders not to admit any of Aragon's 'six faces'. Thin and hollowed out, Sabartés follows them round the huge studios, sniffing at their heels. Triolet asks him when he expects the maître to return to Paris. Predictably, and with the secretive air he has cultivated for all unwanted visitors (practically everyone, including even Dora Maar), Sabartés disclaims all knowledge of his master's intentions.

'Has Madame Maar called in?' Triolet asks him.

He simpers: 'I was instructed not to admit her. In any

circumstances. I believe she is currently *chez elle* in the rue de Savoie committing suicide, but believe me that will take time.'

'Don't be cruel, Jaime' – but Olga notes that Triolet is not displeased since Maar figures high on her league table of deadly-dangerous influences on Pablo, not only mad and predatory but also a former Trotskyite wrecker with friends like André Breton and Marc Chagall, the *atlantistes*. On the other hand, Pablo is more manageable with a woman securely in his bed.

Olga has been foretold about Picasso's legendary clutter but is nevertheless taken aback to witness piles of pictures by famous artists, negro masks, ceramics, twisted pieces of glass picked up in the lava of Martinique, plaster casts, hats, reams of Holland paper, heaps of unopened packets, bottles of eau de cologne, bars of chocolate, loaves of stale bread, cigarettes, matches, old shoes lined up under a table, the retired oil lamp which lit the canvases of the Blue Period, a broken coffee grinder.

'Pablo is a hoarder,' Triolet explains to their Soviet guest. 'He never throws anything away except women. Whatever comes into his hands he considers part of himself.' She plucks out a canvas: 'See here, *Dora Maar with Green Finger Nails*.'

'Dora is a hoarder, too,' Aragon muses. 'If we visit her in the rue de Savoie she will proudly show us the cigarette packets and match boxes she has preserved because Pablo has doodled on them.'

'Or she may not,' Triolet says 'She has persuaded herself – or been persuaded by her Dominican solitaries – that silence is tantamount to profundity.'

Sabartés ventilates his feelings. 'Picasso's bric-a-brac should be preserved but they should not belong to Madame Dora.'

'Would Madame Maar welcome a visit if...she is upset?' Olga asks.

Triolet grips her arm. 'She will certainly be curious about you, my dear, but I don't think a meeting would be advisable at present.'

They come across *Portrait of Dora in a Garden*, 1938. Sabartés has actually turned the canvas to the wall, but Triolet heads for it unerringly and Aragon consents to get dust on his suit by fetching it out. Olga is stunned: the woman in the painting is trapped by zigzagging branches and by the angular forms of a wicker chair, but she remains composed and, Triolet says, 'she could only be Dora.'

'It's so interesting,' Olga ventures, 'to see portraits of Madame Maar in the days when she was radiant with happiness – before the better known "weeping woman" series, I mean.'

Triolet lays a vermilion-painted claw on her arm – as she tends to. 'One thing you must understand. Dora's real tears came some long time after Pablo did his "weeping women". What we see in that famous sequence is Pablo shouting his political rage through the distorted heads and faces of the woman in his life.'

Olga hears herself asking Triolet about Picasso's present companion, Françoise Gilot. 'Has she really left him despite two children?'

'She has and she hasn't. Françoise is an intelligent woman capable of deciding enough is enough.'

'It is not entirely a question of intelligence,' Aragon demurs. '*Au bout du chemin* it's a question of a woman's survival.'

'Very true, Louis.'

They leave the rue des Grands Augustins. Another day passes without word of, or from, Picasso. Mikhail Koltsov keeps calling by telephone. Tempers are frayed. Olga has now come round to the necessity of making the journey to Vallauris with Mikhail. Triolet won't hear of it.

'There is plenty to do in Paris. Laurent Casanova would like to meet you. Perhaps one or two others, André Stil, the editor of *l'Humanité*, they arrested him at the same time as Jacques Duclos, a total frame-up by Pleven's Minister of the Interior – and maybe Pierre Daix, a keen student of Pablo's life and work.'

('They chatter like parrots in a cage,' Koltsov has warned. Olga must avoid general circulation, dinners, parties, receptions.)

'Are all these comrades…I mean, are they aware, do they know,

Madame Elsa?'

'Only Laurent Casanova. He's our Party's cultural chief, totally dependable. No one else. Laurent escaped from the Germans four times in order to lead our Resistance unit.'

To Olga that means the Germans recaptured him three times. Tales of French military heroism do not impress her. She says: 'Mikhail warned me that the Paris comrades are indiscreet. He thinks they lack Soviet discipline.'

This detonates Triolet, her fuse already shortened by worry about Picasso and the rising fear that Moscow will hold Aragon and her responsible for any fiasco. The Generalissimo's birthday is when it is, 21 December, and there can be no excuses. She knows that Koltsov would like to drive Olga south without the Aragons.

'I suppose you know about Mikhail's father, also a Mikhail? Excellent reports from Spain but then found to be a traitor.'

'Madame, I'm surprised at you.'

Triolet stands her ground on pointed heels. 'Surprised, Comrade?'

Olga's eyeballs burn, her tongue is dry: 'Yes, surprised that you still repeat that claptrap in France. Millions of innocent people were executed including my father and Mikhail's father and it's about time you knew it.'

Triolet and Aragon are staring at her, dumbfounded. Has some fatal mistake been made by Kemenev?

'You have been reading Arthur Koestler,' Aragon rebukes her. 'You have been reading *Darkness at Noon*.'

'No, Comrade Aragon, I have simply grown up in the Soviet Union where everyone knows the truth without reading Koestler – not least those like my mother and myself who experienced the Terror.'

Although she is very young, an *ingénue*, what causes them to hesitate is a lifetime of deference to any Soviet comrade. And perhaps she is suddenly conscious of this advantage as she launches a sentence inconceivable within earshot of the Pushkin

Museum: 'I am confident that in a very few years' time, when nature has taken its course, both of you, Monsieur Madame, will be writing articles in *Les Lettres françaises* deploring so many millions of innocent victims.'

Triolet half-recovers. 'Comrade Olga, you may feel yourself free here in Paris, but I must warn you, I mean of course counsel you –'

'So I will go south with Mikhail. My responsibility as a cadre is to the Soviet Party – not to vacillating Parisian intellectuals.' She is trembling, she has blown it, they will send her home, and then no roof over Mamochka's head. But when she goes to her room and looks in the ornate Venetian mirror she tosses her hair and is reminded why she is indispensable. Pyotr has said as much, and Kemenev, and Mikhail too, and you can read it in the muted gaze of Aragon and Triolet. A few moments later she is at the door of the apartment with her suitcase and portfolio.

They stare at her, aghast. 'I will report back to you. *Au revoir Monsieur Madame.*'

∾

Mikhail drives through the night and the little Renault responds gallantly.

'Believe me, Ochka, these acolytes are helpless in the face of Picasso's vagaries. It has always been like that.'

Olga reports Triolet's crude remark about Mikhail's father, and the row that ensued. 'I think I may have blown the whole thing.'

'Not for a minute. Elsa is a tough woman. She will respect you for your outspoken courage. She will probably start writing out a list of Stalin's crimes in code for future use. She will calculate that you can stand up to Picasso.'

'I'm not here to stand up to him. I'm here to lie down underneath him.'

This shakes Koltsov. Women don't speak that way. 'Ochka, please.'

'You men are such hypocrites.'

They circumvent Lyon. Mikhail knows the roads. 'Yes, we are

hypocrites,' he agrees. 'It's just that I have a very special feeling for you.'

'Is that why you took off for Lille on my first night with you? I searched the papers next day, no mention of a CGT strike in the north.'

His gaze flickers sideways, his hands on the wheel jump about in agitation. 'I was afraid I was going to take advantage of you – uncomradely conduct, *povedeniye*.'

They drive in silence for a further five minutes, Mikhail dipping his headlights for oncoming traffic, before she says: 'Maybe I wanted you to take advantage of me.'

'*Deystvitel'no?*'

'*Oui, vraiment.*'

Reaching Vallauris too late to announce themselves at La Galloise, they find a small hotel and treat themselves to escargots, Olga's first ever, though she doesn't want to pile up the disasters with a bad stomach. But Mikhail is confident, relaxed, and she enjoys the sauce of butter and garlic if a little unconfident about the rubbery taste and texture of the snails. She can hear them wail as her teeth close.

They return to their room. Both know it's now or never.

'How can I take advantage of you within a stone's throw of Picasso himself?'

She places both hands on his chest. 'You can try.'

'*May I ask, Madame, whether Picasso's shadow intruded on the two of you?*'

'*Let's say I felt that when I...that with Picasso it must not be the first time. I had changed my mind about that.*'

'*So you felt sure that would be required of you?*'

'*Oui, Monsieur. Thank you for kindly enquiring.*'

Next morning, over a too-leisurely breakfast of croissants, Olga is so nervous that she keeps glancing at her watch, checking her make-up, getting to her feet and smoothing her Lanvin skirt. Mikhail knows that Picasso always sleeps late and is furious if disturbed, so they visit his statue in the town square of Vallauris,

L'Homme au Mouton only recently unveiled to applause from the Party chiefs.

Mikhail is observing her reaction, which is masked. 'Frankly, I don't get it,' he admits, gesturing at bronze man and bronze sheep, 'but of course a Pushkin curator is obliged to get it.'

'I find it totally inexpressive, if you want to know.'

'Let's go and meet Destiny in his pyjamas.'

La Galloise is a surprisingly modest house, both in size and style, but Olga knows that Picasso has workshops in the town for his ceramics and sculpture. The gate is closed, locked. Olga is clutching her precious leather portfolio, her heart literally pounding so that she can hear it, thud thud. Mikhail rings what may be a working bell, time will tell. After some minutes a middle-aged lady appears, not from the main house but from across the yard where you can see a smaller building, a cottage. She does not open the gate but presses her face up close to it, grinning.

'Picasso? Is it he who has brought you here? He's a lousy painter, no talent, take it from me, I've been keeping an eye open for years. You're out of luck, my young friends, his chauffeur Marcel drove him back to Paris last night in the Oldsmobile. Oh yes, there was a great deal of angry shouting from the great man but not a word from Madame.'

Olga is aware of a woman's face at the downstairs window, shaded by half-drawn shutters, though it is deep autumn now and the face, too, looks autumnal. The elderly woman drifts away, chuckling (in former times she had sold the main house to Picasso), and presently a handsome woman of about Olga's age emerges from the front door, unlocks the gate, opens it on squeaking hinges, and stands staring at Olga.

Madame Lepinskaya reached for her chignon. 'I recognised her from a Robert Capa photograph taken on the beach of Golfe-Juan in 1948. In the photo she is walking slender, carefree and smiling along the sand, wearing a sun hat and a long beach-dress, Picasso following behind and holding a huge parasol above her head. But now at Vallauris she no longer looked carefree, quite the opposite.'

'Françoise, do you remember me?' Mikhail begins.

Gilot barely deflects her gaze from Olga. '*Oui. Koltzov, je crois.* And this is the woman, the femme fatale from Moscow? Don't look surprised, Pablo told me all about you and why he will and why he won't go to Russia. I also had a call from Aragon about you both, very agitated. That's a nice skirt, I expect Triolet bought it for you at Lanvin. Well, Mademoiselle Lepinskaya, Pablo and I had our usual altercation, his usual display of rage. I told him to leave me and the children in peace, so it's straight back to Paris for you and your portfolio. Adieu.'

At an upstairs window a young boy has lifted a small girl to have a look. Their mother walks back into the house, stroking a kitten on the way.

On the long road back to Paris, Olga is preparing for a frosty reception from the Aragons. Mikhail keeps reassuring her that Picasso's return to Paris is good news.

'Fear not, Ochka. They are totally dependent on your knowledge of the Pushkin Museum's collection – and on your charms. A good Soviet Communist does not sit around waiting for things to happen.'

'*Khorosho.*' She realises that she despises the French, they lost the war, they collaborated, they are coddled and passive, they couldn't even make a revolution in May, the Elysée was not stormed like the Winter Palace in Petrograd. She will not bend the knee to Aragon and Triolet or to any of them.

Mikhail smiles approvingly. 'That's my Ochka.' He lays a hand on her knee, unaware that she associates this predatory gesture with Dyadya Ilya Ehrenburg and all the other lecherous old predators.

'I am not yours, Mikhail.' She removes his hand.

He drops her off at the Aragons'. By the time he reaches his office identical messages are waiting for him from the editor of *Pravda* and from Ambassador Petrov: 'You are to part company from Lepinskaya and take no further action in this affair.'

The Aragons have known which strings to pull.

In the event, the couple remain tight-lipped about her illicit adventure. They have decided, as the saying goes, to handle her with kid gloves. They have heard that Picasso has now slept off his journey from La Galloise and will receive them that very afternoon. Meanwhile, Triolet will brief Comrade Olga, who has had little sleep since removing Mikhail's hand from her knee, on the nuances of contemporary French literature. Olga will gather that the main agenda of a Communist writer in France is to prevent those fashionable pinks, Sartre and de Beauvoir, getting above themselves. 'Simone dresses like a frump, like a schoolma'am, but Jean-Paul has positioned himself behind the Party since the Ridgway affair† so we have to make allowances for his vanity...'

Olga succumbs to irritation and sleeplessness. 'Should Madame de Beauvoir not dress like a "schoolma'am"?' she asks. 'Should she buy her clothes at Lanvin?'

Triolet's thin mouth curls at the jibe. 'It may be difficult for Soviet women to appreciate what is expected of us in France.' She lights a cigarette. 'I suppose you know that Aragon is writing the definitive history of the USSR with full Soviet collaboration. They have shown him all the secret archives. But Louis is in no hurry to publish, my dear. It may not be the moment. Although we would all like Comrade Stalin to live for ever, we suspect that the landscape may change.'

Well, this more or less echoes what Olga herself had told them in the heat of her indignation. Triolet's long face accords her a penetrating scrutiny as she reverts to the Russian language: 'Come now, tell me frankly what Soviet citizens are thinking about the current crisis.'

'Crisis?'

'My dear, you wouldn't be here in Paris but for the crisis of

---

† A violent demonstration greeted the arrival in Paris of General Matthew Ridgway to take command of NATO forces. The American general, according to the Communist press, was a 'war criminal' and a 'microbe general', having allegedly ordered the use of bacteriological weapons in the Korean War.

succession.'

'Madame Elsa, we learn at an early age in the Komsomol and the Party which questions to discuss and which not to discuss.'

'I fear you may meet Dora Maar today. If Pablo is not with Françoise, he is back with Dora. If she doesn't speak to you, don't speak to her.' Triolet then describes with some relish the nervous breakdown Dora suffered six years ago after it became apparent that she had been supplanted by a woman twenty years younger, by Françoise.

'Well, I met Madame Françoise at the gate of La Galloise.'

'You met her!' Triolet raises her voice to summon Aragon from his study, where he is checking the proofs of his evening newspaper, *Ce Soir.* 'Louis, come here and listen. Tell us what Françoise said to you, Olga.'

'She said several things. She thought you might have bought the skirt I was wearing at Lanvin. She called me the femme fatale and said she knew all about me.'

Only half inside the door, Aragon is sceptically inspecting Olga, 'How did she know all about you?'

'Evidently the maître told her why he was going to Moscow and why he wasn't. I was something to do with it.'

'Pablo is so indiscreet!' cries Triolet.

Aragon reaches for the telephone and beckons to Olga to listen in through a twin receiver: 'You may as well get a preliminary "sighting" of the real Picasso.'

'No, Monsieur, it can't be right for me to eavesdrop.'

'Believe me, you urgently require orientation, Comrade. Your trip to Vallauris now becomes the fiasco we predicted.'

(Maybe one should not wear high heels even when eavesdropping on Picasso. She eases them off.)

Aragon is bickering with Sabartés but eventually gets through to a distempered Picasso.

'I'm working!' Olga hears a bellow.

I could feel myself shaking,' Madame Lepinskaya told me. 'Picasso was shouting down the line because his visit to Françoise had not gone his way, she was refusing to promise him anything'.

Aragon smooths his hair with a spare hand. 'Pablo, we have with us the Soviet curator who will be discussing the Moscow exhibition with you. As I predicted, she has brought with her a splendid portfolio of your early work held in the Pushkin Museum. They have also managed after great difficulty to bring up some hidden pictures from the Hermitage in Leningrad. You must receive her and receive her courteously.'

'*Merde!* I've already had a Russian wife called Olga and don't need another! You know I never do business with women! Is my dealer Kootz a woman? Women are fit for only one thing. If you'd got that into your head, Louis, you wouldn't have had so much trouble with Elsa. She's a *tricoteuse.* She will sit there knitting when they drag me to the scaffold.'

But Aragon is a man used to getting his way, just as he got hold of the great estate, the Moulin de Villeneuve in Saint-Arnoult-en-Yvelines. Even his enemies defer to him. He informs Picasso that Maurice Thorez[†] himself, who might one day be France's Stalin, is requiring that this Soviet comrade be received immediately. After further canine kerfuffle Picasso eventually consents to grant them 'five minutes', mainly because Aragon has convinced him that this important Soviet guest is worthy of a painting and embodies what Aragon describes as 'the kind of translucent beauty you find among the Cossacks of the Caucasus – indeed Mikhail Sholokhov is her favourite novelist.'

'Shocklov?'

'Mikhail Sholokhov, *And Quiet Flows the Don.*'

～

After lunch at the Catalan restaurant – Olga would rather sleep than eat – they drive to the rue des Grands Augustins. Olga now on low heels, they enter the courtyard and head for the door in the corner. Sabartés opens it five or six inches and asks if they have an appointment (he always does, he cannot help himself).

[†] Veteran General Secretary of the French Communist Party.

Reluctantly he steps back to let them through. Once inside the large ground-floor studio littered with everything imaginable, the lean Afghan hound Kazbek comes at them threateningly, followed by Picasso himself, a suntanned Puck wearing a sailor's vest in white and blue – as in the photographs she had been shown in Moscow. His toad-features are set reluctantly in a best-behaviour scowl of welcome. He takes Olga's hand, seems to weigh it, to read its palm, finds her to be taller than he would like – even in low heels her advantage over him is some two inches.

Picasso pinches Olga's cheek to watch the colour rise. 'So who is this Shocklov you so admire, *devushka?* The one who was rude to me at the Wroclaw Congress in Poland? The one who took me aside and asked why I chose to paint in forms that "plain people" could not understand? The one who couldn't tell cubism and surrealism apart?'

'That was Fadeyev, Secretary of the Writers' Union,' Aragon intervenes.

'The Soviet version of Aragon, you mean.'

'Pablo, all that was four years ago. I remember the occasion. I was there.'

'But you didn't say a word on my behalf.' He is calming down and soon conducting his Soviet guest through the sprawling studio spaces of les Grands Augustins, with Aragon and Triolet following in close attendance. Olga notes that he refers to himself in the third person, as 'Picasso'. No one has forewarned her – she has never met a major Soviet artist or academician who refers to himself as Gerasimov, Serov or Ehrenburg. She can't believe Repin did it.

Reaching the first floor, he stops to address them, really her, his eyes scorching. 'For Picasso a painting is a dramatic action in the course of which reality finds itself split apart. What counts is the drama of the plastic act, the moment at which the universe comes out of itself and meets its own destruction.' He grips Olga's wrist: 'Can you understand my French? Elsa tells me it's as thick as my favourite fish soup.'

Olga produces a shy smile: 'Bouillabaisse? Of course I can understand, Maître. Everything you say will prove profoundly helpful for our *exposition Picasso*.'

'*Weh?*' His elfin grin pops up again, sceptical and almost self-deprecating. 'Well,' he continues, gesturing with a muscular arm tanned on the beaches of the Mediterranean, 'see how the green and the violet struggle in this canvas here. The green spot has a tendency to grow, to work out from the centre. It's not contained within a line or form – colour never should be. But the violet starts big and grows smaller.'

She conveys appreciation. Satisfied, he leads them up a staircase and passes through several doorless doorways – sculptures and bas-reliefs everywhere. Olga is conscious of the sharp stiletto report from the pursuing Triolet.

'People forget that nature never produces the same thing twice,' he goes on. 'Hence Picasso's stress on seeking the *rapports de grand écart*: a small head on a large body, a large head on a small body.'

She nods gravely as she writes in her notebook, 'Henry Moore also.'

'Now look out of that window,' he commands, 'and you will see where cubism was born.'

She obeys. Shadowed by the shaggy Kazbek, he is standing close behind her, both hands gripping her waist as she studies the roofline of Paris's Left Bank, the Seine hidden to the north, its existence signalled by the tall outline of Notre-Dame. Yes, the intersecting outlines...but he hadn't bought 7 rue des Grands Augustins until 1938, by which time cubism had had its day? The notes she is writing move from French to Russian. She is still five centimetres the taller.

Then a nasty surprise, out of the blue, his next utterance causes her heart to race.

'Picasso doesn't trust those who sent you, Russian *devushka*, that bastard Kemenev in particular.' His accumulated fury causes her to tremble – oh Mama, nothing we have predicted could be as bad as this! Nervously she strokes the reluctant Kazbek.

'He only bites those he suspects of insincerity,' Picasso says. 'Are you truly convinced that the vaults of the Pushkin Museum and the Hermitage have been prised open to release Picasso's works so long imprisoned?'

'Oh certainly, Maître. I did it myself, I led our team of curators and assistants. Please believe that we are preparing for the great exhibition day and night! The Director was reluctant to let me come to Paris because we are so busy.'

'What about the Hermitage collection?'

'Their Director has promised us.' (She has reason to doubt the value of the promise. The great, bearded Armenian, Joseph Orbeli, who had led the State Hermitage through the years of blockade and siege, has now retired and his successor is an unknown quantity to Olga, if not to Kemenev).

Picasso's scepticism declines to evaporate: 'Will the creator of decadent, filthy, anti-human cubism suddenly be hailed as the fountainhead of genuine revolutionary art?'

'No, Maître, merely as a genius always true to himself.' Aragon and Triolet are listening as if their lives depended on it.

Still his hands grip her waist. 'Picasso sees treachery in your limpid gaze, Olga *devushka*. By dusk today he may have made a series of ten sketches charting your descent into hell – script by Dante.'

'What a beautiful idea,' Triolet exclaims.

Picasso ignores her. 'What do you think of Bonnard?' he abruptly challenges Olga.

'Oh – obviously an artist of major significance –'

'Rubbish. Bonnard is a potpourri of indecision – just another slave of nature, a neo-impressionist, a decadent. Painting is a matter of seizing the power, of taking over from nature. Matisse is always able to make an intellectual choice about colours. Van Gogh was the first – he knew how to assert his freedom by using a range of colours which burst out of nature's straitjacket.'

'Of course, Maître, I shall never again look at Bonnard.'

A woman has positioned herself in the open doorway behind them. Dora Maar stands silent, intense, behind eyes which seem to gaze inward. Seeing her, Picasso abruptly disappears without a word, the dog Kazbek with him.

During the ride back to the Aragon apartment, Triolet confides to Olga that Pablo's dear friend, the poet Paul Éluard, has been 'roped in' to waylay his fears and resentments about flying to Moscow. Éluard's trip the previous year, to commemorate the 150th anniversary of Victor Hugo's birth, had been a great success, a talk in the Bolshoi, a talk on French poetry at the Writers' Club, an invitation to address students, with Dominique Éluard at his side.

'Pablo always listens to Paul,' Aragon adds.

'I am glad to know that, Monsieur Louis.' Olga keeps to herself a little incident picked up by Pyotr and his dissident chums: the other Frenchmen invited to Moscow along with Éluard, the painter Jean Hugo, had been arrested on the Sonysky Embankment while making a sketch of the Kremlin which inadvertently showed the top of the Defence Ministry. His sketch-book had been confiscated, though it was later returned after a protest by Ehrenburg. Jean Hugo had promised not to say a word about this 'misunderstanding' on his return to France and he hadn't.

That night, in the Aragons' luxurious apartment, Olga seeks comfort by imagining herself talking to her mother: How Picasso loves to talk, Mamochka! They say he writes very bad poems and he wrote a terrible surrealist play called *Desire Caught by Tail* in which Aragon, Triolet, Éluard, Sartre and *Le tout Paris* took part.'

The following morning Olga keeps to her room as long as possible to avoid a further *tour d'horizon* of French literature from Triolet. Towards noon, overhearing her host and hostess arguing about what she, Olga, should wear today, she steps out into the hallway and presents herself for inspection.

'Too modest,' is Aragon's verdict.

'Too immodest,' is Triolet's. 'Heels too high.'

126

'She knows when to remove her shoes,' Aragon objects.

They return to the rue des Grands Augustins. Today Picasso is found to be quieter, more watchful. Over a glass of wine, Olga opens her Italian portfolio case (dear Uncle Ilya) and spreads her offprints and slides across a gate-leg rosewood table.

'We have a projector set up in the next studio,' Aragon reminds Picasso, who shrugs his indifference. 'I don't need projectors. I know these images across forty years. Mainly stuff sold to Shchukin, if I recall, sometime before the Revolution.'

Olga continues to lay out her wares. 'Yes, Maître, your work was among the French masterpieces bought by the great bourgeois collectors Shchukin and Morozov. Both fled after the Revolution and their collections were confiscated by the Soviet state.'

He corrects her: 'No, wrong, *devushka*, they fled after they were appointed minor curators of their own collections. Shchukin had bought 54 pictures by Picasso, 37 by Matisse, 26 by Cézanne, 29 by Gauguin, 20 by Derain, 14 by Monet, 13 by Renoir. The Soviet state then proceeded to lock the entire collection away, out of sight, never spoken of.'

'Perhaps it wasn't the right time, Maître. Revolutions are not picnics at the seaside.'

His muscular fingers pinch her cheek so that it hurts. 'That's what revolutions should be, Olga *devushka*. Picnics open to everyone.'

'But now we make amends,' Olga says. 'You will be our picnic, Maître.'

His long accumulated anger refuses to expend itself. 'We all know that Kemenev has been wiping his arse on his own diatribes these past few weeks. You, too, I expect?'

'Pablo, Olga is your guest,' Triolet says bravely.

Picasso reaches for a fig from a brimming bowl of fruit shaped like a conch – clearly from Picasso's recent ceramic series, *Les Fruits de la paix* – proceeds to the world peace movement. He squelches, his lustrous eyes fixed on the small colour slides brought from Russia, his heavy lips parted by these reminders of his own genius at the onset of cubism. Olga plucks up courage to confide that it is now understood in Russia that he had never been either an impressionist or a surrealist – or a decadent.

'And not before time,' he tells her, unsmiling. 'I am the creator of cubism. I and Braque.'

~

'You might care to read this, Comrade Olga.'

It is late afternoon, an idle hour in the Aragon apartment, and Triolet is presenting a book to Olga, who murmurs in appreciation. The book carries the title *Le premier accroc coûte deux cents francs. Nouvelles*. It bears the name of Elsa Triolet on the cover and, inside, on the title page, Olga sees 'Prix Goncourt 1945', which she recognises as France's most prestigious literary prize.

'Thank you, Madame, that is very kind. And congratulations – le Prix Goncourt!'

Triolet smiles modestly and faintly. 'In 1945 the prize was likely to be awarded to a Communist. That would hardly be the case now.'

Olga sees that the first short story in the collection is called *Les Amants d'Avignon* and was first published illegally in October 1943 under the name Laurent Daniel. Triolet explains that she chose the pseudonym as a tribute to her comrades Laurent Casanova and his Communist wife Danielle – she perished in Auschwitz.

Olga remembers hearing from Mikhail about the extravagant dinner for Picasso in St Paul de Vence, the fine wines paid for by the Party that Laurent Casanova and Aragon had to explain away to the bourgeois press as the very essence of patriotic France.

'I will read your book with great interest, Madame.'

'You may find the style differs from the Soviet style. That is to say, less heroic, more naturalistic.'

Alone in her room before dinner at the Brasserie Lipp, Olga discovers that the heroine of *Les Amants d'Avignon* is a young typist, Josette, said to be ravishingly beautiful with the kind of face you find on the cover of the magazine *Marie-Claire*. But Josette is virtuous. She works for the boss of an aeroplane factory yet resists his advances despite his gifts of marrons glacés. The boss admires her firmness of spirit as if (he imagines) she were the actress Clarissa Harlow or the Princesse de Clèves. Olga has never heard of these women but wonders why Madame Triolet had felt obliged to endow her heroine with so much glamour. When Josette dreams of love, the man sometimes resembles Gary Cooper or Charles Boyer. Were they film stars? Olga wonders. Josette adopts a pseudonym, then takes train journeys to Lyon, Avignon and Valence. Her mission is evidently to smuggle ration cards to Resistance fighters.

Josette meets a handsome Resistance commander, Célestin, and falls in love with him. '*Je t'aime à la folie*,' he tells her, '*je deviens fou d'amour.*' Olga notices (Josette seems to take it for granted) that Célestin has a *domestique* who provides them with a good dinner, a bottle of sardines, banana conserve, goose and good wine from his cellar – how the French love food!

Olga is waiting for the Germans to appear, after all this is occupied France. Two Gestapo agents do pick up our heroine, they want her to lead them to her lover Célestin, but they are quite gallant, impressed by her beauty, and she comes to no harm. When she travels by train the German personnel behave correctly towards her and offer her a seat because she is so beautiful.

Olga tosses her head and pulls back her hair, indignant. Banana conserve and goose, indeed! Why has Triolet put this story in her hand? How can a Russian believe that German conquerors can be so chivalrous? On other hand, she finds Triolet's naturalistic vocabulary astonishingly extensive for someone born in Russia. Olga thought she knew the language well but frequently has resort to her dictionary. Of course, if you live in France...

But the characters? – are they not cut out of cardboard, even the heroine Josette? Why is everyone prototypical? In the later story, *Le premier accroc coûte deux cents francs*, set in the summer of

1944, Triolet describes columns of German prisoners, les Boches, *'le bleu des yeux pâle d'humiliation et de panique, les épaules affaissées par la résignation.'*[†] Good – but Olga notices that Triolet never mentions the American soldiers who died on the beaches of Normandy, that wasn't the Communist Party line. These elegant people, Triolet and her husband Aragon, always talking about their six hundred Communist *fusillés*, what did they know of real war? Only six hundred!

Later they go out to dinner at the Brasserie Lipp. Being Spanish, Picasso eats late and sleeps late. They find Dora Maar already seated in the restaurant, wearing a black gown which brings the luminosity of an icon to her unforgiving face; she waits, impassive, inscrutable. It is not clear to Olga whether Madame Maar has been summoned or just waits there night after night for Picasso. He does not greet or acknowledge her. He motions to Olga to sit beside him. Triolet places Maar between herself and Aragon but she looks at neither, her unnerving stare fixed on the wall above Picasso's head. The *patron* hovers, Aragon orders wine to the table, a bottle of champagne heads the parade. He raises a glass in an elaborate toast to Olga which includes something about *notre belle copine soviétique*, our beautiful Soviet comrade, something about *la lutte pour la paix*, the struggle for peace, and something about *les lendemains qui chantent*, the tomorrows which sing.

Picasso's hand has settled on Olga's knee under the table. (Here we go again – but it is particularly disappointing in a genius.)

'Are you happy to be in France with the great Picasso?' Triolet asks her ceremonially.

'*Très heureuse, mesdames messieurs.* And profoundly honoured.'

'Now you must make a speech,' Picasso squeezes her thigh. 'You must say that you fell in love with Picasso the moment you set eyes on him.' His luminous eyes glow provocatively. Olga

---

[†] '...the blue of the eyes pale with humiliation and panic, shoulders sunk in resignation.'

notices that most of the other diners in the Brasserie are looking in Picasso's direction.

'So, *devushka* (he squeezes her thigh yet again), they trained you in Moscow to flatter me, Kemenev has sent me a witch to take possession of my soul. I have heard you likened to a Madonna by Raphael. Well, why not, let me do one now.' He grabs a spare napkin, not bothering to wipe his hands still stained from eating *moules* with his fingers. Everyone remains silent as the sketch of Olga Lepinskaya as Madonna is completed at speed, capturing a hint of high Slavic cheekbones, a sensuously relaxed mouth, the hair no longer severely pulled tight as during the day, but caressing her bare shoulders. Olga emerges all in one unbroken line, the faintest of haloes above her. But the shock is immediate – naked from the waist up, she is dreamily suckling an indulged baby. Olga detects no trace of Raphael but she will be proved wrong.

He makes a gift of it: '*Pour vous*, Olga of the Caucasus, mistress of Shochlov.' Olga registers the suspect formality of the '*vous*' but is spellbound by the portrait.

'You are privileged, Olga,' Triolet says. 'Pablo never gives anything away.'

Picasso emits a snort: 'They say Elsa has not smiled since Mayakovsky shot himself.' He turns to Olga, now squeezing her thigh above her stocking tops. 'The *devushka* can send the napkin to her imprisoned friend in Moscow, "the Dog man" – it may comfort him.'

No one speaks, Aragon and Triolet stricken by the mistake they have made when confiding this to Pablo.

Olga is afraid that she will have to spend the night in the rue des Grands Augustins, *droit du seigneur,* but no such suggestion surfaces. Taken back to the Aragons' luxurious apartment and falling into a light sleep, Olga encounters Vincent himself in his floppy hat sitting on a small fold-up stool, fashioned out of fallen branches from the linden trees, in the middle of a rutted road. A troop of cavalry in burnished helmets is advancing towards him but the emerging canvas shows only two desolate trees and crows swooping beneath a thunderous sky.

– Vincent, what would you have thought of Picasso had you known his work?

– There are so many Picassos, Vincent murmurs as the cavalry pass.

The following morning Triolet greets her at the breakfast table. '*Bonjour.* Did you sleep well, dear Olga?' Triolet is wearing a new day dress, new finger nails and a Russian cape against the falling temperature. A telegram in Cyrillic lies beside the crumbs of her croissant.

'*Bonjour, Madame Elsa.*

'Louis has been called away. He is with Maurice Thorez. He has received this telegram from your Director, Vladimir Kemenev, passed through the Soviet embassy last night. Here, read it for yourself.'

Olga reads: 'In view of what is now known about Davidov's illegal collaboration with American Zionist circles, the continued detention of this traitor is non-negotiable. Comrade Lepinskaya is to make no approach to Comrade Picasso on this subject. Regards, Kemenev.'

'I had no such intention,' Olga says.

Triolet nods. 'Beware your sub-conscious, Lacan[†] always warns us. Now, Olga, we have a new plan. Louis and I are going to keep out of the way. We think you should visit Dora Maar this morning, then go with her to see Pablo this afternoon. Take your portfolio again.'

'Madame Maar? I thought she is your *bête noire*, an *atlantiste* never to be trusted.'

Triolet nods again, lights a cigarette. 'It's Pablo's idea. He left a message with Sabartés. One must play along with Pablo.'

'But what does Madame Maar say?'

'She is not surprised. She can read Pablo. I will put you in a

---

† Jacques Lacan, distinguished psychiatrist who had treated Dora Maar.

taxi to the rue de Savoie.' Triolet is studying the young woman from Moscow. 'You understand what is required of you now – nothing to do with portfolios, nothing to do with paintings sold forty years ago to Shchukin and Morozov. Time is not on our side, Olga.'

'Required, you said?'

Triolet pours her a cup of coffee. 'Pablo would like to see you this afternoon – that is all you or I need to know.' Olga stares at her empty plate. 'Remember: to please him you must resist. He cannot seduce a woman unless she resists. It has to be a conquest against a blood-red sky. It has to be *Olga et le Minotaure*. When the moment comes you must be wearing a light cotton frock with nothing underneath.'

Olga sits paralysed. She has thought about this moment for weeks but somehow never really believing it would happen. The prospect – the place, setting and time – had remained hazy in her mind, blurred. Perhaps she had imagined that Madame Triolet, a writer much admired, 'your chaperone' Kemenev has promised, would protect her, would intervene, no Pablo no.

'Have you taken precautions?' Triolet is asking her. 'I can take you now to our best pharmacy, Gaston's. They will provide an immediate fitting.' Her nose grows longer. 'The Party has an account at Gaston's for such contingencies.'

Olga chokes. 'Madame, kindly desist.'

'Yes or no?' Triolet shrugs impatiently but with a hint of sympathy. 'Well, if you won't accept my advice don't forget, my dear, to wash yourself in a mild mix of vinegar and water – before and after. Not too strong, only one quarter vinegar.' She stubs out her cigarette with today's light mauve nails. 'Dear Dora may advise you further. She is the most recent in his bed – we do not know about Françoise when he visited her the other day – before you and the quixotic Koltsov turned up at the gate like mendicants.'

Olga declines breakfast and excuses herself. At midday she and her portfolio reach the rue de Savoie by taxi. This street runs east from the rue des Grands Augustins, a short distance from Picasso's residence and studio. Maar herself eventually answers the bell, staring at Olga as if she had never seen her before. She is still dressed in black but with a green scarf round her neck.

'*Oui?*'

'Madame, I was told I should visit you.'

'*Pourquoi?*'

'Those were Madame Triolet's instructions. If it is inconvenient for you I shall not bother you.'

Olga half-turns as if to walk away, producing an immediate change of demeanour in Maar. 'Please come in, Mademoiselle Olga. You must forgive the mess, I am a poor housewife.' This woman may be past forty but Olga finds her dark, intense beauty arresting. She is led into a small, cluttered studio littered with easels, brushes, tins of paint and turpentine, cut-outs from Matisse pinned to the wall on a cork board, photographs by Man Ray, two studio portraits of Picasso by Cartier-Bresson, a pile of paint-smeared newspapers, photographic magazines, pages from *Le Monde* and *Le Figaro*. Only a chair is missing. Olga surveys it all slowly, methodically, professionally determined to forget nothing.

'Please sit down.'

Olga looks about her at the chaos. 'Where, please?'

'Oh *mon dieu, attendez.*' She returns carrying two small utility chairs of the kitchen type. Olga sits but Maar doesn't. She produces her long ivory cigarette holder, jamming it between her teeth without a cigarette.

'Pablo likes you.'

'He has been very kind,' Olga murmurs.

'Kind? Pablo kind? Do you mean the napkin portrait he gave you? Do you imagine that means anything?'

'Madame, please explain why you have agreed to receive me this morning.'

Maar ignores the question. 'Shall I tell you something? For Picasso other people, including those who imagine themselves close to him, are merely grains of dust floating in the sunlight.

His entourage of devotees are facile opportunists. Yes, without exception. During the years when I reigned in the rue des Grands Augustins, they fawned on me. *Notre chère Dora*. When we holidayed together on the Côte d'Azur and he took me into the sea with him, the acolytes clustered like flies on the beach taking photographs. Now the same people relish the spectacle of my downfall and humiliation. I have no friend or ally in that ménage. My Catholicism is wrong, my politics suspect. When his first wife, a mad old Russian, comes after me in the streets shouting abuse, Pablo merely shrugs and turns away.'

'I think you are very brave, Madame, if I may say so.'

'Brave? Shall I tell you how I seduced Picasso fifteen years ago? By slicing up my own gloved hand on a table in the Deux Magots. With a penknife.'

'Yes, Madame, I did hear about that, it's quite legendary.'

'But have you seen the picture he painted soon afterwards, *Dora et le Minotaure* – the sovereign Minotaur dark and bestial grabs and plunders the prostrate pure woman against a blood-red sky.'

'Madame Triolet told me he remains addicted to the same image.'

Maar stretches a still-fine little figure. 'Did she? *Mourir de ne pas mourir*. So Moscow wants to take the Minotaur captive? Listen: don't do it. Abandon your cynical conspiracy. Picasso is more important than Communism. His magic is greater than theirs, they can never match it. That is why they will not dare to put his work on display in your Pushkin Museum. That is why dissident artists like your Pyotr – oh yes, we all know about him – will remain imprisoned while Pablo parades around Moscow swallowing canapés and Georgian champagne. True?'

Olga bridles. 'Why did you receive me so coldly, Madame? That curt *oui?* and that peremptory *pourquoi?*'

'Do you imagine I enjoy setting eyes on you, the femme fatale sent by Moscow?'

'Those were the words used by Madame Françoise at the gate

of La Galloise. Do the two of you exchange notes on incivility?'

'My dear young woman, you shepherded yourself into anger by asking me why I received you coldly. If you are looking for a quarrel with me as a way out of Pablo's bed, forget it.'

But that, Olga becomes aware, is exactly what she is looking for. 'I see you read *Paris-Soir* and *Le Figaro*, Madame.'

'Of course, the "bourgeois" press. Aragon and Triolet tell me I am not to be influenced by the Kravchenko trial here in Paris, even though Sartre and de Beauvoir came away convinced that millions languish in Soviet forced labour camps. Aragon and Triolet will tell you it was all CIA propaganda. What do you think, comrade?'

'Maître Picasso can make up his own mind about that.'

'He doesn't have one. Pablo is the ideal Stalinist, ignorant and loyal.'

Maar extracts a Gauloise out of a soft blue packet and inserts it in the cigarette holder, which is moulded like a tiny trumpet with a black Bakelite stem and a flaring bell for the cigarette. She drags at the spark wheel of a lighter. The tobacco catches. She inhales deeply. Her teeth are clenched tight on the ivory stem of the holder, causing it to jut up at an angle of what resembles defiance.

'You haven't answered my question, Mademoiselle Olga. Do you really believe your masters will dare to show Pablo's early work and his cubism to the Soviet public?'

Olga replies '*ça va de soi* – that goes without saying,' but inwardly she is depleted of an answer except *merde*. If Maar knows so much about the project, the planned trip to Moscow, who else? Will she not attempt to sabotage it by chattering to journalists? Olga makes an attempt at conciliation:

'I am told, Madame, that when you are in residence at Ménerbes you often set out early, when the light is good, on your motorbike, your hair tied in a woollen scarf, a rucksack over your shoulder carrying a miniature easel.'

Maar nods. 'So?'

'I am extremely eager to see your work.'

'Why not? I can show you my photography from my surrealist period.' She excavates a pile of large folders but then abandons the quest in exasperation. 'What is the point? I could also show you my paintings which mirror Picasso's "weeping" portraits of myself – you might not detect the difference, except when Picasso's dealers, Klootz *et les autres voleurs*, call here with their bedraggled bunches of flowers – what they want, what they propose fancy prices for, are not my versions, not my paintings.'

'Can I please see them?'

'They are of no interest to Comrade Kemenev. You must understand, Mademoiselle Olga, in life as in art my trajectory is that of a meteorite that came too close to the sun.'

'Yes but I –'

'I could show you my photographs of *Guernica* taken stage-by-stage throughout its composition.'

'Please do show me!'

But Maar makes no move to do so. 'Art historians have identified seven distinct stages of *Guernica* but my photographs show two more. It was in reality a painting entirely influenced by photography – by me. You know it well. The multiple horrors are conveyed in a palette of greys which evoke what?'

'The moral universe of fascism?'

'Yes, perhaps – if Pablo is in the mood he will tell you how Gestapo officers arrived at the studio in 1943, took a look at *Guernica,* and asked him whether he "did" it. Pablo replied, "No, you did." The story might be true, I wasn't there on that occasion. To me the palette of greys also convey the shock newsprint reports of the atrocity. The bare bulb suggests a camera flash.'

'Yes – or the naked truth?'

'I doubt Picasso has ever been interested in the truth.'

'Why should you say that?'

'That summer of 1937, when so utterly "appalled" by the events and massacres in his native Spain, Pablo took me and a dozen others to the Hotel Vaste Horizon in Mougins where he insisted that we engage in nightly "wife-swapping". That was his tribute to the people of Spain.'

'Oh.'

'I have often felt like Don Juan's Elvira. One of Pablo's favourite phrases is *que ça ne te donne pas des idées, ma douce* – don't let this give you ideas, my sweet. Understand?'

'Yes.'

'His women are not allowed to "get ideas" though he calls himself a Communist. He has a paint brush, *un pinceau*, in place of a heart. Do you know the origin of the word *pinceau*? No? It is the Latin word *peniculus* meaning "little penis". Of course in Pablo's case, as you will no doubt soon discover for yourself, the diminutive is more touching than realistic.'

Olga drops her gaze but Maar is now relentless: 'He gave me the old house you mentioned at Ménerbes in the Vaucluse as a present. I felt it was mine but one day he turned up here, demanded the keys, took his new young mistress Françoise down there and conceived a child in my bed. They called him Claude.'

'What can I say, Madame?'

'You should call me Dora. So you and I are now rivals. Shall we fight here and now? He made me fight with Marie-Thérèse in his studio, like two cats – did they tell you that?'

'No.' (She means yes.)

'So you are a Communist, a Party member, Comrade Olga?'

'A candidate member.'

'Let me tell you that when I was with Georges Bataille and the surrealists, we were to the left of the Communist Party. They called us Trotskyists – spies, wreckers, saboteurs. And now they accuse us of working for the Americans. Do you know why?'

Olga thinks of her father. 'Tell me.'

'Because we don't like to see artists and museum curators like your Pyotr Davidov sent to prison. Picasso laughed when Aragon and Triolet told him about your lover's painting name, Sobaka. Yes, he laughed merrily. Dog! He asked his repulsive Afghan hound Kazbek what he thought about that. But forgive me –

you're shaking like a leaf in the wind.'

The telephone rings, buried in the far corner of the room. Maar forces a path through the clutter, takes it and listens. After a while she says 'No.' Then 'No' again. The other party is apparently insistent. Finally she replaces the receiver.

'Pablo wants me to accompany you to his studio.'

'What a happy idea, Madame. I thought that was why I was sent to you.'

'No idea of Pablo's can be a happy one. Believe me, he is not interested in your portfolio and your slides. I know him. No one knows him as I do. He wants me there to watch – that will guarantee his pleasure.'

'Watch?'

'You have a fine figure, Olga. By the way, have you taken precautions? Pablo won't tolerate condoms.'

Olga is on her feet, reaching for her portfolio, her overcoat. 'Is that any way for one woman to speak to another? I shall go to Picasso alone, Madame.'

'But I am compelled by Pablo to follow. He promises to take me with him to Moscow.' The long cigarette holder jabs upwards. 'If I swear to silence about it.'

'May I ask, Madame, why you should want to visit a country you despise and detest?'

'Because Pablo is the Minotaur without whom my life these past six years has been an empty space of anguish.'

Beset by a pity akin to disgust, Olga insists that she will go to Picasso's studio alone. 'I will not share a taxi with you.'

'Then I shall follow. *C'est obligatoire.*'

When they reach the street, Dora looks Olga over quite clinically, from head to toe. Olga imagines that is it her clothes which are in question, causing her hands to flutter nervously down her body.

'You are too tall,' Maar says, 'five or six centimetres too tall.'

'Should we go back upstairs, Madame, and saw some of me off? What would you suggest, the head or the tail?'

Maar hails a taxi. 'Rue des Grands Augustins,' she tells the young driver, '*numéro sept.*' But she, too, is shaking.

The driver smiles in his mirror. 'Picasso?'

Here Madame Lepinskaya broke down. In fact I could see it coming as moisture filmed her eyes and her fingers began to dance in agitation. She stood up, offered me tea then immediately forgot about it. Her distressed body language was inviting me to leave but I didn't want to. How many hours spread over how many months had we taken to arrive at this, the dénouement, the moment that had indelibly scarred her life?

Without looking at me, her attention fixed on her Ming console, she said: 'I think, Monsieur, we may next pass on to Picasso's subsequent arrival in Moscow. If we meet again.'

13

⁓

Olga is back in Moscow. Her fellow-curators' intense curiosity about her trip and its outcome is held in check by the presiding ethic instilled by the Party: you need to know only what you need to know. Keep your eyes to the front. Even so, she gathers that during her absence abroad conversations in the cafeteria have been rife with speculation. Some predict promotion for her; others an unpleasant fall from grace. Gossip has been intensified by Pyotr Davidov's empty desk followed by the disappearance not only of the man but the desk as well. No one knows his fate. In the language of curators, he has been airbrushed out of the canvas. As for what would be required of Lepinskaya in Paris, speculation has been muted by the conventions of decency and comradeship.

She finds Kemenev as she left him, still calculating on his abacus who is Number Two and Number Six. Her persistent questions about Pyotr's fate are met with shrugs and evasions.

'Comrade Olga Maksimovna, bear in mind that Davidov ran to the Americans, to our mortal enemies.'

'But only because of the enormity of Comrade Khrushchev's tirade at the Fortochka! What Pyotr did was not planned. It was the man from the *New York Times* who approached Pyotr – I watched him do it.'

'Every Soviet citizen is responsible for his actions.'

As the calendar marches relentlessly towards the opening of the Picasso exhibition, she works long hours for its success. She is thrilled to unearth from the cellars an Italian print of Picasso's *Vecchio cieco e ragazzo* – Blind Old Man and Boy – from the blue period and quite touching. A man and boy are seated on the ground. The boy is listlessly nibbling an apple; his overlarge downcast eyes register nothing beyond hunger and helpless lethargy. The bearded, ragged man is barefoot, his trousers in tatters, his eyes are unseeing yet uncannily he 'sees' more than the boy. She prepares a new entry for the catalogue: 'Distinguished by subtle colour, plastic form, and, nonetheless, controlled line, these early works constitute a penetrating social and psychological study of the human condition. They are full of an emotional, at times bitter, feeling about man's lost or transient harmony with the universe.'

Ilya Grigoryevich Ehrenburg telephones, inviting her to dine with him at one of his favourite clubs, the Moscow Artists and Book Illustrators. She accepts dutifully, wearied by the prospect of his serpentine evasions and a late journey home through a winter's night. She has to remind herself what an eminent man is *Dyadya* Ilya, a witness to the First World War and the Revolution, a favourite writer for Red Army men during the Great Patriotic War with his message of Kill Germans, 'count only the number of Germans you have killed', the author of *The Black Book* detailing Nazi genocide of the Jews, a writer who knew personally almost every European writer and artist of distinction, including the modernists, cubists, surrealists and other deviationists. He has known Picasso since the First World War.

A waiter leads her to a reserved corner table where she sits for fifteen minutes before her sixty-year-old host appears, his still-thick hair brushed straight back, deep pockets beneath his eyes, putting on weight, kisses her hand, orders champagne with a casual flick of his fingers, and absent-mindedly reaches for her knee under the tablecloth as if it were the gear lever of his Moskvich car. She moves her leg abruptly.

'Picasso does that, *Dyadya* Ilya. I have had enough of it.'

'Ah, I sometimes forget you are supposed to be my niece, Ochka, though only in a manner of speaking.'

Ehrenburg assumes the wounded-stag expression for which she feels affection considering the public ordeal he recently suffered when drenched in dung in the columns of *Oktyabr* – a dangerous Cosmopolitan Jew, a 'masked advocate of Western trends' – and now he confesses that life is getting nastier. On 12

August, twenty-four Jews, most of them well known to him, had been executed. He has heard a reliable rumour that various leaders of the Czechoslovak Party, most of them Jews, are to be put on trial in Prague including his old friend Vladimir Clementis. To Olga all this is rather remote although the deep creases assailing his features confirm his distress. She wishes he would not evade the one subject he knows is breaking her heart – Pyotr. And isn't it always the same with these conceited old men, all they care about are the grand designs, the larger battlefields, the trenches gained and the cities lost? She presses him about Pyotr.

Ehrenburg sighs and calls for a new bottle of champagne. 'It seems that Davidov fell into the clutches of the most dangerous man in Moscow. You know who I mean?' She nods. The first course arrives. Ehrenburg sighs again but with a keen eye on the food. 'As a matter of fact Harrison Salisbury recently came to see me. I shouldn't have taken the risk of talking to him but I was thinking of you. He told me that he had noticed my habit of bowing formally to members of the foreign press corps without speaking to them.' Ehrenburg smiles. 'I confess that rather won me over.'

He begins to eat while her own plate remains untouched.

'Salisbury assured me that he was much distressed by Davidov's arrest. To which I pointed out that Khrushchev's rant at the Fortochka Theatre followed by young Davidov's disappearance is manna from heaven for the *New York Times* and the CIA. Then Salisbury swore that in fact he did not take your Pyotr to the US embassy, he would never put any Soviet citizen at such risk. He swore on the Bible that he merely drove this maligned young artist and his castigated canvases back to his dilapidated attic studio in Cheremushki – no doubt you have spent many loving nights there, Ochka, your toes nibbled by rats – to look at Sobaka's Severe paintings, one of which Salisbury bought there and then with nice crisp dollars. Admittedly Davidov expressed anger and dismay concerning the Pushkin's planned Picasso exhibition, which he called a "fraudulent and cynical charade" – but he most certainly did not ask to be put in contact with American diplomats.'

Ehrenburg dabbed his mouth with his napkin.

'Do you believe the American?' Olga has not touched her food.

'Yes, I do. I have reason to believe the false story was put about by Gorovsky's MGB after they arrested Davidov. Kemenev believed it because he wanted to, and of course it's the Party line for our friends in France, who you now know well.'

Amazing how Uncle Ilya has cleaned his plate of lamb cutlets while talking so much.

'And where is Pyotr now?'

'When people are taken away in our country, Ochka, they are taken away. As you and your mother sadly know – and as my friends Babel and Meyerhold also learned. Habeas corpus we don't have.'

Olga presses. 'You have a line to Comrade Beria. He knows where Pyotr is. Beria is certainly Golovsky's superior in the Organs.' Olga is stunned to hear herself mentioning such dangerous names openly, in a restaurant, in flagrant contravention of the ABC of survival.

'My dear Ochka, how can I swear an affidavit to Beria on the say-so of the reactionary spy and saboteur Harrison Salisbury – who I should not have been talking to?'

Ehrenburg subsides into weariness and a full stomach. 'Tell me about Pablo – did he beg you to resist?'

She is on her feet now, tears in her eyes, distraught to find herself on the verge of the vast impropriety of walking out on her host.

'Please sit down, Olga, don't disgrace me.'

She sits and snatches her napkin, now damp and crumpled. 'You disgrace yourself, *Dyadya* Ilya.'

'I know. Forgive me. To survive an old writer must know everything, more than anyone else.'

'In that case I can tell you something. While I was "resisting", I persuaded Picasso to make a personal pledge to me.'

'He's never going to marry you, Ochka.'

'Picasso pledged that if Pyotr is not set free by the time he reaches Moscow, he will turn round and head straight home, with or without his servile entourage.'

'Was that true, Madame?'

'No. Though this was the first worthwhile lie I had told in my twenty-eight years.'

'Was Davidov released?'

'Monsieur, you must let me describe events in the proper sequence. Otherwise I do not remember what I have already told you.'

Ehrenburg absorbs Olga's threat without responding to it. She is clearly over-wrought and must be handled with kid gloves.

'You'll enjoy this story, Ochka. Perhaps you remember that I did a tour of China last year. The story runs like this: reports of Pablo's quarrel with Chagall reach an all-night Kremlin banquet in honour of Mao Tse-tung. Chairman Mao asks Comrade Stalin what it's all about. "My good friend, you wouldn't want to be in a picture by Picasso," Stalin tells Mao. "You'd come out with at least two noses and one eye."

'Mao chuckles. "What about a portrait by the other one, Jackal?"

"Chagall? He would have you floating in the sky, upside down."

'Mao returns home and commissions Chagall to paint the ceiling of the Peking Opera House. Mao stipulates that he must be shown floating in the sky, suspended above the Confucian universe. Chagall accepts the commission because he can never say no. When he reaches the top of the scaffolding he finds Pablo already at work, painting doves.'

Ehrenburg sighs mistily and refills their glasses. 'The story doesn't amuse you?'

'Every character in your story, Uncle Ilya, is either someone powerful or someone famous. And always an old male person.'

'Ah yes, ah yes, *touché.*' He takes out a pocket diary and turns its pages gloomily. 'I have to be in Vienna in December for the Peace Congress. So does Aragon. I only hope we can get Picasso and Chaplin here and away again before the Congress – it gives us a narrow window of two weeks, quite tight, don't you agree?'

She bids him goodnight. In the reflection of the restaurant's glass door she can see him bringing out a pile of foreign newspapers from his briefcase. You can be sure that Pyotr Davidov's name is not in any of them.

～

Picasso made the dreaded journey to Moscow by air[†] in the company of Aragon and Triolet, along with Dora Maar and the indispensable Sabartés. Of course there is no written record of the journey, which biographers and historians never acknowledge as having taken place. Madame Lepinskaya's description was largely dependent on what she heard from Dora Maar, although I also caught glimpses of Olga's own imagination at work, mainly accurate I suspect. I confess that Picasso's brief dream at altitude is a naked invention of mine.

The world's most famous, in some quarters notorious, artist is discovered in the 'first-class' section of an Aeroflot Ilyushin leaving Prague for Moscow – his fear of flying, the acute ache in his ears during the descent into Prague/Ruzyne, and the tedious stopover has left him distressed and depressed. Triolet and Maar are both alarmed by his condition while Sabartés is close to hysteria. His maître is seventy-one years old, short and stocky, suntanned, with the general aspect of a toad – from the bridge of his broad nose two concentric folds run to his mouth and, when he smiles, persevere until they pincer the chin. The smile may seem provisional because he takes nothing on trust.

Although the plane has not yet left the runway, Picasso is again panicked, as at Orly, by the imminent prospect of take-off. He is convinced – and Sabartés has fed his fear – that planes fail to take off more often than they succeed. The Aeroflot Ilyushin stinks of some nauseating compound of lubricating oil, diesel,

---

† Regular Paris-Moscow flights by Air France and Aeroflot were not inaugurated until the agreement of 1954. Picasso and his entourage must therefore fly from Paris to Prague where they disembark and, after an exhausting stopover, board an Aeroflot Ilyushin of the 11-12 model.

vodka, overworn tyres and yesterday's vomit. Picasso has been given a seat beside a window so layered in grime that a single motion of his thumb could produce a peace dove. Two thickset hostesses are distributing brown paper bags, one to each passenger.

'What for?' he asks.

'*Rvota*. Sick. *Malade*.'

He is layered in sweat. He closes the dark, phosphorescent eyes which have remapped the universe at close quarters but they refuse to stay closed. Fleetingly he imagines an escorting squadron of his peace doves (Indian ink, 1947), also heading for the Capital of Peace. Now airborne, Picasso is finally asleep. The empty seat beside him indicates a monarch. It contains the horns of a dying *toro bravo*, a dying horse bares huge teeth, a light bulb sputters, the whores of Avignon rearrange their astonished profiles, Dora Maar's handsome features and prominent, motionless chin bring with them the portraits *Femme 1*, *Femme 2*, *Femme 3*, all Dora.

Pablo is dreaming about Charlot's mother, the actress Nell Gwynne, a mistress of King Henry VIII. She wanted to marry him so he cut off her head. Charlot is smiling: 'I'm never sure who my father was, Mother had a travelling heart'. But now Dora Maar's chin has intruded. 'You will find Moscow too cold for sex, Pablo.' His huge eyes widen in alarm. He loathes and fears the cold. The hold of the Aeroflot Ilyushin is stuffed with his fur hats and woollen underwear, plus Italian snowboots – a gift from Renato Guttuso – and fur-lined aviator's gloves from Harrods. But he needs them all now. He wakes up shivering and calls for Sabartés: '*J'ai froid. Je meurs* – I'm cold, I'm dying.' He remembers that Ilya Ehrenburg has promised him and his entourage the use of a large, centrally heated apartment and studio in Gorky Street, courtesy of the Soviet Union of Artists, always warm, heated at all hours. Well, you can't trust Ehrenburg.

Elsa Triolet turns from monitoring Picasso to monitoring Aragon 'How long will it take Pablo to get Lepinskaya to remove her furs and model for him?'

'*Huit jours* – at least a week.'

'Eight hours. I don't trust that girl. Her head may belong to us but her heart is in turmoil.'

Triolet does not feel sick, she never does. The latest essays by Sartre, the one-eyed goblin, lie open on her still-comely lap as she broods about Sartre and Simone de Beauvoir, who both desire to endow each other with perfect freedom, so she, the badly dressed school ma'am, is said to be having a gay time with an American writer in Chicago, her skirt over her head. No less irritating is Pablo's soft spot for Sartre. 'I like his squint,' Pablo has told her, always keen to irritate. 'One eye looks at you but the other is studying the ceiling – as if the real meaning of things may have taken flight. I like the way Sartre keeps changing his mind about everything. And he's no taller than I am. Like Charlot. That's why Sartre is so successful with women.'

Triolet mulls this over – of course Pablo was insulting her own good taste since she had chosen the tallest of intellectuals. She sits brooding about her novel-in-progress, which portrays a sculptor with many of Pablo's mannerisms.

The propeller-driven Ilyushin crosses the Soviet frontier to the sound of snapping elastic bands. Perhaps two hours later the plane descends on the Soviet capital in darkness, a freezing winter's night, losing height with such chaotic lack of control over cabin pressure that all their ears, not least Picasso's, are aching and popping. 'Press a finger up under your nose, Pablo, it will soon be over,' Laurent Casanova has advised him but he can't remember that.

The plane has now parked its rotting fuselage off, or on, the potholed runway of Sheremetyevo and stands hissing and groaning, triumphant to have flopped down like a diseased vulture on the socialist sixth of the earth. Swaddled against the cold, Picasso eventually emerges, supported by anxious hands. He is without everything he cherishes except his fame, his value in some counterfeit game on the chessboard of the Cold War. No documents are required at Immigration, no forms to fill in, nothing at all except applause and the embraces dictated by Russian protocol – this cold cheek, that cold cheek, this cold cheek. Ilya Ehrenburg is on hand with his damp, lukewarm kisses for male and female alike. Well, at least, someone I know!

'Elsa, *bienvenue*! Louis, *à nous la liberté*!' A pause. 'Jaime! And Dora, too!'

Ehrenburg takes Picasso's arm and translates the huge banner slogan in neon lights extending across the main airport building. Picasso gazes gloomily at the bulging Cyrillic letters which seem to threaten his spread-winged peace dove and its beaked olive branch. Indeed the bird is missing half a wing.

'My dove looks worse off than I am,' he mutters to Triolet.

Now the visitors are confronted by a line of bulky overcoats and fur hats, clearly arraigned in order of precedence. A man from the Party. A man from the Ministry. A man from VOKS, the All-Union Society for Cultural Relations with Foreign Countries. And Vladimir Kemenev, hat in hand. Picasso doesn't recognise Kemenev from the smudged, passport-style photos accompanying his published diatribes, but Ehrenburg murmurs the introduction.

'Best behaviour, Pablo.'

Picasso forces himself to shake the viper's hand. The creature is attempting to smile but (like the Archbishop's orgasm in the bordello) it won't come.

'You are very welcome, Maître,' says Kemenev. 'I hope we can make your visit to our country an occasion for strengthening international understanding and the bond between peoples through the power of art.'

Quite a mouthful! Olga observes and listens from behind the bulky overcoats and fur hats of the men. She is only an underling but she knows and dreads Kemenev's *plat du jour* that will follow his hors d'oeuvre. Kemenev has now stationed himself behind a bank of microphones. He is about to speak in Russian and Triolet, sizing up the situation with the eyes made famous in Aragon's poems, takes upon herself the translation – she glimpses Olga hovering in the background, a new Olga swathed in furs, in hiding, clearly petrified, as yet undiscovered by Pablo.

'Comrades and friends, brothers and sisters, how can one underestimate the personal contribution of the great artist who has honoured Soviet culture by his first visit to our Motherland? And is it not the first duty of Soviet art historians and museum curators to appreciate that we expect such a genius as Maître Picasso to be a little impatient with the artistic theory and the political ideology to which we, under the guidance of Lenin, Stalin and the USSR Academy of Art, attach primordial importance?'

Triolet translates, her arm gripping Picasso's as if he might run away. The prolonged applause for Kemenev's peroration strikes Picasso as gratuitous. No one seems willing to dare to be the first to stop. 'What are they clapping?' he grunts to Ehrenburg.

'They are clapping Comrade Stalin, dear Pablo.'

'Stalin? Is he here, *ça va, eh?*'

'He's always here even when not.'

'Like Jesus in a church?'

'However,' Kemenev eventually continues, 'we must never cease to remind ourselves what Vladimir Ilyich Lenin had to say on this subject. In a crucial intervention which encapsulates our Revolutionary scientific approach to art, Vladimir Ilyich defined his position to Comrade Klara Zetkin thirty years ago: "The beautiful must be preserved," he remarked, "even if it is 'old'. Why worship the new as a god compelling submission merely because it is 'new'? Nonsense! Bosh and nonsense!: It is beyond me to consider the productions of expressionism, futurism, cubism and others 'isms' the highest manifestations of artistic genius. I do not understand them. They give me no joy."'

More applause. Triolet has been murmuring a French version in Picasso's ear, horrified by Kemenev's oration but loyal to her task.

'Am I an "ism"?' Picasso asks.

'We are applauding Lenin not what he said,' Ehrenburg murmurs anxiously.

'Now you must speak, Pablo – diplomatically please.' He gestures to Aragon, who glides forward on cue and hands Picasso a typed text.

Picasso glowers at it, rubs his eyes. 'But this is one meaningless platitude and cliché after another!'

'Hush, Pablo.'

'I won't "hush". When Picasso speaks he speaks for Picasso. I regard Kemenev's speech as an outrageous provocation. He didn't say a word about staging a Picasso exhibition! I am going to punch his nose!'

Ehrenburg hurries over to Kemenev. They confer urgently. Ehrenburg returns. 'Director Kemenev assures you that the exhibition is almost ready. Just a few finishing touches to be completed, lighting, captions, posters, that kind of thing. The intention is to bring in a selected audience – to gauge reactions – before opening it to the public.'

'And the world's press? I am expecting the world's press. Why aren't they here? We should be blinded by flashbulbs.'

'All in due course.'

'*Merde.*'

Picasso scrunches Aragon's text into a ball and shoves it in the pocket of the Prince Louis' smart blue coat. In doing this he staggers, almost falls. French hands and voices rush to keep him on his feet. A distraught Sabartés is wailing that if Pablo collapses in these zero-minus temperatures he may never rise again. But he will – Picasso has been rising again all his life.

The cortege of cars sweeps along bleak avenues apparently built of grey cardboard. They see pastel-tinted Zims, a few old, high-bodied Zis, which resemble Packards of the 1930s, otherwise the mass-produced Pobedas and whatever they currently call their black limousines with curtained windows. Picasso catches glimpses of broad-backed women shovelling snow. He reaches for a sketchpad but none is to hand. A deep gloom descends on every spirit in the official cortege: the land which embodies all our hopes, the land we would give our lives for, amounts on first inspection to rows of stout women in woollen balaclavas and thick gloves shovelling snow through the night. Picasso nods off. This precious sack will be laid to rest in a comfortable bed all his own in *ulitsa* Gorky. On Sabartés's instructions, Dora Maar will be confined to a separate bedroom. The secretary has taken note: during the two weeks since Lepinskaya's departure, the maître has not once summoned Maar to his bed – although Sabartés can't be sure because he lives with his wife some distance from the rue des Grands Augustins and not being sure is his life sentence.

Olga goes home from the airport on the metro, a long journey, alone. Her mother will have prepared a late meal of *Chanakhi*, a claypot stew of lamb, aubergines, potatoes, tomatoes and herbs from Georgia – and the two women will talk long into the night about Pyotr and Picasso. Olga has opted not to tell Ekaterina everything, not yet. You can be very close to someone yet closer to yourself. She has not yet quite told herself what she has not told her mother.

14

The arrival of the Chaplins at Sheremetyevo is a rather more genial and relaxed affair. Nina Bolsharova has travelled with them. They enjoy her occasional, always deferential, bursts of wit, even Oona.

'I sometimes suspect she is pretending to be me, Charlie.'

The tensions and travel sickness blighting Picasso's trajectory are in marked contrast to the cheery showmanship of Charlie on arrival and the carefree embraces dispensed by his Oona, who has enjoyed three vodkas and tonic during the flight and is intrigued by all the Soviet uniforms and those peaked caps with exaggerated round tops. 'How do they keep them on?' she whispers to Charlie. The Soviet welcoming party from Mosfilm, the Ministry of Culture and the inevitable VOKS is waiting to dispense the customary hugs and kisses. Chaplin recognises a still-handsome Grigorii Aleksandrov, hair still brushed straight back, who had frequented his Hollywood swimming pool and tennis court twenty years ago, regularly calling Chaplin's best shots out when they were manifestly in.

'Charlie! Long time no see! Your plane arrived early.'

'Two hours late.'

'That's early for Aeroflot. On time is three hours late.'

Aleksandrov introduces his fellow directors, currently most in favour, Chiaureli and Romm. Each kisses Oona's hand, as if to remind her they are continental Europeans. Nina hangs back in the presence of the all-powerful Aleksandrov as he gallantly explains to Oona that the airport's slogan MIR VO VSEM MIRE means 'Peace for All the World' – adding (every foreign visitor has to hear this) that the Russian word 'mir' means both 'peace' and 'world'.

'Did they run out of ideas?' Oona asks. 'I mean, when they got to "world" – can't think what to call it – why not "peace"?'

The Russian film directors are too polite to exchange glances – her reputation has run ahead of her. You can't help liking her, if only because she is so manifestly happy to be herself. Now a crumpled figure shuffles on to the scene, unshaven and carrying his body like a sack, hand tremulously extended. Nina steps forward to guide him towards Chaplin.

'Hullo, Charlie.' He pauses for breath. 'Eisenstein.'

'Sergei, old friend! It's really you! Long time no see!' Chaplin's professional smile carries a hint of reservation in the eyes, a cautious scrutiny.

'Can it really be you, Sergei?'

'Who else?'

'How does it feel to be dead?'

'*Nyet* not yet.' That square-jawed, Germanic head with its wild tuft of electric hair is surely unmistakable. Nina senses that Chaplin had never been completely at ease with the great Soviet director's air of knowing all that could be known, now extending to the last word on whether he is alive.

'Oh Sergei you look absolutely dreadful,' Oona greets him, 'I mean dead on your feet.'

Eisenstein, who has never previously met her, gazes bleakly at Chaplin as if to say, how could you make a mistake like this? Chaplin takes him aside and drops his voice.

'I got your letter.'

'Letter? Good. Of course.' He doesn't seem to remember it. Nina is hovering, clearly anxious.

Chaplin appraises him. 'Never mind, Sergei. I don't forget the terrible conditions you Soviets endured during the war. And your own heart attacks.'

'No, no, I lived under privileged conditions while making *Ivan the Terrible*.'

'But I heard that you were summoned to the Kremlin and berated because your Ivan reminded Mr Stalin of Hamlet and because Ivan's praetorian guard, I forget their name –'

'The *Oprichniki*,' Nina helps out.

'OK, I still can't say it. Mr Stalin complained to you that these guys were depicted in vivid, expressionist photomontage, as tyrants drunk on blood, as dissolute thugs resembling the American Ku Klux Klan. You were instructed to re-shoot Part 2 in its entirety.'

'My dear Charlie there is no more truth in that than my subsequent heart attack and early death. Part 2 has been shown and applauded across the Soviet Union.'

Meanwhile Oona, having lost interest as the two old dogs circle each other in mutual tail-sniffing, has wandered into conversation with a tall American who offers a confident handshake.

'Nice to meet you, Mrs Chaplin. Harrison Salisbury, Moscow correspondent of the *New York Times*.'

Nina follows closely, this is going to be a dangerous exchange, two alert Americans in their prime – not the rambling reminiscences of the geriatrics. Salisbury is telling Mrs Chaplin that he is from Minnesota and has gotten through three years of gruelling solitude, ostracism and relentless police surveillance in Cold-War Moscow.

'I have to live in the Metropole but a posting to the South Col of Everest couldn't be more isolated.' He leads her aside, Nina following. Oona is surprised to hear him tell Nina to get lost in Russian.

'Oh no,' Oona protests, 'this is my good friend Nina, she has come all the way from London with us.'

'Mrs Chaplin, I hate to disillusion you but this lookalike lady works for the MVD.'

'What's that? I can assure you Nina works for Mosfilm, our hosts.'

'Maybe she's right now at our elbows to translate from English into English?'

Nina takes Oona by the arm. 'Unfortunately Mr Salisbury is not a truthful or reliable reporter of our life here in the Soviet Union. He represents one of the newspapers which have been persecuting Mr Chaplin. Kindly have no more to do with him.'

Oona isn't too keen on that. She is studying Salisbury's entirely reliable and rather attractive features, a fellow-American after all and that counts for something if you find yourself in a part of the world where dead people are still alive. Now it is she who takes him aside and firmly dismisses Nina (who stubbornly follows, her life may depend on it) as he tells her that he is allowed no Soviet friends, even people he knows like Ilya Ehrenburg give him the cold shoulder or run for cover. The resident US press corps is down to one, himself, plus four Americans working for the news agencies. The few West European correspondents in town mostly represent Communist papers. His despatches and cables are censored and few of them reach West 44th Street, even when they have been culled straight out of *Pravda*.

'When I send a cable marked and priced "Urgent", the girls at the *kassa* count the number of words ten times, after which the cable is delayed by forty-five minutes and is no longer "Urgent".'

'Oh wow, how lonely you must be. Is your wife with you in Moscow?'

'I wouldn't inflict that on her. Janet and the kids stay in Minnesota. I must say, it's an honour to talk to the daughter of Eugene O'Neill.'

Nina calculates that Salisbury must be admiring this Disneyland beauty for having broken all records by holding down the job of being Mrs Chaplin for ten years, despite rejection by her dad, the great playwright, who refused to attend her wedding and who even cut her out of his will. When Chaplin comes across to join them, Salisbury confidently offers his hand again, although the *New York Times*, has recently been giving Mr Chaplin a hard time.

'An honor to meet you, sir. Is it true that the invitation to visit Moscow came to you from Sergei Eisenstein?'

'He's standing right there, large as life. Ask him.'

'The one thing hard to understand, sir, is that Eisenstein was declared dead four years ago, at the age of fifty. Heart attack.'

Chaplin smiles indulgently. 'The same old hoary story. Did you attend his funeral?'

'I read his obituary in *Pravda*.'

'Well, go and ask him if he's dead.'

Oona chimes in: 'He smells of garlic, needs a shave and has wire wool for hair. Does that help?'

'Mrs Chaplin, is that amusing comment on or off the record?' Salisbury keeps his rugged Minnesotan features in courteous neutral.

'Off,' Chaplin snaps, now a tubby, would-be statesman, no longer the flea-trainer who brings chaos to a doss house.

Salisbury nods in acceptance. 'One thing I have observed during my three years in Russia might interest you both. The fastest growing profession in Moscow is the look-alike, the double, the *dvoinik*. I have seen Stalin at the Bolshoi for the first night of *Boris Godunov*, but according to the news agency Tass he was actually vacationing at his Black Sea villa.'

'Wow!' Oona says. 'Did Uncle Joe travel by rocket?'

Chaplin's expression is clouded, hostile. 'So the *New York Times* is going to mark my arrival in Moscow, my first visit to the socialist sixth of the world, by reporting that I am driving around the film studios in the company of a "double" pretending to be the genius who directed *Strike, October* and *The Battleship Potemkin*. Is that it?'

Salisbury's expression suggests that it is.

'Charlie,' Oona says sweetly, but not quite, 'you've lifted millions of dollars across forty years by pretending to be someone else. Who dances Claire Bloom's part in *Limelight*? – Melissa Hayden. You kept the camera at a distance so we don't spot the double.'

'That's a nice point,' Salisbury almost laughs. 'Mrs Chaplin, they say that when you met Picasso recently in Paris he declared himself your slave for life.'

'Everyone falls for Oona,' Chaplin snaps.

'*Pozdravleniya*, Mrs Chaplin – that means congratulations.'

'Did you teach yourself Russian, Harrison?' Oona's upturned

eyes are as wide as they can get. 'You did? I do admire that. I went up Charing Cross Road to buy a primer called *Russian for Half-Wits*. I tried to learn the alphabet but it's all in capital letters and half of them look like garden forks turned upside down. Then they give you a perfectly good "B" but it turns out to be a "V". I mean, does that make for peaceful co-existence?'

Salisbury laughs outright this time. 'Give the Russians due credit, recently they have made great efforts to learn English. So what's the big script, Mr Chaplin?'

'As far as I'm concerned, the Soviet premiere of *Limelight*, nothing more.'

Salisbury nods non-committally then affably offers them a ride into town but Chaplin firmly declines.

'Maybe we'll meet up again,' Oona says, 'if you're really you.'

'Ma'am, I shall follow your footprints through the snow – even if I find two sets.' He hands out his business card, one to each just in case. Nina feels sure this Yankee bastard knows he's on to something. Instructed to liaise, she and Olga have agreed he's a menace, having landed Olga's Pyotr Davidov in prison. It may prove necessary to put him in cold storage – but how?

15

~

The next meeting in Cheyne Walk took place early in 1994 and was at Lady Stears's initiative, a hopeful sign, with no Centre Court or other afternoon engagement signalled. Same Ivan at the door, same spaniels, same warm welcome in the first-floor Georgian drawing room. Lady Stears was wearing denims and grey moccasins below a brilliant white blouse, indicating a solid interview ahead of us. Coffee yes, but otherwise there was no preliminary skirmishing.

I threw down the obvious challenge: 'The biographers claim that Charlie and Oona had already decided to settle in Switzerland – and did so. A trip to Moscow is nowhere to be found.'

'No, you are wrong. Lake Geneva was merely an option. Chaplin had decided nothing. They were living, as the saying goes, by the hour, each hour shorter than the last. Anyway, where and what is Switzerland? You are familiar with Harry Lime's speech during the funicular scene in *The Third Man?*'

I was. 'So you have told me you travelled to London carrying a letter of invitation from Sergei Eisenstein to kidnap Chaplin heart and soul – even though Eisenstein had been dead for four years?'

'My idea, though of course Grigorii Aleksandrov laid claim to it. Vladislav Volkov was a fine actor with the Moscow Art Theatre but past his prime and surviving as a double. Vladislav had known Eisenstein, knew his history, and was one of the boyars in *Ivan Grozni*. You can see from his films how Aleksandrov was always attracted by bold strategies, the riskier the better. Volkov was sure he could pull it off.'

'May I ask this, Lady Stears, I apologise in advance... Were you and Aleksandrov –'

'Of course. Whenever his wife Orlova was preening in front of her mirror. If I hadn't taken precautions my womb would have been quite confused by so many different visitors.'

I was taken aback: not so much by what she had said as by the relaxed manner of delivery– how different from Olga!

'Wasn't Chaplin suspicious about meeting up with a dead friend?'

'No, well perhaps yes. At that time he desperately needed friends, support, praise. Consequently was unable to distinguish appearance from reality when appearances smiled on him.'

Lady Stears then told me about the first trip out of Moscow to the film archive at Belye Stolby (White Pillars). It was designed, she said, to provide Chaplin with his first, chastening encounter with Soviet reality and to bleed his intolerable self-confidence. 'Of course it was a blunder,' she added, 'and I have to take some responsibility – you can put that in your hungry notebook'

16

By ten o'clock Oona has decided which of her four fur coats to wear and they are bundled into a limousine heading for Belye Stolby, the central Russian Federation film archive, some forty-five minutes out of town. Eisenstein and his conspicuously decorative 'assistant' Nina, whose surname he obviously cannot remember, take the jump seats, travelling backwards.

'The story of my life,' Eisenstein mutters.

'Oh Sergei,' exclaims Oona, please swop places with me. 'Nina and I can talk diapers.'

'If you insist,' Eisenstein says gratefully, heaving his bulk into the comfortable back seat.

A contented Chaplin pats his hand. 'Well, Sergei, lovely to see you again. I remember how you arrived in Hollywood twenty years ago with your aide Grigorii Aleksandrov and a young English Communist whose name eludes me.'

'Ivor Montagu.'

(This must be the real Eisenstein after all. Now, as twenty years ago, he reeks of onions and vodka.)

'Ah yes, Ivor. A demon tennis player, I recall. An aristocrat as well as a Communist.'

'You never took more than two games a set off him.'

Chaplin's displeasure at this observation would be apparent to the man in the moon. 'I could beat Douglas Fairbanks. I could beat him in any competitive exercise except golf – and I refused to play golf. As for Montagu, I'm reliably informed that he was a spy.'

Eisenstein shrugs. 'Spies are for the puerile imagination. I have never been interested in spies.'

'You're so right!' exclaims Oona. 'After last year's scandal, Burgess and Maclean running off to Moscow with all our secrets, the British suspect everyone of being a spy.'

Chaplin inclines his head gravely. 'I spoke to Churchill only the other day. He took me aside at a Royal Academy dinner and confided there may be another spy in the woodwork, indeed two more. He thought I might be one of them – or both.'

'What a fib, Charlie!' Oona exclaims. Already busy taking snapshots of birch trees through the car window, she is devoted to her camera and likes to walk the streets of London or Moscow snapping what she calls 'memories'. In Moscow she has found that old ladies may take umbrage for reasons Nina cannot adequately explain to the daughter of Eugene O'Neill.

'OK, what shall we talk about, Sergei?' Chaplin jabs Eisenstein in the midriff. 'The Chaplin Film Festival you are setting up?'

'That we shall discuss when we reach Belye Stolby and review the available archive.'

'But I brought prints of *The Gold Rush*, *Modern Times* and *The Great Dictator* with me from London. I have them with me right here.'

Nina cuts in swiftly. 'It is the Soviet versions we must first consider.'

Chaplin, who has brought to Moscow several suits from Gieves & Hawkes of Savile Row, observes that sartorially his old friend is more of a mess than ever. As for his suit, he might be wearing the one in which he was squeezed into his coffin (if you believed Louella Parsons).

A heavily scented Nina leans forward rather compellingly. 'Maestro Chaplin, the Institute of Foreign Cinematography (Academy of Arts) and the Ministry of Culture (International) have bestowed on Sergei Mikhailovich Eisenstein the great honour of urgently organizing a "Chaplin Festival" here in Moscow. I am in place to assist. Currently working for the Russian Federation Branch of the National Film Institute. Prize graduate of KINO, first class.'

'Are you reading this from an autocue?' Oona asks.

Chaplin winks. 'She knows the ropes, our Nina. Take my word, she'll get things done.'

Oona is brooding. She has not yet found out what happened

between Charlie and this professional lookalike while she was absent in America, tying up the securities and transferring the bank accounts. When she swept triumphantly into the Savoy suite the only greeting she got from Charlie was 'There can't be two of you'. So what do you make of that? Then he told her they were going to Moscow and she said that was news to her and no they weren't, it was time the children had a home and Switzerland was where they were heading. But Chaplin was adamant:

'I have this letter from Eisenstein. It will be a major Chaplin retrospective and we can have the late Duke of Tolstoy's palace and political asylum.'

'Eisenstein is dead, Charlie.'

'So all ill-informed people believe, people who read the Hearst press.'

Nina had taken Oona aside. 'Mrs Chaplin, I want you to understand that this will be the chance of a lifetime for Maestro Chaplin.'

'Well, he's sixty-three so he's had a few chances.'

'Maestro Chaplin and you are promised a great Kremlin reception hosted by the Generalissimo himself. The Hearst press will have scrambled eggs on their faces.'

'Maybe poached.'

'Thank you, I always like to improve my English.'

'In bed with my husband? Make yourself scarce, Comrade.'

But Nina senses that even Oona is coming round to a fêted trip to Moscow, fizz all the way and kissing Stalin's moustache before the world's cameras. The great receptions in London, Paris and Rome have whetted her appetite – after all she is becoming the cherished star of the cavalcade while Charlie is increasingly sidelined as grumpy, paunchy and pompous. Nina reckons that Oona reckons she might even come away from Moscow with a portrait by Picasso – when Oona had pressed her butt against his in the rue des Grands Augustins he had clearly yearned for more of the same.

Now on their way to the Belye Stolby film archive, Oona is

again vexed by Nina's perfect embodiment of Claire Bloom – too many of Charlie's favourite young actresses for the price of one. Nina, of course, reads her thoughts:

'I shall be doubling for Miss Bloom at the first night of *Limelight*, the opening film of the Chaplin festival in Moscow. I am gratified that you feel I look the part. I hope my accent is Old Vic.'

'I warn you, Miss Lookalike, I have a powerful left hook. Ask the real Claire Bloom. She didn't last fifteen rounds.'

Chaplin laughs. 'One round would do. Claire says you taught her how to use finger bowls, she'd never encountered them before.'

Nina retaliates by lifting *Russian for Half-Wits* from Oona's lap. 'You need this? Please say something half-witted in Russian, Mrs Chaplin.'

Eisenstein is still gazing wistfully out of the window at the usual drab clumps of birches and plane trees. 'Leaving the Moscow suburbs behind, Charlie, we now see the Krasnaya Dom sugar-beet factory spreading everywhere the odour of our brave new world.'

'Sergei, don't look so glum,' Oona says. 'Charlie has always told friends that Eisenstein is the greatest film director of all time, not forgetting D.W. Griffith and Pudovkin and Charlie. I mean that pram tumbling down the Odessa steps as the Cossacks descend on the crowd. Wow!'

'You must forgive my wife,' Chaplin tells Eisenstein. 'This is the first time she's been out of the United States.'

Eisenstein sighs wearily. 'I am now the occupant of the pram. What's worse, I know the chalk mark on the step where the baby must topple out on to its head.'

Nina looks vexed. 'Sergei Mikhailovich is not himself today.'

'But you enjoy perfect freedom here in the Soviet Union,' Chaplin tells him.

'I forgot. Perfect freedom, unlimited budgets.' Eisenstein slaps his own hand in rebuke.

'And Stalin, to my certain knowledge, has always been your

greatest admirer. And mine, I'm reliably told.'

'Kindly do not mention that holy name in public. Here in the USSR everywhere is public. Always say "Somebody" when you mean – Somebody.'

Chaplin beams. 'I know Mr Stalin always has the broader picture in view. He doesn't court popularity, he simply does what has to be done.'

'Sergei, would you kindly stop looking at my legs!' Oona says. 'Won't Nina's legs do?'

'Ach, apologies, Oona, it's a habit I picked up in Berlin with Marlene Dietrich. She always took it as an insult if one didn't "pay attention" to her. "Pay attention!" she'd hiss if one took forty winks. It's the same with Orlova, our home-grown Dietrich. You'll meet her with her husband Aleksandrov...maybe tomorrow.'

'On Friday,' Nina corrects him.

'So now you're going to bite the bullet and tell us about *Ivan the Terrible*,' Chaplin says. 'It was a magnificent contribution to the war effort, Sergei. Nothing to be ashamed of even if it arrived after the war was over.'

'I am not nein nicht nyet never ashamed of it. Somebody instructed me to make a great film about Somebody's all-powerful predecessor Ivan the Terrible. That is what I did. In this neck of the woods our only history book is Somebody – just as our Moscow river skyline is now dominated by Somebody's skyscrapers whose crowning ruby stars applaud each other.'

Nina chides him in Russian: 'Might some other time be better to get into that, Sergei Mikhailovich?'

'Charlie, Brecht has written, "Happy the land that needs no heroes." We might add, "Happy the land whose heroes never go to the cinema".'

'But think of all that state patronage you have received. I have to invest my own money in my production budgets.'

'I wouldn't mind if I had your kind of money. I might even make the films I wanted to make. I wouldn't mind if I had to bow to the Queen of England at the Royal Command Performance. I wouldn't mind being Laurence Olivier when Churchill summoned him after seeing his *Henry V*.'

'Soon we will reach Belye Stolby,' Nina announces.

'What a pity Nina wasn't the baby in the pram on the Odessa steps,' Oona tells Chaplin, but he follows his own lines of thought. 'Did I mention that Mr Stalin is a Chaplin fan, Sergei?'

'You did. Twice.'

'The odd thing is, even Hitler, secretly, was a fan though he had my films banned of course. I was a Jewish degenerate.'

Nina's eyes have widened. 'Jewish, Maestro? You?'

'You had a week to examine his foreskin,' Oona says.

'Kindly never disclose this bad ancestry while in the Soviet Union,' Nina admonishes Chaplin, but he only smiles:

'I have always felt a Jewish element in me – I like making money. I never say no when asked whether I am a Jew – it only encourages the anti-Semites.'

They have reached Belye Stolby. Nina produces the passes and attends to the bureaucratic formalities with the guards at the gate.

'It looks like a fortress,' Chaplin remarks as she returns.

'We can take no chances, Maestro. We are surrounded by enemies.'

The limousine edges forward through a succession of sentry posts before finally coming to rest. Oona hops from the car, holding her hair against a fresh wind.

Eisenstein stretches himself, sighs: 'Now, dear Charlie, observe how the redwing are panicked into flight from their birch trees by our coming. Listen! – they release a sound like air held under high pressure and escaping from a valve. It can be explained by quantum physics.'

'Sergei Mikhailovich, we are running late,' Nina says in Russian.

'Look!' Eisenstein utters an awed whisper. 'Perched on a gate in the middle of that field of turnips.'

'Is it a lonely turkey?' Oona asks. 'Only four weeks to

Christmas, fella!'

'A turkey!' Eisenstein is aghast. 'Look at the head slowly rotating the huge eyes – a female peregrine falcon assessing the next family meal. No, wait until she takes wing – that soaring ascent is something no cameraman can miss.'

The falcon not obliging, Nina leads the way into an ill-lit labyrinth beneath spluttering strips of neon. Topcoats are discarded, valuables transferred, felt-overslippers provided for entrance to the film archives. A woman archivist is eventually found, appraises Eisenstein in an odd kind of way, does not greet him (the Chaplins notice), and informs Nina in rapid Russian that the archives have not been 'correctly forewarned' of their visit. *Nyet*, nothing doing today, ничего, *nichego*. While Eisenstein's shame and despondency is clearly genuine, Nina cannot conceal something closer to satisfaction.

But they must, she insists, have lunch before they set out on the return journey. Nina lives for the cafeteria lunches of large institutions since her lonely evening meal normally amounts to remnants of cold food overlooked by the mice. Like Galina forty years later, she adores the canteen food at Belye Stolby, delicious, with a choice, and absurdly low-priced (though Chaplin is always happy to find her hand in his pocket).

An hour later they drive back in a silence which cannot endure, Chaplin seething. Nor is Oona a queen of silence.

'So tell us your life story,' she has a go at Nina. 'We didn't get much of that in London.'

'Oh, I don't have one, Mrs Chaplin, just another ordinary Soviet girl raised in the Volga region during our great collectivization drive and now a war widow, but privileged to fulfil the lofty cultural aspirations of the Soviet people.'

Oona softens and lays a hand on Nina's. 'Tell us about your husband.'

'We hardly had time to know each other, just kids snatching at happiness. I used to read Simonov's poem, "Wait for Me" – but I waited in vain, my Sasha never returned.'

Oona loses interest. 'Would you like my life's story? When I was three my famous father had disappeared but I knew I might find pictures of him in magazines. "It's Daddy, it's Daddy!" I would cry out. "When will he be coming back to live with us, Mummy?" I didn't see the great Eugene O'Neill for eight years. Not so swell. Oh sure, he paid for one smart boarding school after another and a holiday in Bermuda but I was crippled inside. I wrote to him with my bad spelling all the time, can I come and see you, Daddy, but he didn't reply. The last time I was allowed to see him was in 1941, eleven years ago. He's still alive, the newspapers tell me.'

'Maybe a better fate than a Nazi occupation and twenty million dead,' Nina says. 'Tell me, Mrs Chaplin, did you always plan, when you were "crippled inside", to marry a very rich man?'

Oona furrows her smooth brow to ponder this. 'It's a good question. I think, yes, I think I did because I can remember my stepmother Carlotta scolding me for saying that I planned to marry a rich man.'

Oona produces a miniature bottle of vodka from her bag, takes a sip, offers it round, takes a swig.

Approaching the suburbs of Moscow – the sugar beet factory again – Eisenstein suddenly cheers up. 'Charlie, can you guess what is currently Somebody's favourite film?'

'*City Lights?* No? *The Gold Rush?* No? *Modern Times?* No?'

'I'm afraid not. Somebody's favourite film is *Ninotchka*, straight out of Hollywood.'

'Garbo! – you can't be serious.'

'When Garbo's poker-faced, impenetrable Commissar Ninotchka begins to laugh helplessly in the Paris café, Somebody starts to laugh from the belly. He has to see that film once a week, he has even lost interest in Tarzan. By the end of the film he is wiping his eyes on a silk handkerchief. His doctors crowd round anxiously. They beg him to watch *Gamlet* instead.'

'*Gamlet?*'

'The letter H is foreign to the Cyrillic alphabet,' Nina informs her class. 'It is also foreign to the English working class. As a

Cockney you should know that, Maestro. I take it you have read *Pygmalion* by Bernard Shaw.'

Proud to have known Shaw, Chaplin is taken aback by the requirement to have read the old windbag's plays as well.

Eisenstein is musing. 'Somebody himself once told me that the suddenness of Garbo's laughter in *Ninotchka* reminded him of how he himself suddenly thought up the collectivization campaign which was to kill five million people.'

'Sergei Mikhailovich!' Nina protests.

'Mr Stalin told you that?' Chaplin exclaims, awed.

'The lord of the universe squinted at me – no through me – from those yellow slits of his. I looked back as steadily as I could, because Somebody will eliminate anyone he thinks is shifty and his notion of shifty is primitive-Georgian, a deflected gaze.'

'Like this?' Chaplin does a deflected gaze so shifty that everyone in the limousine has to chuckle, even Nina. But Eisenstein's features immediately revert to a soaked washing-up cloth.

'Somebody doesn't bring in his *oprichniki* there and then, to drag you out. No, he bides his time, lets you have one night's troubled sleep, maybe two nights, then they come for you in the dead hours.'

Silence in the car. Nina is leaning forward from the back seat and murmuring something, in Russian, in Eisenstein's ear, something threatening.

'*Nyet, pozhaluysta...*' gasps Vladislav Volkov.

Chaplin, who has fired many actors in his time, understands.

17

Now familiar with Dora Maar's warning that no visitor can be received until late in the morning, Olga arrives at the vast apartment-studio loaned to the Picasso entourage in *ulitsa* Gorky. Maar opens the door with Sabartés at her shoulder, sniffing for British agents.

'I hope I am not too early, Madame.'

'Please come in, Mademoiselle Olga. *Tu es bienvenue.* He's still in bed.'

'Thank you. I hope Maître Picasso has not been too taxed by the long journey and our severe weather.'

'He's not sure how he is feeling yet.'

'We have doctors –'

'It's not a physical question. He is never sure. It depends on his mood and mindset. Pablo typically spends the first hours of each day complaining about his life and health.'

'But, Madame, our medical service is free –'

'It's all in the mind, Olga. Sometimes he holds court in bed like the kings at Versailles. But whereas they dressed up in all their finery for the *matinée,* Pablo is to be found naked, like a burnt sausage, tangled up in a sheet and groaning.'

Olga offers a reserved smile of complicity, woman to woman. Dora pours coffee and leaves the room. 'I will tell him you are here.'

Olga's bag contains today's issue of *Pravda*. It carries not a whisper of Picasso's arrival. Fortunately the maître cannot read Cyrillic, nor Maar, only Aragon and Triolet who will keep their thoughts to themselves.

Maar returns, closes the door. 'He complains that you ignored him yesterday at the airport. Not even a kiss or a hug of welcome. He says he undertook the hideous ordeal of Aeroflot only in order to see you. He says he can find no reason to get up at all today.

Tomorrow we will fly straight back to Paris.'

Maar seems more than content with that. Her cigarette holder is jutting up between her teeth.

'May I please talk to him, Madame?'

Maar shrugs her delicate little shoulders. 'It's clearly you he wants not to see until he does. Expect an initial display of rage – rage is the *spécialité de la maison Picasso*.'

'Oh. Thank you.'

'Didn't they train you for this? I take it this room is full of concealed MVD microphones, am I right?' Maar's pleated skirt swirls irritably. 'In you go, Olga! And make sure you address him as "Vincent".'

'Vincent?'

'Virtually every morning our Grumpy imagines himself to be some other artist he admires. Recently we had a run of Renaissance geniuses and I had to dress like a courtesan of the Florentine Medicis. Today it's his hero Vincent Van Gogh.'

'Oh my hero too!'

'So you told me in Paris. Address our Pablo as if he were a Dutch artist who died a pauper, forgotten, despised, rejected – and with a bit missing from his ear.'

'Madame, I'm no actress! I'm only a museum curator.'

At this Dora's pent-up emotions and humiliations explode in fury. 'Anyone in your job has to be an actress, a whore, or both.'

A hoarse shout is heard from another room, then an outburst in Catalan which Olga cannot decipher. Picasso himself appears in the doorway, a brown toad wearing, or not wearing, a gaudy dressing gown which hangs loose over a pair of bulging shorts. He does not greet Olga or even acknowledge her.

'You have no idea how unhappy I am,' he groans. 'People think I must be happy because I am rich and successful. They are wrong – they are all wrong, including you, Dora. I have stomach trouble, it can only be a cancer. But nobody cares, least of all my rich and famous doctor. I pay his bills, don't I?'

Olga takes a welcoming step towards him. His lustrous eyes

settle on her (though the whole performance has been for her benefit). 'I hate the dawn, Ochka *devushka*. I understand why executions have always taken place at first light. I only have to glimpse the dawn through the curtains and I find my severed head under my arm.'

'Good morning, Maître. Welcome to Moscow.' Olga bows, a touching gesture.

'And why didn't you embrace me at the airport yesterday?'

'Maître, they wouldn't let me get near you.'

'And you know who I am this morning?'

'You are a Dutch artist who died a pauper, forgotten, despised, rejected – and with a bit missing from his ear.'

He addresses Dora: 'This is the one I came all this way to paint. And they don't let me get near her. And now I am near her she won't touch me.'

'You are in Russia now. They won't put up with your charades.'

The front doorbell sounds. 'No, tell Jaime I will not see anybody!' Picasso shouts.

Olga dares to lay a hand lightly on his arm. 'I have brought someone who wishes to convey an important message to you. Please do it for me, Maître. Just five minutes of your time.'

The American had been waiting for Olga early that morning outside the Pushkin Museum. At sight of him she shrank back, glancing nervously about her. 'Go away,' she hissed in Russian, 'not here! You will ruin me!' He was carrying a parcel wrapped in brown paper under his arm, clearly a framed canvas. 'Davidov is on my conscience,' he said. 'Together we must go to Picasso and secure your Pyotr's release, yes, this morning.'

Now Harrison Salisbury has been waiting patiently across *ulitsa* Gorky.

'Trust me, Maître,' Olga pleads, letting her hand wander.

Picasso softens, shrugs. 'Only two minutes. No, one.'

Moments later the tall figure of Harrison Salisbury appears in the doorway and introduces himself. He is carrying his parcel.

'My French isn't so hot, sir, but Olga will translate.'

'Ha! Another Yankee. Didn't your people refuse me a visa?'

'I believe they did, sir.'

Olga translates anxiously.

'And what did the *New York Times* say about that?' Picasso demands.

'A long editorial was highly critical of the decision. It did America no credit.'

Olga translates. Picasso's eyes burn into hers. 'Is that true? When did a Yankee ever speak the truth?'

'It's true, Maître.' (She doesn't know if it's true.) 'I have seen the editorial.' (She hasn't.) Circumspectly she begins to explain the situation concerning Pyotr Davidov. 'He is an artist who remains cruelly imprisoned *à la Bastille*.' The words trigger sympathy in Picasso.

Dora Maar has been listening intently. 'You must help, Pablo.'

'Help that Dog man? Why?'

'He is a young artist, sir,' Salisbury says.

'And you're telling me, Yankee beanpole, that Dog never did run to the American embassy, never told those stars and stripes that Olga *devushka* here was being sent to France to hook Picasso like a big, bloated fish?'

'Emphatically, he did not, sir. I grabbed him during the fiasco at the Fortochka. I drove him to his studio in Cheremushki, nowhere near the embassy. I bought one of his paintings. I have it here. Olga wants me to make a present of it to you.'

Picasso turns to Olga. 'And you want me to put dynamite under my exhibition – your exhibition – by making a public statement? Release Dog or Picasso flies home!'

'No no, Maître, a public statement would be a humiliation for certain circles and merely stiffen their resistance.'

'Then what?'

'You will most kindly, most honourably, write a private message, absolutely confidential, to People's Artists Gerasimov and Serov – and to Museum Director Kemenev. I will carry it by hand myself. You will kindly express pain rather than anger about

Pyotr Davidov's continued detention – he is, was, like myself a junior curator at the Pushkin Museum where you are to be honoured.'

'Hm.' Picasso looks to Salisbury, 'Well, let's see this masterpiece you've brought me.'

Salisbury unwraps the canvas. 'I believe Davidov is a true artist, sir.'

The immediate reaction is scorn: 'Which way up should it be? I suppose this must be the bottom because it carries the signature Sobaka in Western letters.'

'It's an urban landscape rendered in the new severe style, Maître,' Olga says, trembling

'Frankly, this could have been done by one of these new American "abstract expressionists". What's the name of that "drip" man they're all talking about?'

'Jackson Pollock?' Salisbury suggests.

'How much did you pay Dog for this shit?'

'I paid the artist one hundred dollars.'

'Out of charity?'

'Sir, you sound a bit like Nikita Khrushchev when he rampaged through the Fortochka and ordered Davidov's paintings to be ripped from the walls.'

Olga could scream. She refuses to translate. Turning to Salisbury, she speaks sharply in Russian: '*Ya ne ponimayu po-angliĭski – I didn't understand your English.*'

Salisbury nods stoically. 'Point taken.'

'What did the Yankee say?' Picasso demands.

'Maître,' Olga pleads, 'all of Moscow's "unofficial" artists are awaiting – indeed expecting – your intervention on Pyotr Davidov's behalf.'

'I heard the words Nikita Khrushchev, this Yankee was comparing me to Khrushchev, a philistine lout.'

'No, Maître, Mr Salisbury said only you can repair the damage inflicted by Khrushchev – you and your coming exhibition.'

Dora Maar addresses Picasso gently. 'Pablo, give me a moment alone with Olga.' She leads Olga into the adjoining room, leaving Picasso and Salisbury not looking at one another. 'The problem,' she murmurs, 'is that Pablo is jealous of your Davidov – sexually jealous. What has he to gain from having you restored to your lover while he is in Moscow?'

'In that case, Madame Dora, I can promise not to see Pyotr while the maître is in Moscow. On my honour. And you will kindly make him promise on his honour to intercede for Pyotr. You know better than I that he is very sensitive to his Spanish honour – you told me in Paris how he presides over a bullfight in the arena at Arles.'

Maar stands motionless. 'I will try.'

A few moments later Olga has led Harrison Salisbury (and Davidov's rejected painting) out into *ulitsa* Gorky. They both observe the MVD men 'waiting for buses' across the road. She is not going to tell an American journalist what she has said to Maar.

'We must be patient,' she says. 'With Picasso things take time. Kindly do not intercept me again. I will lose my job.'

He lifts his hat, a trilby. 'No, ma'am, you won't lose your job, not while *Operatsiya Dvoinik* is in progress. They can't do without you.' He takes a few steps then turns back with an uncomfortably altered expression. 'The *New York Times* will pay you five thousand dollars for your full story when it's all over.'

'Please go away. You disgust me.'

'I'll be in touch.'

I later asked Lady Stears about Salisbury. She described him as 'tall and quite nice'. Oona 'made a pass at him' – although, added Nina, she did that like drinking coffee and instantly forgot about it. 'Few of his reports reached New York uncensored. He could use the telephone to the London office but only if a line was available. Attempting to send backups by mail was a joke because they too were intercepted and the camel train through Samarkand took its time.'

As she stands waiting for her bus Olga asks herself yet again what she really feels about Pyotr. Their relationship had never been an easy one. Sometimes, too painfully often, you felt his emotional reach was confined to his painting and his ideology. So little personal tenderness. His own opinions alone counted. He and his dissident friends harboured a conceit all of their own – they were sure the wider world was watching them, eager to hail them as heroes. Olga found it easier to admire their courage than to feel affection. They had swallowed too much American culture undiluted and their clothes were an affectation, a claim to individuality within a rather obvious conformity. Pyotr could be possessive, jealous, but is jealousy the other face of love? Could she ever want to marry him?

She watches the MVD men lounging across the street. They will report back, earning their kopeks. You cannot explain why a man has taken possession of your emotions but, by the time her bus trawls through the slush, her heart is aching for my dear imprisoned Sobaka. I will not let you down, Pyotr.

~

She has noticed in the streets of Paris that if passing pedestrians glance at you they do so, particularly the men, as if by right, as if it's natural. This has brought home to her that in Moscow the same glance from a stranger is rare and furtive. People walk the streets and take the metro locked into themselves and their own survival. They huddle. Communism belongs somewhere else, at meetings, rallies, in schools and hospitals, but once citizens are released from places of work or obligatory attendance, from banners, slogans, public exhortations, you find that Communism evaporates and it is each to himself, each pair of boots set intently on its course. That is how Olga travels home to her mother at the end of the day, jostling for a decent pair of fish in the market, her personal resources pitted against scarcity, carefully counting her change, each citizen reliant on a local knowledge and an ingenuity she shares with so many other dark overcoats and their pressing shoulders. Olga can imagine herself married to Pyotr, the small nest bursting at the seams, more mouths to feed. She believes that the Revolution was necessary, and Lenin wise and good, though Ekaterina refers to him as 'the worst of history's bullies'. Without Lenin there would have been no Stalin (Ekaterina says), and but for Stalin they would not have taken Maksim Petrovich Lepinsky away and ruined her life. Yet Ekaterina and Olga had been among those privileged to be evacuated from Leningrad after the blockade tightened and death threatened, the stigma of Papa's arrest unaccountably forgotten (in reality through the intervention of Joffe and Tamm), transported to safety in Christopol in the same plane as the illustrious Anna Akhmatova. The poet had befriended Olga during the flight. She had a hawk-nose and a lovely voice. Olga was seventeen and Akhmatova changed seats with Ekaterina to read to the unhappy girl some of her pulped poems. Later they met again by chance in the Tashkent public library. Akhmatova had put on weight. She smiled and said, 'I remember you, Ochka, but you are not allowed to remember me.' She looked severely but kindly down her hawk-nose and during the months that followed invited the girl to tea and cakes, explaining how great paintings worked and why growing up was a dangerous business – but never mentioning the men, the husbands and the son, they had taken from her. For Olga, Soviet Communism is her education, her opportunities, her job. She is part of it and it is part of her. In Paris she was struck, shocked, by the full force of anti-Soviet propaganda – so cheap, so ungenerous (even though the great Akhmatova is now silenced). She does not want to be a captive of American capitalism – those octopus tentacles stretching out along the Paris boulevards from one fast-food, fried chicken counter to the next rack of vulgar Mickey Mouse T-shirts, from one gaudy cinema display (always someone pointing a gun) to the next neon-lit Coca-Cola sign, everything multiplied. How vulgar! *Poshlyi, grubyi...* Aragon had told her that Paris was more recognisable as the capital of France under the Nazis than under the Americans – though of course the Communist Party was no longer illegal, just persecuted.

18

Today a warm greeting from Madame Lepinskaya – auspicious or not? The lady had still not unbuttoned to disclose what had ultimately transpired in Paris between herself and Picasso. I occasionally hinted that my understanding of her later narrative would be enhanced if she did – but that fraught subject remained not only *terra incognita* to me but also *vetitum territorio*. Did the fact that I was a male person inhibit her? And might I not, as a man, take the view that Picasso's succession of women, each convinced despite his past record that she was the One and Only, got precisely what they deserved?

But her tangential hints were legion. She would for instance digress about the Soviet prohibition on personal relationships with foreigners, and how such a Russian woman could be regarded as damaged goods. Not a few British servicemen despatched to Russia during the war had become engaged to Soviet girls. Sent home, they had not forgotten their Irina or their Natasha but protracted negotiations between Molotov's staff and the British Government proved futile; exit visas were not granted.

'Are you saying, Madame, that this cruel prejudice could possibly extend to you?'

'Of course. Picasso may have been an illustrious figure but still a foreigner, an alien from the West, and if a young Russian woman allowed herself –'

I had as mentioned noticed that only three personal photographs stood on her mantelpiece: her mother, her father, and a sister. No husband, no children. When quite some time ago I had ventured to raise this with Svetlana in the hope of a disclosure, she snapped back irritably.

'Before your arrival she removes Pablo, Pablito and Pyotr. She told me.'

'But why?'

'Ask her.'

But Madame L. was not to be stampeded. She took pleasure in the drift of the wind in her own sails, she enjoyed watching me suppress the questions causing my jib to flap.

She had forewarned me that today she would want to talk about Picasso's *Guernica*.

She had once recalled how Dora Maar had participated in its composition, dismissing as bogus, a charade, the great painting's ostensible pain and compassion. When I now raised this again Madame Lepinskaya looked stricken. '*Vous avez raison, Monsieur.*' After a tussle with her chignon she said, 'I have been holding out about *Guernica* – there is more to confess. Before I went to Paris and while setting up the exhibition, I found on my desk an offprint of one of Kemenev's celebrated polemics, published in the Academy's official magazine *Iskustvo*, on which he had scrawled simply "REWRITE – PEREPISAT". Yet guess who had virtually written that same polemic at Kemenev's bidding.'

'You.'

Madame Lepinskaya huddled into her chair unhappily bemused to find herself volunteering this confession.

'Of course I complied. The original issue of *Iskustvo* was removed from library shelves and pulped, so I can no longer show it to you.'

'Fortunately, Madame, the original version was not pulped in London's School of Soviet and Slavonic Studies.' I produced a photocopy from my briefcase. Madame Lepinskaya looked surprised, then wary. She took it, read, nodded in confirmation, then her eyes became moist behind the pince-nez.

'I feel so guilty, so ashamed ever to have written this.'

Here is an extract from the incriminating original text, drafted by Olga and signed by Kemenev:

'Picasso's *Guernica* has been hailed as a "masterpiece" in the West. This large canvas in black and white is 335 cm high, 783 cm –almost eight metres – wide. Supposedly a condemnation of fascist barbarism, the massacre of the inhabitants of the town by

German fascist warplanes, this painting yet appears so abstract in its outlines, so stereotyped in its symbolism – man, woman, horse, bull, light bulb, candle, severed limbs, a house aflame – as to lack all trace of the humanity it purports to defend. *[Here I skip a long passage of detailed description.]* Since the Great Patriotic War, Picasso's paintings, graphics, ceramics and sculpture have continued to occupy a prominent place in the retrograde formalist movement – *prodolzhaiut zanimat' bolshoe mesto formalistich.* *Guernica* is currently housed at the Rockefellers' showpiece Museum of Modern Art in New York. This may tell us all we need to know about the picture and the artist alike. The wealthiest American families have been eager to validate their rapacity by presenting a cultivated image. Ford, Rockefeller, Carnegie, Whitney all set up immensely wealthy institutes to fund and pervert scholarship, science and the arts.'

'So then, Madame, you re-wrote it at Kemenev's behest?'

'Entirely. I explained that on reconsideration we recognised that "Guernica" was conspicuous for its life-enhancing resistance to the morbid classicism promoted by the Western appeasers.'

I nodded appreciatively – reliving this episode obviously put Madame Lepinskaya under stress and constantly close to tears.

'If I remember,' she went on, 'I emphasized "Guernica's" derivations from Breughel and the progressive German art of the Thirty Years War, plus the debt to Goya's depiction of massacre and rape in Spain under Napoleon. I detailed the symbolism of Picasso's painting: the bull representing darkness and violence; the horse as the epitome of innocence and goodness; the women witnesses, a chorus; the central motif, a head thrown back in agony echoes the open mouths of Greek and Roman masks. Of course I also mentioned Picasso's prodigious activity in the Resistance – which at that time I ignorantly believed to have been nil, apart from his complaints about the difficulty of obtaining chateaubriand steaks on the black market for his Afghan dog.'

'Did Kemenev go along with all that?'

'When I put the revised version on his desk he was almost

asleep from vodka and nervous exhaustion. He had more or less forgotten about his "REWRITE – PEREPISAT".'

'May I ask, Madame, what you genuinely thought of *Guernica?*'

'I could not help viewing it as a celebration of violence rather than the lament, the cry of despair, it was supposed to be. I fully agreed with my mother about that. It was painted the same year they took Papa away. I asked myself how many among those protesting the bombing of a Spanish town also protested the arrest of innocent millions in the socialist paradise?'

'Certainly not Picasso himself.'

She stared at me but her hands began to tremble and her gaze was suddenly unfocused. 'You could never understand Pablo. He came here to see me yesterday.'

I am no drinker but did on this occasion wish that Madame Lepinskaya would produce a bottle of spirits, but she never offered anything stronger than tea from the samovar.

We sat in silence until I had to realise that Picasso's 'visit' to Madame Lepinskaya 'yesterday' was more or less the end of mine today. But then, so characteristically, her mind cleared and she recovered herself – always moved by her sense of duty, of obligation – and threw her mind back forty years to recall quite amusingly the visit to VDNKh on a very cold day, both Picasso and Chaplin reduced to shivering malcontents while their minders, she and Nina, strove to keep the sagging spirits of maître and maestro afloat.

Whenever I left *ulitsa* Sivashskaya 12, kv. 10, Moscow 113149, and walked away through those quiet, solemn residential streets brooding about when next I might return (she would never fix a date), my pleasure at having extracted more of her remarkable story was always darkened by the suspicion that I was being led up, or down, a garden path. Did not Olga's account of the visit to VDNKh, and Nina's, dovetail a little too neatly, dialogue remembered word for word, as if both were working from a common script? If so, who was writing it?

19

Last night all the foreign dignitaries were taken to the legendary Moscow Circus, to watch a handsome, black-haired female lion tamer in black boots, black shirt, black gloves and black riding breeches put her head in the mouths of four male lions (but, as Chaplin remarked loudly, 'not all at the same time'). Nina pointed out to a tremulous Oona that two firemen with high pressure hoses were standing by in case the lions 'acted up'. The beautiful amazon then pulled one of the lions around by his tail before making all the beasts lie down and flinging herself full-length among them.

'She needs a bit of oo-la-la,' Picasso shouted.

Chaplin was so enchanted by the clowns' hilarious nonsense that Nina feared he might leap into the ring and join in. The next morning – whether they like it or not – they are taken by coach for a guided tour of VDNKh, the Exhibition of the Achievements of the People's Economy. Given the freezing weather, Chaplin and Picasso have each offered excuses but discover you can't wriggle out of this special treat, not if you entertain hopes of an exhibition at the Pushkin Museum or a personal film retrospective at Dom Kino. VDNKh is situated in the vast Sokol'niki Park at the north end of Moscow and few of the foreigners disembarking from the slow coach journey through evil-smelling traffic are in good health let alone high spirits. Olga and Nina are wrapping their two elderly, short-legged, wards in extra shawls until you couldn't tell one from the other.

The elderly stagger out of the coach into the snow-covered wasteland of Sokol'niki, where they are informed that their guide today will be none other than the illustrious Professor of Socialist Economic Development, I.I. Tamm (who, it may be recalled, had dared to write in defence of Olga's arrested father and who had later helped to extract Olga and her mother from besieged

Leningrad – but Olga has not yet learned of this, so does not embrace the old professor as she will later wish she had). And here he is, beaming. The mouth above his neat goatee beard speaks every language in the world, so that's not a problem except that it is, because he likes to speak them all at once. A long sentence beginning in English may pass through German, French and Spanish before concluding in what sounds like Mandarin Chinese.

'Could be Urdu,' Chaplin comments. 'His beard seems to know.'

~

Magnificently poised at the entrance to VDNKh is the colossal sculpture by Vera Mukhina, *Worker and Collective Farm Woman*, hammer and sickle aloft, male and female thrusting joyfully towards the Communist future. Professor Tamm explains that this sculpture was originally commissioned for the Soviet Pavilion at the 1937 Paris International Exhibition of Arts, Crafts and Sciences. Tamm's beady eye seeks out a shivering Picasso:

'Your own *Guernica* was of course first on display in the Spanish Pavilion at the same exhibition, Maître.'

Picasso nods politely. 'Mukhina's work is always striking,' he mutters.

'Say you like it,' Triolet hisses.

'Can't bear to look at it.'

They move on at a cautious pace. Laid out with meticulous symmetry, the numerous 'national pavilions' stretch round a frozen pond graced by gilded plaster maidens, *devushky*, dressed in the costumes of each Soviet Republic. This is ice-cream architecture thick with plaster but surprisingly interrupted by an intricate stained-glass window here, a baroque façade there.

'Eight million visitors a year,' Professor Tamm announces. 'And rising fast. Call it the Motherland in miniature.' The vibrant goatee beard runs through the translations.

Once inside, the visitors are invited to absorb an inundation of statistics, graphs and tables chronicling the amazing growth of socialist agriculture. Vivid three-dimensional dioramas with working model trains and tractors give the impression of a toy store. In the Poultry Pavilion a motor-driven procession of stuffed chicks circle a pyramid of eggs, above which a spinning placard announces the annual rise in egg production.

'As you see,' Professor Tamm declares, 'we have developed exhibition culture to its highest level. That is why we ask you to be on your guard against rather desperate British claims, as their empire declines, about the invention of mechanical looms, steam locomotives, jet engines, penicillin and television tubes, as shamelessly promoted at the recent Festival of Britain – I'm sure many of you visited the so-called Dome of Discovery.'

It turns out that not one of the distinguished visitors has heard of the Dome of Discovery and only Chaplin has heard of the Festival of Britain, masterminded by his friend the Labour Cabinet Minister Herbert Morrison. Chaplin now makes the point though not sure what it is – well, he has to.

'No offence to the British, Maestro Chaplin,' Professor Tamm hastens to add, goatee quivering, 'every Western nation has advanced its own spurious scientific claims. Contrary to the received wisdom, the German Siemens in fact stole the blueprints for the telegraph from our Yakobi. You may think that Marconi invented the radio but in truth our Aleksandr Popov demonstrated the first radio set to the Russian Physics and Chemistry Society more than fifty years ago. The Wright brothers usurped the aeronautical genius of our Moschisky, who took to the air near St Petersburg in 1882, fully twenty years before the Kitty Hawk got off the ground.'

As the only American present, Oona feels constrained to intervene: 'What do you mean "usurped"? How far did your guy Mochy get?'

Tamm ignores her (the French have passed him a warning that Mrs Chaplin can be unreliable). 'I may add that the true father of rocket propulsion was our Tsiolkovsky, while our Polzunov built the first steam locomotive ahead of Stevenson.'

'Of course,' says Chaplin, 'building it is one thing but getting it to move is another.'

'And the first submarine was ours too. The first tractor was pioneered as far back as the 1850s by our Blinov. A Russian workman, our Vasili Pyatov, invented the rolling process for the production of armour plate in the 1860s but corrupt Tsarist officials who kowtowed to everything foreign callously transmitted this Russian invention to foreign concerns.'

'Bravo!' says Aragon – but not for long. Professor Tamm's eyes glitter maliciously:

'Our friends from France may be interested to learn that the balloon was wrongly attributed to the brothers Montgolfier, whereas in reality the first balloon was in our skies near Nizhni-Novgorod much earlier.'

This is too much even for Aragon. 'Wait a minute, professor, with greatest respect I can assure you that the Montgolfier brothers pioneered the balloon.'

Chaplin chortles. 'The French have always been the masters of hot air.'

Picasso has half-understood. 'What did Charlot say? Tell him I'll punch his nose.'

A worried Olga glances at Nina: is this an emergency? – Nina rather hopes it is because her feet are frozen.

'For your guidance,' Tamm continues serenely, 'other Russian firsts include the bicycle, the internal combustion engine, the tank, radar, television, synthetic rubber and penicillin.'

'What about the pencil?' (This is Oona.)

'In fact research has proven that Smera, court doctor to Grand Duke Vladimir of Kiev, invented printing a century before the Chinese and four hundred years before the celebrated Johann Gutenberg.'

'Should we tip him?' Oona asks a taxing hour later as the inexhaustible Professor Tamm courteously takes leave of the visitors, thrusting into their hands booklets containing even more 'economic information' in very small, smudged type printed on terrible paper.

'When will they invent paper?' Oona wants to know.

The eminent foreign visitors, the maître, the maestro and their retinues, now carefully steer clear of each other in case they come to fisticuffs over the first tractor to take to the air or the first submarine to walk on dry land. They'd all like a decent cup of coffee. In the coach (invented by Stopoff) on the way back to central Moscow, Eisenstein leans into Chaplin's ear. 'Want a joke?'

'Haven't heard many today.'

'Who created the world? Jehov. Who was the first man? Adamov. Who was his consort? Evarova. Who created the fatal apple? Lysenko.'

~

The following morning Nina returns to the Gorky Street apartment (standing in for Count Tolstoy's promised Romanov-era town house), to which Mrs Chaplin has not granted her the spare key. She bangs a large, brass doorknocker irritably. Oona slips the latch and brings her hello there!, etched into cheery elfin features smooth as porcelain, to the open space. She has been in carefree mood, rummaging through her large leather suitcases, trying on clothes, garments strewn all over the bedroom, perhaps a dress rehearsal for the as yet unscheduled premiere of *Limelight*. The vodka bottle is less than half-full.

'Hi, Nina, what do you think of this dress? Too demonstrative? I don't want to distract public attention from Charlie's film. How about this one? – more *soviétique*, is that what the French say? Where's Pablo? Hey, what do you make of that Olga woman? Something going on there, if you ask me. I really don't understand why Madame Maar puts up with it.'

'Well, Mrs Chaplin, it shames me to tell you, but Comrade Olga has requested Maître Picasso to get her boyfriend released from jail.'

'Wow! Are you kidding me? Jail? Did he say the wrong thing?'

'It's quite deplorable. He's a dissident artist, a *stilyagi*.'

'What's so wrong with that?'

'He made contact with the Americans, contrary to Soviet law.'

'But I'm an American! You've made contact with me!'

Nina hears an unscheduled knock on the door. A further knock follows, louder this time, more insistent. So who is this man – tall, grave, immediately imposing – carrying a vast black leather holdall with coils of white plasticated wire over his shoulder?

'I have come to fix the telephone,' he tells Nina, an educated voice. The stranger turns to Oona Chaplin, evidently aware who he is addressing.

'Telephone Engineer, Mrs Chaplin,' he says in English.

'Is there something wrong with ours?' Oona asks Nina. 'It seems OK to us.'

'Kaput,' the engineer tells her.

'Is that German? Don't German words tend to begin in 'k' – kraut, kohl, krieg, klieg lights, Kafka.' She picks up the ugly black receiver and hears the usual slightly disrupted dialling tone which signals to her ear 'All the lines to London are engaged. Try later.'

'Mister, it seems fine!' she exclaims. 'You listen.'

He shakes his head gravely: 'Kaput.' He really is quite handsome, and quite young too, in a lugubrious way – and removes his outer coat, revealing a one-piece blue overall of a sort she hasn't seen before.

'Nina, who is this nice man?'

'I am a zek,' he says.

'A what?'

Alarmed, Nina tries to take him aside and into the safe depths of the Russian language: '*Vy gavarite na russkom iazike!*' But he isn't having that. It's Oona who interests him.

'Madam, a zek is a political prisoner sentenced under Article 58 of the Soviet penal code, clauses 10 and 11.'

'Oh! Oh really our telephone is fine, really. We can make calls and receive calls, what more do you want?'

'Problem with the bug,' he says wearily. 'I am here to sort out the bug and the new scrambler. The tenth today – a glass of water, please.'

'The "bug"? Do you mean cockroaches? We were warned to

buy powder before we got to Moscow, and we do see a few but my husband does not want to make an issue of it.'

'"Bug" means concealed microphone, listening device – so that they can overhear what you and Mr Chaplin are saying.'

'But – but what Charlie and I are saying to people is private, strictly between ourselves, that's the American way, Mr Zek, it's in our Constitution.'

'My name is Sasha. We have to monitor everything you say and preferably everything you think. Likewise your visitors. Not to know everything including the secrets of the human soul given to us by God is obviously intolerable for the most advanced scientific state in the world.'

Puzzled, Nina is looking him over, reckons his age in the early thirties, not much beyond her own and Oona's, although lines of suffering are visible. She can tell that Oona has already taken a fancy to him, he's more romantic than Mr Salisbury, this might be her first real adventure in Russia.

'The most advanced scientific state in the world, isn't that America?' Oona asks.

'One must say what one must say.' He turns to Nina. 'Water, please, as already politely requested.'

She hurries into the bathroom, lets the tap run (which it is always reluctant to do) and returns with a full glass of misted water. Watching him drain it at a single draught, Nina reckons she would like to see what lies beyond those one-piece blue overalls. Her guess is that Oona would, too.

'How come you speak English?' Oona wants to know.

'I read American technical magazines in my *sharashka*,' he volunteers. 'They cannot withhold them from us if they want to get quick results.'

'Hey, Nina, does Mr Sasha carry any kind of identification?' (This challenge invariably charges up salesmen and repairmen in California. It's like pulling their pants down several inches.)

He extracts a small document from his blue overall and offers it to Oona. She recognises the photograph, a real mug shot, miserable, but the rest, all this ugly Cyrillic, is for Nina. Nina notes the man's surname, one she hasn't encountered before.

'It's lucky for you I was at home,' Oona says.

'We have the key to your apartment, of course.'

'Wow! Is that legal, Nina?'

'For your protection,' Nina says, baffled about the man's identity.

The zek is gazing down gravely at Mrs Chaplin, winding up his English: 'We are all ex-zeks and future zeks, temporarily extracted from the forced labour camps, engineers and mathematicians, linguists and a few philosophers. We debate day and night our moral relationship with our masters. Are we collaborators? My friend Kopelev says yes, my friend Stolobin says no.'

Oona is bridling but quite coyly: 'Mr Sasha, there are no forced labour camps in the Soviet Union. Charlie and I happen to know that for a fact. Isn't that the truth, Nina?'

'None,' Nina says, then addresses the telephone engineer in Russian. 'Finish your work, hold your tongue, then get out, *ubiraisia*.'

The zek ignores her.

'You must meet my wife Natasha, Mrs Chaplin, and explain to her that there are no political prisoners in our country. She is wondering why she can meet me, her husband, only once a month, with a guard listening in to every word. You and Mr Chaplin can explain to my Nadya why she can enrol at Moscow University only by pretending that she is not my wife.'

Oona is studying the man. 'You said her name is Natasha, so now she's Nadya?'

'Diminutive, as with your "Charlie". All Nadya's child-bearing years are going away. I think the term in English is "slipping away"? – "under the bridge"? yes? Possibly that means something to you, Mrs Chaplin, a mother many times I believe.'

'Listen, I still don't know who you are...'

'I told the comrade here. I am Zek number SR 236. You can call me Sasha.'

'Isn't that a girl's name? Maybe that's why I couldn't understand in Russian novels why girls are always hoping other girls will marry them.'

He almost smiles.

Oona softens: 'Mr Sasha, can you tell me why there are so many people in Russia whose names end in "ich". It's confusing. It makes one scratch.'

'Everyone has a patronymic which comes between the Christian name and the surname. The patronymic follows the father's Christian name. The masculine patronymic ends in 'vich', the feminine in 'ova'. You are Oona Eugenova Chaplin. Your husband is Charles Sidneyovich Chaplin.'

'I'm never going to get any of this unless I attend evening classes. It's not only the "ich" stuff at the end but all that "zh" and "khr" and "shch" running ahead of it. Why are you looking out of the window?'

'You will see my MVD guards happily smoking in the street below. Any attempt at escape simply deprives us at Mavrino of relatively privileged conditions and leads straight back to where we came from – the Gulag in Siberia. But of course I am tempted to be tempted.'

'I'd rather you didn't do anything to our telephone until my husband comes home. He's in a meeting with Mr Eisenstein. Isn't that so, Nina?'

The zek nods gravely. 'Yes, Mr Chaplin and Maestro Eisenstein are reliving greater days, probably 1929 getting into 1930. These two geniuses are still wrestling with the tragic demise of the silent cinema. Actually, it was a tragedy from many perspectives. Look what Eisenstein has been forced to do since that time – yet I admire him. He's dead of course. Your husband is swapping reminiscences with a *dvoinik*, a double, an unemployed actor at Mosfilm.'

'Listen, Mr Zek, Sergei can remember the exact scores on Charlie's tennis court in Hollywood twenty years ago. So he can't be a door knocker or whatever you said.'

'*Dvoinik*, madam.' The zek having been steadily at work throughout the conversation, the telephone now lies disassembled on the floor, vandalized, yielding greasy components amid coils of plasticated cable. Nina sees the word 'Zeiss-Jena' printed on the cardboard cartons strewn across the floor.

'This bug is no good, kaput,' Solzhenitsyn tells Mrs Chaplin. 'It was I who installed it shortly before your arrival. To create an error-proof scrambler I have given myself up to the cryptographic octopus – the theory of probabilities, the theory of errors. I have now set up a special scrambler device recently perfected by us zeks at Mavrino so that no one can any longer monitor Stalin's top-secret conversations, not even Stalin himself. Which is why no one in the USSR knows what is happening or where or why.'

'Wow!' Oona says, turning to Nina. 'Maybe me and Charlie don't know either.'

Nina listens helplessly. The men in the street below are clearly MVD. The whole escapade is too outrageous not to be some kind of *provokatsia* – maybe she herself is being tested.

The tall electrical engineer produces a bottle from the depths of his discarded black coat. 'Georgian plum slivovitz. You have glasses, please?'

'Oh, I never touch anything at this time of day!' Oona clasps her hands as if in pious prayer.

'But your father the O'Neill playwright is famous for his drinking. They say now he won't speak to you because he doesn't approve of you, or your Charlie – or anybody.'

Aghast, Oona appeals to Nina: 'Who told him that? I am very close, quite close, sometimes, to my father. It's his current wife who's the nigger in the woodpile. OK, Nina, please fetch some glasses.'

'Not a good idea, Mrs Chaplin.'

'Do it, bimbo, or you're heading for Siberia.'

A moment later Oona is toasting (something) in Georgian plum slivovitz. The zek knocks his back. Nina feels she has to go along with it, just a sip, must stay on top of every situation.

'In Moscow O'Neill is a decadent,' the zek announces. 'We can never hope to see his *Electra* or his *Iceman* staged here in our utopia, but if we graft and beg we can find the text under the counter in the library of the Academy of Arts and Sciences.'

'You are certainly an unusual electrician. I wish Charlie was here.'

'Were here.'

'Sorry?'

'Subjunctive. Essential in any language. "I wish Charlie were here." I have been studying the subjunctive in prison. "I wish I were a free man. I wish I were not hungry all the time. I wish Stalin were King of Spain".'

'Is that telephone "bug" of yours working right now?'

'Bug now operating. Anything we say recorded for ever. You may wish to know that I was arrested while an artillery officer in East Prussia, a few weeks before the fall of the Reich.'

'The fall of the what?'

'Of Hitler. The Great Dictator, Mrs Chaplin.'

'Oh so you know my husband's movie?'

'It has never been shown in Soviet Russia.'

'But it will be! That's why we have come to Moscow.'

'Forgive my ignorance but I wouldn't lay a big bet on it.'

'Tell me why they arrested you, Mr Sasha, though I don't think either of us should be drinking sliv – call it brandy at this time of day but what the hell.'

'Why arrested? I wrote a poem about our Great Dictator. They found it in my possession.'

Oona bridles. 'I don't think that's altogether a fair or progressive way to talk about Uncle Joe.'

'The Georgian dwarf.'

Nina shudders – to be in the same room with this man is worth a ten-year sentence.

'Is that meant to be funny?' Oona asks. 'It was Joseph Stalin – if that's who you mean – who won the war for all of us!'

'Having lost it first.'

'How could he win it if he lost it?'

'Ask the seventy million Russians put under Nazi captivity in the first weeks after 21 June, 1941.'

'It was a great fight-back. Charlie always says so. That's why he campaigned for Russian War Relief. Charlie stood up for you on platforms!'

'"On platforms"? Dangerous! He never put his life on the line in either world war, did he? The paradox is that the English deemed him unpatriotic during the First World War, while the American public was loving him, then during the Second World War the English adored him while many Americans regarded him as unpatriotic.'

'That's a lie! Charlie demanded a second front. His sons fought in the army. Do you people know this? Do you know about Lend-Lease?'

A commotion in the hallway below signals the arrival of Mr Chaplin. Somewhat inebriated, he enters the apartment with the swaying dignity and rotating eyebrows of the drunken Calvero in *Limelight*. But on this occasion there is no door to be smashed down and no despairing ballerina to be rescued from her gas-filled room. Chaplin surveys the tall stranger, who looks suspiciously Russian (they are everywhere). A bottle of Georgian plum slivovitz can be seen on the floor, surrounded by electrical debris.

Chaplin examines his young wife's wide-eyed hello there. She is completely cooked. '*Dobryi dyen*, Charlie my Boy,' she giggles.

'And who is this man engaged in teaching you Russian and wrecking our telephone?'

'This man is Mr Sasha Zek,' Oona very slowly reports. 'He says he's a political prisoner who admires my father.'

'Ah, a fantasist on both counts. He's the kind who hangs around Sverdlov Square near the theatres. Our telephone is fine, Mr Zek. Or was.'

'That's what I told him, Charlie. But he says a bug is hidden in there, a microphone to overhear our conversations. Mr Zek says they won't let him see his wife because he wrote a poem.'

'Well, he'd better not recite his poem in my apartment.'

'You must leave now!' Nina hisses at the zek, 'Go, *idi!*'

The zek is unmoved. 'I shall recite you a stanza from my saga of the rape of conquered Germany in which I took part.'

'Rape?' Oona is aghast, Chaplin conveys outrage by whirring an invisible cane.

'Yes, while an artillery officer serving in East Prussia, I took a lady called Anna against her will. Afterwards she pleaded, her body beneath mine, "Please don't shoot me!"'

'Oh how could you!' Oona cries.

'In this verse composition Red Army units are heading for Neidenburg, burning and looting everything in sight, vacuum cleaners, wine, candles, brooches, blouses, rings of sausage, cheeses, wineglasses, shoes, typewriters – unfortunately we never find ones with Cyrillic typefaces, As we advance we see recently liberated Soviet prisoners of war being marched in the opposite direction, the pariahs, summoned to no victors' feast, necks bowed, heading for the distant parts of a cruel country, *dvizhutsia k daliam zhestokoi strany.*'

'What country?' Oona asks.

'Where I have been and I will soon be again. So I come to the rape of the trembling German woman Anna.' The zek straightens his back to recite seven lines beginning '*Leykii vzdymlivul purok*' and ending '*Pomanil, ne gliadia: "Komm!"*'

The zek surveys the Chaplins. 'You understood the last word, I take it! Komm!'

'Doesn't sound Russian to me,' Chaplin says. 'Well, I never went to school apart from a few years at Eton, but shouldn't it be "kommsky"?'

'And afterwards, disturbingly close to her pale blue eyes, I express regret to Anna, but too late, she answers in an unsteady voice, her face in the pillow, "*Doch, erschiessen Sie mich nicht!*"'

Oona reaches for the plum brandy, now too far gone to change the subject – or know what it is.

'Tell me,' she asks, leaning against the tall zek, 'is it true that a young Russian can win a girl's heart only if he can recite the whole of Pushkin?'

'Every baby born in Russia is Aleksandr Pushkin's,' the zek solemnly tells Oona.

'Oh wow!' Oona burps. 'A handsome suitor like you, Mr Sasha, must know the whole of Pushkin by heart'

'Every word, of course.'

Charlie has now gone into boxing mode, Madison Square Garden, his showdown title fight with Joe Louis or maybe Georges Carpentier (and all the other big guys who have bullied him, film after film). This effectively terminates the electrician's visit. He gathers his equipment then produces a manuscript wrapped in brown paper stamped 'MAVRINO'.

'As a matter of fact, Mr Chaplin, I happen to have a novel with me, a *povest*' written by a friend...which I am inviting you, Mr Chaplin, to carry in your luggage when you leave the Soviet Union. It's called *One Day*.'

'And who's your friend?'

'Someone I trust. He may be a genius, time will tell.'

'Is it a love story?' Oona asks.

'It's one day in the life of a zek who has not seen his woman or any woman for years.'

'Isn't that rather negative? I mean who'd want to make themselves miserable all night reading something like that?'

Chaplin is not to be hoodwinked by this impostor. 'I always admire an optimist but nothing subversive gets into my luggage. Progressive minded people the world over know that no one is more devoted to justice than Mr Stalin. Of course sometimes things happen behind his back but as I used to tell William Randolph Hearst, Uncle Joe is never slow to set them right.'

'The Gulag is rather a large thing to happen behind one's back,' the zek says bitterly, replacing the wrapped manuscript in his electrician's bag. 'Perhaps I should now mend Maître Picasso's telephone. I hear he is more sympathetic to freedom of expression.'

Oona's eyes are alight. 'I butted Pablo's behind, he's no taller than Charlie.'

Charles Chaplin's face is not one of his best. He will now dispose of this cocky tramp. Nina, meanwhile, follows the irregular man down the stairs and into the street, where she beckons the MVD men lounging against their illegally parked vehicle. She flashes her identity card.

'Who is this man? What's his real name? What's going on?'

Their leader stubs out his *papirosa*, pinches her bottom, handcuffs the zek, shoves him in the back of the vehicle, and they drive away in a black van on which she can see the printed the words МЯСО – FLEISCH – VIANDE – MEAT.

I suppressed my disbelief. 'Did you ever discover who the zek was?' I asked Lady Stears.

'Eventually. He was expelled from Russia the same year I defected. His face was everywhere – but twenty years older and by then less appealing to a woman.'

I didn't believe a word of it. After all 'the zek' later published copious memoirs in which no hint of such unlikely exploits surfaces. If he had really been assigned to bug the telephones of Chaplin and Picasso, then Aleksandr Solzhenitsyn would surely have been delighted to recall such episodes. But I held my tongue because I realised the scene was beyond Lady Stears's capacity for invention – and fortunately so because, as we shall see, the fabulous zek will reappear elsewhere in Olga's narrative.

20

E hrenburg and his wife live in a large apartment not far from Red Square (as if to facilitate his periodic, breath-taking, direct appeals to Stalin). This evening they are at home, a *soirée*. Ehrenburg has been showing Picasso and Chaplin his private collection of modern art. As his elegant wife Irina graciously serves a light supper – black caviar, canapés, bliny, borshch – old Ehrenburg is taking obvious pleasure in what he calls a 'historical *tour d'horizon*'. As he listens Picasso's expression is both wary and weary. The conversation is in French so Olga's role is to sit in a corner while Nina stands between the Chaplins as translator.

Ehrenburg smiles foxily. 'Do you remember, Pablo, what you said to me as we waited for the Germans to attack France in 1940?'

'Said?'

'People sat by their radios, even those who knew no German, listening to Hitler's speeches and trying to guess from his intonation what the next day would bring. I remarked to you that France was like a sleek, well-fed rabbit hypnotized by a boa-constrictor. And you said, "*Mon vieux*, I find it difficult to work – we're drowning in filth."' Ehrenburg waits. 'Do you remember?'

'I remember how we got you out of France and back here to write your great book *The Fall of Paris*, which I have no intention of reading. I expect you reached in my pocket.'

At this juncture a new, unexpected guest arrives, Russia's most celebrated composer, said to be the greatest of the modern era. Olga has sat spellbound through performances at the Moscow Conservatoire – until he and his work suddenly disappeared and piles of dung descended on his name (and Prokofiev's, too) in the press. Kemenev scornfully told Olga that Shostakovich aspired to be the musical Picasso. Courtesy to Ehrenburg – and clearly nothing else – here and now obliges the composer to make the briefest of appearances. Wandering in behind thick lenses, he shakes foreign hands like a half-blind mendicant. Chaplin greets him as 'Dmitri!' Shostakovich responds with a silent bow.

'We met in New York two years ago,' Chaplin reminds him cheerily. 'At the Waldorf conference.' Ehrenburg translates. Shostakovich's scathing retort shocks everyone present:

'Yes, I remember, Maestro Chaplin. You had been running around with Henry Wallace during the '48 presidential election. A fellow-traveller of the fellow-travellers.'

Nina tries to soften this in translation but there's no way out. Chaplin is visibly stunned: 'I wanted peace with Russia, your country, Dmitri.'

'And in the cause of "peace" you hotly denied reports of Soviet purges and concentration camps.'

Chaplin has not expected this, not here in Moscow. 'I still do. I wouldn't be here otherwise.'

Shostakovich blinks belligerently behind his porthole spectacles: 'You're not familiar with the case of the German Marxist Margarete Buber-Neumann? She took refuge from the Nazis in the USSR. We Russians handed her back to the Gestapo after the infamous Hitler-Stalin Pact – one of many German democrats we callously betrayed. The Nazis sent poor Margarete to Ravensbruck. By a miracle she survived. Her testimony in Paris after the war rattled even the pro-Soviet blinkers of Sartre and de Beauvoir. Our host Ehrenburg here had to spend hours in the Café de Flore trying to convince them that Buber-Neumann was a dangerous Trotskyist planted by the Americans.'

Chaplin is indignant. 'Why should Ilya do that if she wasn't –'

Ehrenburg intervenes smoothly, in his perfect franglais. 'You mean why should I want to stay alive? I am *citoyen soviétique*, Charlot.'

Silence. The beliefs of a lifetime have been removed from Chaplin (but of course they haven't, you might as well try to remove the boots from the legendary tramp). Shostakovich offers a small apology for his candour:

'As you know, dear Maestro, we composers are tone-deaf when it comes to diplomacy.' Ehrenburg translates. The tone-deaf composer now inclines his head to Oona. 'Madam, please convey my respects to your eminent father, whose plays have been a gift to the world...if not to the Soviet Union.'

Oona is on her feet, radiant. 'I heard Toscanini conduct your Leningrad symphony on NBC radio. It was a great moment for us. Thank you for that.'

'*Spasibo*, Madam.'

Olga is observing Picasso. Clearly he hasn't understood a word of the exchange, except the bad feeling between Shostakovich and Chaplin. Olga is not tempted to venture a whispered translation. Shostakovich now bows to Picasso – my god, what next?

'Well, Maître, we all look forward to your forthcoming exhibition. Of course it is wise here in the Soviet Union not to approach such events with too much optimism.' Moments later Shostakovich drifts out into the Moscow night, twitching and blinking behind his portholes.

Picasso asks Ehrenburg whether the composer's music is often performed in the Soviet Union.

'Sometimes. It depends on the weather.'

'Oh my god,' Oona says. 'Tell us, Ilya, is Dmitri right? I mean what happened to that nice German woman with the long name?'

'Dmitri is always right. One thing he and I have in common is that we both live in fear of being right all the time.'

Chaplin is sulking about meeting the wrong kind of Russians. 'The true Russia is hard to find,' he tells everyone.

But then we come to a more fragmented recall, neither Olga nor Nina fully understanding when Ehrenburg and Chaplin engaged in an exchange about the German playwright Brecht, whom Chaplin had evidently known in California during the war years. We will have to help out here.

'Brecht is a blatant plagiarist, my dear Charlot,' Ehrenburg declares.

Chaplin smiles. 'We all steal.'

'Brecht's dramatic events, figures and emotions are constantly borrowed from other dramatists – Büchner, Lenz, Marlowe, Webster, even the great Goethe and Schiller. And what themes does he steal? – jealousy, incest, castration, infidelity, murdered and abandoned children, violations of women, attractive murderers, burnings, suicides.'

'That's life,' Chaplin remarks. Oona fails to stifle a supportive smile, further irritating their host.

'My dear Charlot, you must be aware that the comic elocution lesson in Brecht's *Arturo Ui* is a straight steal from you! I refer to Adenoid Hinkel's gymnastics with a paper globe in your own, incomparably greater work, *The Great Dictator*.'

'No, I am very fond of Bert's scene when Ui seeks gravitas under the tuition of a motheaten old Shakespearean pedant.'

Now Chaplin launches into performing mode, exactly capturing Brecht's *The Resistible Rise of Arturo Ui*. He begins with the gangster Ui's vain performance in front of a mirror, Ehrenburg's guests soon collapsing in laughter. Picasso is radiant – at last he is seeing the old Chaplin he had once adored, not the weak old man surrendering his loved one in *Limelight*.

Chaplin raises his hands for silence: 'Ladies and gentlemen, I now offer you a moment – or two – from Arturo Ui's elocution lesson. Your humble clown will play all parts and tickets are free. The vegetable gangster Ui yearns for the greater respect which comes with the fine clothes, elegant speech and grand style of the established vegetable merchants. He has sent his underlings out in search of a suitable Tutor, and here the man is hauled in, a shambling old actor called Mahonney.

Chaplin shambles. Picasso claps in delight: no one else in the world can shamble like that.

UI. Look, here's a mirror, full-length. Show me how to walk – how do they do it in the theatre and the opera?

MAHONNEY. Imagine yourself progressing as in Shakespeare's drama, the grand style.

Mahonney demonstrates how the point of the foot must touch

the ground before the rest of the foot.

UI. Excellent! When I proceed I want people to see that I am proceeding.

Ui starts walking, thrusting the toe of his shoe down in an exaggerated manner. Desperate to catch his reflection in the mirror, he is soon tumbling and cartwheeling all over the place. Olga fears that Picasso may succumb to cardiac arrest through sheer delight.

Chaplin bows, is applauded. Only Ehrenburg looks less than pleased.

Oona is into a ravishing smile. 'I was crazy about Bert Brecht in Hollywood. And he smells so bad – I'd love to wash his feet. If he invited me to join his harem I'd just go find a huge suitcase – though I don't want to have my shins kicked again by Helli Weigel under the table. I guess it's her way of making her mark.'

Picasso grips Olga's wrist. 'What is la belle Oona saying? Who is Veegle?'

'Mr Brecht's wife, Maître, an actress famous in the role of Mother Courage.'

Annoyed by Olga's equivocation – isn't that girl a bit too virtuous? – Nina tries her bad French on Picasso: 'Mrs Chaplin was saying that Frau Weigel kicked her under the table in California because she wanted to join Brecht's harem.'

Still gripping Olga's wrist, Picasso is getting excited enough to try his English. 'Leddy Oona why you not in Picasso harem? *Tu affoles Picasso.*'

Chaplin gets most of this. Ehrenburg is mopping his brow in despair – the Peace Movement is disintegrating. 'Pablo,' he begs but Picasso brushes him off. So does Chaplin, now prancing on his feet and imitating Joe Louis at Madison Square Garden:

'Tell Pablo I'll knock him down and out. For the count.'

No one translates because no one can. But Picasso is enjoying the display of aggression, he may not know too much about boxing but he loves the bullring.

'Hey, Charlot, I heard that when Meess Bloom went over to

New York to audition for *Limelight*, you insisted she bring her mother as chaperone so that no one could once more accuse you of oolala. Translate, Ogla *devushka*.'

But Pablo is already asleep. When he wakes up a few moments later he tells old Ehrenburg that he has been dreaming about Buñuel and Dali slitting eyeballs in *Un Chien andalou* in imitation of Eisenstein's woman wearing bloodsoaked lenses in *The Battleship Potemkin*.

'Did you understand that?'

'Very little but Olga and I agreed it was time to carry everyone home. We watched as Picasso groped for Oona's hand from the depths of his chair.'

'Pablo amoureux de la Leddy Oona.'

'Oh Pablo, what a surprise! Ever since we got to Moscow you haven't said a word to me. Why haven't you invited me to your studio?'

'Tomorrow! A new portrait of Leddy Oona in the altogether.' The last word might be English.

On the drive home Chaplin starts fretting about his film festival. Nina can only murmur words of optimism. What she hears at Mosfilm is what she also hears from Olga via Kemenev: Beria is powerful, still making Georgian jokes, and now supported by Malenkov – but Khrushchev and Molotov are working hard to gain the ear of Stalin, who is still unapproachable in his dacha on the Mozhaisk Chaussee outside Moscow.

Later that evening Nina telephones Olga and begs her to fix up the promised invitation by Picasso to paint Oona in the "altogether". Anything to distract and divert the over-active and over-observant Mrs Chaplin.

'What did Olga say?'

'She said she was asleep and neighbours complained if she received calls at all hours. She said she would do her best but I don't think she wanted Picasso to get that close to Mrs Chaplin.'

21

Lady Stears had told me so much during our long day when she was wearing a white blouse, denims and grey moccasins – the maid had brought us crab sandwiches – that when on my next visit I was confronted by a short Laura Ashley print dress, black stockings and high lace-up boots, I feared that the interview would be brief. So I began with a down-to-earth question:

'Please tell me about your background and education, Lady Stears.'

She recrossed her legs impatiently as if to ask was I Professor Plod?

'I prefer to tell you about each art on these walls.' (Why did she use that expression?) 'But okay, who was Nina Bolsharova, why not? First you have to understand that I belonged to a particular generation which owed everything to Stalin. In the West Stalin is simply terror, the massacre of the kulaks in the Ukraine, deportations, show trials, monstrous purges, unending cruelty. For us Stalin was education and technical training. We paraded joyfully as Young Pioneers and Komsomols in our red scarfs and bright eyes. Can you possibly understand that, Oxford?'

'Yes. And your family?'

'I was born in 1928 in Volgograd, called Stalingrad since 1925. Six children, three died in infancy. My father worked in the docks on the Volga, a turner and a Bolshevik. He had been conscripted into the Red Army in 1919, during the Civil War, in Trotsky's time, though dare I mention that name. In 1920 my father fought under Tukhachevsky, the disastrous Polish campaign, and was lucky to escape with his life. My mother was a hospital cleaner who taught us that Lenin and Stalin were our saviours. I got to an elementary school, sixty kids for each teacher – but you won't believe this, we wanted to learn! We feared our teachers but worshipped them. We carried our homework in big canvas satchels back to our rat-infested two rooms and we sat at the kitchen table murmuring the multiplication tables over and over. In my secondary school we learned English, it was quite unusual, but we read about Ford and Taylor and Ferguson tractors. I was one of the few who had the gift for English, for replicating strange foreign sounds. I was bright – and girls were as worthy of education as boys.'

'For which you have remained grateful to Stalin?'

'So you do understand, Oxford man. In 1941 came the Great Patriotic War. The Government sent me to secondary school in the Crimea, my parents wanted me evacuated from Stalingrad. Both my parents died in 1942 during the terrible siege. The whole city was destroyed, did you know that?'

'I have seen Vladimir Petrov's film, *The Battle of Stalingrad.*'

'You won't find my poor parents there. In 1944 I was sent to Language School in Moscow, a Technic. I always received high grades in foreign languages and I wisely majored in English. By that time I had no home, no family, no brother, no sister, no one at all – so I met a young student Sergei, we were engaged, he was conscripted, I never saw him again. A hero of the Battle of Berlin but his aunties kept the medal, I wrote to them but I was nobody. So I never married Sergei but I am always married to him, I have never loved anyone else. Do you know what love is?'

'Please tell me.'

'Love is not there until they take it away. It settles into you later and then it is forever part of you. Did you ever see Grigorii Chukhrai's *Ballada o soladte – Ballad of a Soldier?* I saw it in 1959, fourteen years after Sergei's death. All quite sentimental and boring for you.'

'I remember the scenes of the young lovers parting at the railway station.'

'Yes, that was me and Sergei, always. Maybe I like you more than I should. I call you "Oxford" because that is my highest term of praise. By 1950 I had graduated and to my great joy was taken on by Mosfilm, first as a language assistant preparing subtitles for the export of Soviet films. That meant for me no longer the regular shelter of a student hostel, must find my own room, must have two jobs, every woman did, there were so few young men alive...'

'Not only the war dead but the prisoners of war swept away to Siberia.'

'The MVD knew all that very well, they ran the camps after all, and I was a good Communist, a Komsomol leader, fluent in English so...so.'

'And you loved American films?'

'They had showed us some chosen Hollywood movies during the war under Lend-Lease. *Mission to Moscow, Red Star, Song of Russia, Gone With the Wind, Tarzan*. Paulette Goddard, Betty Grable, Rita Hayworth, Vivien Leigh. Clark Gable but Melvyn Douglas my favourite. Have you heard of Lend-Lease? Not just tractors, tanks and food, but also Hollywood.'

'Was it a shock to you when love of America turned to enmity?'

'We never loved America, just Hollywood, maybe Roosevelt a bit. Always monopoly capitalists, Wall Street warmongers, in Russian we say "Uoll Strit". Did you know Roosevelt and Churchill could have started a second front in 1942, not two years later?'

'It's a point of view.'

She flared: '"It's a point of view" on high table?'

I, too, was losing equilibrium: 'Did you know, Lady Stears, that Britain was at war with Hitler from 1939, for two years, I remember the bombs, while the USSR made friendship with Germany?'

Nina looked sullen, we were relapsing. 'Friendship? Never.'

I couldn't resist pressing on: 'Britain's war against Hitler was denounced by Moscow and the Comintern as an imperialist war.'

'Probably was. Churchill, Empire, why did he send troops to North Africa, guarding the Suez Canal, protecting India, and not help the Red Army?'

'Stalin did not declare war against Hitler until after Operation Barbarossa. Instead he divided up Poland with Hitler – the secret protocol of the Nazi-Soviet Pact.'

'Better than giving the whole of Poland to the Nazis. Anyway, the Polish Government was not a friend of the working masses.'

'It was Stalin who murdered four hundred Polish officers in Katyn forest.'

'That is a lie!' She suddenly sobbed, choked, clutched at her hair and left the room, tottering on her lace-up boots. I had been on occasion an erring party to Olga's tears but had hitherto imagined Nina to be made of tougher fabric – I had come to believe that she relished arguments, thrived on duels. Olga was the more inclined to wear her heart on her sleeve, but Nina's bravado, cynicism and wit, I realised, was little beyond plaster and stucco on crumbling brick. Forty years of silence had become insufferable to both women. The stranger admitted to their sitting rooms came to steal away their long nights of denial.

She was gone for a quarter of an hour while I studied her pictures, her 'art', then she returned smiling in fresh make-up.

'So where were we?'

I asked Lady Stears whether she had seen Chaplin's films when young.

'Early ones, silent era. But *Modern Times* and *The Great Dictator* not permitted.'

'Why?'

'You will find out if you come to see me and my hysterics again.'

'And when they took you on at Mosfilm, you were already a beautiful young woman? Was that ever a factor?'

Nina laughed. 'A what?'

'I mean –'

'I know what you mean. It is always a "factor", Oxford, but my skills were real. I knew the right idioms for English subtitles, sometimes we did different versions for America. I believe that some females have a particular aptitude for foreign languages. Of course I thought I might become a film actress, I had the looks, and I had one small part as a "good" German in Aleksandrov's

Vstrecha na Elba, not at all glamorous believe me. Better, I was substituted for Paulette Goddard in Aleksandrov's re-make of Chaplin's *Modern Times*. I worshipped and feared Aleksandrov's wife Orlova, She had everything, fame and wealth. I shall now tell you about her encounter with Mrs Chaplin, yes?'

'Yes.'

Nina stands, her high heels digging into the Persian carpet, hands on hips. She is now about to perform, and she will ventriloquize both parts, Orlova and Oona, catching the body-language of each – but while Orlova was in reality speaking in her native Russian, to be translated, Nina instead has Orlova speaking English with a heavy, perfumed Russian accent.

'OK, here we go. It was a plush reception for the Chaplins held at the Dom Kino. Oona had had one or two vodkas before setting out and arrived at the party with a ravishing smile.'

'Did Chaplin know about her habit?'

'He turned a blind eye. So Oona grabs a glass of champagne and looks happy. Then who should converge on us but our hostess, the glamour queen of Soviet cinema, but no longer as young as she would like to be. Lyubov' Orlova doesn't grace me with a glance but I am in for some rapid translating. Of course Oona doesn't know who the woman is but you don't introduce Madame Comrade Orlova any more than you would say, "By the way, this is the "Queen of England".

'"And how do you like our Moscow cuisine, Mrs Chaplin?" asks Orlova.

'"Well, we only arrived four days ago but it seems great so long as you don't eat it. No, that's a joke! Don't repeat that! Charlie will kill me."

'Of course I know Orlova will most certainly repeat it all over town.

'"They say Mr Chaplin has a good sense of humour," Orlova says drily.

'"Never heard that one before!" Oona says gaily. "Only if the joke's at someone else's expense."

"'You're not saying he suffers from vanity, Mrs Chaplin?'"

"'No, he doesn't suffer at all. He thinks he's the greatest comic actor of the twentieth century – forget Harold Lloyd and Buster Keaton, forget Laurel and Hardy, forget the Marx Brothers.'"

"'I hear that Mr Chaplin does not favour women taller than himself,' purrs Orlova. "Forgive me, Mrs Chaplin, but what is your own height?'"

"'Well they can go on arguing about that in *Paris-Match* – their photographers accuse me of bending, crouching or even squatting to conceal that I'm several metres taller than Charlie.'"

"'Centimetres, surely?'"

"'If you say so. When we were living at the Pallisades in California, Charlie erected a special bower in our rose garden. Each would-be secretary or nanny applying for a job had to walk under the bower without catching her hair. I used to watch from our bedroom window, laying bets.'"

"'Presumably in the vulgar climate of capitalist America you and Mr Chaplin have needed a large domestic staff to protect you both from intruders?'"

"'Spot on! So much of our life has been spent hiding from bailiffs, debt collectors, Internal Revenue men with extravagant, cooked-up demands, and from actresses claiming insane paternity payments – someone like Joan Barry will barge right in, smashing precious ornaments. Before leaving California, I had to pay off the old retainers, well some of them. The others are claiming a grievance and bringing suit – Charlie calls them 'sharks'. Hey you, waiter, fetch me another glass of the same, will you? Charlie and Picasso agree about servants. They should all be shoved into Samuel Beckett dustbins. Charlie told Pablo that ingratitude is the inevitable result of generosity. 'My few friends are those I have given nothing to,' he told Pablo.'"

"'One question, Mrs Chaplin, please. What is a Samuel Bucket dustbin?'"

"'It's Beckett, I mean it's a dustbin with a woman inside. You can just see her mouth. It's where Western avant-garde theatre is now at. When I met Sam Beckett in Paris he said I would fit nicely and promised to cast me in his next production." Oona almost kisses the young waiter who brings her the champagne. "Oh you lovely boy or should I say Boyar?"

'Orlova smiles and moves regally away.'

The performance over, Nina bowed to me. I applauded. She curtsied. I said I had a problem: how could she possibly remember all that, word for word, across forty years?

'Oh, I don't, not a word of it. I can only advise you that if Nina Bolsharova doesn't perform, she doesn't remember and she doesn't tell. Understood?'

'Imperfectly.'

'So back to my life story. The MVD reached out for me, Beria's Intelligence outfit, you can't say no. I remained at Mosfilm while the Organs took me in for training. They called it "orientation". You British will call it "indoctrination". We were taught that America wanted war against the Soviet Union because monopoly capitalism was succumbing to its own contradictions.'

'Did you believe that?'

'Of course. It was true. Look how they rearmed West Germany and put all those former Nazis in high places.' Nina was monitoring my expression. 'Maybe you can never escape from your own brainwashing. I know you served in the British colonial army. You demonstrated in the streets of Oxford when the Soviet Union intervened to save socialism in Hungary.'

'Is that in the KGB files?'

'How would I know? I was guessing. People in England tell me things.'

'Tell me about *Operatsiya Dvoinik*.'

'The intention was to operate a *prostaya sistema* but nothing can be simple in a Byzantine dictatorship. The operation should have been *prostoi*, you invite two world-famous artists, you give them what they want, you flatter them and offer them scented vaginas, they go home radiantly happy, your friends for life. But we were divided among ourselves, *my sozdali khaos*, we created chaos.'

Later, when leaving, I asked whether I would be at liberty to quote everything she had told me. She lit her first cigarette of the morning.

'I thought we'd come to that. I would need to read your text first. I don't want to discover that I am telling lies.' She paused, blowing out smoke. 'I have a lawyer with chambers in the Temple with two doors, outer and inner like in Oxford. He says "sporting the oak" but I have never understood that. Henry likes contracts.'

'Olga has never spoken of a contract.'

'Olga is Olga. I think you are maybe-maybe head-over-heels about Madame Lepinskaya. Have you ever asked her why she is known by her maiden name?'

'Her state registration and her bank account are still Davidov. For Olga the name Lepinskaya is essentially her professional name.'

'Why do you know more about Olga than you know about me?'

～

That night I dreamed about Nina. I saw her walking away on high heels towards a fine Adams panelled door boasting Ionic orders at the far end of the room. She half-turned:

– You want to see my bedroom, Oxford?

As I obediently followed her out of the drawing room, the pictures, the 'art', seemed to be falling off the wall, spiralling to the Persian carpet but soundlessly, as if descending through sunlit water. Entering Nina's rococo bedroom, ahead of me stood the largest bed I have ever imagined, not only filling the entire room but spilling out of it, squeezing its moving antennae through doors and open sash windows framed by the inset shutters introduced in the late eighteenth century to reduce risks of fire. [In retrospect I interpret this as the bed filling Olga's small, 9'x 9' bedroom, where the Picasso-Raphael Madonna hangs.] Both King Charles spaniels lay like hairy seals on the undulating silk bedspread, alert but sure of their domain. Searching for Nina, no sign of her, I came face to face with an aviary littered with caged birds, a cockatoo, a canary, a South Seas parrot, some kind of hawk sternly surveying the entrails of his mice. I was conscious that I must without delay sell the movie rights in my research to Mosfilm – any delay and Grigorii Aleksandrov would withdraw his offer and the entire venture would die. But where was Nina and where was Olga, without them I had no story to offer? I sensed that both were waiting in another room I could not find, both waiting to present me with legal contracts I could not, must not, sign. While the dream prevails, I am aware of its lack of stable definition, not unlike the perpetual shifting of sub-atomic particles as described by quantum physics and quantum biology – rapid mutation. I am both inside the dream and simultaneously conscious of it being 'only' a dream, even aware of its symbolic nature – yet while it retains possession I am unable to escape the tyranny of the cascading particles.

Then Ivan in his black suit was opening the rear door of the Silver Cloud Rolls, he carrying a huge picnic hamper for Wimbledon, and Nina was whispering in my ear how certain Oxford notables had lost her respect by making 'sad excuses', including (since you ask) 'Hugh, Alan, Isaiah, Stuart, Freddie and (oddly) Iris, 'famous poet and philosopher guilty of serious Sapphic errors.' But who was this woman absurdly wearing a mink coat on a hot afternoon in June? With Ivan impatiently sounding his horn through the tail-backs, the faceless mink coat was making it clear that I was to be its privileged (undeserved) guest on the Centre Court; I was to meet its 'dear friends' from the same wardrobe, the other beautiful clothes who took for granted seats in the royal box, and Pimms, champagne and strawberries, famous suits and gowns who utterly ignored the rallies, the contemptible adventures of the humming yellow ball, while roaming in search of the courtside cameras. But we never got to SW19. The bonnet of the Rolls began to emit smoke and the last I saw of Ivan was his sharp shoes protruding from beneath the smouldering chassis.

'I suppose you have been dreaming,' my wife said.

'Sorry, so sorry. What was I saying?'

'The only word I heard clearly was "inconvenient". You kept repeating that.'

22

The Picasso exhibition is ready, as planned and almost on schedule. The chosen paintings are restretched, reframed, hung, the lighting has been adjusted, and Olga has suspended a peace dove in flight over the entrance to every *salle*. Dual-language captions in Russian and French grace every picture.

Picasso's first visit to the Pushkin Museum has been delayed by Kemenev on one petty pretext after another, causing Olga to run out of plausible excuses. Hearing of the artist's mounting exasperation verging on rage, Kemenev yields to her exhortations.

'This may be the best day of your life, Ochka,' Ekaterina embraces her as she sets out.

'Or the worst, Mamochka.'

Olga accompanies Picasso and his entourage from *ulitsa* Gorky. Wearing a green worsted suit and a broad silk tie inimitably his own design, he has become excited to be in Moscow, happy to visit the famous churches and the Armoury Museum. He enjoys hearing unfamiliar languages in the streets, jovially badgering Olga to translate. In the limousine his hand rests on her knee while she explains the history of the Pushkin Museum, the original classical design by Roman Klein and Vladimir Shukhov, construction between 1898 and 1912, the name Pushkin chosen in 1937 to commemorate the centenary of his death. Arriving in Volchanka, the limousine threads up the curving driveway of the small garden fronting the classical portico of the Pushkin. She cannot understand why the militia have turned out in force.

Nor can Picasso. 'More soldiers than spectators,' he comments as the doors of the limousine are courteously opened. 'Is it the third world war?'

Six girls of the Young Pioneers in white shirts and grey skirts, wearing red sidecaps, are drawn up to present the maître with bouquets of Georgian roses. Even so, it strikes Olga as a depressingly sparse gathering because the general public has not been admitted – and there are no posters on the street although she had made sure that one showing Picasso's *Vecchio cieco e ragazzo* from the blue period has been designed and printed.

Flanked by Aragon and Triolet, Dora Maar in the wake, Picasso is ceremonially received on the steps of the classical portico by Director Kemenev and a small contingent of curators.

Picasso weighs straight in: 'So when does my exhibition open, Monsieur le Directeur?'

'Today, Maître. Or tomorrow.'

'But where are the queues? Where is the public?'

'Today entry is reserved, as is invariably our custom, for a small delegation of distinguished academicians headed by Comrade Gerasimov himself.'

Aragon leans down to Picasso's large left ear: 'Obviously the academicians deserve a clear view of your paintings – without too many heads in the way.'

'Where are the journalists, the art critics?'

'The press? Tomorrow.'

Led by Kemenev and held by Aragon on one arm and by Triolet on the other, Maar still out on her own with her bevy of cameras, Picasso mounts the imposing staircase and progresses into the first salle. He likes the doves suspended over the doors.

'Your work?' he asks Olga.

'Everybody's work, Maître, that is the Soviet way.'

Picasso turns to Kemenev: 'You have a Madonna by Raphael on your staff.' Olga has to dodge a motion of his right hand which she knows will result in a fiercely pinched cheek.

Kemenev's smile is pale: 'Yes, Maître, but please don't tell her.'

A hand gently touches Olga's arm. It is Madame Dora. 'May I take photographs?' Olga has been waiting for this in some trepidation. 'The Director will not permit it,' she whispers. 'But I can promise you the complete portfolio to take back to France.'

'I like to take my own images,' Dora presses. 'I am a

photographer.'

Kemenev has picked up the exchange. He too is thankful for Picasso's good humour. 'Feel free, Madame Maar, you have earned the privilege of breaking the rules by long service.'

Olga smiles radiantly. 'Your art has bewitched Monsieur le Directeur, Madame Dora.'

Picasso had not deigned to accord close attention to the portfolio she brought to Paris, pretending that everything already resided in his mind's eye, but now there is no disguising his vast pleasure at being confronted by what he had achieved forty years ago. He is spellbound to the point of tears.

Pausing at the first emergence of cubism, Olga invites him (as planned) to explain the movement. But explain to whom? To half-a-dozen curators? Olga longs for the warm pressing in of the large crowd of eager students, of young citizens and workers, which lifts her heart to the sky as each new exhibition opens.

Picasso's deep eyes register pleasure at the opportunity and – everyone can see it – pleasure in her.

'What was cubism, Mademoiselle Curator? Well cubism was partly a search for order against Impressionism with its love of colour, emotion, sensation. We wanted an architectonic basis for composition. But after a few years the cubists who were any good were no longer cubists.'

No need to translate. Everyone here understands.

'It has been said that you attempted to displace reality?' she prompts him.

Picasso looks faintly indignant (Olga has seen that puckish pseudo-expression on several occasions):

'We cubists did not try to displace reality. Reality was no longer in the object, it was in the painting. A bowl in a painting has nothing to do with a bowl in real life. The Chinese say, "I don't imitate nature, I work like her. I don't paint a tree, I search for the essence of tree-ness".'

The assembled curators nod politely. Kemenev could be a statue.

'*La réalité, c'est l'impossible,*' Picasso declares, flashing luminous eyes packed with mischief.

'Pablo, you were close to Georges Braque?' This prompts comes from Triolet.

'Yes, I was very close to Braque. I'll tell you a story. One day he was working on a large oval still life with a pack of tobacco, a pipe, the usual paraphernalia. I told him I'd made a dreadful discovery – I'd found a squirrel in his canvas' Picasso pauses for laughter and gets it. 'Braque said it wasn't possible. After a while he too found the squirrel because that kind of paranoiac vision is infectious. Day after day Braque fought that squirrel. He changed the light, the composition, but the squirrel always made a comeback.'

Everyone is breathing easier. There are no squirrels in the Cold War.

Knowing how ardently he would have liked to display samples of his recent work, Olga takes courage despite Kemenev's prohibitory countenance. She invites him to explain his recent *papier collé* technique.

This backfires. 'No point without any examples here!' He looks at her and softens. (So far he has been polite enough not to address her as 'Olga *devushka*', which she dreads. What are they all thinking/whispering about her?)

'The purpose of the *papier collé*,' Picasso explains, 'is to convey the idea that different textures can enter into composition to become the reality in the painting. We tried to get rid of *trompe-l'oeil* to find a *trompe-l'esprit*. We didn't want to deceive the eye, we wanted to fool the mind. The sheet of newspaper was never used in order to make a newspaper. It became a bottle or something like that. This estrangement is what we wanted to make people think about.'

This reminds Olga of Pyotr's devotion to 'alienation'. She has carried by hand Picasso's personal appeal for Pyotr's release to Gerasimov and Serov – that is to say to the sullen secretaries who guard their outer offices, no admission beyond that point. And to

Kemenev himself. She does not know the outcome and Picasso himself has shown no further interest in Pyotr's fate.

Beaming, he scans the attentive faces. He chuckles: 'When I was a child, my mother said to me, "If you become a soldier you'll be a general. If you become a monk you'll end up as the Pope." Instead I became a painter and merely wound up as Picasso.'

Appreciative laughter. Olga has heard it before but it never fails! But where is Academician Gerasimov and his party? Anxiously she murmurs the question to Kemenev.

'Maybe tomorrow. One step at a time. So far so good, eh?'

She has been hoping to persuade Picasso to take Gerasimov and the inevitable Serov aside and put in a word on behalf of Pyotr. As they leave the Pushkin an hour later, she feels sick with despair for him.

The following morning, when she arrives at the apartment-studio in Gorky Street, a revived Picasso insists on being conducted by metro to Tretyakovskaya, the nearest stop for the hundred-year-old Tretyakov Gallery in Lavrushinsky Pereulok. The proposal is evidently the Aragons', anything to divert Pablo from brooding about his own exhibition at the Pushkin, still not open to the public or mentioned in *Pravda* or *Kommunist*. They set off. He loves the descent into the metro, the heroic marble columns, the bas-reliefs and uplifting mosaics of happy Soviet workers and peasants. He stops to examine everything. It is always to Olga that he turns for information, no one else will do. Short, stocky, swathed in fur, he swivels to right and left, beaming.

'I am planning a new dove built by the constructivist method out of the word "Mir" in Cyril lettering. You see how I am already speaking Russian! I am making a gift of the new dove to all Moscow's public buildings.'

His 'Russian' sounding like increasingly Catalan French, he has brought them to a halt. Some curious Soviet citizens are shyly listening in – foreigners are a rarity and this short, squat man is obviously a someone, a notable.

'Let me tell you the true story of the peace doves. Matisse had four large Milanese pigeons in his aviary. Their feet were not bare like most pigeons. They had feathers right down to the ground covering their claws, as though wearing white gaiters.' (The joke isn't new, but it's newish in Moscow.) 'Matisse gave them to Picasso. Early in 1949 Picasso made a lithograph showing a single dove, and succeeded in avoiding a mottled *peau de crapaud*, achieving a transparent grey wash with wonderful gradations. Aragon (he gestures, but without emphasis, to the long-legged princely figure shadowing him) came to the rue des Grands Augustins, found the lithograph lying in a folder, and that was that. By the end of the day the French Party had the poster up on the Vélodrome d'Hiver.'

He beams, enjoying the total attention of a crowd which hasn't understood a word.. 'How am I doing, Olga *devushka?*'

She flinches at the word, it had to surface sooner or later. '*Epatant, Maître.* Now that you are among us, we all want to sit at your feet.'

'We should move on,' Triolet intervenes. 'The Tretyakov staff are expecting us.'

He waves her off dismissively. 'I'll tell you all a story. When Matisse and Picasso had a joint exhibition in London immediately after the war, Alfred Munnings, President of their Royal Academy, encountered Churchill and Field Marshal Montgomery somewhere in one of their parks. They all agreed that if they ran into Picasso they would kick his backside. That's why I visit London only when the weather is bad enough to keep these homicidal old men indoors.'

Olga remembers being instructed by Kemenev to rewrite her own official Soviet account of the 1945 Matisse-Picasso exhibition staged at the Victoria and Albert Museum in London. Relying heavily on sardonic letters to *The Times* written from the Tory gentlemen's clubs of St James's, Junior Curator Lepinskaya had conveniently concluded that the vast majority of ordinary English citizens utterly rejected the degenerate art of Matisse and Picasso. The odd thing, she discovered (but could not possibly say), was that the "Tory clubs" seemed to share the aesthetic canons prevailing in our Soviet Academy. She had been fascinated to read a report of a dinner given at the Royal Academy, attended by Churchill and Field Marshal Montgomery. During his speech the President of the Academy, the noted horse painter Sir Alfred Munnings, had described Picasso and Matisse as incapable of drawing a tree that looked like a tree. In fact Munnings greatly admired Soviet art – though himself no socialist. But Kemenev had recently directed her to change her text by revealing that the great mass of the ordinary English working people welcomed the Picasso-Matisse exhibition of 1945 – in vain Olga pointed out that the Victoria and Albert Museum in Kensington was mostly patronized by the bourgeoisie and the intelligentsia.

Kemenev had listened while she argued with herself about it. He told her he had headaches enough. 'If all this all comes off, Olga Maksimovna, I shall arrange a Black Sea holiday for you and your mother.'

'*Did you rewrite it, Madame?*'

'*Oh, I couldn't be bothered. That man was falling apart. He was incapable of remembering what he said from one moment to the next.*'

'Listen,' a smiling Picasso declares, 'when Picasso reaches the Tretyakov Museum he will buy a ticket like any other visitor. He's not asking to get in free and break the budget of the Soviet State!'

He is persuaded to move on and take the train. He leans on Olga's arm the whole way. 'Don't worry, they think I'm your Spanish grandfather,' he chuckles. Half an hour later they reach the Tretyakov. Now fatally fatigued, Picasso is shepherded to the Director's office and plonked in a deep armchair, where he promptly falls asleep.

'It will be a short nap,' Triolet assures everyone, sipping tea. 'Pablo always jokes that he can sleep for less time than his fellow-artist, Churchill.'

At the word 'Churchill', Picasso is wide awake, shrewdly taking stock of his surroundings. 'Why are we sitting here?'

Curators of the Tretyakov have been anxiously conferring

with Olga about her list of bygone artists whom Picasso is demanding to view, including 'closed' collections. Such short notice! At a later date, perhaps? Why not view the permanent collection on display today?

'Bring me my Olga *devushka*,' he demands.

'Maître, I am right beside you.' Smiling sweetly (and sweetly scented), she bends to him in his chair. 'The Tretyakov is a vast collection, Maître, many eras and schools of painting. Too much for one day.'

'So let's head for what I want to see, the modern movement. The rest can wait.'

'I'm sorry, Maître, it cannot be arranged today. The Director promises a future viewing especially for you.'

He hauls himself to his feet, his fury mounting, and Olga takes a step back.

'No, Pablo, please,' Triolet entreats.

'*Vas t'en!*' he snorts – 'get lost'. He walks, a little unsteadily, out of the Director's office and places himself in the main foyer where a scattering of curators and unforewarned visitors, including babies in prams, is treated to the most astonishing oration heard in Russia since Ivan the Terrible overturned his chess set and decided to massacre the Boyars. Olga notices that among the 'unforewarned' visitors stands the tall figure of Harrison Salisbury of the New York Times. (He has been excluded by the militia from the display at the Pushkin Museum).

'So! Here is Picasso! You can see him? He has come to Moscow. They keep telling him "tomorrow tomorrow tomorrow". We Communists in France are devoted to a famous phrase from the Resistance – "*les lendemains qui chantent*". But here in the workers' paradise, *les lendemains ne chantent pas*.'

'Pablo, that American journalist is listening,' Triolet hisses.

'But the tomorrows do not sing to Pablo Picasso here in Moscow. He is promised that his own exhibition at the Pushkin Museum will open to the public soon – maybe. *Peut-être, peut-être*, eh. And here in the Tretyakov he is promised a maybe-maybe private viewing of the moderns not open to the public! When will they allow the people in? When will they allow the people to form their own judgment on the hidden collections of great Russian artists, Malevich, Filinov, Kandinsky, El Lissitzky, Rodchenko, Tatlin, Falk, dear Goncharova, Popova? Will they let the public see Goncharova's *Women with Parrots*? Will they even show the public Chagall's *Above the Town*? What about Petrov-Vodkin's *Bathing the Red Horse*? Where is Pavel Filinov's *Ships* and where is Mikhail Larionov's *Soldier Resting*? Why hide these treasures? It is a crime! Why hide the Russian cubists like Ivan Kliun, how does one pronounce his name? Why can't we inspect Kazimir Malevich's *Black Suprematist Square*, do many of you realise that it isn't as black as you'd first think? If you look hard you'll find an animal with legs composed of delicate white lines. I once asked Kazimir what kind of an animal it was and he said it was an absent animal.[†] Do you all realise everything happened throughout Europe in that one decade, the 1910s, the revolution in consciousness beside which the great Lenin Revolution proudly takes its place? Why do they want to hide it all from the ordinary working people I met today, so happily, in the metro?'

Harrison Salisbury catches Olga's eye, his raised brows asking a question which can only be, 'Any news of Davidov?' She dare not approach him but fractionally shakes her head, no. From his distressed expression it now dawns on her that the American's silence about what he is witnessing, a great story, is perhaps guaranteed by the guilt he feels about having gotten a young artist arrested and detained. But if Pyotr is released...the guilt may evaporate. The American wants her story, five thousand dollars.

Exhausted now, unsteady on his feet, Picasso turns to leave the Tretyakov, searching for the way out. He grasps Olga's arm. Reaching the street, he announces: 'Since 1917 spontaneity has

---

† Malevich's *Chernyi Kvadrat* (1915), later displayed in the Tretyakov. On inspection the black square now reveals whitish specks of mortar beneath.

been a dead dog in Russia.'

~

That afternoon, Olga finds Dora Maar manifestly at the end of her tether in the Gorky Street studio.

'Pablo has been counting his money again. He never gets the same result. It drives him mad.'

'Why not let him, Madame? Do you have to become involved?'

'Naturally. *Ça va de soi, chère Olga*. He wants me to go out loaded with dollar bills from his Hermès trunk to buy expensive presents for you. I don't know my way and I don't speak Russian.'

'Madame, the shopping centre is *ulitsa* Gorky, Petrovka, Kuznetsky Most, Stoleshnikov and Neglinnaya.'

Maar held her hands to her ears. 'Such impossible names! You must accompany me.'

'Oh, I don't want presents.'

'Please! – you must think of something – anything as long as it's prohibitively expensive.'

Olga drops her gaze. 'Yes, there is something I do want. You remember the evening in Paris when the maître did a napkin sketch of me in the restaurant, the Brasserie Lipp – or was it Les Deux Magots? You may remember he made a present of it to me and I was overwhelmed by the honour.'

'I remember your radiant expression.'

'The night before my departure from Paris I found the napkin sketch had disappeared from my travelling suitcase.'

'That was Triolet. The comrades feared it might compromise "operation Pablo" if you brought it home and proudly showed it to your friends. I know that Triolet has brought it with her to Moscow. If all goes well with the Pushkin exhibition, she intends to place the precious portrait in your hand.'

'Thank you for telling me,' Olga says stiffly.

'If you people don't exhibit his paintings to the public as promised it will break his heart. He keeps asking why the opening date is repeatedly postponed – "vaporized" is Pablo's word for it. *Picasso est mort à Moscou* – how would that headline suit you?'

Olga bridles. 'Kindly inform the maître that I don't need anything from the shops. I would like the beautiful portrait he gave me.'

'Tell me, Mademoiselle Olga – are you pregnant?'

'Perhaps.'

'Then I am sad for you, I mean *vraiment triste*.'

Olga makes an excuse, abruptly departs. Here as in France la maison Picasso is a nightmare. Finding herself in *ulitsa* Gorky, she realises she does not know where she is going. Not back to Kemenev – before leaving the Museum this afternoon she had been yet again summoned by the Director. An array of dummy newspaper headlines prepared by his own staff lay across his desk.

'Take a look, Olga Maksimovna. We have to prepare for every contingency.' He reached for the vodka bottle. 'They say that Comrade Khrushchev has been admitted to Somebody's dacha. It occurred at midnight.'

Olga beats back tears as she leafs through the odious dummies: COMRADE PICASSO RELUCTANT TO RECOGNISE SOVIET ARTISTIC ACHIEVEMENTS (*Pravda*). PICASSO CALLS SOVIET ART A 'DEAD DOG' (*Literaturnaya gazeta*). BYELORUSSIAN WOMEN'S GROUP FINDS ANTI-SOVIET TENDENCIES IN PICASSO EARLY WORKS ON DISPLAY AT PUSHKIN MUSEUM (*Kul'tura i zhizn'*).

'Who wrote these headlines, Comrade Director?'

'I did. Just in case.'

'Just in case what?'

The sallow Kemenev is observing her. 'Frankly, Olga, outbursts like the one at the Tretyakov undermine all our – your – work.'

'In that case, Comrade Director, the solution is not to frustrate him further with pre-arranged delays.'

'My dear Olga Maksimovna, Soviet society must follow well-proven procedures. I have to confess that the women from Byelorussia –'

'But those women were handpicked Party activists. They wear blinkers made of thorn bushes.'

'Listen. We show a certain kind of "adult" film to adults – but not to children. Right?'

'We are not talking about children!'

'Kindly allow me to finish. The Party is the vanguard of the people. We must test the water. Unfortunately, the initial reaction is cold feet. Frankly, I have had telephone calls from –' he gestures towards the stucco decorations adorning the ceiling. 'Everything I hear is negative. Is the Soviet public ready to understand a complete reversal of our long-standing position on modernism? Did I tell you that Khrushchev –'

'Yes, you told me. But where is Beria?'

'They say Beria is at his dacha in the Crimea. Or here in the Kremlin. They say he made a Georgian joke to Khrushchev who took offence – a bad sign. You must persuade Picasso to be patient. He trusts you, doesn't he?'

'I haven't told him that our Museum secretly holds the gold of ancient Troy, seized in Berlin by the Red Army in 1945. Nor that it holds works by Degas, Renoir, Goya, El Greco and Tintoretto which we allow the world to assume are lost forever.'

'Olga, scientific history, dialectical materialism, does not recognise the concept "forever". Now go home and rest. I hear you are pregnant.'

'Who said that?'

'Madame Triolet. She thinks you remain our only hope.'

~

The following morning Olga leads a select group of students, two Russians and a Latvian, who have been invited to the Gorky Street studio to watch the maître at work. Climbing the stairs and entering the studio, she finds to her astonishment that the nude model today is Mrs Chaplin – and utterly at ease with her naked state.

'Hi,' she greets Olga. 'I wondered when you'd show up, *devushka*.'

Nina comes across and murmurs to Olga: 'So far so good.'

Dora Maar is standing frigidly in the background, wrapped in her blank expression, an unlit cigarette jutting up from the ivory holder.

'Why does Maar torture herself?' Nina whispers to Olga.

'Well, she has to. Picasso compels her. She compels herself.'

'Olga, they're saying you're pregnant.'

'I expect I shall be the last to know.'

Pablo has not turned his head from Mrs Chaplin or acknowledged the arrival of Olga and her students. He is using no palette. To his right stands a table covered with newspapers – mainly *Pravda* and *Izvestiia* – and a cluster of large cans filled with brushes immersed in turpentine. Each time he takes a brush he wipes it off on the newspapers, which are quickly reduced to a jungle of coloured smudges and slashes. Whenever he wants pure colour he squeezes some from the tube onto the newspaper. From time to time he mixes small quantities of colour. Around the base of the easel a medley of cans contain grey and neutral tones as well as colours he has previously mixed.

Olga speaks softly to the awed students, in French, because the maître has been showing signs of paranoia when Russian is spoken behind his back. Actually, in Olga's view it is not paranoia at all, he fears nobody, he simply wants to hear the odes of praise.

The two Russian students and the Latvian gather round her. 'Maître Picasso can stand before the canvas for four or more hours at a stretch,' she discloses. 'I have seen him do this in his great studio in Paris. One thing that surprised me was to discover how he will often switch from one painting to the next. You can see here how he likes to surround himself with several half-dry canvases. At home in France he may work like that from two in the afternoon to eleven at night. Watching him, in the end it was always I who collapsed from exhaustion.'

Oona Chaplin is clearly listening in but does not get the French. How thin she is, Olga notices, for a mother of four. You could mistake her body for Nina's if Nina wasn't standing over there in the corner looking like the witch in *Snow White*.

Picasso throws down his brush and turns to survey his visitors. 'Olga's French is so much better than mine,' he tells them with a big wink. They laugh. 'A Russian *devushka* arrives in Paris from Moscow, she makes the usual nuisance of herself, she is persistent, and she is clearly keen to get on close terms with Picasso. But why should Picasso stop his work simply to gratify her?'

His dark eyes swim with darting malevolence. Olga has turned away shattered. Nothing could have prepared her for so cruel a rebuff.

The reclining Oona orders Nina to fetch her robe. 'I don't speak French and I need to stretch my legs.' On bare feet she glides across to join Olga's group.

'Hi.'

Olga tries her English. 'Good afternoon, Mrs Chaplin. I hope you are enjoying the sitting. It is a great privilege.'

Oona strikes the high American female pitch which knows no equal in the world: 'I hear you hooked Pablo in France. Tell us all how you did it.'

Olga's English is up to the insulting echo of 'hooker'. 'I travelled to France, Madame, to ...'

Nina has come to help: 'To show the maître some slides of his early work which we intend to exhibit.'

'Go away, bimbo, you're surplus to requirements. What else did you show him?' Oona asks Olga.

Olga loses self-control, Nina cannot contain her: 'Frankly, Madame, not as much as you have been showing today.'(Oh, Mama, she's so slender, so assured, so rich and I'm frankly jealous of this pretty woman.)

'Well get your tank off my lawn,' Oona says, giving Olga a shove with surprising force, given the size of the shovel.

Dora Maar has been studying the image on Picasso's easel. 'Take a look at the portrait,' she advises Oona.

Oona does so and immediately shudders as if electrocuted. 'Hey, Pablo,' she screams, 'this isn't me. It's her. It's your hooker dressed up as a fucking Madonna!'

Picasso chuckles. '*Provisoire, Leddy Oona, ça dépend. Tout dépend de toi. Je peux toujours imposer la belle poitrine d'Olga devushka.*

Picasso adore la oo la la.'

'What the hell is he saying?' Oona asks Nina. 'I got the "oo la la" bit.'

'Mrs Chaplin, I don't speak French.'

Oona turns to Olga. 'What's he saying?'

'I fear you would be insulted, Mrs Chaplin. The maître did not speak politely.'

Oona grips her arm. 'Tell me what he said.'

'He said you are too thin for his brush...he expects women to have breasts.'

Oona trembles with the humiliation. 'Get me my clothes, Nina.'

Olga is too proud to look at the portrait, still unfinished. Is it full-length in the style of Ingres or Manet? Is it a reclining woman pregnant? Can it be a Madonna with Child by Raphael? She leads her three students from the studio. 'With Picasso you never know,' she tells them, smiling sweetly (she hopes). The students do not look as if they need consoling, having witnessed a scene they may recount to their grandchildren: 'He pretended to be painting one woman but he was really painting another!'

Olga risks a telephone call to Ehrenburg: 'Uncle Ilya, I am so worried. The maître is not happy.'

'It will blow over. Just sit tight, we need time. And Ochka – I hear you are *enceinte*. Who should we congratulate?'

23

We are at the Dom Kino, the House of Cinema in central Moscow, *ulitsa* Vasilyevskaya 13, headquarters of the Soviet Filmmakers' Union. The event has hastily been laid on, under the aegis of the Ministry of Cinematography, at the instigation of Stalin's current favourite film director, Grigorii Aleksandrov. Flanked by his wife Lyubov' Orlova, he is the first to greet and shake the hands of the Chaplins and Picasso's entourage. Georgian champagne circulates beneath the chandeliers of the reception hall.

Aleksandrov himself would have liked to invite the Soviet press to the Dom Kino, and some foreign comrades too. After all, a good spread of handshake photographs, of smiles and embraces – would this not achieve the main aim of confirming that Picasso and Chaplin have embraced the Soviet system and Peace? Nina managed to pass a message to the mighty Aleksandrov that this 'main aim' was not Mr Chaplin's and not what had been promised to him. She believed that the same held true for Picasso but of course Aleksandrov must ask Comrade Lepinskaya about that.

Grigorii Aleksandrov did not take this message from an underling well, in fact he took it badly. In Orlova's frightening (to Nina) presence, he summoned Nina to his office in Mosfilm and accused her of having made false pledges to Chaplin – 'promises utterly unauthorised'.

Nina wasn't having it: 'Do you imagine Maestro Chaplin came all the way to Moscow to shake your hand and sip champagne, Comrade Aleksandrov?'

'Such insolence!' exclaimed Orlova, slapping Nina's face. Nina felt as if her whole life, from her time in the pram when her mother pushed her to and from the Stalingrad hospital where she cleaned the wards – as if every moment of her existence had been in preparation for knocking Orlova to the ground. And the wish was no substitute for the deed. Cornered, indeed fearful for their necks, the nomenklatura had no resort now but to follow custom and blame subordinates. Eyes narrowing, gripping Nina by the wrist, Aleksandrov accused her of posing for Picasso in the nude, pretending she was Mrs Chaplin, then heinously promising to sell her story to the arch-enemy, Harrison Salisbury of the *New York Times*.

'Five thousand dollars! Confess!'

'*Had Salisbury approached you?*'

'*Of course. But Chaplin was in bad odour in the USA so he only offered me two thousand. Frankly, I wondered what had happened to my support structure within the MVD. Suddenly I was out on my own.*'

'*You were frightened?*'

'*Extremely dangerous situation. It's precisely at such moments you are never seen again. Must capitulate.*'

'Comrade Aleksandrov, why not show Chaplin and Picasso your own masterpiece, *Vstrecha na Elba*? They will be lost in admiration, Comrade.'

'*But that would scarcely satisfy Chaplin?*'

'*Of course not. I was living by the hour, Oxford.*'

Aleksandrov lets go of Nina's wrist. Orlova almost apologises for the slap but doesn't. 'We hear alarming rumours, Comrade Nina,' he explains. 'Shostakovich is said to have barged into Ehrenburg's apartment and been thoroughly rude to Chaplin. And some fool is said to be planning to send Picasso and Chaplin out to Peredelkino to munch biscuits with Pasternak. That will get back to that dissident bitch Anna Akhmatova and to Mandelstam's aggrieved widow, I forget her first name.'

'Nadhezda,' Orlova says. 'She is always hoping!' (Nadezhda is Russian for 'hope'.)

'Now, Nina, look at my proposed guest list, where is it?'

'Under your nose,' Orlova says.

'Ah yes. To impress Chaplin and Picasso we must go the whole hog, *vsyu katushku*, eh? Now, the music crowd: Khachaturian,

Prokofiev, Oistrakh. The film people, me, Chiaureli, Romm. The actors – usual crowd. The writers: Sholokhov, Simonov. The scientists, Kapitsa. Lysenko. The runner Kuts. Who is a good footballer?'

'Anatoli Vasilievich Bashashkin,' Orlova says.

'What team does he play for?'

'I always feel he plays for me.'

'Good. Ballerinas, Galina Ulanova if available. What do you think, Nina?'

'Excellent, Comrade Aleksandrov. Don't forget Eisenstein.'

'He's dead. Ah, you're right, get hold of Volkov. Is he still alive?'

'It's a matter of opinion.'

'Though of course no Jews apart from Ehrenburg. All these illustrious Soviet guests will issue cordial invitations to the foreign guests, offers of hospitality at this Conservatoire, that Institute, and before you know what, Chaplin will be waving to 50,000 at Dynamo Stadium and someone will have built a bullring for Picasso!'

Aleksandrov (a talented director but flamboyant) then hatches the Great Idea of bringing Somebody himself to the occasion (the famous Stalin-impersonator Gelovani is on standby, always eager to go). The real Somebody has not appeared in public since the 19th Party Congress at the beginning of November, so the gullible foreign guests will instantly part company with their sanity. Imagine the Generalissimo genially asking Picasso how many noses a man should have, then cordially inviting Chaplin to imitate his friend Winston Churchill laying a brick wall round Chartwell. Imagine (continues Aleksandrov) Charlie lifting an invisible bowler hat, lighting an invisible cigar, scooping up invisible bricks and cement at frenetic speed, dropping bricks on his feet, getting cement full in the face, all while erecting a wall out of *A Midsummer Night's Dream* – then delivering a final, Churchillian V-sign!

'Imagine Somebody beaming genially and shaking the clown's hand. "*Khoroshoi, Charlee*".' Aleksandrov strides round his desk.

'What do you think of our Great Plan, Nina?'

'I am not paid to think, Comrade.'

Conveyed late at night to Moscow's sleepless Party bosses, this scenario encounters distinctly straight and sombre faces. Aleksandrov is snatched from Orlova's bed and whisked through empty streets to the Kremlin. He emerges ten minutes later without the Great Plan.

So the prime event of the hospitality evening at the Dom Kino, 13 Vasilyevskaya Street, is to be a viewing of Aleksandrov's prize-winning film *Meeting on the Elbe* (*Vstrecha na Elbe*). Expecting to wear the black tie and dinner jacket he has brought from Savile Row, Chaplin is politely advised by Nina that this is not the Communist custom – but Oona's gorgeous attire, a long gown of dazzling white silk and satin from Harrods, violates no revolutionary principles. Nina also apologies in advance for Eisenstein's absence 'indisposed'. Picasso arrives at the Dom Kino sporting a wide silk tie in psychedelic colours designed for him by Dora Maar who, for this occasion, he has decided to present as his chosen companion. Of course Olga and Nina are on hand, but dressed not too competitively (competition being exclusively Orlova's province, unwise is she who forgets it).

Grigorii Aleksandrov (once assistant to Eisenstein and famous for his Hollywood-style musicals, girl-meets-tractor) addresses the company before the screening. People's Artist of the USSR, with two Stalin Prizes under his belt, he brims with confidence:

'Honoured international guests, Maître Picasso and Maestro Chaplin – comrades. The film you are about to see was first shown to the Central Committee of our Party before general release. I shall not forget the occasion. The General Secretary himself, the Father of our People, was present. I was, to put it mildly, nervous. My heart beat was so irregular that I thought it must belong to someone else. (*Laughter.*) How does one dramatize our international relations in the correct Party perspective while entertaining our great Soviet public? When at the end of the screening the lights went up in the viewing room, our great leader rose and declared in a flat, matter-of-fact manner, *"Fil'm sniat s bol'shim znaniyem dela* – the film was shot with great knowledge of the facts.' (*Prolonged applause, no one daring to be the first to stop.*)

Aleksandrov then recalls his lightning tour of East European capitals carrying boxes of film. 'Naturally the warmongers were enraged by the success of *Meeting on the Elbe*. May I quote a sardonic report by Harrison E. Salisbury of the *New York Times*: "Muscovites see Americans Portrayed as Mata Haris, Thieves of Russian Science and Super-Knaves in Germany." Mr Salisbury also claimed in his wisdom that it was the charms of Lyubov' Orlova which brought the long queues of fans outside our cinemas. Nothing to do with the film and its exposure of American imperialists machinations – of course.'

Aleksandrov smiles down at Orlova in the front row, then glances up to the projection room and nods. The 32mm spools bring up the credits. Oona whispers to Chaplin, 'Are we going to understand a word?'

'No.'

A few moments later Picasso complains to Dora Maar and Olga, seated either side of him, that he doesn't understand a word.

Chaplin is enjoying a scene in Germany where GIs are discovered carousing in a nightclub called NIGHT CLUB. He is also amused when oddball American officers start drilling Germans in the goose-step outside the Rathaus.

Picasso, meanwhile, is taken by a scene in which the American General's wife poses for a portrait by a local artist so poor that his skeletal frame barely supports his frayed clothes. General and Mrs McDermott are seen trading cigarettes to starving Germans in return for art treasures, gold and furs. When chalking a white cross on requisitioned works of art, the Yankees apply the chalk to the canvas rather than the backing. While posing for her portrait, the General's wife (the actress Faina Ranevskaya) wears a fixed grimace like false teeth and a greedy gleam in her eye. She keeps rotating her grin back to the servile old painter, whose ludicrously flattering version of her she does not reward in cash since a can of pork meat and a packet of cigarettes will do.

'What does she say?' Picasso squeezes Olga's thigh. Olga tells him. 'Well, tell them, *devushka*,' he declares in Catalan French louder than the soundtrack, 'Picasso is not that servile old German artist and Picasso does not prostitute his talents for a tin of Yankee pork meat!'

Now the telephone rings to inform the American General that there's a fuel crisis in England. His wife advises him to cut down the local German forests and sell the wood to the English. (Too much dialogue here for Picasso and the Chaplins, despite Olga and Nina's whispered attempt to explain that the English fuel crisis is a result of capitalist collapse.)

By this stage of the film Chaplin is asking who was on whose side in which war. Chaplin hasn't forgotten that the suave Aleksandrov used to beat him at tennis when visiting Hollywood with Eisenstein. Oona likes the Shostakovich score but is less than happy to see American soldiers depicted as crass philistines with a neurotic, jack-in-the-box tendency to fidget with their pockets, their little gadgets, their cigarettes. She supposes that fidgeting is film language for guilt – but about what, she whispers loudly, saving the world from Hitler?

Now Orlova appears caked in make-up as American super-vamp spy Jeanette Sherwood. Orlova's sideways and upwards seductive glances at the Soviet hero eventually cause Oona to whisper, 'With spies like that how can we Americans lose?' A few moments later Oona loudly describes Orlova's performance as 'part-Garbo, part-Dietrich and maybe part-Orlova.' In a state of panic, Nina begs Mrs Chaplin to keep her voice down.

The film depicts the Russians as giving every encouragement to the good, democratic Germans who have survived the Nazi years. The Chaplins are loudly asking each other in which locked cupboard you find these good Germans.

During the reception that follows the screening Oona tugs Nina over to where Orlova is holding court. 'I hope all American women aren't as bad as that,' Oona says to Orlova. Nina translates. Orlova looks at Nina as if she were responsible for the remark (another slap coming?).

'I have observed such American women abroad,' Orlova tells everyone gathered around her. 'I mean women who are well groomed, well dressed, spiritually empty, without lofty strivings – *bez vysokikh stremleniĭ*. Their fluctuating loyalties are attached only to worship of the dollar. I'm sure you have met similar types, Mrs Chaplin.'

Chaplin is telling Aleksandrov that *Meeting on the Elbe* is a strange reversal of the war we fought. 'The Germans are all good and honest, except the pro-American ones, and your erstwhile allies come across as decadent vulgarians when they are not outright crooks –'

Aleksandrov begins to explain politely the necessary class perspective but Oona, on her third glass of Georgian fizz, tells everyone that Charlie has hit the nail on the head – and does anyone want to go 15 rounds with her? (During the return journey from Belye Stolby, Charlie has explained that early in their marriage Oona had picked up the Joe Louis stuff from him, and that she had never understood that a fight can go less than 15 rounds.)

By now this face-to-face is closely attended by anxious officials from the Ministry of Culture, from VOKS, from Mosfilm and whoever else. The situation is happier over in Picasso's corner, he'd loved every minute of the Yankee-bashing. Aragon and Triolet are confiding to their Russian hosts their disapproval of the Chaplins – forty years working in America, then expelled by the witch-hunters, *la chasse aux sorcières*, yet Charlot is still blinkered! Dora Maar (whether Madame Picasso or not) has drifted into her own space with her ivory cigarette holder. Quick to spot contagion, no Soviet woman approaches her.

'OK, Grigorii,' Chaplin gently takes hold of his lapels, 'when are we going to cut the crap and show *Limelight* to the great Soviet public?'

'Charlie! Charlie! We are working night and day on the sub-titles!'

'Which night and which day? And what about *Modern Times*? What about *The Great Dictator?*'

'We have Soviet versions to hand. We can show them, Charlie. Tomorrow!'

'I mean my versions.'

'Ah. I suspect that our young comrade, Nina, may have misunderstood our proposal.'

'And why did you plant a double on me pretending to be a dead man we both revere, you and I, Grigorii, yes the greatest film director of all time.'

'It was an error of judgment, Charlie. We thought meeting Sergei Eisenstein again would cheer you up. He thought so too.'

24

~

O ut of the blue, without premonition, like an unheralded vomit-attack, I heard myself asking her an utterly destructive question obviously precipitated by a mounting revulsion. And perhaps I was irritated, even humiliated, by the spectacle of her arrogantly pacing her drawing room on stiletto heels while I sat with meek knees pressed together to support my notebook. She was wearing a blue overcoat and matching hat from Harrods this morning, dressed for going out, she didn't disclose where; from the moment of my arrival she was letting me know that this interview was on a short fuse and not due to run its course. When on high heels Lady Stears was usually looking for an argument verging on a quarrel; whereas sporting jeans and moccasins, or her Kazakh slippers, she was capable of unloading a large cargo of history in a short space of time. On high heels the trials of her past were for her irritating intrusions on the important business of today and tomorrow.

My utterly destructive question was this: 'Can you be proud in retrospect, Lady Stears, to have worked for Lavrentiy Beria?'

She froze. I might have been Orlova slapping her face.

'Ah. I see. We must continue to inhabit the Cold War, is that it? Did I not defect? Isn't that enough for you?'

I remained perversely loyal to my vile question. 'Perhaps only part of you defected.'

'A historian from Oxford should understand that it wasn't all black and white for those of us living under *sauve qui peut*. I had lost my husband Sergei during the war. One learned to spell "survival" backwards. Try that with *vyzhivaniye*.'

I said that Russians born into the Soviet period have always found it difficult to come to terms with a key term in Western political science, namely 'totalitarianism' (Orwell, Arendt, etc.), which is widely regarded as the common factor linking the Nazi and Soviet regimes.

'Oxford, I don't think we can ever understand each other. Frankly, British democracy has not been so hot. What about India? What about Ireland? What about your Boer War? What about your great Empire? Who sent troops to support the White armies in my country? Who gave Arab Palestine to the Jews? Did you not yourself serve in the colonial army, massacring poor Africans in Kenya?'

'I have never been in Kenya and I have never written a word in defence of the British Empire.'

'But I am told you fired many shots into an innocent African crowd. George told me.'

'That was fiction, a novel, and not me. I was conscripted...like your husband Sergei.'

'There can be no comparison! He died for his Motherland!'

'Yes, of course.'

'Frankly, I had hoped that you would possess real wide knowledge of these things, real understanding. After all... I mean, why otherwise am I now talking to you?'

She sat down and to my surprise removed her coat and hat, throwing them on the floor as those who have servants once did. But her heels remained high.

'I will tell you something: I have been approached by two Russian historians since the collapse of the Soviet Union. They are both young men not even born at the time hoping to make money out of our tragedies. For them the Great Patriotic War is merely the favourite story of geriatrics. Terror is historians like Mr Conquest counting heads in the Gulag. They can scarcely conceal their contempt for my generation, we who had never heard of glasnost' or perestroika, of Gorbachev and Yeltsin. Why should I stuff manna from heaven into their dripping mouths?'

I had reason to suspect that her young Russian historians (if real) had been bought up by a well-funded Ivy League university press currently launching an archival blitzkrieg to set the seal on America's Thermopylae – in short by Abe Kahnleiter's CAP.

'I am grateful for your frank recall, Lady Stears. I may have said it before, but I would not have believed much of what you have told me had not Olga corroborated it.'

'But you believe Olga straight off? Is she still so beautiful? Has she shown you that famous portrait of her by Picasso?'

'Yes.'

'Frankly, Olga is much less likely to tell you the truth than I am. That experience with Pablo permanently screwed her up. I don't think Olga's life has been a happy one. Perhaps that is to say she has no wish to be a happy person. It is not her project in life. We all have a project, don't you agree, even when we don't fully recognise it. We are not alike, Olga and I, but always good friends perhaps due to a shared experience – actually I don't think she has ever felt at ease with me, she distrusts doubles. No, she despises them. They are *nekultturny*. For some time after I defected in Canada she did not answer my letters. Too dangerous for her, perhaps.'

'That was in 1974?'

'Quite so. I was working for the KGB covering Baryshnikov's tour of North America. When the dancer defected, so did Nina. It was high time.'

'You knew Mikhail Baryshnikov well?'

'Of course.'

'I believe you settled in Hollywood?'

'Settled, no. I met Marcus Epstein, a major producer with MGM. I was graduating from the female jobs, translator, gofer, costume adviser and wife – an Orthodox Jewish wedding for which I obligingly converted – but already with a small production company of my own. We moved to New York, got involved in off-Broadway theatre, staged a musical – have you heard of *One Fine Day*? – got divorced. I had moved into art fakes and Marcus thought it could damage his name. '

I remarked that I could see his point of view.

'Henry knows better. He understands what is legitimate.'

'Your present husband? You both regard fakes as legitimate?'

'You are behind the times.' She laughed in anticipation of her coming joke. 'Historians always think that today is yesterday.'

'Or more likely that yesterday is today?'

Her almond eyes registered polite appreciation. 'Believe me, Oxford, now is the time of the fake market. Henry immediately understood the potential for investment in my company. A skilled fake can be worth more than the original. It is not a hoax. Every top-class faker attaches his name as the Imaginer. "Modigliani Imagined By Leszek Kolakowski". I employ Leszek on a commission basis. There is no deception. Aficionados now recognise the inspired imagination of the artist who can create a Vermeer more Vermeer than Vermeer. The market has gone crazy for it. The Getty people in LA have taken a stake. If my friends came into this room and suspected that the Modigliani you see over there was the original, they would lose interest and zip up their pockets.'

(I wondered whether this was any better than working for Beria. Had she not always been, at root, addicted to deceit?)

But surely Sotheby's and Christie's don't go along with that?

'Not quite yet. And the big museums remain stuck in the past. But that will change. One day soon the New York Museum of Modern Art, the Tate Modern and the Beaubourg will open great new spaces devoted to Fakes. They will display the Fakes alongside original works and the public will go wild. I know all the Directors and Senior Curators – many of them. Even at the Louvre they are now interested in hanging a modern fake Mona Lisa beside the boring old one. Leszek Kolakowski may do it.'

I had to smile.

'I can see you don't believe me, Oxford. You have been trained to believe nothing. It is part of your training. That is how you have been trained. That is why so many sterile eunuchs come out of Oxford. No balls.'

I laughed and Nina laughed, too.

'What nationality is your Kolakowski?'

'None. Stateless. Polish once. He lives in Brno, Czechoslovakia.

But that was yesterday.'

'I suppose this leads on from your Moscow days as a double?'

'Could be. Requires immense skill and imagination. Would you like to see one of his latest?' She walked to an art deco wardrobe, tapped in an electronic code number, the doors grudgingly swung apart, and Lady Stears produced a painting shrouded in colourless bubblewrap.

'You can unwrap it, Oxford. I'm going to enjoy watching your face.'

They say that faces 'fall' when dismayed. If so, mine must have been through the floor. I was looking at what appeared to be a perfect copy of the portrait in Olga Lepinskaya's bedroom, the 'Small Cowper' Raphael Madonna she attributed to Picasso – with the onion domes of St Basil's in the background. I was shaking with rage.

'How did you acquire this?'

'Kolakowski. Olga once showed it to me. By the sixties we were occasionally seeing one another, no great friendship. Recently I described it to Kolakowski – easy enough, copy the "Small Cowper" and stick in St Basil's.'

'Is this meant to be by Picasso or *après* Picasso?'

'Oh Kolakowski never does the *après* stuff. It's valueless. He's not Jacques Villon. What people pay real money for is a fake.'

I studied the painting, trying to remember every detail of Olga's – the colours, the poses, the position of the baby Jesus's hands, the Virgin's hand supporting his standing position – all identical.

'Lady Stears, how much would this fake sell for?'

'For you, darling? For you, sir –' she broke off laughing. 'For a nice gentleman like you –' She doubled up. Eventually she told me that it would be beyond my means and would I like a drink.

'A double whisky.'

'And I will have a vodka tonic. Please press that bell behind you.'

The Estuary maid appeared. 'The gentleman will have a double whisky. Mine the usual.' The maid bobbed and went.

Nina refolded her legs. 'All right, I'll tell you. Do we really know who the Madonna is? If we can prove that Picasso's model was your Olga, a woman still alive, that would send the price up.'

'Who else could it be?' I asked angrily.

Nina did one of her twirls, a spinning top. 'Who knows, Oxford? It could be Oona Chaplin. If so, the price would go through the roof. Say five million dollars.'

'How much did you pay Kolakowski for it?'

'When did you last sleep with your wife? That I don't say. Lezsek is currently moving country every week and not in a position to bargain. But I might make a gift of it to you if I go on liking you.' She smiled her cat smile. 'Which do you enjoy more, talking to Olga or talking to me?'

I thought the question might go away if I didn't answer, but she was enjoying herself. The maid brought the drinks with a small Jugendstil jug of iced water. I told her half-and-half.

Lady Stears raised her glass. 'Is this to Olga or to me?'

The whisky hit my throat and flushed up into my head. 'You are very different people, you and Olga. Madame Lepinskaya doesn't have a Kolakowski. She is not wealthy. She is not well connected. She doesn't have a seat in the Centre Court at Wimbledon. She doesn't inhabit a Georgian mansion in Cheyne Walk.'

'Is that an answer, Oxford? Tell me, when you were a spotty schoolboy only a few days short of sixteen, which of us would you have hidden in your tuck box?' But then she relented (in her fashion). 'Maybe you should work for me composing catalogues. Of course even in your field there are great fakers.'

'Plagiarists, you mean?'

'No, no, a literary plagiarist never acknowledges his theft. He conceals it. I am talking about historians and scholars who write pseudonymous reviews lauding their own work. They invent spurious allegations to discredit their critics. When the ruse is discovered and they are threatened with legal action they become more famous, more in demand on television. True?'

'True.'

'So right and wrong is old stuff, cobwebbed morals for Christians. What counts now is High Profile, Fame, Celebrity, bigger sales of their books, lecture appearances round the world, television series – anything for money. Agree?'

'Yes.'

'I am already advising several notable scholars. They invite me to dine with them in their Oxbridge colleges. Of course I prefer Oxford, I wish the annual boat race came past us here in Cheyne Walk – imagine what a party we could have in this room.'

'Your view would be blocked by the trees shielding the rich from the heavy traffic along the Embankment.'

She looked startled. 'Then you are not invited. Secretly you resent "the rich" without whom there would be no culture, no art, no civilization.' You are one of those helots who go to Wimbledon to watch the tennis, your heads swinging on your rubber necks like pendulums. You are lucky to watch the boat race alongside the plebs of Hammersmith.'

I must admit I laughed. 'Please tell me, Lady Stears, these notable scholars you mentioned, do they pay for your advice?'

'Not yet. Not up-front. For good promotional results I will take a percentage of their royalties and residuals. Would you like to join my stable?'

'And that too is "legitimate"?'

'You can take a view. The law must always catch up with the market. Henry calls it the iron law of the law.'

'I would like to meet him.'

'I don't think you would. Now all the time you are asking yourself why has this Bolshevik woman settled here as Lady Stears, wife of a Bullingdon Club barrister, a silk? Does she truly love Sir Henry – or untruly? Well, I confess that I find it quite amusing to be a Lady. I have always been one of those women, you know, Bob Hope would say, "She's no lady". Now I can be lady and no lady. I can sleep with Lucian Freud one day, hobnob with ambassadors the next. Have you seen Lucian's portrait of me?'

'No. Where is it to be seen?'

'He keeps it, won't give, won't sell. I am Russian so I am always a doll, very convenient because which one. I don't look Slavic like Olga, people think I'm Italian, even Spanish, so I am always big surprise. Lady of a certain age who looks...how old do you think?'

'It depends on what mood you're in. Perhaps forty-five when happy?'

'So you mean perhaps fifty-five. Believe me, no man who has been with me will ever remember my true age. London, New York and Paris, these places are littered with men who are never forgetting me. I think Charlie Chaplin, too, but long ago. I adored his stories of Hollywood and all the famous actresses he'd known. I could mime his former wife Paulette Goddard or his present wife Oona until he didn't know which wife was pleasuring him.'

I asked whether she had ever truly believed that Chaplin would be granted the film festival she had promised him.

'Who says he didn't get it?'

'Well, I —'

'I haven't finished the story, have I? I am in Paris next week, then meeting Leszek in Vienna to discuss which Klimt to fake next, Egon Schiele too, you can come back the first Tuesday of next month. Don't look so clouded, Oxford.'

25

To play for time – and time is a variable gift of life – it has been decided that Picasso and the Chaplins should visit an eminent poet in his woodland dacha at Peredelkino, a colony granted to the Writers' Union by Stalin. The chosen poet is Boris Pasternak who remains on the approved list, his fatal novel *Doctor Zhivago* still below the radar for a further four years. Pasternak is also a noted translator of Shakespeare and of his play *Gamlet*. The only visible fly in the ointment is the internment in a concentration camp of his beloved mistress Olga Ivinskaya.

Approaching Pasternak's dacha in two large Zis limousines, they see a van departing along the narrow road, its sides carrying the printed words мясо – FLEISCH – VIANDE – MEAT. Nina calculates that the zek from Mavrino has been here setting up the microphones to record the visit of so many guests. She wonders how the zek, the self-styled writer whose surname on his identity card she remembers, gets on with a real Russian writer, a great name in the land – so unlike the naïve, untutored guests from England and America. She can imagine the zek's outrageous heresies gradually persuading Pasternak to confide, to drop his guard – and there he is, seated at Pasternak's kitchen table, coils of electronic cable littering the floor, while he devours the secret pages of Boris Leonidovich's new manuscript with the speed of a starving man offered a plate of food. Nina has heard Ehrenburg say that these secret pages are of concern to the security organs, some of whose entrapment operatives believe Pasternak is setting himself up for martyrdom and deification in the West, a dreamy, other-worldly lyric poet cruelly shouted down – an outcome to be avoided at all costs.

Pasternak is now a distant figure taking a stroll in the woods. He turns himself in their direction, waving them to join him. Oona is keen on that and out of the car, trotting ahead through the trees, a medley of evergreen firs and deciduous, panting up to the surprised poet and kissing him three times in the Russian fashion. Nina follows.

'You must be Mrs Chaplin. I am delighted to greet you.'

'Wow, you speak English.'

'Not well but I may have translated Shakespeare.'

She slips her arm though his as if she has known him (and read him) all her short life. Chaplin arrives out of breath; the tramp is wearing fine shoes but is willing to get genuine Russian mud on them.

'Maestro, welcome,' Pasternak shakes his hand. 'You and I were born within a few months of one another...a bond.'

'Well, I never met the Tsar,' Chaplin chuckles, 'he wouldn't receive me.'

'My father painted a portrait of Tolstoy,' Pasternak tells him. 'I can show it to you.'

Picasso has been grunting recalcitrantly, like a powerful Boxer dog arching its muscles to resist the lead. Olga is trying to coax him from the limousine while the rest of the French party – Triolet, Aragon and Maar – assess the prospects for their shoes. Picasso loathes scenery like this. He should be circulating the museums followed by large crowds. He observes the treetops bending under a mild wind, raindrops sparkling in the branches. He decides he is ill.

'Please come, Maître,' Olga begs. She can see that Nina has already caught up with the Chaplins and a silver-haired man of perhaps sixty who must be their host; she has heard the name Pasternak during her childhood but he is only a name.

'Come, Pablo,' Triolet leans into the car. 'In this countryside I grew up.'

'Is this where my exhibition is open to the public? In this mud patch?'

Aragon informs Picasso that Aleksandr Fadeyev can be seen approaching through the woods, a neighbour here at Peredelkino and the boss of the Soviet Writers' Union.

'The one who insulted me in Poland?'

'There was a *malentendu* in translation, Pablo.'

'Well, tell that bastard I'll kick his shins and that will be a *malentendu*.'

Aragon murmurs to Olga: 'Keep the maître away from Comrade Fadeyev.'

Pasternak is rather enjoying the company of Oona. She is light on his arm, does not disturb his knotted walking stick, and keeps tilting her smiling face up at the swirling birds – utterly charming.

'I remember the redwing during a visit to England,' he tells her – 'in the distant days when one could travel. They make such a lovely sound. Birds are far wiser than we humans. But sometimes a gale gets up and they are blown off course like we are.'

'That's so true,' she says. 'They say your poetry is profound, Boris. Of course I don't read Russian.'

He smiles. 'I have bad news for you, Mrs Chaplin. Much of it has been translated into English.'

She looks faintly disappointed, a bit burdened by this information, like a schoolgirl called back to class from her skipping rope. She has a period right now. On reaching Moscow she had briefly thought she might be pregnant, number five, but then the blood came, a little splatter, it turned out that number five was back in the pending tray. Nina has told her that the young woman Olga – you can see her over there, supporting Picasso, old grumpy – may be pregnant and is upset because she isn't sure who the father is. Nina says it could be Picasso. Oona says wow, you certainly notice how she dotes on him. It would be nice to talk to her but I messed up over Pablo's portrait, I was canned. She's quite shy about her English which is really quite OK though you wouldn't want to discuss Shakespeare with her (or with anyone actually not even nice Boris here). Well (Oona is thinking, or Nina is sure she's thinking) that Olga is quite unlike Nina who couldn't spell 'shy' if her life depended on it, it's interesting how she turns Charlie on then switches him off when his tank gets too hot but the real question is whether Nina is on the level about the

Chaplin Film Festival or about anything, you don't entirely trust her though she wouldn't steal from your purse. Maybe Russians don't exist to be understood.

'All of that is Olga's stream of consciousness according to Nina?'

'You have to remember, Oxford, that if I could be Mrs Chaplin in Charlie's bed, I could pretty well be Oona in every circumstance. It's the Stanislavsky method. Do you know about it?'

'I've read his An Actor Prepares, *published in 1936 I think.'*

'I never read,' Lady Stears says. 'Books are for squares.'

'Tell me, Boris, do Russians exist to be understood?' Oona is asking Pasternak, who looks surprised, smiles, how nicely he does that.

'Russians are enigmatic,' Chaplin intervenes. 'If you're casting a Russian character in a film you need an enigmatic actor. He'd better be Russian. There's no shortage in Hollywood.'

Oona walks at the poet's side, Chaplin trailing and falling sullen about spending a wasted day out here. Oona is telling Pasternak how Russians are really very human, they fall in love and shed tears and their children are lovely, those bright blue eyes, so questing though not entirely trusting.

Fadeyev has converged. He and Pasternak shake hands. Oona doesn't follow the exchange but gathers that this fellow Fad-something, he's an Alexander like the zek, was he a dream I wonder, I wouldn't mind bed if the zek asked me. Mr Aragon told me Fad-something had one famous novel banned, *The Young Guard*, he had to write it all over again, but then it won a Stalin Prize and now Fad-something rules the roost and you can watch him bullying Pasternak in a sort of comradely tone but I think Pasternak wishes he would go away and leave him in peace and maybe never come back.

Fadeyev moves off to join Aragon and Triolet, who greet him like royalty, the top writer of World Communism until he isn't.

Pasternak points to an old man walking some distance away but heading towards them in the company of a woman younger but not young.

'My neighbour and very dear friend Kornei Chukovsky,' Pasternak tells the Chaplins. 'And of course his daughter Lydia, also a wonderful writer although' – he drops his soft voice – 'she is currently out of favour, cannot be published, and is very close to my dear friend Anna Akhmatova.'

'That's a lot to take in,' Chaplin says. 'In favour out of favour, that's the big question here in Russia. They promised me a film festival but there's no sign of it.'

'*Did* they?' Pasternak exclaims politely, feigning ignorance. 'Something for us all to look forward to. But of course things tend to take time in Russia, Maestro.'

Chukovskaya and her father are now only fifty yards away, their faces are beginning to come into definition under the shifting shadows of the trees. Pasternak is telling the Chaplins how his dear friend Lydia wrote a novel set in these very woods here at Peredelkino, a story about a woman writer with a tragic life behind her, they'd taken her husband and executed him. She's staying at the Writers' Union resthouse down there just out of sight in the woods, and she meets a man, another writer, a war hero, and she becomes attached to him but then one day when they are out walking along these paths he stops in his tracks ashen-faced and says he has to tell her something he can no longer conceal from her – that when he was in a Soviet labour camp he did the worst possible thing because he was so hungry and needed the extra rations they gave to informers. So he informed on someone who had said to him that Stalin lost the war before the Soviet people won it.

Charlie is listening intently and Nina, trailing discreetly behind, can see from his expression that he is thinking the man in the story had been right to inform because the other man shouldn't have been saying that sort of thing about Stalin. Oona has told him that the zek said the very same thing about Stalin losing the war, so there you are.

The Chukovskys, father and daughter, are now slackening their stride because they can guess that Boris Leonidovich is telling the story he is telling, if only out of chagrin that it was suppressed by the authorities.

Anyway, in the story the woman writer never speaks to the informer again and in fact never leaves her room in case she should run into him in the corridor or the refectory, then she packs her bags and leaves the Writers' Union resthouse. But afterwards she condemns herself as narrow-minded and no better than all the others whom she thought she despised, the anti-Semites and boot-lickers.

Men like Fad-something, Oona supposes, you can see him talking to Aragon and Triolet, Oona doesn't like them, too stuck up.

Oona watches a disgruntled Picasso pulling Olga away towards the dacha. Pregnant by him? – wow.

Now Ehrenburg joins Pasternak and the Chukovskys and there are warm embraces and they are all taking care to speak English, not to let the Chaplins feel left out. Ehrenburg is explaining to them why Picasso refuses to talk to Fadeyev who had insulted him at a conference in Poland by saying why didn't he paint people who looked like people.

'You can see' (says Ehrenburg without pointing or even turning to look.) 'Aragon and Elsa Triolet trying to persuade Aleksandr Aleksandrovich to make amends to Picasso, to assure him it was all a misunderstanding.'

Oona can see that Pablo and Olga have stopped now, he with those frightening searchlight eyes of his, bulging with contempt, Charlie's the only one who isn't frightened of him, Oona thinks. Me neither ever since I butted his backside in Paris. But he got his revenge in that fucking studio of his and how I bet that woman Olga's conception wasn't too fucking immaculate.

'You look troubled, Mrs Chaplin,' Nina says.

'We should head home,' Pasternak says.

'I heard about your wonderful story,' Oona tells Lydia Chukovskaya. 'I'd like to read it.'

'I am so pleased to meet you, Mrs Chaplin. And I do hope to

wangle a ticket to your husband's film festival. My father and I would love to see *Modern Times* and *The Great Dictator* in the original.'

Oona grips this good woman by the arm. 'Tell me, Lydia, do you think they'll go through with it?'

'Isn't that why they invited you?'

'It's becoming a case of yes but.'

Nina comes up now and reports to Oona that poor Olga is having a hard time with the maître, he's rooted to the spot and demanding to be taken straight home to Paris. And Dora Maar is just standing immobile and apart, neither here nor there. Oona is sure that bitch Olga won't allow herself to break down and cry in front of guests from the West, I just know I could never be a Communist, not after meeting Mr Zek. Charlie should have accepted that brown paper parcel but he gets furious if I say so.

Pasternak is walking on with practised strides, prodding tufts of grass with his knotted stick, heading up to the dacha in the company of Ehrenburg. The Chaplins catch up, the Chukovskys following, Nina nowhere in particular but never out of earshot, that's her job, always. And reading Oona's mind, that's almost a hobby, jealous of Olga can you believe it.

'Ilya and I were talking about the German playwright Brecht,' Pasternak confides to the Chaplins.

Chaplin laughs at Ehrenburg. 'What Brecht again, Ilya?' Ehrenburg bridles a bit and says they are discussing Brecht's play *Galileo*. Pasternak smiles in his gentle way, he's extremely handsome, and says he has translated some of Brecht's poems from the German into Russian. Ehrenburg explains that the Vachtangov Theatre had wanted to produce *Galileo*, and they came to me, did I know the play? I told them it could not be staged in Russia. And do you know why? Ehrenburg is smiling licentiously (Nina thinks) at Oona, inviting her to give an opinion why *Galileo* cannot be staged in Russia.

'That's obvious,' Chaplin says, although the only obvious thing is that Pasternak and Ehrenburg seem to prefer talking to

Oona rather than to him, which Oona is happy about, and why old men prefer pliant females preferably pretty ones who don't contradict everything as I do when things don't plan out my way. So Oona is now saying she thinks *Galileo* is a progressive play and after all the Soviet Party believes in science and the earth rotating round the sun, doesn't it? I mean Galileo is a lone scientist bravely defying the authorities, the Church, isn't he?

Pasternak and Ehrenburg glance at one other, as if each wants the other to tell her, then Ehrenburg cups his hand under Oona's elbow: 'Well, Oona, Galileo defies the authorities who threaten him with the instruments of torture.'

'But it was the medieval Catholic Church!' she protests.

'It still is,' Chaplin says. 'And my friend Bert Brecht knows it. Rule One: nobody must step out of line. Not even if his name is Chaplin.'

They have arrived at the front door of Pasternak's 1930s-style dacha, fronted by two storeys of bay windows in the style of the bridge of a modern liner. The upper one is Pasternak's study.

'Please come in. My wife hates mud brought into the house. I can lend you all some slippers, or most of you, I can't guarantee they'll fit. I think we may be able to find some green tea.'

There are rather a lot of them for slippers: Ehrenburg, Fadeyev, Chaplin, Oona, Nina; Picasso, Maar, Aragon, Triolet, Olga; the Chukovskys.

While discarding his muddy shoes Kornei Chukovsky is addressing Chaplin in wonderful English, 'We're all pretty much contemporaries, Maestro. I was born in 1882, the year after they assassinated Tsar Alexander. I remember seeing *The Tramp* shortly after our Revolution but for the life of me I can't recall where.'

So they all crowd in and are greeted by Zinaida Pasternak, a homely figure who ushers them into slippers and chairs and speaks only Russian, enlisting Olga and Nina in the distribution of biscuits and glasses of tea, she being the kind of senior lady whose bidding it is a pleasure for young women to accept. Olga has never set eyes on Pasternak but from rumours filtering through the

Pushkin Museum she can guess how Madame Zinaida feels in the presence of guests well aware of this cruel domestic façade, the legendary poet's heart aching for Madame Ivinskaya, deprived of her job at the literary magazine *Novyi mir* then sent to Siberia even though a mother and pregnant with Pasternak's child. Olga knows herself to be pregnant by another great man whose heart manifestly does not ache for her or for anyone. They say Madame Ivinskaya had aborted in her prison camp. Olga is handing round biscuits. Everyone is chewing biscuits.

They drift upstairs to Pasternak's spacious study overlooking the woodland which extends down to a narrow road where an MVD car is parked day and night, watching. Fadeyev has already positioned himself in Pasternak's private workspace, taking down one book after another from the shelves. Instead of placing them back where they came from, he tosses them onto the writer's desk as if accumulating a pile for an indictment. Shakespeare of course but here is James Joyce's *Ulysses*, here the works of Franz Kafka, the plays of Frank Wedekind, some Hemingway, Proust of course, Eliot and Pound, Thomas Mann, plays and poems by Brecht (with Pasternak's translations). Ehrenburg watches Fadeyev as if reminded of the unacceptable paintings which cover his own apartment's walls in Moscow. Fadeyev is the writer currently closest to Stalin and worth observing. He has denounced Jewish cosmopolitans, his goose-step is highest. It is little comfort that the writer closest to Stalin may not expect a long life in the role, or a long life. They say that Fadeyev's novel-in-progress is called *Ferrous Metallurgy*, what a promising title! Two Orders of Lenin already! Ehrenburg gets this on the grapevine which runs through the Writers' Union to the major publishing houses, but editors are not above feeding him false information to see what he does with it when he travels abroad under special license as the figurehead of the Peace Movement. This same year, 1952, Ehrenburg has been awarded the Stalin Peace Prize. He has denounced Israel and Zionism (though he will secretly bequeath his papers to Israel), but there is no guarantee, no security: on each occasion he could return to Russia with his snowy old head under his arm.

Ehrenburg takes note that the author of *The Young Guard* has not yet spoken to the Chaplins, partly because they have never heard of him, partly because he finds talking through an interpreter aggravating. Mrs Chaplin's high, vacuous laugh belongs to just another American birdbrain, a poop. Fadeyev has been monitoring this Picasso-Chaplin enterprise and Ehrenburg's seminal part in it. He is not so powerful that he can yet make a move or know which one to make. Beria is out there, somewhere, the spider at the centre of a vast intelligence web, of an MVD 'police' force equipped with tanks, and neither Fadeyev nor his vodka bottle (yes, he too) can be sure from hour to hour where the chess pieces lie on the board. Examining Pasternak's incriminating library is a substitute for action, therapy almost, but Aleksandr Fadeyev is burning with chagrin over Picasso's ostracism. After all, the rebuke he conveyed to Picasso in Poland four years ago, urging him to paint humans like humans, was merely socialist common sense. Pasternak's precious books are flopping onto the table, tossed down regardless of their age or the condition of their spines. Picasso's outburst – 'I'll kick his shins' – could determine the outcome of this frivolous little adventure.

While walking in the woods, Louis Aragon has been explaining to Fadeyev the uses and abuses of indirect monologue. 'Indirect monologue allows the characters to act as porter for the author's luggage, very useful and tailor-made for socialist realist fiction.' Fadeyev is not really listening but Aragon ploughs on: 'I'm currently planning another big novel about popular resistance in France to American penetration; *les dockers* of Toulon will bring to a halt arms shipments to Indo-China, along with importations of Coca-Cola. Of course Elsa has more than once warned me that I'm no good with proletarian characters, I don't seem to have the ear for it.'

Fadeyev knows that. Aragon is more at home excoriating the rich – he can live with that, and with being rich. Fadeyev reckons that since Napoleon's time the *frantsuzyi* have always lost their wars though invariably found sipping champagne at the victors' table.

'*You divined all this, Lady Stears?*'

'*Me and you together, Oxford. Ehrenburg liked to talk to me, he explained more than I wanted to know but I'm relying on you to invade the heads of the old literary men, the heavyweights. They're out of my league.*'

Ehrenburg reads Fadeyev's thoughts accurately enough but cannot know that Fadeyev, who has called Stalin the world's 'greatest humanist', will lose his job and his life after the death of the great Helmsman. He will shoot himself here at his dacha in Peredelkino. Pasternak will offer a token epigram.

Fadeyev, the self-appointed master of ceremonies, invites their host to tell them about the novel he has been working on for years. Pasternak stands embarrassed, a lock of fine, silvery hair falling forward over high forehead. He shrugs diffidently, he must not say anything to worsen the predicament of his beloved companion Ivinskaya in her concentration camp.

'I am probably discovering, Aleksandr Aleksandrovich, that I am not a novelist only a poor poet.'

'But you have shown some pages to Fedin,' the tall Fadeyev insists. 'When I asked to read them, Konstantin Aleksandrovich made excuses to me, your General Secretary and Chairman.'

He means the Writers' Union. Pasternak gazes out of the window.

'Tell your foreign guests about the foreign writers you have most admired,' Fadeyev persists in Russian. 'Do you admire the pederast André Gide, for example?'

Olga and Nina whisper translations to their guests, though Picasso's eyes are closed.

'*L'Immoraliste* and *La Porte étroite*, yes certainly,' Pasternak nods.

'Suitable for Soviet youth, would you say?'

Ehrenburg murmurs to Olga, 'Nothing is suitable for Soviet

youth.' Pasternak's embarrassed answer is lost. He takes down from the shelves one of the few volumes to have survived Fadeyev's desecration. It is a collection of Brecht's poetry into which he has inserted, leaf by leaf, his own translations not only into Russian but also into English.

'Here I have Bertolt Brecht. May I crave your attention for a moment?' he says softly. He begins to read from his English version:

'Last night I dreamt I saw fingers pointing at me

'As at a leper. They –'

Fadeyev immediately breaks in, always in Russian:

'Well, if Comrade Brecht chooses to call himself a leper, who are we to argue with him?'

'But he doesn't,' Pasternak says firmly. '"As at a leper" is what he writes.'†

'Your shelves are full of Franz Kafka,' Fadeyev continues. 'Did not the Jew Kafka depict Man as helplessly lost to forces beyond his control? Is he not admired by Sartre and the existentialists?'

Pasternak nods politely. 'I expect so. I have never met Sartre.'

At this there is an unexpected disturbance from the chair on which Picasso is uncomfortably perched. He has picked up the word 'Sartre'. He pinches Olga and demands to know what has been said. She whispers that esteemed Comrade Fadeyev has likened Monsieur Sartre to the decadent Franz Kafka.

'Who's that?'

'I haven't read him, Maître. He may be dead, forgive my ignorance.'

'But Sartre is not dead!' Picasso protests loudly. 'I had dinner with him only last month. So did Friend Chaplin here.'

'And he's no taller than either of us, Pablo,' quips Chaplin.

Fadeyev, who has been following this with difficulty, decides to

---

† In fact this Brecht poem, 'Nasty Morning', was certainly written at a later date. Lepinskaya remembered Pasternak opening a book to recite but could not recall what, only Fadeyev cutting him short. I have chosen a line from 'Nasty Morning' because it provides Fadeyev with the word 'leper'.

drop his interrogation of Pasternak. Ehrenburg emits a far from inaudible sigh of relief. He has not been shown a page of Pasternak's manuscript novel and can only go on rumour from Konstantin Fedin, Pasternak's friend and neighbour (but not here today, why?). If you listen to Fedin, a member of the editorial board of *Novyi mir*, then Pasternak is engaged in a disastrous enterprise whose nature he does not fully grasp. He innocently believes himself to be relating the story of a fictional doctor-poet, Yuri Zhivago, who just happens to write poems written by Pasternak and who suffers (Pasternak modestly puts it), his 'ups and downs...perhaps mainly downs'. But – Fedin confides to Ehrenburg, 'and this must go no further, Ilya Grigoryevich' – the emerging novel is in obvious danger of amounting to 'an indictment of our entire Bolshevik Revolution. Yes, from the heart and from the head.'

For example: post-Revolutionary Moscow is depicted as descending into squalid filth and anarchy, leaving decent citizens at the mercy of any bunch of ruffians calling themselves Bolsheviks.

For example: when during the Civil War the Red partisans kidnap this doctor, the reader has to share the deep revulsion he feels.

For example: Zhivago is deeply religious (Pasternak is a Jewish convert to Christianity), and a 'White' to the depths of his murky soul.

For example: The woman Lara who Yuri Zhivago loves, the heroine of the novel, denounces Lenin and his colleagues as 'power mad despots' – or words to that effect. Lara is destined for years in a Siberian labour camp.

'I am sure,' Fedin has told Ehrenburg, 'that even Boris Leonidovich's friends, people like Lydia Chukovskaya and her mentor Anna Akhmatova, will find the novel fatally flawed as a work of literature.'

'Have you tried to persuade him to abandon it, Konstantin Aleksandrovich?'

'He is stubborn. He surely cannot have forgotten what happened to his friend Mandelstam.'

'I know he hasn't forgotten. Boris Leonidovich may be in quest of martyrdom.'

'The darling of the West, yes.'

Some of this Ehrenburg will confide to the Chaplins during the slow, traffic-congested drive back to Moscow, his hand on Nina's knee; some of it she will leave, forty years later, to her Oxford inquisitor's appetite for exegesis. Not a ghost of it would flicker through forthcoming volumes of Ehrenburg's memoirs. The man by then in power, Nikita Sergeyevich Khrushchev, was too predictably unpredictable.

Fortunately, much of this account was confirmed by Olga, who remembered adoring Pasternak while detesting Fadeyev. I did in fact show a draft of this chapter to Lady Stears, mainly for accuracy, but she said she couldn't remember which of these conceited literati had been saying what or why. Oona had enjoyed herself immensely but Chaplin himself was 'utterly freaked-out' by the whole event.

26

Early in 1995, at Lady Stears's firm request (excuses not on the menu), I took her to dinner in All Souls College, where I was a *quondam* and women guests were no longer subjected to the prevailing misogyny of the late Warden Sparrow regarding the Ladies' Nights he loathed. The prospect excited her enormously. She asked what she should wear and I chose (or counselled) her dark silk japonaiserie jacket over a sleeveless scarlet dress to guard against the draughts in the great hall where dinner would be served. Ivan drove us up through the Chiltern gap and, on reaching our destination, mistily recorded by Turner, had to be persuaded not to park the Silver Cloud on the quadrangle lawn made famous by the trespass of Svetlana's husband Mitya. The incoming Rolls was in fact thwarted by a stout medieval gate and a stout medieval porter.

All the way from Cheyne Walk, Lady Stears had chatted about fake art deco and its limitless commercial horizons. She had seen an exhibition that traced the 'style', as she called it, from the time that art nouveau slid out of fashion through to its zenith at the 1925 Paris Exhibition – although in commercial terms (we were passing Northolt aerodrome) that had been 'mouse cheese' compared to the 1939 New York World's Fair, when deco went 'through the roof'.

And why was I wearing my usual 'Oxford long face'? Was I too ignorant to realise that deco had transformed the look of everything, from factories and cinemas to fashion and photography: from painting and sculpture (Fernand Léger and Sonia Delaunay), to glass, metal, Cartier jewellery, to industrial design, fashion (Jeanne Lanvin and Coco Chanel). And film. Had I never passed through the glittering foyer of the Strand Palace Hotel?

(No.)

'You can't abide anything that's popular, Oxford. That's why all English snobs are anti-American while scuttling across the pond to collect their lecture fees. Oscar Wilde, yes? You can bet those Bloomsbury characters looked down their noses at deco. Over Virginia Woolf's dead body would you see any deco in Tavistock Square or wherever she gazed at her navel.'

'Almost certainly true. No chrome for Virginia.'

I had discovered that Nina was a magpie for validated literary names but there was no evidence that she had ever read anything, anywhere, in any language. I was far from sure that she had ever learned to read the English she spoke so fluently. On the rare occasions when I accompanied her to an exhibition she would ask me with a distracted air what the captions said as if she were too busy looking at the artworks themselves. There were no books or newspapers visible in her home though I was never invited to penetrate Sir Henry's study in what she called the Library.

The painting Nina most adored (we are through the Chiltern gap and passing the village of Watlington, hidden from view) was *Jeune fille en vert* (1927) by Tamara de Lempicka. She had plans for Leszek Kolakowski to mass-produce Imagined versions, each one subtly different. 'Deco shouted a tribute to the age of film,' Nina told me. 'It echoed yet defied the recent cubist heritage.' But the green woman's bare left arm was the mystery, it troubled Nina. It was too big, too swollen, and its culminating hand resembled a creepy claw of disease-thinned fingers within a white glove.

'But Leszek is adamant – you have to copy all that faithfully.'

I commented that the presiding female image in *Jeune fille en vert* was listless, vulgar and decadent; it was everything a good Soviet girl was taught not to be.

'I expect your friend Olga would agree with you. She's still a "good Soviet girl" at heart.'

As Ivan commanded the fast lane at speeds up to 100 m.p.h., I tried coaxing Lady Stears back to Chaplin's *The Great Dictator* and *Modern Times* – why exactly had they been banned in Stalin's Russia? Nina dismissed all such probes with a contemptuous 'Do you never stop working, Oxford? Nothing better in your life?'

Her eyes misted over as she described Lempicka's extravagant parties whose guests were invited to lick titbits off the bodies of naked servants, snort cocaine from silver teaspoons, and crumble pellets of hash into sloe gin.

I dared to point out that the house she currently inhabited in Cheyne Walk was scarcely art deco, apart from a few items of furniture.

'I am always telling Henry we must do a makeover. But he thinks dubious investment when we may have to scuttle any minute.'

(I should have taken that remark more seriously, but dismissed it.)

I asked whether she had ever gone in search of Oona Chaplin while living in America.

'Not on your life! Is she still alive?'

'She died in September 1991.'

'What a pity! Oxford could have made a pilgrimage to check out my story.'

(I had indeed thought of that but *Operatsiya Dvoinik* had most unfortunately been unknown to me while Mrs Chaplin had been alive.)

I warned her that in the course of the evening ahead she might meet the real Leszek Kolakowski, a renowned philosopher in exile from Poland who believed that we learn history not in order to know how to behave or how to succeed, but to know who we are. Nina re-folded her legs at that and said she knew who she was without diving into the archives. Only squares tied themselves in knots in tormented pursuit of the truth.

'And what is true? Was I untruthful with Chaplin when he mistook me for Oona? Did I ever say, I am your wife? A fake is always true to true.'

She was certainly more fun than Olga, who could sometimes

be likened to a Madame Tussaud's waxwork of Princess Grace, with press-button tears. Unlike Olga, Nina was not to be petrified, turned to stone, by any one episode in her life. She resisted the stifling embrace of passing time, she hijacked each new year offered to her.

I began to fear that this deco monologue and its naked servants might continue to run its course over pre-dinner drinks and right through dinner in All Souls. But I need not have worried, Nina always knew where she was, she had a sense of occasion. Admittedly an old philosopher clutching a glass of sherry was informed that F. Scott Fitzgerald admired Lempicka, who was now collected by Madonna, Barbra Streisand and Jack Nicholson. The old philosopher shook with delight, you could have licked him off the carpet. Indeed some of the Fellows began to glance at me with a hint of admiration never previously manifest.

Arriving in the hall, where the tables were loaded with silver, Nina studied the portraits of former fellows and *quondams* keenly, clearly weighing up the opportunities for fakes. She wanted to know whether any of the distinguished gentlemen portrayed in gilded frames around the hall might be interested in a sitting for Kolakowski (hers). I had to confide that most of them were dead, notably Prime Minister Salisbury and the Viceroys Curzon and Halifax, who had earned their place over the high table by grinding Indians into submission.

We were now seated, she on my right. I noticed she declined to read the menu card.

'But who is famous dining here tonight?' she whispered. 'Who's a real celebrity?'

'Do you mean who is most likely to present a television series about Hadrian's Wall?'

'A celebrity is someone who's in the news even when he or she hasn't done anything. The journalists invent a story as a pretext for posting a pic of the celebrity.'

'I assure you none of these people here fit that description except perhaps Isaiah Berlin – though he would cavil, despising the press while adoring it.'

'Well, where is he?'

'He's that one up there on the high table beside the Warden.'

'The ugly one in horn-rimmed glasses?'

'Yes.'

'Does he know he's a celebrity?'

'Yes.'

'Does he like it?'

'He regards it as a disaster which somehow overtook him while writing an indecipherable paragraph six pages long.'

'Is that a lot or a little?'

'A little of it is a lot.'

'Has anyone done his portrait in oils?'

'Sir Lawrence Gowing, oil on canvas, 1982. There may be others.'

'Worth faking?'

'You can view it in the National Portrait Gallery.'

When over coffee I introduced her to a nice young Fellow who knew more about Pushkin than Pushkin, it was a pleasure to hear Nina burst into her native Russian. When he asked her whether she had ever visited Aleksandr Pushkin's schoolroom in the former Imperial lycée at Tsarskoye Selo, she lightly lifted his lapel.

'No, never, I was raised in the Caucasus, but do you know Konstain Simonov's poem "Wait For Me"?'

'Yes, I remember it,' he said.

'But not as I do.'

She then launched into a charming rendition, in Russian of course, her high voice turning the old grey heads in the Fellows' common room where women's voices had rarely been heard – or when heard not raised. Even Salisbury, Curzon and Halifax (though no longer visible from their eternal stasis in the Hall) must surely have stirred from their long reverie about dealing firmly yet compassionately with massive Indian famines induced by British tariff policy.

So Nina, Lady Stears, in Russian:

'Wait for me, and I'll come back!

'Wait with all you have!'

But then longevity and the evening's wine made a grab at her, she faltered, gallantly recovered – but some lines later:

'Wait, though they with whom you wait

'Doubt if I'm alive.'

In the smoking room overlooking the Fellows Garden I showed her some portrait sketches of T.E. Lawrence of Arabia which awakened Nina's interest because she had seen the David Lean film starring Peter O'Toole. I failed to restrain her when a miniature Minox camera disguised as an onyx cigarette lighter emerged from her handbag – clearly Lawrence was destined to take his fatal motorcycle ride while heading for the studio of her Kolakowski.

Ivan drove us home at speed constantly flashing his lights at any vehicle impudently observing the speed limits. Putting Simonov behind her, she began to hum Bob Dylan's 'Desolation Row', which she'd heard him sing at a gig in California, 'You belong to me I believe' painfully echoing Simonov's 'Wait for me'. She then confided how she was planning to sell a fake Lempicka to a jejeune member of the Monaco royal family in a back room at Colnaghi's. Then, as the street lights of outer London and red-ringed speed signs signalled an obligatory reduction (but not to Ivan), Lady Stears dreamily asked whether there had ever been a homosexual Fellow of All Souls.

I laughed.

Always pleased with her own prejudices, she declared that Russians had no time for homosexuals – too many of them in London. I commented that Russians and Muslims shared a special gift for intolerance.

'That is decadent Western permissiveness. You will be overrun by immigrants. Your civilization will not survive it.'

I felt constrained to point out that only one of my four grandparents was British by birth. 'My mother is Jewish. Her parents were from Galicia. They fled from the pogroms.' Sensing the shock in her silence, I added: 'Your Oxford is a mongrel.'

Nina absorbed this. 'Tell me, Oxford, do you believe in *The Protocols of the Elders of Zion*? True or false?'

'A forgery.'

'But forgeries can be more true than the truth.' Her finger touched my chin, 'Like the book you are writing about me.'

'Have you thought about giving me that painting, Kolakowski's version of the "Small Cowper"?'

'Please don't spoil a lovely evening. Ask me when I'm awake.'

The rest of our journey passed in silence. As Ivor sped us under the Hangar Lane roundabout, the drowsy head of an exotic anti-Semite of seventy years had come to rest lightly on my shoulder. I had never before imagined her as someone who ever slept.

27

~

F or the benefit of the distinguished foreign guests, but to
Chaplin's mounting exasperation, we are back in Kino 1 for
a private screening of Chiaureli's film *Padeniya Berlina, The Fall
of Berlin*. Nina has warned Aleksandrov that Chaplin is close to
packing his bags, but has been curtly told to mind her own
business and to keep 'the old man happy by any means'.
Picasso's French contingent have turned out in force, in happy
expectation of further massacres of the Anglo-Saxons and their
dastardly plotting to do a deal with Hitler at Russia's expense.
Between the French intellectuals and the Chaplins a minimum
of cordiality now prevails, you might as well try to swim the
Channel in a blizzard.

As usual the select audience is small, no journalists present.
Soon the projectors are humming.

At the Yalta Conference a bloated, oily-eyed Churchill, wearing
a sky-blue, Latin-American version of an RAF uniform, is found
making machiavellian predictions while puffing at a cigar.
Unmoved, Stalin, also a smoker, calmly unfolds his plan to win
the war, with FDR nodding in benign agreement.

Chaplin is already restless. 'That is not the Winston Churchill
I know,' he says loudly.

As the Russian troops approach Hitler's bunker, the Führer
finally marries his mistress. Before the couple commit suicide Eva
Braun first feeds the cyanide sandwich to their dog. A fanatical
Frau Goebbels does the same for her many children.

'Did that really happen?' asks an appalled Oona.

'That's fascist motherhood,' Nina whispers.

Celebrating victory, the entire Red Army assembles on a Berlin
airfield and gazes up in awe as Stalin's fighter-escorted plane
descends. Adulation reaches religious proportions while a white-
tunic'd Stalin (Mikheil Gelovani) walks in slow inspection of
banners dedicated to Himself, to the sound of Shostakovich's

messianic choral music. Hero and heroine, Alyosha and Natasha, are reunited, embrace, and are then led before Stalin. Natasha half-touches him (or his hem) as if he were the living god.

Aragon and Triolet lead the prolonged applause. After the screening the proud director, Mikheil Edisherovich Chiaureli, explains to his foreign guests the superiority of Soviet film stock, the colour-palette richness of the scene which honours 'the standard-bearer of peace, the leader and teacher of toiling mankind, the torch-bearer of freedom.'

Chaplin is still gnawing the Churchill bone: 'I know Winston personally,' he keeps repeating.

Chiaureli offers a gesture of consolation: 'But we know him as the man who thwarted the desperately needed second front. You yourself, Maestro Chaplin, were nobly calling for that second front from American platforms.'

Chaplin is further roused: 'Don't forget that Churchill resisted Hitler for two years, by land, sea, and air, while Russia stayed out of it. Where was the "second front" while my native London was burning?'

'That was the imperialist phase and the phoney war, *la drôle de guerre*,' Aragon declares loudly.

Chaplin then points out that Stalin's descent from the sky over Berlin in 1945 was entirely fictitious.

'Wow!' exclaims Oona. 'I never knew that!'

'Poet's license,' Mikheil Gelovani, no longer Stalin today, winks uneasily at the French.

'*Symbolique,*' Aragon is heard. 'Socialist realism in art,' he goes on, 'is aspirational, it transcends banal naturalism. It speaks of today, it sings of tomorrow.'

'That's all crap, whatever it means,' Chaplin says.

'It's crap,' Oona says.

Chiaureli struggles to explain. 'The scene of Comrade Stalin's descent on Berlin was inserted to inspire the broad masses. Sometimes history requires a little assistance from the imagination.'

'You certainly directed this film as if your life depended on it,' Chaplin says. 'With a lot of help from Shostakovich's score.'

At this an odd thing happens, no, astonishing. From an obscure corner of the screening room a man stands up who bears an uncanny resemblance to Dmitri Shostakovich. Twitching, peering from behind porthole glasses, a sardonic grimace etched into his prematurely eroded features, he has to be the usual double – but is he? Can he be the great composer who had kept a bag packed night after night in 1936 and again in 1948? The defeated figure who had read his servile speech to the Waldorf Conference like an automaton? He is now addressing Chaplin, no doubt about it.

'My friend Chiaureli is tone-deaf and can't distinguish a bassoon from a clarinet or a piano from a toilet bowl. I remember when they first showed *Padeniya Berlina* to Stalin. Our friend Mikheil Chiaureli was brought in to the screening room along with Gelovani and searched fifteen times on the way. As usual, Stalin was seated in the back row, behind the members of the Politburo he has dragged in – he likes to watch the hair on the necks standing upright. Chiaureli sat petrified. He had turned into a giant receiver set – every squeak and cough from the back row seemed to seal his fate. Then Stalin's secretary, Poskrebyshev, came in with a despatch. The director heard Stalin growling, "What kind of rubbish is this?" Chiaureli thought he meant the film, fainted, fell to the floor, and was given the kiss of life by Gelovani before being carried out. And they didn't give him a new pair of pants for the ones he'd soiled either.'

No one speaks. Dmitri Shostakovich walks out looking like an ageing schoolboy. No one moves to intercept him. No doubt he will walk home, he chooses to walk because music fills his ears.

On their way back to *ulitsa* Gorky, Chaplin asks Nina whether that was the composer himself. 'I mean the real one.'

'Real.'

Oona says: 'I shall never forget hearing Dmitri's Leningrad Symphony when Toscanini conducted it across America on NBC.

Dmitri even appeared on the cover of *Time* magazine wearing a fireman's helmet.'

'Yes, so you told us at the Ehrenburgs',' Nina says coldly.

'So maybe I did! And what have they done to the man? We're told that yesterday *Pravda* condemned Dmitri's new symphony for "crude lapses into cacophonous... something".'

'Cosmopolitan cacophonous formalism,' Nina says. 'I think today was his little bit of revenge...perhaps.'

'It will blow over, it always does.' Chaplin offers the male's consoling wisdom. 'Stalin is not vindictive, he can ride with the punches like Joe Louis.'

As they reach *ulitsa* Gorky through a blizzard giant snow ploughs can dimly be seen lumbering from nowhere to nowhere. Nina will have to struggle home alone – once the Chaplins have disembarked, the chauffeur no longer recognises her.

***

Ekaterina and Olga are walking in Gorky Park on either side of a young man with a consumptive pallor, Olga supporting him, re-wrapping a long scarf which persists in drifting loose from his gaunt neck, guiding his feet away from the deeper snow-puddles. Smaller than Sokol'niki and more intimate, Gorky Park is a fairyland in winter, filled with music and ice-rinks and hundreds of shouting youngsters. Here Pyotr as a Moscow boy used to come for Pioneer choral concerts and skating. This year the park's fountains already threaten to freeze solid, an apt symbol, Pyotr comments too loudly, of the Stalin era on its last legs. Wearing the rubber boots popular since the war, although the old *valenki* felt boots were warmer, if ugly and clumsy, his breathing is laboured following a bout of pneumonia in Lefortovo prison. A week longer in there, Ekaterina has told him, and you wouldn't have survived.

'How are you feeling, Pyotr?' Every few minutes she asks him how he is feeling. She has not noticed the two MGB men who now shadow him everywhere.

'The same as a moment ago' he murmurs through raw lungs, impervious to the dementia progressively stealing her mind.

'How are you feeling?' Ekaterina asks him. 'Do you have enough to eat, Pyotr?'

Olga says, 'Hush, Mamochka. Madame Maar has been giving me extra rations to build Pyotr up, she has been very kind.'

Pyotr nods from within his swaddling scarf. 'Dora Maar bought two canvases and showed me some of her own sketches of Moscow. She has a good eye and is afraid Picasso will carry Olga back to France.'

Ekaterina does not understand, or pretends not to. 'And will you marry Ochka?' she asks him.

'Oh Mama,' Olga protests, 'Pyotr doesn't believe in settling down.'

'Nor did our beloved Vincent,' her mother muses. 'Many women would have liked to be Vincent's "devoted companion". Oh yes, when our Vincent comes in from a day's work with easel and canvas, I always meet him with a chicken bubbling in the pot, fragrant with thyme, rosemary, garlic, tarragon.'

Ekaterina is chuckling while watching Vincent eat.

'Oh blessed Provence,' Pyotr murmurs caustically. 'Olga's chosen heaven.' (No better proof of his coming recovery than the revival of sarcasm, Olga thinks.)

Although her mother may not exactly remember how they travelled to Gorky Park, and may confuse Kemenev with Khrushchev among her ogres, she retains a sharp sense of the geography of human relationships. Ekaterina wonders why Olga and Pyotr never seem to meet alone; they need a buffer and Olga is clearly – in an unclear world – not as happy with Pyotr as one might hope. He too, but he's always been like that. Ekaterina knows from Olga that his sudden release is down to Picasso, even if the sequence of events eludes her, and she suspects that Pyotr is resentful of the gratitude expected of him. Indeed she has heard him claim that the untimely intervention of 'beau monde meddlers' had let 'them', his jailers, off the hook.

'And what can I expect from them when the great maître goes home to France?' he asks rhetorically.

One thing Ekaterina does recall quite clearly is the arrival of a taxi disgorging Dora Maar during Olga's working hours at the Pushkin. Maar has ventured on a secret visit, how on earth did she contrive it without the language, to find the tiny apartment lost in the grimly uniform façades of a *ulitsa* barely visible on the smudged street map? She brought with her a large, heavily laden bag. Despite the surprise and the embarrassment of being discovered in old clothes, Ekaterina's rusty French proved up to it and she found herself charmed by a small, handsome woman who pretended not to notice the miserably cramped conditions in which she and Olga live.

'*Of course, as I've said, Monsieur, I was not there when Madame Maar arrived, so I have to paraphrase what my mother told me afterwards. Dora never spoke of it.*'

'*Understood, Madame. Perhaps you have also imagined your mother's thoughts in Gorky Park?*'

'*I could read her thoughts as if they were my own.*'

Dora Maar does not divest herself of her fur coat. It is not warm in here despite one of those big Russian stoves.

– You must be pleased about Pyotr's release, Madame Lepinskaya. Picasso himself is delighted, he thinks his exhibition can now go ahead. But please tell me, I am concerned for Olga, have she and Pyotr been happy together since his release?

Ekaterina freezes like the hedgehogs at her now sadly disused dacha. Olga used to bring them milk.

– Hm. Olga and Pyotr, you ask. It takes time. Men come home from wars, or from the Gulag, but the first embrace doesn't last for ever.

– Does Olga speak of her time in France? Do you think she might be in love with Picasso?

– In love! Thank you for explaining your visit. Good heavens, no! The man's seventy something! When Ochka and I fantasise it's about Van Gogh – safer with the dead. Mind you, no woman could avoid vertigo seated in Vincent's high-backed chairs all at odds with gravity.

– Yes, but Olga is hardly likely to be pregnant by the blessed Van Gogh.

– Pregnant?

– I just wondered.

– *Enceinte?* My Ochka!

They sit in silence, sipping tea, Ekaterina trying to remember her visitor's name. Then she smiles her crooked smile.

– Tell you what.

– Yes, Madame?

– If you can persuade Picasso to visit Pyotr's studio, we can destroy the Soviet regime.

– *Vous croyez vraiment?* The Soviet regime is the most powerful on earth. I don't mean armaments, I mean its grip on the souls of the people.

– No, no, the Gulag regime is brittle, fragile, a dinosaur about to suffer a stroke. When the heart stops the largest beast on earth falls down. It was the same thing with Hitler – how he toppled into the dust. In the end he had to burn himself and Frau Eva Braun with the help of cans of gasoline. Our Führer will be no different.

Maar gazes at her in bewilderment. – But Madame, your daughter is a Party member. She told me, most severely, that Trotskyists are wreckers and saboteurs.

– I'm sure she's right. But who's a Trotskyist? My late husband? Do you know about Maksim Petrovich? Believe me, the only real Trotskyist was Trotsky.

– Madame, please tell me, has Picasso ever come here to see Olga?

– Here? Never. Mind you, I'd like to meet him. I suppose you feel privileged to have slept with him.

Maar nods politely, without any indication of sentiment, sits for a while longer in silence, then presents the large bag laden with groceries and tinned food.

– I hope these may speed Pyotr's recovery. Thank you for receiving me without warning.

She rises, puts on her gloves, gives Ekaterina a shy embrace, explains that her taxi is waiting outside, and gropes for a light in the ill-smelling stairwell. There is no bulb because each of the warring tenants, floor upon floor, has blamed the others for not switching off the communal light. Ekaterina feels ashamed to have been discovered inhabiting such a dwelling by Picasso's chosen lady.

~

You might expect Aragon and Triolet to be invited to give an informal talk at the Ambassade de France, with the French diplomatic corps in Moscow in full attendance, always eager to advance French culture, but there has been that recent crackdown on Communists in Paris and the Aragons have steered clear of the French Embassy. This is war. So their talk, 'Picasso chez nous' (The Picasso We Know), scheduled at short notice, takes place in a large amphitheatre of the Ministry of Culture. The Министерство культуры, having been stormed by Beria's acolytes, has packed in not only every available academic dignitary but also scores of students studying Art or French, an audience of perhaps five hundred with a spillover into the corridor – a constituency of well-informed Muscovites eager to know why the opening of the Picasso exhibition to the public has been repeatedly deferred.

The pendulum of power is swinging back into the hands of the calculating adventurer Lavrentiy Beria, who can be seen occupying the aisle seat in the front row of the audience.

How will Aragon and Triolet handle the situation, how will they play it? They too desire that the Picasso exhibition be opened to the public and the press – but the Aragons are elegant cakes layered in the marzipan of diplomacy.

Triolet speaks first, a figure of fascination as she deftly alternates between French and Russian, with her youthful recall of pre-revolutionary years, the writers she met, how she brought the young Vladimir Mayakovsky home only to see him fall passionately in love with her elder sister, Lilya, then on to Lilya Brik's tempestuous life with the young poet, although she was already married to the futurist critic Osip Brik – thus Triolet opens the curtains to the legendary bohemia nowadays shrouded from view yet wonderfully validated by Mayakovsky's status, mysteriously granted by Stalin, as *the* poet of the Bolshevik dawn.

'Would you like to hear about Mayakovsky?' Triolet asks her audience.

Of course. Mayakovsky.

Seated in the front row, Olga tries to forget her own Elsa Triolet, the Stalinist with the vinegar for the vagina, and what she hears now is (perhaps) a different woman born into a long-ago avant-garde, an orchid among the thorns. Olga listens intently, translating the passages in Russian for Picasso, he wrapped in inscrutability beside her as Triolet steers with practised hands through the thickets of Mayakovsky's iconoclasm, his brush with futurism, his suicide – all the way to the statue now standing in Pushkin Square, the idol in stone.

On the way to the Ministry of Culture, the Aragons have dragged Picasso to pay his respects to the statue, producing a grunt, a shrug, it's cold.

Olga notices that Triolet only briefly mentions her family but not their Jewish name, Kagan, or their cosmopolitan culture which opened up foreign languages to the sisters. Born Elsa Kagan, a graduate from the Moscow Institute of Architecture, Elsa had been the first to translate Mayakovsky into French. She had married André Triolet in 1918, then Aragon in 1928 – she is now fifty-six, a year older than her husband, her face long and usually solemn or disapproving. Dora Maar has confided to Olga that Triolet has been discreetly taking notes on Picasso's most minor mannerisms for a novel in progress about a Czech Communist sculptor who is commissioned to do a sculpture of Stalin for a public square in Prague. She has not quite decided on the outcome of the novel – or of Stalin.

'You might not guess it now,' Triolet tells her audience, smiling faintly, 'but Lilya and I were both considered beautiful by artists of the time. Our portraits were done by Rodchenko, Tyshler, Léger, Matisse and Chagall...among others. But these past twenty-five years I have been blessed by the companionship of Louis Aragon.'

She smiles at him, he smiles. The audience applauds politely.

Olga calculates that Triolet has deftly opened the gate to Pablo by introducing the moderns, the suppressed modernists.

'Today we took Picasso to see Mayakovsky's statue in the square named after him. He gazed at it and did a sketch – remarkable. Everything he does is remarkable. Then he turned to me: "Elsa, why did Mayakovsky shoot himself? Ought I to shoot myself right here?"'

(But Olga was there and knows that is not exactly what he said. 'I expect,' Olga heard him quip to Triolet, 'Mayakovsky did himself in because you were following him around.')

'You may have heard one or two untruthful rumours,' Triolet continues. 'It is not true that Maître Picasso has called Soviet art since 1917 a "dead dog". It is not true that he refuses to recognise Soviet artistic achievements. It is not true that he spoke disparagingly of Vera Mukhina's celebrated epic statue. We ask our well-meaning Soviet comrades to be on their guard against provocations. You see, Pablo can never forget past diatribes against him and his work. We beg our Soviet comrades to open his exhibition to the general public – as always promised.'

This is in Russian, Olga holds her breath: has Triolet gone too far, further than she intended? Olga's eye swivels to Aragon: he is nodding so it was a pre-planned throw of the dice. She glances at the utterly immobile Dora Maar seated beside her and picking up Olga's translations from the Russian. When Olga had come home the previous evening and heard from Ekaterina about Maar's surprise visit, Ekaterina had remarked that whenever Trotsky was mentioned the Frenchwoman was unable to hold back her tears.

'But I don't think she was crying about Trotsky, Ochka. I think she was crying about you. She thinks that ugly old man will want to take you back to France with him.'

'Perhaps.'

'So what aren't you telling me? Haven't I been both mother and father to you?'

Elsa Triolet is making a farewell offering to her audience. 'Would you like to meet Pablo Picasso? He is here with us. *Oui, vraiment, sa première visite à la Russie neuve.*'

Hesitant at first, the applause swells because Beria is clapping. Picasso is navigated on Olga's arm up the steps of the platform. His luminous yet leathery skin appears to be incandescent. He is offered a chair but refuses. He quivers. You could hear the silence in Irkustk, in Murmansk. Olga glances at Triolet who indicates that she herself will translate – if Pablo consents to open his mouth. Triolet will translate because she is more adept than Olga at censoring the translation even down to altering it completely.

Finally he is persuaded to speak: 'They want me to be diplomatic, my dear friends Elsa Triolet and Louis Aragon. But is art "diplomatic"? No! I grieve for all my dear colleagues who failed to be "diplomatic" enough to satisfy the commissars. What happened to them? Poor Malevich, poor Goncharova, Poor Larionov her lover, poor Popova, poor Kandinsky, poor Falk, poor Lissitzky, poor Rodchenko, poor Chagall though he is not my friend.'

Triolet does not waver. 'I think everyone here understands Maître Picasso, or they should do. I think everyone here can grasp the passion and pain in his heart.'

But Triolet's diplomatic tones only rouse him further – they always have. He extends his heavy arms expressively:

'Now I say this to the commissars who are the self-appointed guardians of the people's souls. You have not only buried your national treasure underground, but every day you feel the obligation to stamp on it. Why? In case it thrusts up out of the earth like a virgin spring of water to slake the dry tongues of the people?'

A silence deeper than Lake Baikal. Then Beria claps (probably a split-second decision but hasn't he prospered on split-second decisions?) and everyone applauds.

'Now listen to this! I had no sooner set foot at your airport than I was treated to a homily by my host, Professor Kemenev. The professor hectored me by quoting Lenin about modern art. May all of you here be reminded what Hitler said when opening the new House of German Art? "Cubism, Dadaism, Futurism, Impressionism, Expressionism, none of this is of the least value to the German people." Does that ring a bell? That was the year that Picasso painted *Guernica*, which Professor Kemenev has denigrated to the world.'

Everyone in the hall has forgotten how to breathe. Lungs suddenly lifeless. Triolet stands immobile, as if cast in plaster. She cannot translate. Aragon sits ashen.

Picasso chuckles from the deep throat, but not amiably. 'Of course Hitler seems to have left out my old friends the surrealists. I don't suppose Salvador Dalí caught a wink of sleep after that!'

A small group of art students laugh nervously because they can't help themselves.

'Let me remind you, my friends. When the Nazis' Exhibition of Degenerate Art opened, it contained precisely the *Kulturbolschewismus* artists who Professor Kemenev condemns as capitalist degenerates. May I mention Klee, Kokoschka, Nolde, Ernst? When the collection in the Kronprinzen was closed, the painters purged and banished included Van Gogh, Gauguin, Matisse, Kandinsky, Chagall and Lissitzky not to mention a few second-raters like Picasso.'

Picasso now holds up a sheet of paper on which he has imposed a sketch in a single line, never lifting his charcoal crayon:

'I have been sketching Professor Kemenev from memory. I have restricted myself to a single continuous line in the hope that art itself, the magic we all worship, will help me discover *homo sovieticus* in his "lofty climb".'

Picasso slowly swivels in appraisal of the five hundred people stretching to glimpse his charcoal drawing of *homo sovieticus*.

As Lavrentiy Beria abruptly rises from his seat in the front row, so do the members of his staff – Olga counts eight. Poker-faced and menacingly solid, Beria briskly leads them out of the hall. Witnessing this, the audience abandons all thought of a discussion and files out in complete silence, all five hundred.

Harrison Salisbury has been standing at the back of the auditorium. He watches as Picasso fastens on to Olga Lepinskaya's arm – nice girl, worth five thousand if she ever comes clean. PICASSO BURNS BOATS IN MOSCOW would be the next day's headline in the *New York Times* if the Soviet censors let the despatch through – but Beria will make a phone call: 'Bury Salisbury.' Anyway, the girls in the *kassa* will still be counting the words an hour after Salisbury's cable to New York marked 'urgent' is submitted – and the phone lines to the *Times*'s office in London will also be unavailable, *nedostupen*.

28

C haplin and his wife are ushered to a gilded box raised above the stalls of the Bolshoi Theatre. Picasso's considerably larger contingent are conducted to the adjoining box whose advantage in size seems to vex Oona. Tonight Galina Ulanova will be dancing *Swan Lake* – or she won't (usually). The prima ballerina assoluta appears increasingly rarely these days, audiences often go away disappointed, she is rumoured to be well into her forties though no date of birth can be found in any official Soviet gazette or almanac.

Moscow, evidently, is not Paris. The Chaplins' recent visit to the Paris Opéra had been an occasion for white tie, evening dress and medal ribbons in honour of *liberté, égalité, fraternité*. The audience had risen in welcome – the progressive press had already greeted the arrival of 'The Great Charlot, Political Refugee from McCarthyism'; even *Le Figaro*, staunchly wedded to the Atlantic Alliance, had been unable to stifle its enthusiasm: *Il est chez nous, il est chez lui.* But he does not yet feel quite 'at home with us' here in Moscow. Mr Chaplin has once again been advised by Nina that white tie and tails are not in order here: a lounge suit for Mr Chaplin; for Oona – after a fraught consultation – a simple little number from Dior cut decently below the knee.

The Moscow audience barely glances up as the guests of honour take their places, for here Picasso's glowering visage is unknown and Charlie no longer resembles Charlie – could be a minor bureaucrat or banker. Prepared to wave and blow kisses, he finds himself gently tugged into his seat by Nina. One or two Soviet ladies in the stalls detect that the young woman in the box with the luminous smile and the hair parting down the middle is foreign: maybe the man beside her with the swivelling, smoothly brushed head is her father.

Chaplin has been forewarned by the VOKS people that the box

reserved for the Kremlin leadership may not be filled tonight. Waiting for the orchestra to strike up, Chaplin observes that the plush, embossed seats in the Kremlin box remain empty. But look, surely that is Molotov with his pince-nez coming in, the veteran Foreign Minister and former Prime Minister with whom Charlie may yet negotiate a peace deal in Korea. He has already fixed the terms in his mind: everyone stops shooting and goes back to where they started. Plus a Chaplin Film Festival garlanded in white flowers from Seoul to Pyongyang (difficult to spell, maybe Pynyong). But, having inspected the empty seats, Molotov goes out again. Now this one must surely be fat boy Malenkov, a bit jovial – he too abruptly leaves again. A moment later a grinning stout potato bustles in, a crafty peasant – surely Khrushchev? Now he too turns on his heel and steams out. Charlie would like to catch a glimpse of Beria, they say he's the real mover and shaker, but elusive, rarely seen, makes bad 'Armenian' jokes. Here's one: 'Why are Armenian jokes so bad? Because Russians make them up.' A broad-chested figure in khaki uniform and dripping with medals has now plonked himself in the front row of the Kremlin box, staring rigidly at the stage curtain as if waiting for a fight – Voroshilov the war hero! Or one of them! (Charlie recalls Eisenstein describing Voroshilov as 'the man who couldn't find the horse he was riding'.) So where, Charlie wonders, are the other war heroes Konev, Zhukov, Rokossovsky how do you spell that, sounds faintly Polish?

Enter the lead violin, applause. Enter the conductor, applause. First chords of Tchaikovsky's overture, curtain up on a huge stage and traditional painted scenery fit for swans. Prince Siegfried is prancing across the stage, launching himself into huge leaps and twists because he has come of age – could have had him for the ballet scenes in *Limelight*. Chaplin glances at Oona, she is riveted, always wanted to be a ballerina she says. His gaze swivels towards Picasso's box. Chaplin remembers Pablo once designed avant-garde scenery for Diaghilev's Ballets Russes in Paris, music by Igor Stravinsky... Pablo is already asleep. That Maar woman sits beside him, her gaze rigid but into empty space, as if refusing to be in Communist Russia. Aragon and Triolet don't look too happy, they never do, maybe happiness is not the done thing in their circle. That pretty young Olga sitting behind them looks to be terribly worried, what an exhausting job looking after old Pablo! Ten to one he climbs into bed with her though she's too tall for my taste.

Scene 2, now here they come, the cygnets in white, twinkling toes, delicately arched necks, all perfectly synchronised. And now here is Odette herself, the Swan Queen, Galina Ulanova, the audience applauds excitedly, she looks like a ghost, so pale, so thin…no longer young, not pretty, the *Limelight* camera crew would have had to steer clear of close-ups.

'*You are guessing his thoughts, Lady Stears?*'

'*Not hard to do if you were sitting beside him and knew him as I did.*'

So hot in here! Chaplin tugs at his collar, don't those bespoke shirt makers Gieves and Hawkes know that collars require that bit extra for over-heated theatres? Well, London isn't what it used to be. Nothing is. A few pirouettes and arabesques later, Chaplin is asleep. He awakes at the first interval (the intervals being the best part of *Swan Lake*). Immediately he checks the Kremlin box – empty. He feels a tap on his shoulder, light but confident, even commanding, call it a heavy light tap. He leaps up! It's Somebody Himself, no less! Looking exactly like the photographs, the same wrinkly eyes, the same broad mouth broken by the same reassuring benediction – the world's uncle – though there are small surprises in the pungent odour of pipe tobacco and the nicotine stains on the moustache.

'Honoured guest Chaplin.' Stalin is pumping his hand, 'I have come to greet you on behalf of the Soviet nation.'

A thick voice, from the chest. Nina is translating. Well, it makes sense, if you think about it. Stalin has not reached the Bolshoi Theatre until the first interval because he has been wrestling with affairs of state, more war or nor war. Oona too has risen with a delicious rustle of her silk dress, lips parted, as if pitched into paradise. It's Uncle Joe.

Chaplin bows. 'Comrade Stalin, I am honoured to be so honoured.'

'I trust you are being well treated.'

'Your hospitality is prodigious, Generalissimo. I cannot thank you – the great Soviet people – enough.'

Stalin chuckles. 'Sometimes we try too hard.'

'I cannot tell you how I look forward to Your Excellency "cutting the tape" for the forthcoming Chaplin Film Festival – a world event.'

The yellow wolf eyes swivel: '*Da*. I shall be there – if I am invited. Weather permit.'

(Yes, he has a sense of humour, it's legendary even in Hollywood.)

'I would be delighted,' Chaplin smiles, 'to hear that the Chaplin Film Festival will be going ahead, as planned: *The Gold Rush, Modern Times, The Great Dictator*. My friend Eisenstein –'

Stalin's brow has clouded. 'We have been viewing the prints you brought with you from the West. They do not coincide with our own prints which of course have been corrected to conform to the laws of progressive cinema.'

Nina hastily translates. Stalin continues: 'However, as I once told Churchill, everything is negotiable so long as nothing is conceded.'

And then he is gone. Vanished. Slumping back into his seat, Chaplin resembles the victim of a gas attack.

'Don't jump to conclusions,' Nina whispers.

'Why not jump to conclusions? Why not jump straight back to London?'

'Because the Somebody who has just left us was not the real Somebody.'

'A hoax, you mean? Here in the Bolshoi Theatre in front of hundreds of spectators!!'

'The actor Mikheil Gelovani is the busiest of Somebody's official doubles, Maestro Charlie. The joke about the English words "weather" and "whether" was pure Gelovani. He had recently been performing Oscar Wilde at the Mali Theatre.'

'We are not amused. Let's hope it was all a dream, I must have fallen asleep due to the heat. Let's get out of here.'

Nina reacts anxiously. 'We cannot leave now. Mrs Chaplin, please remind the maestro that you are both due to be received by Prima Ballerina Assoluta Ulanova in her dressing room after the performance. A privilege rarely granted. I have brought the orchids and the little gift.'

'Is Picasso joining us for that?'

'Comrade Lepinskaya informs me that the maître says marrying Olga Khokhlova in 1918 cured him of ballerinas for life. She still stalks him. See, his box is now empty.'

'Charlie, we're staying to the end,' Oona says.

~

Accompanied by a massive spray of orchids, a book of photographs and the small gift, gift-wrapped as gifts should be, the Chaplins are conducted through the interminable labyrinths of the Bolshoi Theatre – a swan could get lost – to Prima Ballerina Assoluta Galina Ulanova's dressing room. They are received politely but with obvious reserve by a small, skinny woman who speaks no English on principle. Pale and pinched, with high Slavic cheek bones, the world's prima ballerina is frankly extraordinarily plain, you could ask for your money back. Ulanova passes the orchids to one of her dressers with a barely audible *spasibo*. The Chaplins are invited to sit, Nina stands.

Mr Chaplin begins by explaining that his new film, *Limelight*, just released worldwide, includes a sentimental ballet sequence which he hopes to show to Madame Ulanova in the near future. Ulanova says she has heard about it – as if hearing sufficed. Oona tells Ulanova that she has always wanted to dance Odette in *Swan Lake*. Ulanova politely enquires which company she is with.

'Madame, I've never danced in my life.'

Ulanova dourly assures Mrs Chaplin that Odette-Odile is one of the most demanding technical parts in classical ballet, *ochen' trebovatel'ny.*

'Oh gosh yes, and what a generous, full-hearted person you must be to bridge the age gap.'

Nina is choking but Ulanova does not seem offended. 'Age is in the mind. Contrary to the hostile Western reports, I shall not reach thirty-five until next year.'

'Thirty-five!' Oona exclaims. 'Wow. Is that using the old Gregorian calendar?'

Chaplin produces a folder of photographs taken from 'bygone days' when the Russian émigrés Diaghilev, Nijinsky and Pavlova visited Hollywood. 'We loved them all, Madame Ulanova.'

'I did not have the occasion to meet Maestro Diaghilev. He deserted the Soviet people during my childhood.'

Oona is spreading the photographs across Ulanova's dressing table, pushing aside powder puffs and tubes of cosmetics:

'Charlie fell in love with Pavlova when she settled in America, here's a photo of them together – before I was born! So I'm only a bit jealous! – look, she has signed on the back, wasn't she lovely? They say she had no equal, isn't that so, Charlie?'

Picking up *nyet ravnykh* from Nina's translation, Ulanova remarks that jealousy is something that Soviet women learn to rise above. Chaplin's gaze is fixed on her as she flips through the photographs as rapidly as courtesy allows – almost as fast as Monsieur Verdoux counting his ill-gotten gains! He has imagined she would be proud of her uncontested ranking as successor to Anna Pavlova – even if Pavlova had given offence by settling in the West.

'I believe you have never performed in the West?' he beams congenially. 'We all await your arrival with such anticipation.'

'Yes, but when will you come?' Oona adds. 'We can't wait, honestly.'

'You may have to wait, Madame, with the way the world is going. On occasion I perform in Budapest or Prague, the People's Democracies.'

Chaplin wrings his hands. 'If only I could have coaxed you into

Limelight, what a coup!' Then he is back to Pavlova. 'Anna had no equal in her day just as you have none in yours. Both of you – sublime. The sublime has always affected me deeply. Pale and luminous, as delicate as a white rose-petal, the moment Pavlova made her entrance I wanted to weep. I remember being invited to a testimonial dinner for her at the Russian Consulate. What an occasion!'

The Bolshoi's *prima ballerina assoluta* is not impressed. 'I think you are mistaken, Mr Chaplin. When you say "the Russian Consulate" you must mean "the Consulate of the White émigrés". There was no Soviet Embassy or Consulate in America until 1934.'

Chaplin inclines his head: 'You are a better historian than I am, Madame Galina.'

'I am simply a Soviet patriot and People's Artist for whom our history since the October Revolution of Lenin and Stalin is the most important thing. I dance for the Motherland, Mr Chaplin.'

Oona intercedes: 'Charlie also got to know Nijinsky, we're sure that will interest you.'

'Of course, if you wish.' She turns back to Chaplin coolly.

'Nijinsky came to my studio in Hollywood. I judged him to be an intensely serious man, with high cheekbones and sad eyes, a monk at heart. He watched me at work on a scene in *The Cure* which I thought was funny but Nijinsky never smiled. The more others on the set laughed, the sadder he looked.'

'Smiling is not one of the skills required in our ballet schools.'

'Ah.'

'What we strive for is *chest'*. No word is more dear to Soviet man than is *chest'*.'

'Honour,' Nina translates.

'Except perhaps for *vozvyshennyi* – I have learned the word in all main languages. In English, "loofty".'

'Lofty,' Nina murmurs.

Chaplin is now back with Diaghilev while Ulanova's discreetly shifting motions indicate a degree of restlessness. Luckily she isn't wearing a watch or she might glance at it. Ehrenburg has confided to the Chaplins that Ulanova has never recovered from the trauma of finding herself, as a young ballerina, on stage wearing a wristwatch.

'I think Madame Ulanova is perhaps a little tired after her performance,' Nina ventures.

Chaplin produces their gift, a pair of the very latest American stretch-tights – actually several pairs. Ulanova turns them over without attempting to remove the cellophane wrapping bearing the words 'Simply the Best at Bloomingdale's'.

'They are said to be simply the best,' Oona explains earnestly.

Ulanova flicks a fleshless finger at her dresser, who hurries forward from the shadows. 'Have these put in our Dancing Arts and Sciences Museum as a gift from Distinguished Visiting Artist Maestro Chaplin.'

Nina dutifully translates.

'We hoped you'd wear them,' Oona says.

'Thank you, the thought is appreciated, but our Soviet stretch-tights are "simply the best" in the world. *Spokoynoy nochi* to you both.'

~

The Chaplin party heads for a laid-on late supper in the Metropole, two hundred yards away and not laid-on. Sergei Eisenstein, recently reported to be in a coma on the Black Sea, is waiting for them in the famous marble lobby of the art nouveau hotel. Shambling in their wake (Chaplin is already snapping fingers at recalcitrant waiters), Eisenstein is suspiciously well informed about Chaplin's meeting with Stalin in the Bolshoi Theatre.

'Gelovani has played Somebody in not less than twenty top Soviet films. But he wanted to do the *dvoinik* especially for you, Charlie.'

'That's enough,' Chaplin snaps. 'What do you want to eat, Sergei?'

'Omelette – with or without eggs. Or chicken sandwich – with or without chicken.'

Oona says she isn't hungry. 'Just a litre of vodka, please. I wouldn't want to meet Ulanova every night of the year.'

Chaplin fingers Nina's chin and asks what she wants to eat.

'For you, Maestro, I can eat anything, even a very large rib-eye steak with onions, mushrooms, French fries, Dijon mustard and apple pie. I think I can eat Mrs Chaplin's portion, she does not want to put on weight.'

'I haven't any weight to put on,' Oona says.

Eisenstein is rambling on about Gelovani's career: 'Mikheil grew bored after playing Somebody at the front line in our great epic *The Battle of Stalingrad*. Of course Somebody never went near any battle.'

'You mean the Battle of Somebodygrad,' Chaplin says, maddened by the studied inattention of the laziest waiters in the world (like Aeroflot cabin crews they prefer their own company to that of their customers). But now a waiter reluctantly approaches them across the new carpet, smartly dressed in a white jacket and dark trousers. He shakes his head: no eggs left, no chickens in the yard, bread running out, no apologies. Nina takes the smart waiter aside and speaks to him in a certain tone of voice, MVD written all over it. Within five minutes their table is laden with cold pork, sausages, pickled mushrooms, blini, black caviar, vodka and slivovitz. She hopes for a word of congratulation from Mr Chaplin but he is pressing Eisenstein for a firm date for the Chaplin Film Festival. The answer (there is none) is interrupted by the arrival of a stout, jovial figure now standing before them, dressed in a dark cloak and clearly hungry.

Chaplin waves him away, 'No beggars or tramps here, please.'

'Gelovani, Mikail Georgievich, greets the Maestro.'

The actor settles into a chair and begins nibbling, rather vigorously. A quick shot of vodka and he is addressing Chaplin as one veteran actor another:

'You know, Charlie, sometimes I will wake up late in the morning, never before eleven, examine my medals, feel restless, climb into the Generalissimo's uniform, summon an entourage of limousines and MVD men by telephone, and set about creating policy at the highest level.'

Chaplin is shocked. 'Without authorisation, you mean? Was that the gambit this evening at the Bolshoi?'

'Well, yes and no but more yes.'

'Isn't that rather dangerous work you do?' Oona asks.

'I always wear a bullet-proof moustache.'

Chaplin turns to Eisenstein: 'A thought, Sergei. Maybe when you were summoned to the Kremlin in dead of night to be roasted about *Ivan the Terrible*, Part II –'

'Do not go on!'

'Maybe it was really our hungry friend here – not Somebody – who complained that you had portrayed Ivan's *opri...opricheeky* – to resemble Ku Klux Klanners.'

'*Oprichniki!* Don't try and be funny, Charlie! You were never any good at it!'

Oona claps her hands in delight: 'Oh I so love to hear that joke.'

At this juncture another hungry actor presents himself. This is Vladimir Savelyev, who bears such an uncanny resemblance to Hitler – sallow features, haunted eyes, a wet lock of hair over the forehead, everything except the moustache – that Chaplin momentarily imagines himself to be visiting Berlin at the wrong time. Hitler shakes Chaplin's hand.

'Maestro, I am proud to say that I played Adenoid Hynkel in the Soviet version of *The Great Dictator.* Of course it never reached the cinemas.'

Chaplin leaps to his feet: 'Heil Hynkel! Wiener schnitzel! I veel all off Europa verstorben und crushen!'

Gelovani and Savelyev applaud but Eisenstein merely sighs.

Nina, too, is nursing a reality of her own. She is no longer paying attention to these vain old men with their self-applauding jokes. Her new MVD controller, Aleksei, to whom she must report twice a day and who must remain invisible, a voice on a coded phone line, says she must take the Chaplins back to Belye Stolby tomorrow for a new search for nothing. She protests: 'толкать на дурной путь – I can't go on leading him up the same garden path.' Aleksei snaps back, 'принять мужчину в постель' – take the man to bed, Comrade.'

Now arrives in the ornate art nouveau foyer an Englishman (clearly) wearing an Eton collar, a tail coat and a smart briefcase loudly embossed 'HMG'.

'Ah, Chaplin, settling in, I hope. Good to see you after so many years.'

Chaplin does his exaggerated blink. 'Didn't we meet at Eton?'

'You were in Pop, Chaplin, when I was a freshman. I remember the thrashings you gave me for making jokes. Our Ambassador has instructed me to deliver to you this personal telegram from the Prime Minister.'

Chaplin takes the yellow envelope and eagerly scans the message: 'Dear Chaplin, while in Moscow lose no time in negotiating with Marshal Stalin a test ban on nuclear weapons, armistice in Korea on a no-surrender, no victory, no advance, no retreat basis, plus favourable trade terms for Yarmouth kippers. I grant you complete discretion and full support of HMG. As ever, the Bricklayer.'

Chaplin's expression is that of Joan of Arc when called to serve by St Catherine and St Michael. 'I really must forget about my film festival, it's trivial,' he tells the tail coat.

'Oh, don't do that, old boy. The Ambassador and Lady Chatterley feel sure we can fit everything in.'

'Lady who? – well she certainly knows how to fit things in.'

Oona asks who she is and what he means. 'I'll show you later,' he winks.

Arkady Raikin is now divesting himself of the Eton collar and tail coat (for it is none other than the great Raikin who has won Olga's heart for his joke about wearing out his shoes while standing in the queue to buy a new pair). Chaplin recognises the legendary Jewish actor-comedian from Leningrad.

'Arkady! It's you! By Jove!' They embrace.

'Welcome to Russia, Charlie. Did they tell you that's where you are?'

'You haven't lost your touch, Arkady. Or your head.'

'Well this one's only on loan. I'm your own eternal tramp, begging funds for our Miniature Theatre in Leningrad. They told me I might find you here disguised as Ulanova.'

While nibbling what's left of the food, Raikin fondly embraces Eisenstein, Gelovani and Savelyev. 'I went to see Ehrenburg,' he reports to them. '"How do you survive, Ilya, I said, I keep expecting you to surface in *Pravda* as one of the Cosmopolitan spies." Ilya nodded in that resigned way he has. Poor Ilya, is two Stalin prizes enough?' He turns to Chaplin. 'Now listen, Charlie. Come without delay to our Miniature Theatre. You will be the star attraction. Many of our audience are Jews who once saw *The Professor of the Fleas* and *The Gold Rush* and still remember how to laugh.'

At this proposal Oona is over the moon. She wouldn't want to go home and tell her father she hadn't visited the Leningrad Hermitage, though of course if she does go home she won't be allowed to see him or tell him anything.

'How about a double-act with the famous fleas!' she claps her hands.

Raikin lights up: 'Did you bring them from London?'

'They travelled economy class,' Chaplin says. 'When we got off the plane all the seats at the back were empty.'

'You will be a sensation,' Raikin promises. 'Bring the fleas. Contact me through Ehrenburg without fail.' Moments later he is gone from the Metropole, stuffing his tail coat and Eton accent into a bag. The MVD men loitering in the street outside will of course be tailing his tail.

Arriving back in the *ulitsa* Gorky, the Chaplins confer. Against every law of common sense Chaplin is drawn, via the deep pocket of a lifetime's applause, into the prospect of a double-act with Arkady Raikin. The script is hazy, the consequences lost in another city he knows only from postcards, but the siren call beckons him into the kind of fatal mistake he finds irresistible. And Oona, bless her, will always go along with the sirens. That night he keeps his promise to show her how Lady Chatterley knew how to fit things in.

'*Forgive me, Lady Stears, but how could you know that? You weren't there.*'

'*Charlie told me two nights later, in the MVD's special suite at the Hotel Moskva.*'

~

The following morning they must again endure the long drive to Belye Stolby, the fumes of crudely refined petrol inducing sickness in the Chaplins. For half an hour Nina scurries in and out of the storerooms while her clients are kept waiting in a viewing room – Chaplin and Oona, plus Eisenstein, now joined by Gelovani and Savelyev. Morosely they observe a vast female weightlifter wheeling in cans of film, then hurling them down sullenly in a bedlam of screaming zinc.

'Charlie,' Oona whispers, 'I'm sure that's the Soviet woman at the Helsinki Olympics, the *LA Times* said she hurled a discus and it landed outside the stadium.'

Nina works desperately, fitting the reels into the projector (the bulbs have failed of course, the discus thrower shrieks it's no business of hers) while Chaplin, Eisenstein, Gelovani and Savelyev sit like sulky emperors, legs apart, waiting to view the edited Soviet versions of *Modern Times* and *The Great Dictator* (*The Fascist Beast*) in the vain hope that Chaplin might find them acceptable. Gelovani quips in Russian to Eisenstein that the Maestro's temper hasn't been on so short a fuse since Mack Sennett tried to keep him at $280 a week in 1911.

Eisenstein nods sombrely: 'They say Sennett is still alive.'

Nina is called to the telephone in the Manager's office. It's Aleksandrov.

'You won't find the reels you're looking for.'

'Where are they?'

'Right here on my desk. Tell Chaplin we are working on them.

Promise him a screening tomorrow.'

Nina returns to find the three Russian eminences from Mosfilm snoozing uncomfortably in metal-framed fold-up chairs too small for Mickey Mouse. But Chaplin is wide awake and hears Nina's apologetic report with mounting rage. Nina slumps down exhausted, covered in dust.

'Don't just sit there!' Chaplin yells at her.

Oona decides she needs the 'bathroom'.

'It's me who needs the bath, Mrs Chaplin. Can you imagine an apartment without hot water? That's mine.'

Oona exits into the steel corridors of Belye Stolby from which (Chaplin calls after her) 'few return alive'.

Nina checks that Eisenstein, Gelovani and Savelyev are all asleep, heads lolling. 'You look troubled, Maestro,' she says, her hand brushing his as she leads him aside in Oona's absence. 'Charlie, if I could bring you special pleasure, perhaps in the guise of your old flames, Lita Grey, Paulette Goddard, Joan Barry, whoever you want – I think you may be a little bit lonely here in Moscow – we have a private suite at the Moskva Hotel, you name the time and any woman you desire will be yours.'

'And "any woman" will be you?' Chaplin almost goes into sparring mode then remembers she is a woman.

'No strings attached.'

Chaplin places a few large-denomination rouble notes in her hand and squeezes it. 'But I like strings! They're always my undoing.'

Presently Oona returns, her expression registering horror at what she has found in the 'bathroom'. Nina has instructed one of the blue-overall maintenance staff to find a large rat, preferably only half-dead, and to put it in the toilet marked *tualet zhenskiy*. Mrs Chaplin must be persuaded to leave Russia.

'Did Chaplin accept your invitation to that private suite in the Moskva Hotel?'

'I already told you, keep awake, Oxford. Charlie's head was still full of Lady Chatterley "fitting things in", and he said I must be "Connie"

for an hour. I must lie face-down on the bed and beckon him in a posh county accent while he played the rough-tongued gamekeeper. At the end of it I was covered in bruises. He wanted to humiliate me.'

Lady Stears began to cry helplessly. When I tried to console her she told me how she spent every night alone in the cold single room she hated, how she had to use an old kitchen cabinet to hang her clothes and disguises – and no hot water.

Moscow's dry cleaners cost the earth, 44 roubles or five US dollars to get any of her ten outfits cleaned in four days. Her vindictive MVD controller Aleksei refused to cover the costs. She remembered lying awake far into the night, wishing she had a family of her own and scheming how to capture Chaplin from his wife.

'I thought a mansion in Switzerland overlooking Lake Geneva would be a nice start to a new life. Oona told me they had pre-booked into the Beau Rivage hotel in Lausanne and their agent had his eye on a mansion with fifteen rooms and forty acres, the Manoir de Ban. I thought how maybe she could fall victim to a tragic street accident in Leningrad.'

'Seriously? You hated her?'

'Of course I couldn't help liking her, everyone did. But she was in the way.'

'And the tragic street accident – we know she survived forty more years?'

'Wait and see.'

29

The slush-splattered limousines slowly crunch in through thick snow, between lines of militiamen wearing the red-and-blue caps of the MVD. The Academy of Arts of the USSR, *ulitsa Prechistenka*, is a long, red-toned building raised on two main levels. Over the brilliantly illuminated main entrance hangs a huge slogan: *'Da zdravstvuet Stalin!'*

'It was once known as the Morozov Mansion,' Olga tells Picasso. 'You remember how I.A. Morozov collected your early works.'

'Three. I have little to thank Morozov and his English bowler hat for. Shchukin was my patron.'

As President of the Academy since 1947, Aleksandr Gerasimov is presiding tonight over a grand reception to greet the distinguished foreign guests (who include a visiting delegation from Mossadegh's anti-imperialist Iran and a dozen Chinese).

Madame Lepinskaya laughs (rare). 'Fifteen years later the Chinese would have been sporting Mao buttons and brandishing the Little Red Book but they were still quite modest in 1952, our "junior cousins" as we called them'.

'So Picasso and Chaplin were not exactly the guests of honour?'

'Well, we had to wait in line with everyone else. They noticed that.'

Standing in line in freezing cold, stamping their feet, Ehrenburg advises Picasso that *le Tout-Moscou* is attending.

'Best behaviour, Pablo,' Triolet warns. 'There is a price for everything.'

Ahead of him in the long receiving line Picasso catches glimpses of Oona Chaplin's ivory silk-clad derrière beneath a fur wrap. Well, to hell with her. Why hasn't she moved in with him and resisted? (He is conscious of Dora's vexingly silent presence at his side – she puts on weight when unhappy.) Olga stands at his other flank, closely monitoring his gaze.

'You may find the most recent period of portrait and landscape painting somewhat academic, Pablo,' Ehrenburg murmurs. 'But I know how you admire Ilya Repin's work of sixty years ago and you will not cause offence if you choose to detect a clear heritage.'

They have reached Gerasimov, flanked by Serov, due to succeed to the presidency. Cold hands are shaken. '*Ah, Maître Picasso, vous êtes très bienvenu.*' And that's all, nothing about opening the Pushkin Museum exhibition to the public. An indignant Picasso and his worried companions pass on into the Academy where glasses of wine on silver trays await them.

Oona grabs and gulps. 'Do they have anything stronger?' she asks Nina.

Ahead of the Chaplins, Louis Aragon pauses to admire Fedor P. Reshetnikov's *Dear Stalin*. Nearby Elsa Triolet is admiring Fedor S. Shurpin's *The Morning of our Native Land*, which shows Stalin standing alone shortly after dawn before a countryside vista of distant tractors and refineries. Aragon progresses to another giant canvas, heavily gilded. This turns out to be *Leading People of Moscow in the Kremlin*, 1949, by Academician Vadil P. Efanov. It depicts a great marble reception hall, under vast chandeliers, where Moscow's top people in glittering uniforms and gowns have evidently gathered beneath a podium to applaud themselves.

'Stalin Prize, first class,' Aragon points out.

Picasso remains painfully silent. His expression is being anxiously inspected from all sides and angles.

But now the President himself, Aleksandr Gerasimov – clearly he has eaten a few dinners in his time – has joined them and is conducting the French guests to his own painting, *Stalin at a Meeting with the Commanders*, an enormous postwar canvas streaming with light within a palatial, pillared room.

Groping for something genial to say, Picasso remarks that Stalin's modest attire, without braid or medals, contrasts with the glittering uniforms surrounding him. Olga translates rapidly.

'*Da, da,*' Gerasimov beams, 'I think I have captured the inherent modesty of our Leader, Guide and Friend.' Gerasimov slips away with an apology.

'Velasquez was less servile,' Picasso declares loudly to Aragon, 'when offering his talents to the Hapsburg kings of Spain.'

Ehrenburg lowers his voice in mild rebuke, the habit of a lifetime. 'In the thirties Soviet realist painters frequently showed Stalin mingling with the people but the prevailing style since the war in both painting and sculpture has been classical.'

'Did he ever "mingle with the people"?' Picasso enquires.

'He wouldn't be with us if he had.'

Triolet edges in past Olga: 'Hush, Pablo, please.'

'Look, you can see your Louis trying to catch his own reflection in the glass of *Stalin and Voroshilov in the Kremlin.*'

'*Merde à toi*', Triolet hisses. 'They understand everything you say.'

Picasso's grin broadens: 'Sorry you brought me to Moscow?'

But silence, please, for Aleksandr Gerasimov has now mounted the podium to welcome the guests. He hopes they like the Georgian wine and the caviar from Lake Baikal. He speaks of the *zadachi* of Soviet art so repeatedly that Picasso demands an exact translation of this word from Olga.

'What does it mean – "weaknesses"?'

'It means "tasks".'

Gerasimov also uses the word *gniyuschiĭ* frequently enough to engage Picasso's inquisitive nature.

'It means "rotting",' Olga whispers.

'Ah. And explain to me what keeps on "rotting"?'

'President Gerasimov is describing the current art of pseudodemocratic capitalism. He is reminding us that our Soviet Academy must be regarded as the most progressive in the world. He is attacking proponents of "art for art's sake", artists who paint *dlia izbrannykh* – for the elite. Where, President Gerasimov is asking, do you find the workers and peasants in the so-called cubist canon? He is saying Western freedom is *mnimaia*, a sham, entirely dependent on the money bags. He says he was shocked during a recent visit to London to find artists of talent using chalks on the pavement and dressed in rags.'

'Probably Chagall down on his luck – or our Charlot.'

Olga smiles, feels a small eddy of shame at doing so, longs to tell him she is carrying his child.

'What Gerasimov says would be true if it were true,' Ehrenburg murmurs.

Academician Serov has joined them, smelling of jasmine. He greets Ehrenburg who introduces him to Picasso.

'So happy about your visit,' Serov says. 'May I have the honour to show you one or two of my recent canvases?' They stop to admire Serov's *Lenin Proclaiming Soviet Power at the Second Congress of Soviets*. Diplomacy, never his closest friend, deserts Picasso.

'It could be a photograph – why bother to paint?'

Serov takes this in his stride, largely because Olga has translated 'why bother to paint?' as 'amazingly photographic'.

'You had no inhibition about that, Madame?'

'I believed that Pablo's relentless candour would sabotage his own exhibition. And do you know something? – Pablo once told me that he expected me to twist his words "for the good of the cause". He said that he was freely expressing himself only to me and those who understood French.'

I did not comment because I did not believe.

'Yes,' declares a smiling Serov, 'the photographic effect is the one sought after now by our advanced artists in this kind of history-painting. But in arranging the composition the Soviet artist must always allow space to insert a new figure at a later date – or to remove one. History moves on, you know. Not all of our foreign critics understand this.'

Olga translates faithfully, though Triolet wants to.

'Tell him I am one of them,' Picasso says.

Serov quickly excuses himself and the jasmine wafts away. They arrive at Arkady Plastov's lyrically illuminated *Tractor Drivers' Supper*. The sixty-year-old artist shyly steps forward and offers his hand.

'Pastoral-lyrical,' Picasso lights up, delighted. 'It moves me. Courbet a hundred years later.'

'I'm flattered,' Plastov says. 'Of course Corot and Courbet have been a great influence although, frankly, we are not encouraged to say so at the present time.'

'*Pourquoi?*'

Plastov glances to right and left. 'Well, you see, Maître Picasso, Russian art must be *sui generis*, home-grown. We have now discovered by scientific research that if and when Repin's generation travelled to Paris or Venice or Rome, they kept their eyes tight shut.'

Picasso then asks Plastov about the technique he uses and the two painters are soon lost in a conversation they are both enjoying, Olga too.

Entering the next *salle*, they are in the company of the esteemed Aleksandr Deineka, whose constructivist *The Defence of Petrograd* excites Picasso enormously. It depicts workers armed with rifles, male and female, marching across a bridge.

'It reminds me of Eisenstein,' he shakes Deineka 's hand. '*Magnifique, Maître.* You have brought great art and the insurgent workers together.'

'*The Defence of Petrograd* was finished in 1928,' Deineka explains, 'when we were all still free to give our own artistic expression to the great Revolution. But now contrast it with my more recent *The Relay Race* here, executed twenty years later. What change do you see?'

'You want me to be frank?'

'No value otherwise.'

'*The Relay Race*, if I heard the title correctly, could be a poster by Soviet State Railways inviting us to vacation on the shores of the sunny Caspian. To be frank, all Soviet art is now poster art.'

'May I quote that, Mr Picasso?' The intruding voice belongs to Harrison Salisbury, who has been edging closer.

Picasso is incensed. 'You again! Do you know that during the war the English had a saying, "The Yanks are overpaid, overgrown and over here". Ha! Nylons and *shooing gum!*'

'Oversexed not overgrown, actually. We planted vegetable allotments around our airbases in East Anglia – when we weren't at 30,000 feet over the Ruhr or Berlin. Some of us were amateur painters, indebted to Andrew Wyeth.'

'Who?'

'Wyeth was an American artist if that isn't a contradiction in terms.'

Salisbury is careful to offer no recognition to Olga. She can sense that he feels he has acquitted his debt concerning Pyotr Davidov, and is now grimly on the warpath, as she had foreseen. 'Please go away,' she murmurs to him.

Presently they are conducted along devious corridors to a room where a beguiling surprise awaits Picasso – works from the defunct Moscow State Museum of New Western Art have been put on display for this one evening only. Picasso sighs with pleasure – and Olga, too, is radiant.

'This display is a personal tribute to you, Maître.'

'To me, *devushka?*'

'Normally these works are never shown.'

Picasso's eyes glow. The frigid and silent Dora Maar, always alone, has at last come to life, her petals unfolding. She sighs with joy and almost embraces Olga. Here is Van Gogh's *Walk in Arles* and his touching *Portrait of Dr Félix Ray* (1889), the doctor who treated his rising madness in the hospice at Arles. Here is Gauguin, the friend with whom Vincent had quarrelled. A series of Tahitian scenes confirm the artist's assured grasp of the timeless world of his becalmed islanders, yet Dora persuades Olga that the best canvas of the lot abandons his typically strong, flat colouration for a technique closer to impressionism: this is *Man Picking Fruit from a Tree* (1897).

Agreeing with Dora, Picasso accords her a shoulder hug. 'Look out for the two goats,' he says, beaming appreciatively, his eyes phosphorescent. 'So life is worth living after all, my Olga. Do I detect your hand in the emergence of these masterpieces from the cellars? Yes?'

'I have done my best for you, Maître.'

'You have worked a miracle,' Dora says.

Perhaps fifty people pressing in behind them are watching Picasso's eloquent gaze when confronted by the early Picassos and Matisses on display. The spectators are watching him looking.

'And the State Museum of New Western Art,' he asks Olga, 'who decided to close it?'

'A decree of the USSR Council of Ministers,' Ehrenburg intervenes, 'but never published in our country. The decree stated that the display of this collection to the broad masses –'

'Yes, yes. The broad masses might want to go off to Gauguin's Tahiti and lie under palm trees while polygamous wives brought them coconut milk. They might want to be caught by Van Gogh making love in a haystack. They might want to be found dancing a rite of spring in primary colours by Matisse.'

A crowd has gathered around *Woman with a Fan* and *Three Women*. As Picasso approaches his legendary paintings Olga begins to clap and cry and instantly the applause breaks out like a fire on the taiga and everywhere people are emerging from the formality of the occasion to applaud with spontaneous, overspilling pleasure.

An old lady has pushed through the throng and is gripping Picasso's hand, her expression radiant:

'Do you remember me, Pablo? Paris 1916.'

He doesn't, yet he does. 'I know you – help an old man's memory.'

'Of course you remember Madame Goncharova,' Olga urges him softly.

His heavy features are gashed by joy. 'My god! Goncharova! Natalia! *C'est toi*! It's really you! My favourite of all the constructivists! And we both worked for Diaghilev alongside the choreographer Massine! We designed sets and costumes for Stravinsky's ballet *Parade.* You are still alive!'

'Only just, Pablo,' the old lady says. 'Of course you have

become the greatest since that time. For those of us born in Russia, it has been a rather different story.'

They hug and kiss amidst a small storm of applause in which Triolet and Aragon join with genuine enthusiasm, both of them privately yearning for a new Party line on the arts.

Goncharova is smiling shyly. 'Did you know, Pablo, that you and I were born in the same year?'

'Where have you been hiding, Natalia, all this time?'

'In France. I have been allowed back to Moscow to visit relatives.'

'In France! Why did I never hear from you?'

'You are a celebrity and I am shy.' She smiles mistily at Olga. 'It was dear young Olga here who arranged a ticket for me tonight.'

'*Vraiment?*' He pinches Olga's cheek distractedly but his thoughts remain in the past. 'Show me your paintings, Natalia! Show me your divine *Women with Parrots*! Show me your unforgettable *Pillars of Salt*.'

Goncharova can get by in Catalan Spanish and now takes refuge within it, very softly. 'Well, there are none on display here because I am not a "foreign artist". We Russian modernists remain beyond the pale. We are indeed "pillars of salt".'

'Dear Natalia. Things will improve,' he says weakly, embracing again the tiny almost unrecognisable old lady – who was once, so long ago, the glory of innovative art. Yet she is calmer than he. 'Pablo, may I tell you something?'

'Please.'

'Don't be fooled by this private display. The Soviet Union is a forest of bolts and padlocks. If they ever show your work to the public, as we have been promised, the queues will stretch all the way along the Moskva River and round Sokol'niki Park and half-way to Irkutsk.'

He beams. 'Why not?'

'That's why they won't do it. No chance. You are the *toro bravo* snorting flames at the gate. They are the *picadors* on their caparisoned horses who dare not let you in to the arena. Anyway,

Pablo, there is something else...'

'Tell me, chère Natalia.'

She stiffens with resolve: 'It must be your duty to refuse your exhibition to the public while we Russian artists remain buried.'

His smile is awkward. '*Tu penses?* Not step by step?'

She kisses him again. 'I mustn't keep you from your hosts, Maître.' The tiny, bent figure vanishes in the crowd, carrying with her his memories of a time when everything was possible. He seeks consolation from Olga.

'Why did Natalia say "they won't do it", my exhibition?'

'I have no idea, Maître. Perhaps Madame Goncharova is out of touch. It is an incorrect perception.'

'I reckon the old lady got it in one,' says Oona Chaplin, who has been closing in with Charlie.

'Greetings, Pablo,' Chaplin smiles. 'You must now regret selling your early work to Russian collectors. I never let go of anything. Not even my wife.'

Later, when the Georgian wine has eased osteoarthritic tempers, President Gerasimov returns at the head of his college of cardinals – small metal emblems of Soviet honour glinting in their lapels – and cordially delivers the *coup de grâce*: he is inviting Maître Picasso to execute a portrait of Comrade Stalin for his seventy-third birthday. Having been forewarned, Elsa Triolet grabs the role of interpreter, wreathed in smiles at last.

'You mean he will sit for me?' Picasso asks, opening his hands.

Gerasimov shakes his head. '*Nyet.* Currently the Father of Peoples must regrettably guard his health.'

Picasso gestures bafflement. 'Why me? Olga, what does this mean?' Aragon begins to answer but Picasso won't have it. 'I am asking Olga.'

She has not been forewarned but rallies: 'Maître, your portrait of our leader will be a great event in the struggle for peace and the freedom of people. It will of course appear across the world, Maître.'

Gesturing helplessly, he roams back and forth between French and Catalan: 'Friends, comrades, I'm honoured – I have always admired the great Soviet experiment – but honestly I've never set eyes on Comrade Stalin. I know he wears a uniform with big buttons down the front, with a military cap and a prominent moustache. But I cannot work from photographs.' He gestures expansively: 'I possess a *catalogue raisonné* from the Tretyakov Gallery. In it I found a large number of portraits of Comrade Stalin – by Maître Gerasimov, for example – but how can I be true to life unless the Generalissimo consents to sit for me? Ten minutes would be enough. I could capture you, Friend Gerasimov, in ten seconds.'

Olga translates. President Gerasimov smiles warily: 'Is that a threat, Friend Pablo?'

Olga is familiar with the paintings in the Tretyakov: Stalin and Voroshilov walking along the Kremlin walls; Stalin surveying the new industrialised countryside. She knows they were never done from live sittings. Soviet official portrait art – like cinema art – is about faking the figure, faking the background, faking the event.

Picasso whispers in her ear: 'I would need only ten minutes in his presence with a sketchpad.'

President Gerasimov is now approached by an aide who murmurs in his good ear. Evidently they have made the necessary phone call; Gerasimov again takes possession of Picasso's hand:

'Rest assured, Good Friend, it will be a painting from life. After all, who has more life in him than our great Helmsman? Esteemed Comrade Picasso, we envisage that Comrade Stalin will receive you in his dacha, in his beloved orchard, with your peace dove resting in his hand and another perched on his shoulder. The theme: "He who bears fruit for mankind".'

'Ah, good! When?'

'You will be notified. You will kindly take Olga Maksimovna with you, no one else.'

Smiling serenely, the academicians move away, confident of having achieved a Stalingrad in the cultural Cold War. Picasso observes a new restlessness in Olga. Her pleasing eyes are dancing on hot coals.

'I must now ask a favour of you, Maître. Will you please meet my mother?'

'Your mother? Of course. Where is she?'

'She is waiting for us outside the Academy.'

'Waiting in the cold?'

'Yes.' Olga leads the way past *Stalin at the Siege of Leningrad.*

'He never went near it,' Ehrenburg mutters to Aragon. 'Never went anywhere.'

'He went in spirit and soul if not in body,' Aragon demurs, 'as when he descends on Berlin in Chiaureli's film. Don't forget, Ilya, we are both Stalin Prize winners.'

Once outside Olga leads Picasso through the departing crowd to a grey-haired old lady waiting patiently in the snow in the company of an emaciated youth unknown to Picasso. Dora Maar embraces Ekaterina. Aragon and Triolet register visible concern. What is Olga up to? The MVD have reported that 'the renegade Maar' has not only called on Ekaterina Lepinskaya at home but has also visited Pyotr Sobaka's attic studio, emerging with a wrapped canvas.

Picasso advances to kiss the hand of Olga's mother. 'I am honoured to meet the lady who has produced so remarkable a daughter, Madame.'

'Thank you, Maître. Of course she had a father, too – before they took him.'

'I heard. In his sad absence I have come to regard Olga as a daughter.'

'In that case you must surely wish her good fortune in her forthcoming marriage.'

Olga winces. Mother, you are outrageous! Olga dare not look at Picasso, nor at Pyotr. But Ekaterina presses on, sure that age brings with it all the answers. 'Ochka's fiancé is most anxious to meet you – he's here, let me introduce him.'

A shabby, bohemian figure, long-haired and emaciated, wearing Western jeans beneath a denim top, stands absolutely motionless, looking at no one.

'Maître,' says Olga, 'please meet Pyotr Davidov, who your goodness of heart set free from unjust imprisonment.'

Picasso's features darken: 'You love this ragamuffin? You plan to marry him?'

'We are just good friends and Pyotr has a modest request to make of you.'

Several paces away Triolet is venting her spleen to Aragon. 'This is our Dora's sweet revenge on Pablo. What can Olga possibly see in this scruffy "Dog" man? Nothing, you can be sure. A woman can tell. The CIA could be holding one of their spare-rib barbecues right here, on the steps of the Soviet Academy of Art. As for opening Pablo's exhibition to the public –'

'It's already history,' Aragon sighs. 'Call it a virtual reality. To blame Dora is merely scapegoating, my dear. It has always been a virtual reality *au fond* – in the current climate.'

Maar has put her arm through Pyotr's, a gesture of solidarity lost on no one. 'Speak to Pablo, Pyotr, speak now.'

Pyotr begins, stumbles, gazes at the snow-laden sky for help, and is suddenly eloquent. Picasso listens, his eyes cold as glass, without a hint of affability.

'Maître, I ask you to understand. Artistic degenerates like myself are refused membership of the Union of Soviet Artists – so any work we produce cannot be sold. When we attempt to hold an exhibition – no one is forced to come! – our paintings are ripped from the walls and those of us employed in teaching or as museum staff are kicked out into the street, penniless.'

Ekaterina is gripping Pyotr's elbow. 'Come to the point. Tell him what you are asking of him.'

'Yes,' says Maar, 'you tell him, Pyotr, or I will.'

'Please visit my studio!' Pyotr blurts out. 'All the unofficial artists will greet you with their work in the street outside. The Moscow City Council will not dare to bring in the bulldozers while the great Picasso is *sur le terrain*. Your presence among us will echo round the world.'

Picasso's normally mobile features are of stone. If there's one thing he cannot stomach, it's to be cuckolded by some young cock of the walk claiming to know how to use a paint brush. He and Sabartés are agreed – young rivals are vermin! In Paris they have passed occult notes to each other on the subject, comparing methods of strangulation, garrotting, citing Jacobean plays, using elaborate codes in case the housekeeper deciphered their plans.

'Young man,' he declares for everyone to hear. 'I don't know why you dress yourself like that. Take a look at photographs of the Vienna Secession or the Parisian avant-garde, even the surrealists, during the twenties and thirties – always impeccably turned out. I don't have to prove I'm an artist by presenting myself in public as one of the *stilyagi* – a scarecrow. It's a matter of mutual respect, isn't it? I do not intend to fall in with your nefarious schemes. I have been invited to paint Stalin's portrait. I am honoured. I await the opening of my exhibition to the public. I do not listen to riff-raff who run around with American spies and – he is looking fiercely at Maar – women disappointed not to be my choice of the moment.'

So saying, this man of 5ft 4ins is already climbing through the open door of the limousine. There will be no seat for Dora Maar nor, it becomes apparent, for Olga either. Pyotr stalks away with long strides through the rain, alone. Together Olga and Dora support Ekaterina on the walk to the metro. The old lady is now chattering erratically about Vincent's ear.

30

There were occasions when, on my arrival at Cheyne Walk, Lady Stears simply could not sit still. We must go somewhere, she always knew where. Today she was wearing a Harris tweed pleated skirt not unlike a kilt and playing with a long, tartan scarf. She could have been mistaken for a young fresh-air-loving belle of the nineteen-twenties, from buttoned beige shoes to black bucket hat. Heading by taxi for Tate Modern to view a new exhibition of Russian modernists, she asked if I had ever heard of Elmyr de Hory.

'De Hory the faker?'

'A genius.'

Having ascended the giant escalator, her arm through mine, she was examining Malevich's black square and sighing over the waste of space because it is beyond doubt by Malevich. Just as Popova is lamentably Popova and the Goncharova is, disgracefully, the original. Lady Stears regretted never having met Elmyr de Hory but she had taken his life to heart: how to acquire old paper with pre-war watermarks from Left Bank supply shops, or the blank endpaper of French art books and picture albums, particularly if beginning to yellow round the edges; how to rub Lipton's tea into the paper, where to acquire suitably old frames. But forgeries in oil (Lady Stears assured me) were generally more lucrative than drawings, although oil took an unconscionable time to dry right through 'to the bone'. A watercolour or gouache dries quickly under a hot lamp, but oils long remain exposable to tests by needle points or cotton soaked in turpentine. Nina was excitedly telling me all this with her hand tucked into my arm as if we were already, well, business partners.

'Old unpainted French canvas for oils cannot be found. This leaves us the expensive option of purchasing oil paintings from the required period then soaking off the paint down to the priming.'

'You have people doing that? Where?'

'Where? In World's End, Chelsea. They work in disused garages. I call them my mechanics.'

'And your man Leszek Kolakowski has mastered the entire bag of tricks?'

'Please not sardonic, Oxford. I am paying good money for his fakes but the curators here at Tate Modern are quite incredibly blind to art and becoming quite nasty, too...'

'Nasty?'

'They have forbidden me to step inside this building.'

Indeed I got the impression that she was venturing into the Turbine Hall of this converted power station heavily disguised as the late dancer Isadora Duncan, her long tartan scarf wound round her neck and up to her indignant eyes.

Leading the way to the coffee bar, I bought her an espresso and a large slice of non-fake carrot cake, which she abstractedly said she wanted but didn't touch. It all made gloomy listening, her love of fakes. One had to ask whether her whole Chaplin story from 1952 was a bogusly stretched canvas sprayed with a flit gun or a 'mouth atomizer' (whatever that was). Not that I was completely out of sympathy with her. I knew about the prevailing fetish of identity, of big names. In any museum you could observe patrons who barely glanced at the picture before bending and screwing up their eyes to discover the name of the painter, offering admiring attention only if the signature or caption said 'Nolan' rather than 'Nobody'. They could not decide whether the painting was a masterpiece or of negligible interest until reassured by the caption 'Reynolds' rather than 'Unknown Artist'.

Back in her first-floor drawing room, her long, Isadora Duncan scarf lay at her feet, a mobile object of fascination for the two sparring spaniels. Still brooding about Tate Modern, her mood was restless, even belligerent. Unbuttoning and casting off her beige shoes, she announced that the workers alone understood value in art.

'I am always a proletarian, you must understand that, Oxford. I once queued for hours with my Sergei in Red Square to see the embalmed corpse of our great Lenin.'

This established, she jumped to her stockinged feet and led me upstairs into a dressing room assigned to her husband. Here she threw open a Jugendstil wardrobe to display Sir Henry's splendid hunting clothes and high brown boots, plus an impressive array of foxes' tails hanging like regimental ties. A framed photograph captured Oxford's Bullingdon Club arrayed in white ties, fawn waistcoats and blue tails, during the young Henry Stears's undergraduate days at Christ Church where (she told me) he had occupied one of the prime sets in Peckwater Quad. Solemnly Lady Stears told me that Henry had 'sported his oak' – but then she giggled engagingly and said she had never known what it meant. He was to be seen in the photograph, very tall and fifth from the right in the back row (perhaps sporting his oak).

She gazed at me intently to gauge my reaction. 'Life is double,' she chided me. 'Nothing more true than other true.'

'No.'

'Can you imagine Chaplin's dream when he lay next to me in the Savoy or the Hotel Moskva?'

Since Nina's hand was now firmly in mine I squeezed it. 'Tell me his dream.'

As we settled back in the drawing room, the spaniels still in attendance, she began to impersonate Chaplin describing a dream after coitus with his Russian 'strumpet' (her word). The Little Tramp's comic boots drop to the carpet, along with hat, cane and trousers, he ardently embracing the strumpet like the undone hero in one of his mother Hannah's favourite penny dreadfuls, oh mother, you of the 'wayward heart', how your madness afflicted me and why is this nymph lying in my arms so like Louise Brooks and all the others? Is she infected with the clap? Have I painted my thing bright red in iodine or is it too late? – no, let's have that take of the blind flower girl again, again I say! I don't care what footage I have to bin, take it again! and let's steal the sound track from Jose Padilla's 'La Violetera', he doesn't deserve a credit or payment, if he sues I'll fight his claim in court that lousy Spaniard. OK, Virginia, you're fired, you left the set without my say-so for a hairdressing appointment, is that your story? Fired! Off the set! No, hold on, come back Virginia. So it's a raise you want now! Do you promise to show *City Lights* in Moscow, Nina, does Uncle Joe know about it? You've got to realise, Oona, that on this studio floor those who are gone away are gone away. Cut.

Lady Stears dropped the affectionate impersonation. She was now curled up at my feet in her Harris tweed pleated skirt not unlike a kilt, the button shoes, the scarf and the bucket hat for the spaniels to play with, and about to fulfil her long-standing promise to open the window into the affair of Chaplin's *The Great Dictator*. The two spaniels circled her, tails wagging, jealous of the attention I claimed but soon succumbing to the heat of the log fire that Ivan had kindled in a grate designed, perhaps, by Robert Adam. (Of course burning wood is illegal in the smokeless zone of London, but Ivan had no doubt violated more serious laws in his time.)

'Have you thought about lending me that painting, Nina, Kolakowski's "Small Cowper"?'

'You are very persistent, Oxford. First you wanted a gift of it, now only a loan. Does a fake by Kolakowski mean so much to you?'

'For the cover of my book. Olga won't let me make a print of hers.'

'The cover of your book! So Olga is to be the queen of attention? I see! As I suspected, you are in love with her! What poor Nina has been telling you is to be just a footnote, is that it?'

~

When I returned to Moscow in April 1995, it was Galina herself who laid her cards on the table when she took me to the local version of the Groucho Club. Abe Kahnleiter was offering her a higher salary plus guaranteed employment throughout the year.

I placed a hand on hers and said she must accept.†

'I have already accepted, John. I hope you won't feel I'm ungrateful to you, it has been a privilege to work for you but I have to face the fact that you're in Moscow for only a small part of the year, and I need the full-time security Abe is offering.'

'Of course.'

'I know, I know, you and he are at daggers drawn, I wish you weren't.' She leaned forward, dropped her voice. 'Abe would really like you to sign up for his Project. Abe says if you agree then I will always be at your service here in Moscow.'

Sure enough who should then breeze in, with wheelchair and Ivy League minder, heartily hailing each member of the club's staff, then attaching himself to our table.

'What are you both drinking?'

Even more affable than usual, Abe went straight to the point. He had talked to the editors and finance managers of his Harvard-Yale-Columbia Consortium (CAP), and was now authorised to offer me full-time employment at senior professor's salary, minimal teaching obligations at H, Y and C, travel expenses paid, complete freedom of movement – plus Galina's full-time

---

† Abe Kahnleiter. Pseudonym. Born 1935 in New York. German-Jewish antecedents who emigrated in the 1860s and established the clothing firm Kahnleiter Wholesale. His father Solomon Kahnleiter (b. 1899) became a distinguished social scientist and demographer at Columbia, serving in the OSS Intelligence unit during World War II. After the war he interviewed Russian refugees and defectors in the US Army's West European holding camps. Author of *They Prayed to Stay*. Abe attended Hunter College then Harvard (1959-64) and was appointed assistant professor in the time of Dean George McBundy, for whom he acted as an informant on faculty members judged to be of unsound or unproven loyalty to the USA. At a young age Abe became an informant for the CIA in the time of Allen Dulles and Frank Wisner. This connection was maintained for more than thirty years. As tenured Professor of Political Science at Harvard, Abe Kahnleiter served as adviser to Secretary of State Henry Kissinger and later as adviser to Ronald Reagan's Secretary of State George P. Schultz. Confinement to a wheelchair was the result of spinal damage while playing football for Harvard Crimsons. Neo-conservative contributor to *National Review, Commentary, US News & World Report, New Republic*. Was said to be an influence on Allan Bloom's seminal *The Closing of the American Mind* (1987). Publications include *Out of Darkness: American Historians of the Cold War* (1981). Close colleagues include Gertrude Himmelfarb, William F. Buckley Jr., John Podhoretz, Samuel P. Huntington. Member of Americans for Democratic Action (ADA).

assistance whenever I was in Moscow.

'In return for what?'

'John, any and every project of yours will become the property of, and under the full copyright of our publishing outfit, Combined Academic Press, New York. You will not publish elsewhere. CAP will pay you a royalty on sales of your books and articles in the normal way.'

'I am already signed up with Oxford.'

'You simply speak to them, we simply speak to them, we buy them out plus a small premium on the deal. But you are asking yourself why we want to do this?'

'Since my work is so erroneous and indeed dishonest.'

'Harsh things have been said which maybe should not have been said. The fact is we recognise you as a major player in the cultural history field, and maybe *the* major player. So we want you on-side.'

'My dear Abe, I write what I write – and always shall. The only "side" I'm on is what I perceive to be the truth. Isn't that so, Galina?'

'Of course.' (How could she know, poor, loyal woman?) She rose and put on her overcoat. 'But you must both excuse me, I'm running late for my class.' With the benevolent wave of the hand I knew so well as we parted each evening, she left us.

'And so it shall remain,' Kahnleiter picked up the thread. 'No changes to your text without your authorisation.'

'Then what do you gain by publishing me?'

'John, let's be grown-up about this, let's be the adults we all too obviously are. As things stand, you are a major obstacle to our Revisionist project.'

'As I said at your conference, your so-called "Revisionist" project is quite clearly, to anyone who knows the field, "anti-Revisionist". You aim to turn the clock back to the old Cold War certainties.'

'John, the Left has ruled the history faculties for twenty-five years – and not only in the USA. For a quarter of a century the university presses and sometimes the trade publishers have been turning out books that tell our young people, several generations of students, that American foreign and domestic policy have since 1945 been gravely misguided if not downright evil. The West is engaged in a capitalist global conspiracy. That has been the all-powerful consensus – we love Fanon and Fidel, we love Mao's Little Red Book, we love Ho-Ho-Ho Chi Minh and maybe Mugabe. Via Che! Viva Sandinista! That, my good friend, is what we of CAP wish to revise. In short, we are the true Revisionists.'

I shook my head emphatically. 'I do not belong to the New Left or any other "school". You don't find my name in their periodicals.'

'But sometimes we do. You published an appreciative study of Fanon. That's the whole point, John, you are doubly dangerous because you are half-mainstream. Most of your books have gone out from Deutsch, Macmillan New York, McGraw-Hill, Viking, Weidenfeld, Secker, Harper, Simon & Schuster, and now a new one from Faber and OUP New York. You were in Conor Cruise O'Brien's faculty at NYU. You took a course at Columbia. You were a Henry Fellow at Harvard. You have been, dare I mention it, a rebellious Fellow of All Souls College, which they say is a ticket for life. You always receive mainstream critical attention. Your books have been reviewed by H. Stuart Hughes, Arthur Schlesinger, Jr., Hugh Trevor-Roper, A.J.P. Taylor, Max Beloff, Denis Brogan, Eric Hobsbawm, Sidney Hook, Richard Cobb – need I go on? And you will continue to enjoy this attention if you join up with us at CAP.'

I laughed. 'CAP not OUP, is that the formula? Yet you pledge that I will retain entire editorial control over content and form – is that remotely credible?'

Kahnleiter smiled his wide one. 'That's the point, John. You will boost our academic credibility. An article in the *TLS* recently accused CAP of being an American propaganda outfit with CIA connections. That article appeared under whose name? – yours. And I happen to know that in the distant days when *TLS* reviewers were anonymous you were prominent among them. Deputy Editor John Willett was your pal.'

'You've done your homework.'

'I have and I rather think that you will have to drop your disgraceful smears against CAP if your own work is to appear under our imprint. More important, a whole lot of younger historians who take their lead from you will have to stop smearing CAP as a CIA conduit, the successor to the ill-fated magazine *Encounter.*'

'They would simply conclude that I had sold out.'

'John, the freelance's existence is always precarious, always in debt, always burdened by expenses, always liable to receive letters from publishers demanding their money back because of repeatedly late delivery. Correct?'

'I survive.'

'There's one other thing – your present, highly secret, project. I made that point during the recent conference. You told us that the evidence is indecisive. You said that as of now you remained sceptical. That, if I may say so, was disingenuous. Our reliable sources confirm that you currently believe you are onto one of the great scoops – and you are no fool,' he smiled, 'whatever else you are.'

'Abe, you and yours are currently the source of most of the world's ills. Global capitalism run amok, America imposing the outreach of the Roman Empire.'

'Do you know how much foreign aid the USA donates in any single year? More than the rest of the world added together. John, CAP earnestly wishes to take your new project under its wing. A generous advance payment will be offered when you provide us with a detailed synopsis. Deadline for delivery flexible. That's only fair, my friend.'

'Fair blows the wind for France, blow gentle gale/ Till Edmund be arriv'd for England's good!'

'Is it a deal?'

'My sources have withheld permission for any disclosure.'

'Let me ask this: are your sources the kind of people who would get wind of it if you provided CAP with a detailed synopsis? From the little I know you are talking to two old ladies, one in Moscow, one in London, both utterly detached from the world of academic publishing. I mean, you don't have to confide in these old birds and I can guarantee absolute non-disclosure by our editors.'

'No you can't.'

'We can even give you an *ad hominem* editor of your choice, we can bring in any relevant academic you would care to confide in.'

'And you, Professor Kahnleiter, the guiding hand of the project who can whip up salaries from nowhere – you would be none the wiser?'

'Of course I would be the "wiser" – that's my job. John, this is what comes of working alone, in isolation. The ego becomes fearful, enlarged, misshapen, paranoid how many adjectives do you want.'

Kahnleiter turned to the silent minder standing behind him (who was beyond shadow of doubt the fellow who had followed me on the metro to Nagatinskaya).

'Time to scramble, Joe? Excuse me, John, we have people flying into Sheremetyevo tonight and I must go greet them. Think over my once-in-a-lifetime proposal, my good friend.'

$\sim$

Galina, now working for Kahnleiter like Sergei, gave me one day a week but it was not enough. I flew to London for the full operation at the Western Eye Hospital in Marylebone. Two days later my wife drove me up to Richmond Park for a walk. I clung to her every step while the sky insisted on revolving under the landscape and the speckled deer seemed to be grazing with their legs in the air. By the end of the week I could read a car registration plate at thirty yards and I could drive. By the time I returned to Moscow for the next interview with Madame Lepinskaya I was able to manage without Galina in the archives. She still offered me one day a week but by now I suspected that honourable woman of acting as Kahnleiter's spy, and said so.

'You should be ashamed of yourself!' she exclaimed. 'To say such a thing about me.'

Perhaps this parting remark was justified; I couldn't know; nor perhaps could she. I have earlier indicated that I always regretted the manner of my falling out with a woman who had meant so much to me and my work. But of course the same thing had happened in London with a succession of literary agents, all women, all loyal, all deserving of kinder treatment.

31

Chaplin addresses a sparse audience of two or three dozen film workers and actors in the Institute of Cinematography. Again, no members of the press are visible. Before this 'public' viewing of the original print of *The Great Dictator*, Chaplin has prepared some background information for the benefit of an audience he had expected to be much larger. Nina can feel him struggling to mask his indignation.

'Good morning! I should first explain that the storyline took two years to develop. The film involved miniature models and props, otherwise it would have cost five times as much. I spent half a million dollars before I began turning a camera.'

He is interrupted by Grigorii Aleksandrov: 'Is the film in your view a fictional documentary?'

'Definitely not, Grigorii. Had I known of the actual horrors of the concentration camps I could not have made the film, I could not have made fun of homicidal insanity. However I was determined to ridicule the Nazis' mystic bilge promoting the idea of a pure-blooded race.'

This said, Chaplin veers off in a different orbit and Nina senses that he has been thrown by Aleksandrov's calculated question.

'At the end of the film, finding himself Dictator by mistake, my humble barber declares: "I'm sorry but I don't want to be an emperor. That's not my business. I don't want to rule or conquer anyone. I should like to help everyone – if possible – Jew, Gentile, black men – white. We all want to help one another. Human beings are like that".'

Nina wonders whether anyone could be taken in by such vacuous idealism.

'At the very end of my film I say, "Look up, Hannah! The clouds are lifting! The soul of man has been given wings and at last he is beginning to fly. He is flying into the rainbow – into the light of hope!"'

You could hear a pin drop in the Institute of Cinematography.

Chaplin's delivery becomes more rapid as he informs his audience that the film opened at the Capitol in New York City. It stayed fifteen weeks in New York, playing at two theatres, 'and turned out to be my biggest grosser'.

Nina translates a question from the audience about Chaplin's contribution to Russian War Relief.

'Yes, I told a big crowd in Madison Square Park that Russian mothers were doing a lot of weeping and that a Communist mother was like any other mother. I told them: "On the battlefields of Russia democracy will live or die. What are we waiting for? Let's open a second front now!" My friends, there was uproar and joy in Madison Square Park. Women were weeping.'

Applause breaks out in the Institute of Cinematography. Aleksandrov stands up, clapping. 'Comrades,' he says smoothly, 'let us now see the Maestro's film as adapted for a Soviet audience. We will have a five-minute interval before we begin.'

A confused Chaplin is abruptly being conducted by Aleksandrov, Eisenstein and Gelovani to the Director's office, Nina following.

Eisenstein is wearing a face like a bruised dishcloth. 'We need a word with you, Charlie. Bad news – unfortunately the print you brought from London doesn't fit our projectors. Wrong sprockets. Wrong millimetre.'

Aleksandrov silently observes Chaplin's horrified reaction. Nina can guess that the 'wrong sprockets, etc.' has been his decision following one of his lightning midnight visits to the office of Moscow's Party chief, Nikita Khrushchev.

Chaplin is so incensed he lapses into incoherence. 'Go on, say it, Sergei, you wish you were dead, all those maggots crawling in the sailor's meat and eyeballs slit open on the Odessa steps and killing off half the cast of *October*.' He tries to rise but Nina grips his arm and pulls him down.

Gelovani is less apologetic. 'Let's face a few facts about *The*

Great Dictator, Maestro. You remember when your Adolph Hitler, I mean your Adenoid Hynkel, is ranting to the Nazi rally?'

'I do.'

'And how the clapping is turned on and off with ritualised precision?'

'Nicely done, I have always thought.'

Gelovani glances nervously at Aleksandrov: 'May I say it?'

'It has to be said.'

'Now, Charlie, please understand that when...Somebody addresses a Party Congress no one dares be the first to stop clapping.'

'But that's entirely different,' Chaplin protests. 'It's genuine, spontaneous emotion.'

'It is?' Eisenstein's jowls sag. 'Listen: you remember how Hynkel takes a little blond girl in his arms?'

'She pees on him.'

'It happened to Somebody in 1936. He has never again tried it.'

Gelovani: 'Another thing. You recall the great comic scene when Hynkel negotiates with Napoloni of Bacteria – of course that's meant to be Mussolini – about troop movements on the Austrian frontier?'

'One of my favourite scenes, I do admit.'

Eisenstein sighs loudly: 'But not one of Somebody's favourite scenes. We assume news of the 1939 Nazi-Soviet Pact has by now reached you?'

Gelovani: 'And how Hitler and Stalin divided Poland between them?'

Chaplin again protests: 'But the Soviet Union had no choice – have you forgotten the Western appeasers?' (Nina notes that this had not been his line when Chiaureli's *The Fall of Berlin* was shown – Britain fighting alone for two years and all that.)

Eisenstein: 'You may think so but Somebody doesn't think the Soviet public will think you think so.'

Gelovani is shaking his head eloquently: 'And what about the

Jewish ghetto in your film? Don't the Jews finally decide to resist Hynkel's stormtroopers until they are broken and deported?'

'They do indeed.'

Eisenstein comes in: 'Are you familiar with Somebody's deportations of Jews, Chechen, Tartars, need I go on?'

'Renovation of populations,' Gelovani adds.

Chaplin waves his arms angrily as if swatting wasps. 'Gentlemen, I am growing weary of all this quibbling about details, about how many angels can stand on a pin's head. Your ordinary, everyday cinema audience will notice none of this!'

'But Somebody will,' Eisenstein says. 'In fact he noticed ten years ago.'

Gelovani: 'Your film also features a principled and almost decent Nazi who defies the Führer in order to help the Jews. He openly challenges his Supreme Leader.'

'Of course!' Chaplin protests. 'There are some supreme leaders top-down, by crude force, and other supreme leaders bottom-up, by consent.'

Gelovani: 'Maestro, you deserve a chair in political science.'

'Charlie,' Eisenstein sighs, '*The Great Dictator* cannot be shown to the Soviet public, not in any version. After the Nazis attacked us in 1941, Molotov asked me to attempt it under the title *The Fascist Beast* and I'm ashamed to tell you, Charlie, with a heavy heart, that I did as I was told. But that film has never been released and shown only to Somebody.'

'But we can show it to you now,' Aleksandrov says.

An incensed Chaplin refuses to view it – as Aleksandrov had anticipated, because when Chaplin is led back from the director's office to the auditorium, every seat is empty.

'*You haven't mentioned Oona, Lady Stears. Where was she?*'

'*She didn't come. She was convinced something like this would happen. She refused to witness her husband's humiliation. Mr Chaplin brushed aside her fears as women's tittle-tattle and told her to go shopping.*'

32

~

I stood in the doorway of Apartment 12, second floor, the tidily
dressed Englishman returning yet again with his briefcase and
a small bunch of flowers, a stranger who might now know more
than Madame Lepinskaya could remember telling him (we had
reached 1995). A lingering resentment was obvious: why had she
let this foreign intruder unfasten secrets she had guarded (she
believed) for forty years?

She sighed. 'How can you come from England, where nothing
ever happens to people, and understand us Russians? Pablo was
a fugitive from Spain, he had painted *Guernica*, he had lived under
the Nazis in Paris, he understood us.'

'Of course I, too, understand, Madame.'

'Have you told anyone about me, Monsieur?'

'No one.'

'What about those friends and enemies of yours, what were
their names? Sergei Panov, Galina I forget her name, Professor
Kahnleiter and that little girl you foolishly fell for?'

'I have told no one about you, Madame.'

'Not even Svetlana? I believe she is no longer seeing you. Of
course she is the cat who will never get killed by curiosity. I'm
afraid she has been talking to the wrong people, friends of yours
about whom you never speak. People who would like to know
more about our conversations, some of them Russians but others
American, am I right?'

'Perhaps so.'

'Of course,' she said, her fingers tangling, 'Svetlana can never
get over the fact that her husband has been in love with me.'

'Mitya?'

'Mitya. Dmitrii Nikolaiovich Tairov, architect, wit, admirer of
England.'

It immediately came to me that if she now felt driven to open the door into her private life post-Picasso, she might at last be prepared to talk about her son.

'Madame, what is your son's full name?'

'Maksim Pablito Pablovich Davidov. He has always been Pablito to me.'

'Forgive me, but why is he not up there on your mantelpiece?'

Madame Lepinskaya had doubtless long since been prepared for the question. 'I do not wish to wear my heart on my sleeve for strangers. You may have noticed other missing cards in the pack.' She now rose, extracted the 'missing cards' from the Ming console, and placed them on the mantelpiece. 'Since you are no longer a stranger,' she smiled nervously.

It was the first time I had seen any image of Pyotr or Pablito. Picasso himself was restored to the mantelpiece in the form of a joint photo with Olga, both smiling, another of Dora Maar's snaps – I wondered if there were more, and asked.

'You have now seen all thirteen of them.'

'Your son went to school here in Moscow?'

'Of course! Where else? At school he was known as Maksim by his teachers and Maks by his friends. His great friend was Yuri Tairov, son of Mitya and Svetlana. I would be grateful for one thing, Monsieur. If you ever meet Pablito in Paris, please bring me news of him and recent photographs of my grandchildren. Pablito is not very good at that. He doesn't write often.'

'I will.'

'Do you promise?'

'I promise.'

'You won't forget, I know how busy you are.'

'I won't forget.'

She lightly touched my arm. 'Perhaps, Monsieur, if...if you saw Pablo, I mean Pablito, oh dear...but...let us imagine you were not immediately due here in Moscow...perhaps you could post the photographs to me?'

'Madame, no – the photographs will ensure a further invitation from you. To be frank, the long intervals between our meetings have become a source of acute worry to me.'

Her contrition was touching. 'Yes, I understand. I am not always in good health but we needn't go into that. I promise you I will do my best, Monsieur, you have been a true friend to me.' She wrote out Pablito's address and handed it to me with a radiant smile. Then, as if in celebration, she brought out a selection of my own books and laid them on the coffee table between us, several in French translation and two novels. When I registered genuine surprise she told me that they were a gift from Yuri Tairov, son of Svetlana and Mitya:

'I've known and loved Yuri since he was born. He's a fan of yours and my dearest friend.' She nodded to herself. 'Despite his mother.' Then despondency returned to her still-lovely features and what I took to be dementia began uncannily to replicate her mother's. She told me that she sometimes travelled by train to France, to the sea, to meet up with Picasso, whose naked arm gripped her waist as he reminded her why he admired Van Gogh – because Vincent had imposed his palette on nature instead of creeping about in the dappled sunlight obedient to nature as it comes to our eye.

'"That's why Picasso has no time for the Impressionists," he told me. "Even if you are soft on them, *devushka*."'

She chuckled to herself. 'One day I may show you the portrait Picasso painted of me, what they call the Raphael Madonna.'

'I would like to see it, Madame.'

'Not today, Pablo has taken it to restore the Italian church in the background.'

We sat for some time in silence.

'Madame, would you please tell me about Picasso's portrait of Stalin. You will remember that he had been invited by Gerasimov to –'

'Yes of course I remember.' Once again her gaze had become unfocused. 'You want the episode of Stalin's garden-orchard but why should I reveal it to a foreigner, a stranger, a spy?'

We sat. She gazed into space, both hands trembling on the

arms of her chair.

'Yes, Pablito and I did go to see Stalin. I remember now.'

'Pablo, Madame.'

'Yes, Pablo!' She sprang up and began to pace the room as if restored to herself by treading on the lava of an eruption long extinct.

33

~

Shortly after ten in the morning (when the Generalissimo is normally asleep), the *équipe* Picasso receive a message like no other message. It comes from the Generalissimo's private secretary, Poskrebyshev, via the Ministry of Culture, via VOKS: Comrade Stalin has granted Maître Picasso a sitting in an hour's time! As promised by Gerasimov, President of the Soviet Academy, it will take place in the garden-orchard of the Generalissimo's dacha. Comrade Picasso may not bring his French 'companions' – only Citizen Olga Lepinskaya. The great painter's brushes, paints, solvents, wads of newspaper, crayons, charcoals, easels, whatever, will be transported by members of the Generalissimo's private bodyguard.

The journey takes place in a vast limousine equipped not only with curtains covering the rear-seat windows but with darkened glass permitting nil visibility out or in. Picasso is swaddled in the back with Olga.

'It's fortunate I'm not a landscape painter today, a Repin, one of your Wanderers.' His magical hand, which can turn an old bicycle handlebar into the Venus de Milo, a scrap of newspaper into a soaring dove, is now squeezing her thigh above the tops of silk stockings donated by Uncle Ilya after his Italian trip.

'Pablo, you will bruise my leg!' (Has she ever before addressed him as Pablo?)

'No one can be allowed to know where Comrade Stalin lives, is that it?'

'I know no more than any other Soviet citizen, Maître. We are told that he lives on the Mozhaisk chausee outside the city. I have seen his cavalcade sweeping down Arbat, roaring through Arbat Square on singing tyres, past the big Art Movie cinema and on down Kalinin Street to the Kremlin. The Arbat, or "Orbat" was the ancient medieval trading settlement. A system of traffic lights flashes red several minutes before his limousine appears. Special traffic militia stand duty night and day to divert all traffic when he is coming. They say his usual working day is from 3 p.m. to 3 or 4 a.m.'

He squeezes again, oblivious to her protest. 'And who is "they"?'

'People as ignorant as I am.'

'Tonight, *devushka*, you will resist me?'

She is mute. Ehrenburg has now made a comfortable room available at a secret address where the only prying eyes (Olga does not doubt) belong to Beria. Wine, supper and a hot stove are to be provided by an old woman who was among those storming the Winter Palace thirty-five years ago and is so marinated in discretion (Ehrenburg says) that she can no longer remember who she is.

They have arrived. Guards in blue uniforms open the doors of the limousine. They salute. There is snow on the ground.

'Please follow, comrades.'

They now enter a huge glass pavilion of the kind you find in botanical gardens, a vast conservatory, a Temperate House, a blast of warm air, a benevolent sunshine irradiating a perfect lawn, fruit trees and beds of flowers from Georgia. No snow here.

Once inside Olga is dumbfounded to find Stalin himself, alert and apparently genial, seated in a wicker garden chair. An artist's easel has been placed near him. That unmistakable figure known the world over is wearing a simple buff-coloured tunic, high-collared round the neck, unadorned by medals. He carries a pipe in his left hand, offering the other to Picasso while remaining seated.

Trembling, almost bent double out of deference, Olga observes the handshake, the grip of two dwarfs born within two years of one another.

Stalin smiles. 'Summer surprised us,' he quips. 'Eelyot.'

Olga hesitates. 'I believe the Generalissimo is quoting from T.S. Eliot, an English poet, maybe American.'

Picasso shrugs, bemused, but Stalin takes evident pleasure in the painter's ignorance. '*Da*. The Waste of Land. Very good, though banned here of course. April is the cruellest month, very true, high hopes always dashed – I make sure.'

Picasso's equipment is now laid out on the lawn, whose lush green and warm temperature and humming fireflies and cavorting butterflies and sploshing plums so contrast with the snow and sub-zero temperatures gripping the Moscow they have left behind. Olga notices that Stalin has remained seated, tucking his booted legs beneath his wicker chair. Although she knows that the Generalissimo's height should match Picasso's there is as yet no confirmation of it.

Stalin is addressing her with (she notices) slanting wolf's eyes. 'Tell the Frenchie to make sure the portrait shows me tending that copious Georgian vine with this precious little trowel in my hand. It once belonged to Lenin. Of course no one thought such a grapevine could thrive in our harsh northern climate.'

Hearing this translated, Picasso shrugs in bafflement. 'Either the Generalissimo remains seated or he tends the vine. He can't do both.'

'What does Friend Picasso say?'

She trembles. 'Generalissimo, the maître is asking do you wish to remain seated...while tending the vine?'

Stalin does not budge and Picasso is already at work. All he needs is a charcoal crayon. Olga watches the magic hand pass across the page and into a series of interlocking loops – but not in the famous single, unbroken motion. A burst of subsidiary motions of the crayon suggest the maître is somewhat puzzled by his subject and decreasingly convinced that he exists.

Picasso shrugs and reluctantly shows the sketch. The wolf-eyes scrutinise it.

'Is that me, Frenchie? A bit quick?'

'*Oui*.' Pablo's expression remains reticent, troubled, as if he regrets the cruel power of his art to unearth the unreal in the real.

Stalin is troubled, too. 'Why am I only twenty years old in your sketch? How can I be Father of All the Peoples with a baby moustache like a bushy squirrel's tail and not a line of accumulated wisdom across features known to all the world? It reminds me of my days as a youthful seminarian and poet in Georgia – yes, I was a dreamer then but now I have created the Soviet Union and I have Adolf's skull on my desk in the Kremlin.'

Her head burning, Olga struggles to translate. The wolf eyes are on her.

'You are not doing well, young citizen. Tell the Frenchie to give me a portrait in oil or tempera in the style of the old Dutch masters. There's the easel. Tell him to use it and be quick about it.'

Olga translates. Picasso sighs, unable to disguise his contempt.

'Rembrandt, plenty of chiaroscuro?' he asks sardonically. 'But I warn you it will take longer. The Generalissimo had better settle down think about...whatever he thinks about. I want him deep in contemplation.'

Olga herself is in a form of deep contemplation about Stalin's booted legs, which have now emerged impatiently from under the chair. They are too long. If he stood up he would be measurably taller than the maître. A curator's eye can spot such details. She busies herself helping the guards to lay out the palettes, tubes of paint, brushes, cans for solvent, old newspapers. Stalin observes this with restless wolf eyes and then a strange thing occurs – he loses interests and issues a staccato order to the guards, bringing a new figure into the scene, a tall, youngish man wearing prison denims and carrying a large holdall heavy with electrical equipment. To Olga's astonishment the wolf eyes soften. 'How's your writing, Sasha?' He turns to Picasso. 'Have you met my zek Sasha? He's my favourite political prisoner – even though I have twelve million to choose from.'

Trembling, Olga staunchly translates, word for word. Picasso looks puzzled while continuing to paint. 'My comrades in the French Party tell me there are none.'

'Well, they can't count, can they? Hey, Sasha, what do you think of this sketch by the Frenchie?'

The zek wipes his hands on his overall before examining it. 'Do you really want my opinion?'

'*Da da.*'

'None of your dirty tricks if you don't like what I say?'

'Promise.'

'Not ten more years in the Gulag?'

'Cross my heart. Once a seminarian, always.'

'You still haven't crossed it.'

Stalin complies.

'Well, to be frank, what I see here in this sketch is a young idler with a moustache, smoking a pipe under a plum tree.'

'But is it me?' Stalin jabs his pipe at the portrait. 'Will the world recognise me?'

'Why don't you engage a real artist?'

'What has the electrician been saying?' Picasso demands of Olga.

'This miserable zek Sasha thinks he's writing a novel about me,' Stalin tells Picasso before she can reply. 'He has already given birth to filthy poems revealing himself as an enemy of the people and earned himself ten years but I think he is talented. I can spot a literary gift. I am not going to punish this fellow by setting him free – that would be the death of the artist in him. So would death.' Stalin beams jovially. 'Don't you agree, Sasha?'

Not attempting to comprehend this, or to command his subject to keep still, Picasso is working rapidly on his 'Rembrandt' while Olga hovers at his shoulder, but not nearer than he likes, rapidly servicing him with brushes, newspapers, tubes of paint. What she sees emerging is distinctively Hollandish, perhaps a glimpse of 'The Night Watchman'. And is the Great Helmsman not also the Night Watchman?

'Tell me, Sasha,' Stalin continues with obvious pleasure, 'are you one of those suffering from "writer's block"?'

'No. I am writing even as I stand here observing your Byzantine pretensions, wolf eyes.'

'Well, you know, writer's block is becoming increasingly

common, I don't know why. I keep asking Pasternak on the telephone, "So where's this novel of yours, *Doctor Zhivago*, how long does one have to wait, Boris Leonidovich?"'

'What does Pasternak say?'

'He says his paper refuses his pen until I release his mistress Ivanskaya from the Gulag.'

'And what do you say?'

'I say, you're the one who's supposed to be writing the novel, not your shameless girlfriend.'

The zek lays down his holdall and folds his arms. 'To be frank with you, Iosif Vissarionovich, I'm having difficulty with a scene from a novel in progress.'

'Yes, go on, don't beat about the bush.'

'It's dead of night in the Kremlin and State Security Minister Abakumov is trembling as he waits to be received by Stalin. He is kept waiting for an hour every month and he never knows whether he will emerge alive or dead.'

Stalin nods. 'Good. I like it. I expect he fouls himself.'

'How does Stalin decide who must die? Is it a deep decision or just a whim of the moment, maybe a twinge in the gut? I must know that.'

'You're the writer, Sasha, it's your job to decide. I don't expect Sholokhov or Fadeyev to come running to me bleating, "What shall I write next?"'

'But you do. You bully them round the clock, wolf eyes.'

Stalin shrugs shyly. 'Well, I do and I don't. It's just natural curiosity – well, mainly. You, Aleksandr Isayevich, are frankly the only writer who has ever ventured to understand me – and you alone can bring me everlasting life.'

'So restore my wife Nadya and my freedom to me.'

'You too? Just like Pasternak. Always Olga, Olga, Nadya, Nadya. If I made you happy you'd never write another word about me. You'd go back to teaching calculus in some quiet provincial school. When I'm gone I shan't mind being denounced, denigrated, detested – but being forgotten is not an option. You are the only writer who can keep me on the front page long after I'm gone. Take it from me, Sasha, they will want to pretend I never existed. They'll ship my embalmed body away from Lenin's and hide it under the Kremlin walls. Khrushchev, he's the one! Remind me to execute that Ukrainian potato tomorrow.'

'I have gone on strike, wolf eyes.'

Stalin gestures to the guards. 'Take him away and give him no food until he can show me that chapter about Abakumov soiling himself once a month.'

Olga winces as the zek is dragged out with a brutal show of force.

Stalin abruptly stands up and walks in his high brown boots to examine the easel. He is indeed much taller than he should be but Picasso doesn't know that – he has probably always assumed that Stalin is the giant in physique that he is in action.

'Da, da, good. Comrade Stalin by Rembrandt. Excellent! Lifelike! Classical perspective! Father of my people!' He shakes Picasso's hand warmly, a long grip. 'This will hang in my tomb.'

Picasso is nonplussed. 'I didn't say you could have it, Generalissimo. Isn't it destined for my exhibition at the Pushkin Museum?'

'Da, da, we will display this at the entrance to your exhibition, Maître Picasso.' Stalin is pacing his vast Temperate House in what appears to be a troubled state of mind. He stops. 'Tell me, how much would this Rembrandt fetch on the international art market – today?'

Picasso bridles. 'You must mean this Picasso?'

'Yes, yes of course. Otherwise the dealers in Paris would raise trivial historical objections.'

'You mean you want to sell it?'

'Well, it's mine!' He almost grabs it off the easel, Olga utters a cry of 'Wet paint!' and he desists, the wolf eyes running lovingly across the chiaroscuro. But then without warning the actor Gelovani begins tearing off his make-up and complaining pitifully about his poverty, about never being paid properly for any job he undertakes, not in films, not on the stage, not as the most highly esteemed Stalin-double.

'The name's Gelovani, a humble admirer of your life's work, Maître. May I keep this portrait? Please, I beg you. I have been approached by an art dealer in New York – Kootz or Klootz.'

The guards panic and hustle Picasso and Olga out of the Temperate House, back into the fallen snow. The zek is waiting, unguarded, beside the giant limousine, a parcel or manuscript under his arm, with an expression of ardent expectancy. He asks, he begs, Picasso to take it out of the country in his baggage.

'They will not search the great Picasso. Kindly post it to the address written on the package.'

Picasso snorts dismissively, pushes the package away as if it were a carrier of plague, and clambers into the rear of the limousine.

'Tell this saboteur to get lost,' he commands Olga.

The zek yells back: 'Your exhibition is dead, Picasso. *Mertvyi.* You're just another vainglorious fellow-traveller – like Chaplin. You complain about nothing in our utopia except your own exhibition.'

They are driven out through the perimeter gates and back along the road to Arbat and Kalinin. Only then does Olga notice that the maître has the sketch in his hand although the oil is left behind. She can imagine the sketch being subjected to the frigid, inquisitorial gaze of Comrade Triolet – she has the knack of needling Picasso, indeed she could needle a needle.

'A moment, Madame. What became of this Stalin sketch?'

'Pablo gave it to me.' Madame Lepinskaya produced it from a folder. 'Of course it is worth nothing but I cannot allow you to photograph it.'

It struck me immediately that this signed sketch closely resembled the one published by Louis Aragon in the edition of Les Lettres françaises *marking Stalin's death in March 1953, only three months after the scene described by Madame Lepinskaya. I asked her whether she had ever seen it.*

'*The Pushkin library subscribed to* Les Lettres françaises. *I could see that Pablo had done the same drawing from memory after news reached France of Stalin's death. They say that when Aragon telephoned him in Vallauris, Madame Gilot took the call and Picasso grumbled that he had never set eyes on Stalin.*'

'*That's in the memoir she published.*'

'*Well, he would tell her that, wouldn't he? He had to keep lying to everybody…because of me and our son Pablito.*'

By the following day Picasso has convinced himself that they have never intended to open his exhibition to the Soviet public. It was all a charade like Stalin in his garden. By way of revenge he decides to put in an appearance at Pyotr's 'severe style' street exhibition. 'To kick those bastards in the cojones.' Olga unflinchingly carries the message to the attic studio in Cheremushki. By now she knows that she loves Picasso and is ready to beseech him to take her and the child in her womb away to France.

'*Which is not to say that I liked him. If any man ever gave genius a bad name it was Pablo.*'

I reflected – but did not say – that she had not hanged herself like Marie-Thérèse Walter. Or shot herself in the head like Jacqueline Roux. She had merely retreated into total seclusion like Dora Maar.

Whom I now became determined to find in France.

34

N ina has not slept such is her apprehension about the ordeal
ahead. On the morrow Chaplin will be shown *Modern Times*.
But which version and in the company of what kind of audience?
Following the wipe-out of *The Great Dictator*, and Chaplin's threat
to fly home by the first available Aeroflot 'crate', Aleksandrov has
authorised an offer which might placate an incensed and
medically unstable maestro – a palliative or (as Eisenstein calls it)
a 'placebo'. If *The Great Dictator* is politically out of the question,
too much haunted by history, then a screening of that other
masterpiece of the post-silent cinema, *Modern Times*, might be
feasible.

To bring Chaplin to Kino 1 he must be promised (Aleksandrov
impresses on Nina) his own original print brought from London
(the smokescreen about 'wrong sprockets' having been
abandoned). To persuade Chaplin to believe he will be shown his
own film unredacted, to cajole him into abandoning for a few
hours his soaring incredulity, Aleksandrov has instructed Nina
to organise a shopping expedition for Mrs Chaplin in the
charming company of Lyubov' Orlova, no less, and an interpreter,
and a correspondent from the magazine *Soviet Woman* – while
Nina shows Chaplin the delights of the Hotel Moskva's special de
luxe bedroom suite.

So no wonder she is lying awake in that awful room of hers.
She wishes she could fall asleep but dare not swallow a pill
because the grey winter morning is already seeping through the
window, her alarm clock.

During the past day or two, a further problem has been
gnawing at that part of her skull which descends to her pretty
nose. Chaplin is, frankly, not well in body or mind. Increasingly
he displays an obsessive need to meet the real Stalin, the real
Uncle Joe, not that bounder Gelovani – in fact the humiliating

incident at the Bolshoi theatre has only whetted Chaplin's manic obsession. He has even asked her whether Stalin will attend the screening of *Modern Times*, and if not why not. Nina, who sincerely fears that Chaplin may suffer a physical collapse during the screening, has therefore sat herself down with the lazy Gelovani in the Mosfilm canteen he haunts.

Hearing her proposal, Gelovani can only stare in astonishment. She is very pretty, he notices not for the first time, but no less frivolous and foolish than a woman should be.

'An ambulance driven by Somebody! I have been taught how not to drive!'

'It'll only be for ten minutes. The ambulance won't exactly go anywhere.'

A slow sigh of relief.

She takes his lathery hand. 'So Charlie will have his ardently desired encounter with Someone after all. Speaking as one double to another, I advise you to mug up on your Bernard Shaw.'

'Ah – ah yes, I remember when he – I – invited Shaw to visit the Soviet Union. Wait: do I get paid for this? Show me a chit signed by Aleksandrov.'

It so happens, most awkwardly, that Oona's shopping expedition with Aleksandrov's wife Orlova had resulted in an unanticipated friendship between the two women, Orlova being captivated by Oona's descriptions of her family life, her four children, her tales of modern Hollywood, the glamorous visitors received in Summit Drive, the parties and games of tennis, not forgetting 'true stories' of Chaplin's love-life and his painful prosecution under the Mann Act. Orlova has even learned to say 'Wow'. The upshot being that in a dizzy moment of peaceful co-existence Orlova has confided to Oona that Chaplin is to be shown a Soviet revamp of *Modern Times*, not the real thing at all – and only a few dozen cinema workers have been summoned. Oona is aghast: Charlie's blood pressure has been running high despite the pills anxiously prescribed by Soviet doctors who have been heard murmuring about dangers that Oona cannot exactly remember or spell right – angina, occlusion, myocardial infarction, cardiac arrhythmia, coronary thrombosis.

The upshot of the upshot is that over breakfast on the morning of the screening Oona begs Charlie not to go through with it. He is in high spirits and dismissive, even of Orlova's reported warning (women). A fatigued Nina joins them for the special advance breakfast he has demanded, including waffles in syrup, fatal for every kind of heart condition. As with *The Great Dictator*, a tearful Oona is yet again refusing to accompany him to this morning's screening.

'This is going to be your worst day ever, Charlie, and I don't intend to share it. For God's sake, Charlie, don't go. They are set on humiliating you like they did last time. I bet Aleksandrov has not forgiven your public comments about *Meeting on the Elbe*. I bet Chiaureli feels no better after your derisive remarks about *The Fall of Berlin*. You have made enemies here, Charlie.'

'They will never dare tamper with *Modern Times*,' Chaplin snaps, pushing his plate away.

'I bet they've been doing nothing else for the past week. Isn't that so, Nina? You know the score, come clean.'

Coming clean is not Nina's *spécialité de la maison*. She firmly believes she wouldn't be sitting here sharing the Chaplins' breakfast if she had ever 'come clean' about anything. When Oona tries tears, Chaplin says he has known better actresses.

'Let's go.'

Nina can tell how hurt he is by his beloved wife's boycott as soon as soon they settle together into the limousine. He falls silent, pensive, his profile has aged by ten years, her sidelong gaze watches the chins multiply.

They enter Kino 1. Aleksandrov and other notables (not many, mind you, and no sign of Orlova) are waiting to greet the maestro, all very affable. Eisenstein shuffles in and flops heavily into an empty seat directly behind Chaplin, a bag of gloom seeping at the seams. A chirpy Chaplin turns to pat his knee, the divine hand.

'Up and running, Sergei? Well, at least we can die laughing.'

'Charlie, I am both delighted and distraught to see that you have learned nothing from your time among us.'

The lights remain up but dimmed. No one is in a hurry. Perhaps hurry is a Western invention. Eventually a shabbily dressed, faintly professorial figure ascends a short flight of steps to the stage, closely observed by the portraits of Lenin and Stalin. He introduces himself in serviceable English, as Boris Z. Shumyatsky, whom Chaplin remembers, yes, welcoming to Hollywood when he led a large delegation of visiting Soviet cinéastes in the mid-thirties.

'You told me that Shumyatsky is dead, Sergei.'

'He doesn't know.'

Shumyatsky begins lugubriously by recalling how a Soviet delegation first met Maestro Chaplin, 'who we welcome in our midst today,' in his Hollywood home in 1933. He had most courteously screened for their benefit a preliminary cut of *Modern Times*. Hollywood had deserted silent pictures. The art and insouciance of pantomime was in decline. Caught between the silent film era in which he thrived and the onrush of talkies, Maestro Chaplin had astutely devised a middle way – a soundtrack with few spoken words and avoiding lip synch. The basic strategy was to leave Charlie true to himself as the silent clown. 'Marvellously achieved,' adds Shumyatsky.

'Thank you, Boris,' Chaplin says loudly.

Shumyatsky promises to be brief. The Soviet delegation had found the ending of *Modern Times* unacceptably pessimistic. They had found the hero's class consciousness lamentably weak and hesitant. They had found little sense of solidarity with the American working class fighting for the future of humanity. Maestro Chaplin had received all these suggestions most courteously and indicated that he, too, had been deeply concerned about these defects and intended to rectify them.

'We in Moscow waited expectantly. Unfortunately, nothing came of this. "No one tells me how to make films," Mr Chaplin was quoted as telling the *New York Times*. "If William Randolph

Hearst cannot buy me, nor can Moscow's gold.'"

'Misquoted,' Chaplin loudly tells Eisenstein.

Shumyatsky ploughs on. 'For that reason we have invited the great director, whose presence here in Moscow is a source of joy for all peace-loving mankind, to view a version re-edited – and to some minor extent re-enacted – in our Mosfilm studios under the expert guidance of Grigorii Aleksandrov, always a devoted admirer of Charlie Chaplin's work. Comrades, let us hope that in ninety minutes' time Maestro Chaplin himself will be able to tell us that this is the version he always wanted to make – but for the reactionary pressures of the Catholic Church, the National Association of Manufacturers, and their lackeys the American Federation of Labor.'

Nina's gentle hand lies on Chaplin's pulse, probably up from 100 to 130, thumping with rage.

'Grigorii Aleksandrov always cheated on the tennis court,' he tells Eisenstein (who has lost count of the number of times he has heard this since Charlie's arrival). 'I had to buy an umpire's chair and persuade Douglas Fairbanks or Mary Pickford to call the lines.'

Eisenstein nods. 'I remember. We all cheated, Charlie, it was obligatory.'

The lights dim, the screen comes to life, a projector whirrs, normally the most promising sound in Chaplin's life. The era of silent cinema and subtitles partially reasserts itself, but the captions are in Russian, hastily doctored-in at the Mosfilm studios on the brow of Lenin Hills.

Lady Stears and I had recently viewed a DVD of the film. Modern Times *was Chaplin's satire about the new conveyor belt (or 'Taylor') system made famous by Henry Ford. Big industry was luring healthy young men off America's farms, training them to behave like machines, and turning them into nervous wrecks. This was the time of strikes, riots, unemployment.*

The film had opened with montage – a herd of jostling sheep juxtaposed with a throng of workers in fedoras surging up the stairs of a subway station.

The sheep are gone and with them the entire impact of the opening montage. Eisenstein stirs in response to Chaplin's groan of protest.

'Charlie, I warned you that Soviet culture cannot tolerate animal metaphors – when Vyshinsky vituperates at the UN, the imperialists are running dogs, jackals, hyenas, vipers, etc.'

Proudly surveying his futuristic machinery, interlocking cogs, wheels and levers rising level upon level, the capitalist president of the company introduces a two-way TV hookup which imposes his bullying face on the workforce while enabling him to monitor their every move (as when he catches Charlie smoking in the washroom).

No sign of the factory washroom! Gone!

Eisenstein heaves: 'Too modern, too luxurious, to show to Soviet workers, Charlie.'

Comes the famous feeding-machine sequence. Little Charlie is inevitably chosen as the guinea pig for the lunch-break machine. The inventor's assistants strap him into a seat that places him at chin level with a rotating tray. All goes well until the switches begin to short. His chest is drenched in hot soup, whipped cream from the charlotte russe is smeared across face and neck, roundhouse blows from the napkin buffer all but knock him out, a maniacally revved up cob of corn scours his teeth and the underpart of his nose. Two metal bolts are shoved into his mouth.

Most of this sequence – regarded by the world as the film's supreme comic achievement – has gone.

Chaplin is on his feet, shaking his fist at Aleksandrov. Nina gently coaxes him back into his chair. Eisenstein sighs.

'Charlie, the idea of a capitalist obliged to provide a lunch break for his workers is out of the question even if the capitalist is intent on cutting their free time. As for the meals provided by the robot, they are in any case too good to convey the real plight of American workers.'

'Why? American audiences didn't think so.'

'Because the meals provided are offensively superior to the

Soviet reality. Charlotte russe with whipped cream! Napkins! Three courses – I ask you. Did the sailors of my *Battleship Potemkin* enjoy three courses?'

'Their meat was ridden with maggots but that was in 1905 under the Tsar.'

Eventually little fellow Charlie is driven to defend his sanity by becoming a crazy prankster deliberately causing mayhem and squirting oil in the faces of bullying managers and foremen. Here Chaplin displays a Luddite frenzy with balletic grace, disrupting production all over the plant by spinning valve wheels and reversing master gears in the control room. He is carted away to a psychiatric hospital.

My god, all gone! Not a trace.

'Charlie, please understand that one man's destructive revolt on the production line is out of the question. Such anarchic individualism cannot be displayed to a Soviet peasant audience recently herded into the towns.'

The reels turn. Chaplin is beginning to wish they didn't.

The sentimental episode during which Paulette Goddard and Chaplin inhabit a derelict and isolated waterfront hut in idyllic togetherness – *gone*.

'Charlie,' moans Eisenstein, 'the Soviet urban masses craving for a separate dwelling – that's the problem.'

'But it's a hovel! The little fellow keeps falling through the upper floor.'

'To fall through the upper floor you have to have one.'

In an extended scene, the little fellow finds a job as night watchman in a large department store. He secretly brings his girlfriend into the store and together they play make-believe among the luxuries on offer – she cannot resist the pretty clothes and super-beds, the lovely fabrics.

All gone. Not a trace of it.

'Good Communist women do not hunker after luxuries,' Nina whispers.

'Hanker,' Chaplin says coldly. 'Hanker is what we all do.

Anyway, the young gamine played by Paulette is not a Communist.'

'She is now,' Nina whispers. 'She has joined the striving masses and their lofty aspirations. Look, Maestro, it's your Nina!'

Et toi, Nina? Chaplin tries to rise, clutching not his heart but his throat – so it often goes with myocardial infarction, cardiac arrhythmia, coronary thrombosis. His head strikes the back of the seat heavily and he slumps to the ground. The world's most beloved rubber man, survivor of a lifetime of tumbles, vanishes beneath the anxious forms bending over him. A murmur of consternation passes through Kino 1. This could turn into an international scandal! Aleksandrov is ashen. No one notices the greatest film director of all time, Sergei Eisenstein, motionless in his seat, stricken by shame, properly dead this time. Vladislav Volkov will never again say 'Charlie'.

Chaplin remembers nothing of this commotion. They must have carried him to an ambulance already waiting outside. He becomes vaguely aware of an oxygen mask and concerned faces peering down at him from a complex scaffolding of tubes – modern times! Nina is giving him the kiss of life, surely? Convinced that Uncle Joe himself is driving the ambulance, Chaplin draws comfort from the presence of this solid figure behind the wheel, wearing a simple tunic reeking of pipe tobacco, onion, vodka, moustache, leather boots and is it urine?

'Uncle Joe, are you there?'

'Call me Iosif Vissarionovich.'

'And we have friends in common, sir, I'm sure you remember George Bernard Shaw. He came to see you twenty years ago. He went away tremendously impressed by your Five Year Plans and collectivization.'

'A good larf, Shaw.'

'"Stalin is no mere politician, he's a genius," GBS once confided to me. He came to believe that we in Britain urgently needed our own Uncle Joe, I mean our own Iosovitch.'

'*Nyet*, there can only be one.'

'That's what I told George Bernard. "Only one Stalin" is rather like "socialism in one country", I mean "socialism in one man". Is that the formula?'

'Da.'

'*Saint Joan* is in my humble opinion Shaw's best play.'

'The saints speak to her – I know the feeling. Maestro Chaplin, in anticipation of my seventy-third birthday I award you a Stalin Prize first class. All of your great films shall be shown to the great Soviet public without interference by the Jewish Zionist saboteurs.'

'Uncle Joe, I'm very much obliged, common sense at last, and I'd like you to know that in my time I have met Churchill Wells Macdonald Cocteau Cripps Edward Prince of Wales Lady Astor President Vincent Auriol of France Sir James Barrie Shaw Harry Bridges the boxer Georges Charpentier – I beat him on points over ten rounds – Casals Chaliapin Chou En-lai the tennis player Henri Cochet William Randolph Hearst Cecil B. DeMille Sergei Diaghilev Theodore Dreiser Einstein (twice and we correspond regularly). Did I mention Mahatma Gandhi Pandit Nehru his daughter Mrs Gandhi Sir Edwin Lutyens Frank Harris Clara Haskill Jascha Heifetz D.W. Griffiths Sam Goldwyn Elinor Glyn Graham Greene J.B. Priestley Aldous Huxley W. Somerset Maugham Pola Negri Vaslav Nijinsky the marvellous Anna Pavlova Sergei Rachmaninov Sir John Barbirolli FDR Herbert Hoover Arnold Schoenberg Mack Sennett Gertrude Stein Alice B Toklas. Did I mention Franklin Delano Roosevelt?'

Chaplin subsides, clapped out and out for the count. When some time later his eyes and ears open, the answering voice seems to belong to Nina – no sign of the Generalissimo or of the ambulance. Nina is leaning over him but no, it could be his wife.

'I warned you not to go, Charlie Boy, and you told me to go shopping. They brought you back from Kino 1 in the limousine but you have been insisting it was an ambulance driven by Mr Stalin.'

'Iosofvitchvitch promised to restore the eating machine

episode, and the little fellow sabotaging the automated leviathan, and the big department store scene – and everything else.'

'Charlie.'

'And Uncle Joe is restoring the little fellow falling through the floor of their love nest.'

She is clutching his hand. 'Charlie, when we first got to Moscow I kind of thought, well all this is grand guignol and a big joke like a Sam Beckett play or maybe Ionesco. I mean I'm naturally an easy-going sort of person, aren't I, Charlie? Wasn't that why I married you?'

'Uncle Joe said we can have the sheep montage at the beginning. And the little fellow can be against strikes because he is.'

'But now the guignol is looking rather too grand. Charlie, I've never been so frightened. We're caught in the middle of a byzantine power struggle – I mean, these are desperate people, fakes and doubles and god knows what, all struggling in the darkness to stay alive. To survive. I had lunch with Harrison Salisbury today. He's been here three years and he says it's never been so bad. Harrison reckons that Lavrentiy Beria has made a bid for the succession, a detente with the West, a kind of push –'

'Putsch,' Nina says.

'OK, I'll give you a putsch, Deanna Durbin. Harrison says Beria is now being outgunned by the diehards. Harrison can't find a word about you or Pablo in the press or on Moscow Radio.'

'Perhaps you should avoid further lunches with Harrison Salisbury. I'm sure I'll be in all their papers as soon as Uncle Joe gives the word.'

'Charlie, Harrison says you are in denial. Maybe I should leave Russia tomorrow to look after the children – I mean if the worst comes to the worst.'

'I will arrange it,' her husband says coldly. It's the voice which has dismissed scores of United Artists actresses and wives. 'Go if you think you should.'

He gazes at Oona's translucent beauty, her elfin features, the strong eyebrows, the hair meticulously parted down the middle, and remembers all those home movies of the family she likes to take. 'Stay with me,' he murmurs, gripping her hand.

'He almost gripped mine by mistake.'

'Charlie my Boy, I've got to tell you this, while you were at Kino 1 this morning that electrician Sasha, you know, the zek, he came here again, fixed the telephone bugs again, and asked me to stay in Russia and share the Gulag with him.'

'Sounds promising.'

'Sasha tells me you have to make your own bed in this Gulag thing and do your own laundry and ironing and cook your own meals and even cut your own toenails. He says you have to stand in line in the snow to see a gynaecologist, a masseuse or a psychiatrist. Sasha says that if you step out of line or even stumble in the snow, the guard dogs tear you to pieces. That happens to you every day, he says! That's what I've been missing all these years with you, Charlie, I mean real life.'

'Did that rogue give you his manuscript to take back to London?' Chaplin asks her with a sigh of resignation.

'Well actually he did.'

'Lady Stears, no offence but how can we possibly enter into Chaplin's deliriums and dreams?' (She was still chewing the same piece of gum, sometimes displaying it on the tip of her tongue.) 'Isn't all this a bit beyond belief?'

'Charlie always told me everything. He was very much in love with me, if you can imagine me forty year ago, Oxford.'

'I expect you were now advising Oona to return to her children?'

'No, no, that street accident had to be in Russia.'

35

Pyotr Davidov's attic studio is located in a shabby area of the Cheremushki suburb – the name means 'bird-cherry' and Shostakovich later set an operetta in this area of south-west Moscow. Pyotr's dwelling is to be found amid broken paving stones, cesspools of water from dysfunctional drains, donkeys feeding in courtyards and a noisy elevated commuter railway – the *elektrichka* – clanking from somewhere to nowhere. Two MVD cars are escorting Picasso's limousine whether he likes it or not. Splattered by slush, they hoot haughtily at street urchins playing 'wheels' with old rubber tyres.

A few (not many yet) uniformed men have already formed a protective half-circle opposite a dozen unofficial painters and their canvases waiting to be unwrapped, plus what could be fifty intrepid supporters determined to show solidarity, not a few attracted by the rumours that Picasso himself might show up.

Alighting from the limousine, Olga catches sight of her mother among the supporters, leaning on the arm of Dora Maar, both wearing heavy sheepskin coats and boots. Olga also notices Harrison Salisbury stationed among the artists, taking notes, the only journalist on view. She sees Pyotr talking animatedly to him (as if a fatal mistake is worth repeating).

'It is wrong to bring a distinguished foreign guest here, Comrade,' the MVD captain reproaches Olga. 'What will he think? Imagine the international scandal if he is bitten by a rat.'

'But Comrade Captain, this is how this famous artist began his life in Paris fifty years ago, when he and his friends were so poor that a fresh egg dropped on the staircase meant hunger for a week.'

'I hope you realise where this *pirushka* may lead. Davidov over there is hell bent on a *provokatsia*.'

'Comrade Captain, we should not be ashamed of our working

people.'

'Ha! When did any of them do a day's work? *Parazity*.'

Picasso climbs out warily and surveys the scene, bemused. Olga guides him across the cobbles – she hears mounting applause – and into the huddle of waiting artists, swaddled against the cold.

'Maître, please meet my colleague Pyotr Davidov.' (She does not say 'meet again', the memory of the encounter outside the Academy is too fraught.)

'Ah, the "Sobaka", the Dog.' Picasso does not offer his hand and Pyotr evidently does not expect him to. The great man turns to Ekaterina, bowing to the old lady but his eye is resting on Dora Maar.

'*Bonjour, Dora.*'

'*Bonjour.*'

'This street is mainly inhabited by railway workers, Maître,' Pyotr tells him in his vigorous if imperfect French. 'That's how I now earn a living. They dismissed me as a curator at the Pushkin Museum, you know, so I'm now a trainee signalman, can you believe it?'

Picasso's eyes twinkle though his mouth remains firm. 'I wouldn't want to be a passenger in a train with you in charge of the points.' Turning to Olga, he indicates the solid rank of militia. 'Why are these soldiers here?'

'To protect us against ourselves,' Pyotr answers.

'Well, let's view your work.'

The artists begin to introduce themselves and unwrap their pictures, propping the canvases, some framed but mostly pegged to boards, on old chairs and fold-up stools. Short and broad, Picasso moves quite rapidly through the display.

'I'm afraid magical realism has only just caught up with you, fifty years late,' he tells Pyotr. 'In the wider world it's *vieux jeu*.'

'But not here in Russia, Maître. *Au contraire*, we are ahead of our time! You may be surprised to learn that our best supporters are our new breed of nuclear scientists. I've sold a few canvases to the Research Institute at Dubna.'

Picasso's phosphorescent eyes take in canvases in the style (clearly) of Pollock, Rauschenberg and Rothko.

'The Yankees are coming to Russia, eh? Along with Tarzan, Cola-Cola, American Express, drugstores, Voice of America –'

'Careful, Maître,' someone laughs, 'or you may sound like Khrushchev.'

A ragged but ardent chorus of voices launches into a vigorous defence of American culture, some requiring translation by Olga. 'Yes, VoA! That's where it's at, man. Jazz. *Dzhaz*. Glenn Miller's "Chattanooga Choo-Choo". Duke Ellington. Louis Armstrong.'

Picasso stands bemused. These are grown men with the minds of schoolboys. Voices compete to inform him how the popular jazzman Eddie Rosner was arrested and sent to the Kolyma Gulag.

'He's still there – if alive. They banned the saxophone here. On a specified day every saxophonist was required to bring his instrument to the State Variety Music Agency, where it was promptly confiscated.'

'Identification papers were altered to remove any reference to the sax.'

Picasso gently lifts his hand as if requesting quiet. 'Rosmer? Rosner, have you heard of this man, *devushka?*'

'Yes, Maître, he's a great talent and we all miss his music.'

Pyotr adds his bit: 'The tenor-sax Yuri Rubanov emerged from the State Agency's office as a bassoonist, though he told me he had never held a bassoon in his hand. Everything was banned as cosmopolitan filth.'

'Is this the Voice of America?' Picasso asks Olga.

Pyotr answers: 'The Voice of America hosted by Willis Conover has restored the sound of the sax to us. Did you know that Willis is from Buffalo, New York? Listen, I have records brought back from Berlin by Soviet officers and sold on the black market at 23 roubles each. *Da*, the tango, the foxtrot, boogie-woogie.'

Picasso shrugs. Wandering among the paintings on display, he allows himself to register pleasure when versions of Malevich's suprematist *Black Square, Black Cross* and *Black Circle* surface.

'My good friend Kazimir! Such a genius. Now you are claiming your true heritage – the great European tradition. American shit does not interest Picasso.' He says something about 'shooing gum' and the assembled artists try to suppress laughter.

Pyotr asks him what he thinks of the severe style. 'Do you like our new *surovyi stil*'? – translate, Olga.'

She does so: 'Pyotr means flat spatial composition, outlined forms, and use of similar shades of the same colour. Facial expressions become stereotypical and emotionally neutral, reminiscent of the old icon paintings.'

Restless on his feet, wearing torn jeans, Pyotr talks rapidly in a mix of Russian, French and American English. 'Icon paintings are our future! Please look at this one by my friend Igor – a Da Vinci Madonna juxtaposed with a Moscow slum, you probably recognise this very street. And now this one by my friend Ludmilla – a sensuous Titian nude is impaled on the Kremlin's Spassky Tower. Here you see my own empty vodka bottle floating past the Taj Mahal.'

'I am not a surrealist,' Picasso tells them. 'I leave that to Dali.'

The painter Ludmilla presses forward shyly: 'Maître, we use the *realia* of our life, slogans, banknotes, identity cards, newspapers with typical headlines. You know the parallel work of Andy Warhol and Jasper Johns –'

Picasso waits while Olga translates. He shrugs and grunts irritably. 'The only artist I respect over there in the so called "New World" is Diego Rivera, who is Mexican not American. Why should Matisse, Braque or Picasso care about Pop art, kinetics, movie queens, and Frankensteins?'

Pyotr almost grabs his arm but Olga gently deflects Pyotr's hand. 'Pablo, our new art is coming up from what they call "the sewers". We will send our viruses and pus pouring through their academies and institutes. Vodka, Pablo?'

Picasso accepts a thimble of the liquid – one must – and immediately becomes more benign. He even picks up a couple of

Pyotr's canvases. As Olga watches her 'morning sickness' returns, Ekaterina says she should be granted time off work but 'Impossible now!' Olga cries, summoning her courage to confront the day. Now she would like to cling to Pablo, the source of her sickness, but no woman is allowed to do that.

'Actually, Maître,' she says, 'I remember seeing your portraits of your first wife, the Ballets russes dancer Olga Khokhlova. Your images of her in the early twenties are in this same severe style, don't you agree?'

'*Tochno!* Exactly!' cries Pyotr reverting to Russian. 'Yes, you, PP, are the father of our Russian renaissance. That fact alone makes the two pictures in your hands бесценный, priceless! Although they stupidly bear the signature "Sobaka", they should be valued as Picassos.'

Olga does not translate the last sentence because everyone is laughing and because she feels sick. Pyotr is now eagerly unwrapping a severe-style painting of a herring lying on a copy of *Pravda*.

'Our official press is not without its uses, Maître Picasso.'

Everyone laughs. The vodka bottles circulate. The crowd of friends and supporters have been pressing in, anxious not to miss a word. Picasso feels goaded into raising the subject of values and prices.

'And how much is a new "Sobaka" one metre by forty-five centimetres worth?' he asks.

'Two hundred dollars each!' Pyotr is quivering. 'That is what your friend pays me.'

Picasso is puzzled. 'My friend, you say?'

Olga murmurs, 'He means Madame Maar.'

Picasso searches for Dora among all the taller people. 'Is that true, Dora?' She nods almost imperceptibly. 'You never told me you are so wealthy, Dora.'

'She admires my work, Maître.' Pyotr drops his voice to reveal to Picasso that he is planning to get married. (News to Olga but she cannot demur.)

'Some muddle-headed *devushka*,' Picasso remarks to Olga, pinching her cheek so that it hurts. 'Congratulations, Dog. I'll go to two hundred dollars if you show me a portrait of your fiancée in the nude.'

Harrison Salisbury watches as Olga turns away.

'Why do you hesitate?' Picasso presses the emaciated young artist. 'Doesn't every painter worthy of the name keep several portraits of his beloved hidden behind bric-a-brac in his studio? Here's a man who calls himself an artist but his own mistress won't model for him!'

'Maître,' Olga says shyly, 'how many nudes have you seen by Russian artists from the time of the icons to –'

'Never mind the middle ages! Never mind your monk-painter Andrei Rublev. We're here in the modern world. Go and look at Egon Schiele.'

'But there were nudes in Western art right back to classical times,' Olga says. 'It's a question of tradition. You have been in Moscow for a week, you have visited all the museums and galleries, but when did you see a nude by a Russian artist?'

Picasso's beautiful forefinger is under Olga's chin. 'Don't be too clever with old Picasso. In Catalonia we have a proverb about hares which show their ears above the corn. I never said anything about nudes.' (Though he did, everyone heard him.) He stands with powerful arms folded across his chest.

'What is this *devushka* to you, Dog? Why should she consent to marry a pauper of low principles who can't paint?'

Harrison Salisbury is listening and taking photographs. Everyone ignores him because everyone knows who he is and how he got Pyotr into dire trouble. He wouldn't expect otherwise.

Swiftly Pyotr unwraps an acrylic on canvas. 'I've been executing a perfect copy of Dalí's *Portrait of Picasso*,' he declares defiantly, eyes wild. 'Here, Maître, have it for free!'

Picasso snorts disdainfully but his eye registers a degree of recognition verging on admiration. It's good, a remarkable echo of the original. He is on the retreat. He makes a small gesture which has the effect of gathering the artists close in to him, in a semi-circle. His mood is thoughtful, benevolent – suddenly these disadvantaged fellows are his children, he has seventy-two years in the bank, he has known Apollinaire, perhaps he can rub off on them through the barriers of time and place one of his multiple skins.

'*He delivered quite a long talk, too extended for me to remember word-for-word, and I was constantly distracted by ominous motions among the militia and the construction workers I could see gathering with their hateful bulldozers at the far end of our space in Cheremushki. These were the notorious* druzhiniks, *the vigilantes. So I can give you only the gist, Monsieur.*'

'*Please do.*'

'We have to go back to the Egyptians and the Greeks,' Picasso begins, 'and let's not forget the Romans and the divinely gifted Chinese landscape artists and calligraphers. Their canon of art and beauty was circumscribed by strict rules, by watertight conventions. You get the same thing during the Renaissance, the Quattrocento, and in the Dutch masters from Van Eyck to Vermeer. But then in the late nineteenth century, at the time I was born, perhaps that was a coincidence though I've never been sure, all the rules broke down. Observe the passage from Corot to Van Gogh, from Manet to Klimt. Every artist could quite suddenly do whatever he liked. The rule now was to break the rule. You could say that painting as such died on its feet and the galleries were clamouring for individuality. The new movements pursued one another like happy children galloping along the seashore, leaping on each other's backs and throwing sand. And, you know, that has been both good and bad. We have been searching for a new architectonic order in composition, wrestling with our palettes to escape from the imitation of one fad by the next. And you, my friends, with your sub-American styles, and your "severe" style, strike my old eye as prisoners of imitation. Of course nothing repeats itself exactly but I do warn you about Western fashions. Of course Picasso himself is a Western fashion, the dealers crawl over each other's backs clawing and biting to possess any small bit of him. But while they are sticking dollar signs on "Picasso yesterday", Picasso himself shuts himself away in his atelier in search of "Picasso today", never knowing what he will find.'

'*Of course I translated. The Russian artists listened, transfixed. But I was observing ominous movements and infiltrations across the cobbled square. Gangs of "construction workers" in black leather jerkins and armed with large spades, the famed subbotniki who give their labour voluntarily on Saturdays (yet today was Sunday), were forming up in semi-military phalanxes. Municipal cleaning vans, even bulldozers, were suddenly upon us. The subbotniki and druzhiniks were beginning to close in, shouting coarse street insults. I was now very afraid for my mother and Madame Maar.*'

'*And for the child in your womb? And you felt sick?*'

'Pablo,' Olga says softly, 'I'm afraid they are about to attack us. We thought you would be our safeguard but we were mistaken.'

'Poof. You have the MVD people here. They will telephone the authorities.'

'The MVD, the authorities and the rabble are one and the same,' Pyotr tells him.

Olga approaches the MVD captain who has escorted them from Gorky Street. 'Is this what you meant by "bitten by rats", Comrade Officer?'

'This gathering is unauthorised and illegal, *Grazhdanka.*' (She is no longer 'comrade.') 'You informed us that Monsieur Picasso was to visit a private studio. The Moscow municipality is closing this so-called "street exhibition". We'll give you all five minutes to be gone.'

'Pablo, we must hurry,' Pyotr says. 'We ask you to ship two dozen of our best works out of Russia. We will arrange transport to your studio in *ulitsa* Gorky. Each painting will be properly cartoned, you need only carry them to the airport in your privileged luggage. No one will dare search you or examine the parcels at Sheremetyevo. Your dealers will sell them on our behalf. The world will then know about the real art of Russia.'

Picasso has been taking in the scene and its implications. 'By all means I will do it,' he tells Pyotr, tells everyone. 'I am not invariably in love with your work but I defend your right to paint freely according to your vision. I lived in Paris during the Nazi occupation, you know. The Gestapo used to visit my studio, inspect my "degenerate" work, and ask whether I was a Jew. Although I don't have that privilege, I never said no. In view of what has been going on here in Russia, I offer the same advice to you Muscovites. Never say No, I am not a Jew. So I will send several taxis to collect your paintings and I will take them to France.'

He still does not fully understand the situation.

The high-booted MVD captain strides across the cobbles and through the muddy puddles, followed by the limousine, and addresses Olga. 'This unauthorised and unlawful gathering is now terminated.' He opens the rear door of the limousine. 'Kindly invite our honoured French guest to step inside.'

Olga dutifully translates. Picasso takes a small sketch pad from his coat pocket, moving several paces away from the open car door and into the crowd.

'Tell them that Picasso intends to record the event, this new Guernica.'

The MVD understand defiance when they see it and at a signal the *subbotniki* wade in with flailing spades, attacking artists, canvases, spectators. A water canon opens up while an antique bulldozer rumbles in only thirty paces from where Picasso is standing. A *subbotnik* of no great height but commanding physique takes Pyotr by the collar:

'You have nothing but contempt for working people. You invite celebrities from the West to ridicule us and our Party. We gave our lives fighting fascism yet you call us fascists. You flout our socialist laws. You sell your souls for dollars. You are nothing but parasites, vermin infesting the Motherland.'

Pyotr chokes and wriggles in the man's iron grip. 'Go away, comrade! Leave us alone! You understand nothing!'

The grip tightens. 'Know something? We are volunteers, we don't get paid for working Saturdays. We like to be doing something constructive, the new Komsomol metro station or the new television tower at Sokol'niki. Something vermin like you should be proud to be part of, to call your own. Get this straight: my parents were illiterate peasants under the tsar but I am a qualified construction engineer. I thank Comrade Stalin for that – he has given us the H-bomb ahead of the Americans. Let them tremble before Soviet power. No need to kow-tow to foreigners. Comrade Stalin will never let us down.'

He throws Pyotr to the ground like an empty paper bag then spits in his face. The *subbotnik* then finds Harrison Salisbury and grabs at his camera but receives such a blow as to knock him to the ground. Aware that Salisbury is protected by the MVD's department of Foreign Affairs, the captain intervenes, fearing an international scandal.

Olga sees Picasso gripped by both arms and almost lifted off his feet as the MVD bundle him into the back seat. The militia have also got hold of Maar, they have been following her around Moscow and are well aware who she is. She too is bundled into the limousine. The door slams, the car takes off at speed on skidding tyres, it is Olga's last glimpse of him, ever. As the artists are beaten and scattered, Olga runs to her mother and with Pyotr's help carries her away out of danger, stumbling across the broken cobbles through the slush. As violence mounts Pyotr, bruised and trembling, clutching only a few of his canvases, hustles them up the stairs into his attic studio where the three of them huddle shivering from cold and fright. Pyotr strikes a match and lights several candles.

'Must protect the baby, Ochka – our baby.'

I laid down my notebook as a gesture of protest, so improbable, so totally out of character, was this remark.

36

I laid down my notebook because Pyotr, from all I had heard
about him from Madame Lepinskaya, seemed to me clever,
perhaps talented, decidedly immature, vain, conceited, ungrateful
to Olga for getting him out of detention, and an unlikely prospect
as a husband and adoptive father. At that juncture he would have
been raging: the militia and the *subbotniki* hooligans had foiled
his attempt to enlist Picasso in the smuggling of the paintings out
of the USSR.

Olga nodded sympathetically. 'I can read your thoughts,
Monsieur. Perhaps you are right, perhaps Pyotr did not say that.
I suppose I've always been tempted to believe that at that moment
he and I understood that our lives were now joined. But neither of
us knew what the immediate future held. To be more frank than
I need to be, I still thought Pablo might take me back to France
with him. Ridiculous – but you are convinced that my heart ruled
my head and every woman in Picasso's life had always thought
she would be the final one.'

'May I guess the sequel, Madame? Kemenev dismissed you?'

'He suspended me on full pay. He ordered me to clear my desk
and to take nothing away. Uncle Ilya intervened otherwise it
would have been instant dismissal. Kemenev accused me of
provoking a public scandal in concert with "criminals" and
"enemies of the state" like "the vermin Davidov". He said that
Picasso and his "gang" had been ordered by the Ministry of the
Interior to leave Moscow by the next available flight to Prague.'

'You never saw any of them again?'

'My mother and I received a final visit at home from Dora Maar
later that evening. What a plucky little lady! She brought with
her Picasso's sketch of me, the napkin stolen by Madame Triolet
– and ten thousand dollars in new banknotes from Picasso.'

'So much?'

'You think so? To last his own child a lifetime? From a man worth millions? And Madame Maar was quite frank – he wouldn't have sent me anything if she and Madame Triolet had not bullied him into it. These two women felt responsible for what had happened to me – and they were quite right!' Madame Lepinskaya burst into tears. 'What else must I tell you?'

I had to be severe, time was running out and that incipient dementia always lurked round the corner. 'Well, of course, Madame, you have never told me what happened between yourself and Picasso in Paris.'

Her eyes were red now. 'Why should I? What do you think happened? And you know what was even worse?' Dabbing her face, she waited for my response.

'What was worse, Madame?'

'Before handing over the ten thousand dollars Madame Maar sweetly explained the price – Pablo's price, her price, Triolet's price – my oath of silence forever.'

'Did you agree to abide by that, Madame?'

Lepinskaya hesitated, then almost smiled through her tears. 'It seems I did – but only while Pablo was alive. Then Madame Maar took out her ivory cigarette holder and said I had to stay silent until the day I died, even when, as she put it, I "ascended to Heaven".'

'But you have been talking to me.'

'Yes! Yes I have, and I am! And I want you to tell the whole world!'

'You never heard from Dora Maar again?'

'Never. But of course she became a recluse and when my Pablito first visited France she could not be contacted, not in the sixth arrondissement, not at Ménerbes, no trace. They say Madame Dora had taken vows in a Benedictine convent but really I don't know, I think she was just hiding from herself behind drawn curtains. Of course Aragon and Triolet were still alive at that time, but when Pablito tracked them down to their vast country retreat the gates remained closed to him. I believe I told you how Madame Triolet boasted to me in Paris about their new great estate, the Moulin de Villeneuve in Saint-Arnoult-en-Yvelines. "Six hectares of countryside allow us to write," that Communist woman said to me.'

I hesitated. 'Madame, Elsa Triolet had died there in 1970 of a heart-attack, several years before your Pablito arrived.'

Olga sighed wearily, dabbing at her eyes, embarrassed when she had to blow her nose. This was probably the most blatant lie she had told me, she felt stupid to have imagined that the sentinel of my knowledge would fall asleep. She wanted, needed, the old witch Triolet to have turned Pablito away.

'Monsieur, I think I have told you all I am ever going to tell you.'

'Will you never tell me how...you became pregnant'?

'If you don't know the facts of life, Monsieur, I'm sure there are books and manuals even in England.'

I waited. We sat in silence.

I said, 'I am asking you what happened in Paris, Madame.'

She stood up: 'I am tired, very. Perhaps you could come back some other time.'

So we did not talk about her Pablito, as she usually wanted to do ever since he had gone back up on the mantelpiece. I was in a way relieved because my previous encounter with Pablito in Paris had been a disturbing one. He had told me about his childhood. We had walked around the rather depressing streets near the Gare du Nord, stopping for a coffee on the high stools of a seedy bar. Pablito had the broad nose and the lustrous eyes of his natural father but in life – as distinct from Olga's chosen photo – his facial expressions lacked both the inveterate confidence and the mischievous gaze of the great Pablo. He had been born with the surname of the young Russian painter Olga married, Pyotr Davidov, a consumptive who had died young, in 1965. Twelve years later Olga had sent Pablito to France along with a dozen paintings by 'Sobaka'. I asked him whether he had managed to sell them.

'*Eh bien*, Monsieur, that was to please Mamochka. You know those stalls dotted along the Seine opposite Notre Dame? I found *un type* who took the lot for a thousand francs. He was a Russian émigré.'

'Not a lot for twelve paintings.'

'If you say so.'

Pablito's attempts to legally re-name himself in France had failed, one reason (I gathered) being that he was suspected of fraudulently attempting to pass himself off as Pablito Picasso, the only legitimate grandson of the painter, an unfortunate, tormented youth who had committed suicide in 1973 by drinking bleach. Pablito Davidov told me that he had made intermittent attempts to sell his personal story to *Paris-Match* and the like but had been dismissed by the magazine's editor with the remark, 'There are hundreds of men and women claiming to be Picasso's heirs.' No one was to be fooled by the truth.

I asked him when his mother first revealed who his natural father was.

'She did not reveal. At school I was always Maksim or Maks Davidov. I used to go to play with Svetlana and Mitya's children, I mean Yuri, he had an electric train set and was only a year or so older than me so we could play together, sometimes with Uncle Mitya who loved setting up the railway lines, the points, the bridges, the signals. He was always making jokes. They had foreign newspapers in the house and one day Yuri said he had seen a picture of my father in the paper. I stared at him blankly and he ran to fetch it. It showed an old man I had never seen. He was smiling and had his arm round a beautiful woman much younger. I said that's not my father, are you out of your tiny mind. Yuri laughed and asked why my mother called me Pablito at home. He said it was because I was really a Spaniard and only half-Russian.

'So then Uncle Mitya came into the room. I asked him who was this old man Picasso in the French newspaper? Uncle Mitya said he was the most famous, as well as the richest, artist in the world.

I asked what had that to do with me.

'"Because, my dear Pablito, Picasso is your father."

'I said that Pyotr was my father. Uncle Mitya said yes but now that he had died Mitya could no longer hurt his feelings by telling me the truth.

'I protested, "How can this old Picasso be my father?"

'Uncle Mitya blew out smoke from his lungs and asked whether anyone had told me the facts of life? I said yes of course what facts. I wondered how many facts Yuri knew. He was sitting there looking smug.

'Uncle Mitya lit another cigarette from the burning stub of the old one, I was always fascinated watching him do that. He then took a sheet of his favourite draughtsman's paper and drew a diagram showing a father's penis entering a mother's vagina. Then Uncle Mitya pulled down his trousers and showed us his penis, his scrotum and testes, the place where his prostate was, where all the tubes were. I thought there was something odd coming out in Uncle Mitya the way he did this and even more creepy when he began to explain that when Picasso went to bed with my mother his testes sent sperm within fluid semen to this penis, by first-class mail he said, so that the penis became long and stiff and he put it in the hole that every woman including my mother for some reason has between her legs. Then his seeds came out of his erect penis into her womb and she gave birth to her child nine months later. He said that was how everyone in the world was born, even the Chinese and Eskimos. He said everyone had *seks* and most of the animals. I said to Uncle Mitya, "Not my mother, no one could do that to her".

'"But once she did, Pablito, with your father Picasso. In France. Because she loved him. He came here to Russia and your mother organised an exhibition of his paintings. She saw him every day and some nights and they had *seks* because he loved her as well. She was very beautiful, Pablito. Then he went back to France and she never heard from him again. And you were born after he'd gone. If you went to France and said you were his son and wanted some of his money you would be quite right."

'"Then I will," I remember saying.

'"But who would believe you, Pablito?" Uncle Mitya was smiling in a curious way I didn't like. Then I think I said that my mother could give me a letter saying it was true.

'"Yes she might or she might not, but who in France would believe her?" Uncle Mitya sort of chuckled. Anyway, when I got home I was close to tears, I was probably nine or ten. I told my mother, "Yuri says I am a Spaniard and showed me a photograph of an old man called Picasso with his arm round a woman".

'Mamochka turned pale and sort of stammered that I shouldn't listen to Yuri but later I overheard her on the phone to Svetlana, obviously very cross about it, she kept using the word never, *nikogda*. Sometime later Uncle Mitya told me that my mother was always afraid I would be "stigmatised", *stigmatizirovannïe*. I asked him what the word meant, I'd never heard it before. Then he tried ostracised, *podvergnutyi ostrakizmu*, and I didn't know that either. Then he said, "Tell me honestly, Pablito, how would you be treated if you took that name to school and said your father was a Spaniard who you had never met and who had deserted your mother?"

'I suppose I just stared in horror. Uncle Mitya smiled and said in English "You would be sent to Coventry". He loved English expressions. I said no one at school could send me to a town in England.[†] Of course Uncle Mitya was younger then, more active, and you didn't know him. He told me and Yuri that he was fascinated by the, I don't remember, vaguenesses of English architecture –'

'Vagaries.'

'Yes perhaps, he said the deadly classical influence of...someone I can't remember "put an end to it".'

---

† I did not burden Pablito with my best guess. In his *The History of the Rebellion and Civil Wars in England*, Edward Hyde, 1st Earl of Clarendon, recounts how Royalist troops taken prisoner in Birmingham were sent to Coventry, a Parliamentarian stronghold, where they were not received warmly by the locals.

'Inigo Jones? I expect Mitya raved about the erratic splendour of the Jacobean country houses with their ogee turrets and tall chimneys, their Flemish flamboyance and their wonderfully half-hearted deployment of religious images?'

'No, he didn't get into that.' Pablito was becoming irritated but I was for a moment carelessly enjoying a surrogate conversation with Mitya, whose enthusiasms had been one of the rare delights of Moscow – at least until it all went wrong.

'Did he say that in the age of Francis Bacon, for the length of a heartbeat aristocratic England had stopped believing in God? Did he say no wonder they got it in the neck from the Puritans, a terrible tribe of unforgiving believers?'

God knows what prancing demon had got into me.

Pablito was now angry, he probably felt I was putting him down (which I probably was). 'I wouldn't have known what you are talking about, Monsieur. But if you wish to learn something serious from me, I can tell you that sometime after all this, when Yuri and I had graduated to senior school, Yuri confided to me that his father, Uncle Mitya, had been in love with my mother.'

'I expect many men were. She was the beautiful woman who had spellbound your father Picasso.'

'Yuri said that Uncle Mitya even proposed to my mother after Pyotr Davidov died, promising to divorce Yuri's mother, Svetlana. Yuri said his father had been quite open about it though my mother had never breathed a word to me. But it made sense because Uncle Mitya had been so often in our apartment and I could never fathom why. When I came home from school I would find him there and mother sitting at her typewriter because she was doing freelance editing for Mishkin at the Tretyakov gallery. Uncle Mitya usually left soon after I came home and mother went round sweeping up his trail of cigarette ash but she never seemed too cross about it. I once said to her that since Uncle Mitya stopped working as an architect he seemed to regard it as his duty to stop everyone else working. She hushed me in a fond way but I felt the fondness was as much for Uncle Mitya as for me. So when I was grown up, a student at Moscow Central, one day when I was visiting Yuri's home, well, Auntie Svetlana was in a bad temper with Uncle Mitya and said quite openly in front of us that she should probably have let him marry Olga after Pyotr died, if only "to prevent years of hide-and-seek, years of pretending". Mitya, she told me, had been besotted by my mother Olga. When I remember Auntie Svetlana, I always think of her nose and how ugly she was, with her eyes screwed up against her cigarette smoke.'

'I presume Mitya was not in his usual chair at the time?'

'Oh he was, he was sort of shrugging and smiling at Yuri and me as if to say "Women!" He cleared his throat and told us that an ageing man would be likely to have a "low sperm-count" even if his semen was so plentiful as to "drive him to excess" – unfortunately this did not apply in Picasso's case. I felt extremely angry. Really I never wanted to see Uncle Mitya again and because of that my friendship with Yuri ended after so many years.'

'When you refer to "Uncle" and "Auntie", are you saying that one of them was your mother's sibling?'

'I think Auntie Svetlana was Mother's second or third cousin, something like that. They were the nearest we had to relatives in Moscow, though Mother had a sister we never saw...somewhere.'

～

I never wanted to discuss any of this with Olga, although she herself has confided that Mitya had been in love with her – but not a word beyond that, the indiscretion highlighting the prevailing discretion. Late in 1995 I flew from Moscow to Paris propelled by a conviction that (a) Dora Maar's testimony was crucial and (b) she wouldn't agree to receive me. Madame Maar, who according to my informants now preferred her Yugoslav family name, Markovitch, was not only the prime witness outside Russia to Olga's story, but also a leading participant in that story – though I did not as yet know the full and rather appalling truth about what she had done. I had been forewarned that she gave absolutely no interviews; that she was into her eighties, hermetic, proud, even haughty, bad tempered, scornful of error – and practically everything written about her painting or photography by younger admirers of the next generation she deemed to be wrong. She had even cancelled a scheduled exhibition at the Pompidou Centre, the Beaubourg, because the written material sent for her approval earned her disapproval. I was of that next generation and damned in advance. I was told that she hated people to see her bent by old age and arteriosclerosis – which was one reason why she favoured the telephone. She would talk on the telephone for hours with those she trusted, but I feared that an approach by a stranger over the telephone would get no further than her carer. By the 1980s and 1990s Dora Maar had studiously made herself news from nowhere.[†]

Having booked myself into a small hotel in the 7th arrondissement not too far from the rue de Savoie, I left a message for Pablito in Neuilly, requiring his presence if summoned at short notice, *très urgent*. To verify the time of Sunday Mass, I walked down the rue du Bac as far as 136-40, the convent Maison des Filles de la Charité de Saint-Vincent-de-Paul. Once inside I headed for the Chapel of Our Lady of the Miraculous Medal, according to my informant one of Madame Markovitch's favoured places of worship.

On the Sunday, a good forty minutes before Mass, I took up position some yards down wind on the pavement opposite her apartment building in the rue de Savoie. It was raining lightly but with heavier squalls accompanied by lashing bursts of wind, not pleasant. Of course I feared the nasty weather might deter her from attending Mass. I had plenty of time kicking my heels to anticipate the scene when she emerged if she did. Old men and old ladies enter the street in different but typical ways. An old man will come out carrying his stick or crutch, slam the door and head off at a slow but steady limp without glancing to left or right. An old lady will totter out, stop, recoil from the weather, turn to her

---

† I cannot name my informant, who is still alive and now occupies a prominent position in, shall we say, the Paris art world.

companion and engage in a flutter of exchanges, has she brought this, has she brought that, should the companion go back inside to fetch it? It may be a case of one step back for every two steps forward. Which was more or less what happened when Madame Maar emerged with a young companion. Not that she came unprepared, indeed she appeared to be swaddled for God's journey – she was wearing an *impermeable* over a thick overcoat, a heavy skirt to the ground, a headscarf and a waterproof hat over it. Even so, she engaged her companion in the routine and predictable shilly-shallying. Finally a taxi drew up, clearly commissioned by phone, and the diminutive Maar was helped into the back by her companion, a pretty young woman who (I had been told) was called Rose.

And I was thinking: that small bundle now fighting off death once lay in the muscular arms of the great Picasso. For him she parted her legs. For him she sat for hours while he produced one startling, innovatory portrait after another. The entire collection would be worth millions now, she knew it and the dealers who pestered her knew it. One favourite excuse for not selling a Picasso (my informant had told me), was that it was worth much more hanging on a former mistress's wall than anywhere else. Hearing this from Madame Maar, the dealer would reply yes, yes – but, Madame, it is not worth anything until you sell it. She formed a relationship with a dealer called Gérard Blanc[†] who, when he was grudgingly admitted to that same apartment across the street from where I was standing, found plates piled high in the kitchen, layers of dust, and the famous insects Picasso had made by gouging out little legs in the plaster around protruding spots of paint near the fireplace. But then she broke with Blanc about a photograph he used for his 1991 exhibition 'After Duchamp'. A crucifix appeared next to Duchamp's famous urinal, *Fountain*, which had shocked the world in 1917. Maar was angry: the juxtaposition was 'blasphemous' and she never saw Gérard Blanc

---

† Pseudonym

again.

I began to walk rapidly to the rue du Bac. Of course she would arrive at the Chapel of Our Lady of the Miraculous Medal ahead of me but that suited me, I would be able to take a chair where I could study her postures. Indeed she barely moved throughout the service, she was old, until the moment came to walk forward unsteadily on her carer's arm to take the body and blood of Christ. I followed some moments later and took the wafer on my tongue with a feeling of disgust at this appalling superstition. Had God existed I could not have loved Him. As Maar and her young companion left the Chapel of Our Lady, I was waiting in steady rain (which I cursed). I stepped forward, having decided to address her in English, her favourite reading language, thus hoping to gain a gauche foreigner's grant of indulgence among fellow-Catholics.

'Madame Markovitch, I believe?' She stopped, they both stopped. 'Madame, I carry a letter for you from Russia.' (No apology for intrusion, no self-introduction, be brazen, never go on the defensive, it's fatal.) 'It's from an old friend of yours. I am on my way home from Moscow to London. I have also brought you a novel by Graham Greene which you may not have read.'

'I have read them all,' she said – what a beautiful voice, dark and mellow like my favourite pipe tobacco. 'Which one is it?'

'*Dr Fischer of Geneva* or *The Bomb Party*.' She reached to receive it, scanned the jacket. 'Why should you give me this, Monsieur? Who are you?'

'We are both of the Faith, Madame. There are not so many of us in England.' Yes, I thought, she believes devoutly in the Father, the Son and the Holy Ghost, the Trinity – and so must I today. If she was moved by this spiritual link she was not going to show it – Graham Greene's Catholics, after all, were not above sin, where would they be without it?

And it was raining, chilly, squally. The umbrella held by her young companion blew irritably in the wind over Madame Maar's head.

'What is the letter you spoke of?'

I thought how I would love to be invited into that old, unrenovated house of hers up the hill in Ménerbes, to view the kitchen she treasured because Picasso had stepped inside it, and the chair in which he had sat. Her jet-black hair was white now, barely protruding from her headscarf.

'The letter? Here, please take it. You have a friend in Moscow who admires you, but she did not have your address so she asked me to place the letter in your hand.'

'Show me.' She glanced at the back of the envelope, at the sender's name and address. While looking she was thinking more rapidly than during the service, you could tell that.

'Who is this person?'

'Madame Olga Lepinskaya.'

'An old friend, you say?'

'Yes, from 1952. Madame Lepinskaya's son now lives in Neuilly. He would like to meet you.'

'His name?'

'Pablito.'

'His full name?'

'Maksim Pablito Davidov. The Pablito is in memory of his father, Pablo Picasso.'

Maar did not flinch, she stayed on her horse. 'The world is full of people claiming to be Picasso's children.' I could tell that her young companion was bemused, anxious, not understanding English.

'The name Davidov,' I said, 'belonged to the Russian artist who Madame Olga married. You may remember buying a painting by Pyotr Davidov. You visited his attic studio in Cheremushki. You were present when the dissident artists held a meeting in the snow and Picasso came to address them.'

'Is this your fantasy, Monsieur, or Madame Olga's?'

'Madame, I know only the little she tells me.'

'I have no memory of her. Do you have a photograph?'

'No, she does not allow photographs...just as you don't,

Madame.' (Yes, she was bent and shrunk by arteriosclerosis.)

'Do I read this letter now? You must realise I am getting cold and wet standing here.'

'I am so sorry, Madame Markovitch. Then take it home, perhaps we could discuss it on the telephone?'

'I do not give out my telephone number. But you can give me yours if you have one.'

I wrote down the hotel number and room extension. Her carer-companion took it and murmured politely. *'Ah oui, votre nom, Monsieur?'* I took back the sheet of paper and wrote my name and London address. And off they went, slowly, battling the squalls of rain in the afterglow of the Mass.

I found myself too restless during the afternoon to do anything useful like visiting the new exhibition at the Pompidou Centre or buying presents for my wife and children. I felt that Maar might telephone anytime because the letter I had written on Olga's behalf (she had insisted on some changes) was designed to alarm and even frighten Madame Markovitch. I had of course retained a copy but knew it word for word:

'Chère Madame Markovitch, I'm afraid I shall always think of you as Madame Maar – or as Madame Dora, because you were always so friendly to me in Paris and in Moscow. I shall always gratefully remember how you, a true Christian, carried supplies of food to my old mother Ekaterina. We last met in Moscow in December 1952. As you may know my son Pablito was born seven months after his father, Pablo Ruiz Picasso, was expelled from Russia along with yourself, Monsieur Aragon and Madame Triolet. At our last meeting you brought me ten thousand dollars as the price of my eternal silence about Picasso's paternity, which is why I have been unwilling to discuss the matter with anyone with the sole exception of the bearer of this letter, a man I trust completely. He knows that Pablito is my son and Picasso's son. I have also shown him the thirteen photographs you took in Moscow under grey skies in November-December 1952, and which you so kindly gave to me.

'I do ardently hope, Madame, that you will agree out of your kindness as a devout Christian to receive my son Pablito. I enclose his address and telephone number in Neuilly. If you, a lady greatly esteemed in France and wherever true art is appreciated, were willing to confirm in writing that you know Pablito's father to have been Picasso, I am sure this would validate Pablito's claim to be one of the heirs to the estate. Imagine how much that would mean to him, his wife and their two children. But if sadly you are unwilling to grant what I ask, I must with deep regret convey to you that I shall no longer feel obliged to honour my vow of silence. I shall no longer feel constrained to forbid the Monsieur who brings you this letter from publishing what I have told him. My first duty, of course, is to my son and I must help him in the only way I can.

'I still treasure the portrait in oils of me painted by Picasso while he was in Moscow. It has become known as the 'Raphael Madonna'. I'm sure you remember it.

'Affectionately and with the greatest respect, I have the honour to be, Madame, your friend Olga Davidov Lepinskaya.'

The afternoon carried a long silence like drifts of sand stirring, settling, dying across the desert. The phone did ring in my hotel shortly after 9 p.m.

'Have you yourself read the letter?' that deep, beguiling voice began.

'Yes, Madame, she asked me to read it. As you can see Madame Lepinskaya implores you to receive her son and to help him.'

'Have you met him?'

'Yes I have. He is entirely genuine just as his mother is entirely honest.'

'How do you know she is?' The beguiling voice speeded up a fraction. 'What is this fanciful story she has told you? Why should you believe such nonsense, and an obvious attempt at blackmail? To bring damage to Picasso's reputation and mine.'

Almost all of the dark charm of Dora Maar's voice was lost in the distemper, the outrage. I thought: Picasso scarcely has a reputation to damage with regard to women. I said: 'I believe, Madame, that Madame Lepinskaya is asking you from the bottom of her heart to help her son Pablito.'

'Don't play the Christian idiot with me. This woman, of whom I have never heard, threatens to claim before the world that I gave her ten thousand dollars to remain silent because I knew that she was with child by Picasso. She threatens to claim falsely that I accompanied Picasso to Moscow but have always hidden the fact. Is that not damaging to me or are you without intelligence?'

'I can only hope it's not damaging to you, Madame. I know so little.'

'And what evidence do you have for this farrago of lies? You have either been taken for a ride or you are a co-conspirator looking to take your cut from the Picasso estate. I would rather believe the former.'

I waited. I could hear her companion whispering to her. Then Maar said: 'Ah yes – by the way, the so-called Picasso portrait of this woman, have you seen it?'

'Yes. It is done in the style of the "Small Cowper" Raphael Madonna and signed by Picasso.'

'Obviously a forgery.'

'None of the leading curators in Moscow think so.'

'Who?'

I named the who.

'What do they know? I expect they're all in it together. The fact that Lepinskaya had been a curator in the Pushkin Museum does not make her an expert on Picasso.'

My pulse raced! How could Maar have known that? I hadn't told her that Olga had worked in the Pushkin and the letter did not mention it. Should I ask how she knew? No, better not to put her on the defensive. This after all had become quite an extended conversation, and why had the famously reclusive, hermetically sealed lady even telephoned me? Was she not properly alarmed?

Maar now altered her tone to allow her voice its melodious quality. She enquired politely how much I thought the portrait of

Madame Lepinskaya (no longer 'this woman') was worth.

I said a lot.

'Are you familiar with the art market? Do you read the auction catalogues?'

'No.' Adopting a stratagem I knew that Maar herself often used (quite sincerely). I said that I thought the portrait would be worth much more if Olga, the mistress depicted, could be seen with it.

Dora Maar did not argue with that. 'Could she be persuaded to bring it to France for examination? Obviously I know the experts in the field. I may even be one of them.'

'Perhaps she could if you, with your high reputation, were to write inviting her...as a friend who had not seen her for forty years.'

'Who says she was my friend! Who says I ever met her! Who says she was Pablo's mistress! Who says Pablo ever visited the Soviet Union! Who says I had any dealings with him in 1952! Who says I led this Russian woman into his arms in the rue des Grands Augustins?'

My spirits soared again – who, indeed, had said anything about the rue des Grands Augustins or about Olga visiting France? Not me, not the letter I gave her.

Madame Maar's peroration continued, uninterrupted by my quickened pulse.

'Everyone in France knows that after Picasso turned his back on me in 1946 I did not meet him again until an unpleasant dinner given by Douglas Cooper in 1954 – unpleasant because Picasso was intent on humiliating me. I refused to weep. And I have never set foot in the Soviet Union.'

'Madame, will you agree to meet Pablito?'

'Of course not, why should I, he's obviously another impostor, there's no shortage.'

'But if you met him and talked to him, Madame, you might not think so.'

A pause. She was breathing heavily, her frail strength taxed to the limit.

'When could you arrange to bring him to your hotel? I am very busy at the moment, I am writing an article for *La Croix* about the blessed Saint Jerôme, I have little energy these days.'

'I could arrange it for next Tuesday evening.'

'What is today?'

'Sunday.'

Another pause, an audible sigh. 'Tell me something. How old is this woman Lepinskaya?'

'She was born in 1924, so she would be seventy.'

'How old is this Pablito?'

'Forty-one.'

'How long has he been in France?

'Since 1977, I believe, seventeen years.'

'Why has he taken so long to claim the inheritance?'

'No, he began some time ago. As you may imagine, Madame, the league of lawyers responded much as you have.'

'Can you give me any of their names? I would like to make contact with them. I sense that I may be an affected party to this. This Lepinskaya woman is clearly intent on revealing things which should not be revealed. The waters of history have closed over them. *Requesciat in pace.* I would not want any of this resuscitated, I am too old to stand up in a court, under the gaze of my Maker, and...'

She did not finish. She could (I thought) have mentioned her regular visits to the confessional, but her religion and her frequent chiding of others for non-compliance were for pride's locker. The telephone went dead. She did not conclude with '*A mardi,*' but on the off chance I summoned Pablito to my hotel for the Tuesday evening. He came obediently, looking tired and disconsolate, I fed him a double vodka-and-tonic, we waited in the rather tawdry little lobby of the Hotel de la Paix. I had no wish to talk to him about my conversation with Madame Maar and he was content to ventilate his recent frustrations in quest of his inheritance and how he was short of money. He drank and dozed.

After god knows how long the receptionist beckoned me to the phone. It was Maar's young companion and did I understand French? Madame Maar wanted to know whether she was due to meet me this evening because it was Tuesday – and did I have Pablito with me as promised? I said yes, the hotel was not far away, a short taxi ride, but we could come to the rue de Savoie if convenient. I could hear her conferring and indignant snorts in the background. *'Non, non, Monsieur, aucune difficulté, aucun problème, nous arriverons à l'heure.'*

Old ladies! I wondered whether Maar was already dressed to go out in her mauve-grey wig or whether there would be an hour of fluttering, fussing and fidgeting before she reached her front door in the rue de Savoie. Half an hour later the lady herself walked into the lobby warily, looking around her with the abrupt, stiff movements of an old bird, clinging to the young woman's arm. (She was reportedly the only carer sent by the charity Atmosphère that Maar had tolerated.) Pablito and I stood up. She stopped and stared at him, then went straight to him, gazing into his dark, luminous eyes.

'*Mon Dieu,*' she said, then clasped her hands on his face and held them there, as if about to sculpt him.

'Do you paint, Pablito?'

'No, Madame. I wish I could.'

'Do you like to watch bull fights?'

'No, Madame, but I have heard that my father did.'

'Do you like to surround yourself with bits of old wood, pieces of metal, old ploughs and bicycle wheels, bric-a-brac?'

'I am a rather tidy person, Madame. My wife –'

'Who was your natural father?'

'Picasso, Madame.'

'You have the forehead, the eyes, and the nose – but not the mouth. What has happened to the mouth?' Her wrinkled, taloned hands were still splayed out, gripping his surprised face.

She released him, took a seat in the sofa, and ordered Pablito to sit next to her. I asked whether she and her companion would care for a drink, but she ignored the question, her attention still fixed on Pablito.

'Say something to me in Russian about your mother.'

He did, fluently of course: he said she was kind and beautiful but all her life saddened that Picasso never wrote to her, never sent money.

'When did she stop working for the Pushkin Museum?'

Ah, again! Pablito could not realise it, but neither the letter nor I had imparted that information. How did Maar know this?

'I am not sure about that, Madame, I was not yet born at the time.'

I intervened to suggest that I could provide the answer to her question, but she wasn't having any of that. 'I want to hear everything from the boy!' she announced, though Pablito, *un père de famille* passing fifty, looked rather abashed at the description.

'Who is this Monsieur?' she asked him pointing at me. 'How often has your mother met him? How much does he know about her?'

Pablito was disconcerted by the succession of questions. 'Monsieur is a distinguished historian from Oxford, Madame, the author of many books.' But some instinct informed him that his future fortune hung in the balance now. He leaned forward rather earnestly, brought his fingertips together – how fascinated she was, mesmerized, by his hands! – and said softly, 'I believe my mother has talked to the professor on many occasions. In Moscow.'

'What does the professor know about these events, Monsieur Pablito?'

'Excuse me, Madame, but what events?'

Mentally she shied on to her hind legs. Her hesitation was palpable. For a moment her eye caught that of the pretty young companion, who had of course understood everything now that we were all speaking French.

'What has your mother said to you about me, Monsieur Pablito?'

'What a wonderful artist and photographer you are, Madame. Mamochka remembers visiting your studio forty years ago in the rue de Savoie. She remembers you talking to her about observing the composition of *Guernica*.'

'Was that the last time she saw me?'

'No, soon afterwards, when you accompanied my father to Moscow.'

'Could she be mistaken about that?'

'Madame, I was not even born! Mamochka told me how you took food to my grandmother Ekaterina. My adoptive father Davidov told me how you witnessed the exhibition of dissident artists in Cheremushki, and how the police bundled you into the limousine beside Picasso. They told me all this many years ago while I was still a boy, so of course it's all true.'

Maar was thinking this over. She turned to me reluctantly with a gaze that flickered. 'I will get in touch with my *avocat*. I believe there are special forms for legal affidavits.' She turned back to Pablito: 'If I ask you what I should say, you will answer "the truth"...but still I ask you.'

'Yes, the truth but I think you should ask Monsieur, Madame.'

At this juncture I made another of my notorious mistakes. By now over-confident that my meeting with Maar was exceeding my expectations, I unwisely intervened instead of letting her fascination with Pablito run its slow, muddled but ultimately fruitful course.

'Madame, may I suggest that you kindly put in writing a record of events in chronological order. How you came to know Madame Lepinskaya in Paris in October 1952, how you travelled with Maître Picasso to Russia, how Madame Lepinskaya was Picasso's Soviet guide and helper, how you gave her ten thousand dollars to guarantee her silence – and why you are convinced that her son is Maître Picasso's.'

Yes, that over-confident tone of the academic, the succinctly ordered demands – fatal. Moreover, I was in effect inviting her to admit that she had been lying to me. I'm sure I have already said that this very old Dora Maar did not like or trust those who came later, like myself, but I suspect that it was the last demand, about the ten thousand dollars silence money, that fatally threw Madame Maar back into naked indignation. Yet how could I have avoided the money issue since it was uniquely relevant not only to Pablito's cause but also to mine? Yet imagine the frightful impact on the old lady, a French intellectual who had all her life spoken up for freedom of expression, protested against censorship, an icon of liberty. The payment of silence money was always going to stick in the craw. A proud recluse now, she could no doubt imagine the newspaper headlines, the crass crowd of hacks banging on her door, the raised eyebrows among her friends in the Musée Picasso. Maar could probably visualise the next pained encounter with the leading Picasso biographer who remained one of the few friends privileged to be admitted to her Paris apartment and her house in Ménerbes. And in dollars! – the currency of Coca-Cola and *franglais*! Hadn't Picasso chided Chagall for working in America for dollars? How could Dora Maar reveal that the famous Hermès trunk that went with him to Moscow was stuffed with dollar banknotes? It was too much to ask, it was *de trop*.

So now Dora Maar, née Markovitch, signalled to her companion to help her to her feet. Again she looked around her like an old, arthritic bird, the grey-mauve wig slightly askew over her white hair. That famous chin of hers was less prominent now because it had multiplied, but what she still retained was her dark, velvet voice.

'My sincere regrets, Monsieur Pablito, I have lost my memory of those times. Therefore I cannot help you, I wish I could. Adieu.'

She did not offer him her hand because, I assume, she felt too ashamed. What would she disclose in her next confessional, what would she tell Saint Jerôme, what would she think of herself when she turned on the radio for the Catholic Mass surrounded by walls she had painted grey in pursuit of purity? Would she take solace in re-reading her favourite books, Fanny Trollope's *Paris* and the Parisians (1835) and her *Domestic Manners of the Americans* (1832)? Would she take refuge in re-reading Gabriel Garcia Marquez's *Love in the Time of Cholera*? Or would she bury herself in the society magazines she subscribed to, particularly those from England (where Picasso's friend and early biographer had been knighted as Sir Roland Penrose, much to Maar's delight)? She would continue to browse the auction catalogues, deciding and un-deciding which Picassos to sell off next as she struggled to support herself at a level allowing her to take a taxi all the way from Paris to Ménerbes instead of the train from the Gare de Lyon to Avignon. She could not know (nor could I) that in 2006, nine years after her death at the age of eighty-nine, Picasso's painting *Dora Maar au Chat* (with cat, 1941) would sell at Sotheby's for 95.2 million dollars. The tiny black cat is just there, perched in silhouette behind (not on) her narrow, sloping shoulder. The woman's long, taloned hands are spread on the arms of her chair like restless claws. It can be argued that the cat appears again in her lap, even more miniscule, its wide, apprehensive eyes almost indistinguishable from the dot-motif garment winding round the woman's waist and thighs. One is reminded of Picasso's story of Georges Braque and the squirrel that would not go away. *Dora Maar with Cat* is also the kind of 'two-noses Picasso' that Munnings, Kelly, Montgomery and Churchill jeered about at Royal Academy dinners.

When Maar and her companion had gone from the hotel, braving the wet and windy night, an obviously distressed Pablito asked: 'Did she not believe me? Did she think I was lying?'

'She was ashamed of the truth, Monsieur Pablito.'

Yet much had been achieved: what Dora Maar had unguardedly revealed, and her initial consent to writing an affidavit, had at last confirmed Olga's story.

But confirmed for how long? As the new Eurostar service plunged – my first uneasy experience of this – into its twenty-minute trajectory under the Channel, it most horribly came to me that Maar's apparent *faux pas* about Olga having worked at the Pushkin Museum was perfectly compatible with Olga having visited Paris in quest of a visit by Picasso which never took place – likewise Maar's question to Pablito as to when his mother had ceased to work at the Pushkin could be down to the perfectly understandable curiosity. But why had she repeatedly denied all knowledge of Lepinskaya?

Equally bad, I had not succeeded in persuading Madame Lepinskaya – I virtually fell to my knees – to let me bring to Paris even one of the thirteen Maar photographs showing Picasso and Olga together in Moscow. How perverse! Why? 'Madame, they constitute incomparable evidence!' But no – nothing that portrayed her at the height of her beauty (I suspected) would she release to a callous world. As for Maar, I had to admit that what now emerged (perhaps) was a very old lady gradually remembering the name and identity of a Soviet girl she had known only briefly in Paris forty years ago, perhaps unaware that the girl had stolen Picasso's affections, let alone had a child by him. By the time the Eurostar drew into its Waterloo terminus, I was absolutely sure of only one thing: Picasso was the father of Olga's son Pablito. And perhaps the surrounding dire doubts were brought on by the claustrophobia of the Channel tunnel and the clouding presence of the mighty deep sea swirling and pressing down above, awaiting its moment.

37

~

Chaplin and Nina are driven through the freezing winter night to the Kremlin in a convoy of MVD cars whose flashing lights make the city (as Chaplin remarks) 'turn quarter-somersaults, like a clown at the end of his tether'. Nina has dressed herself soberly, flat heels, a minimum of makeup, her hair tied back in a 'Soviet bun', all traces of her usual exuberance wiped from her suddenly plain features. She is by appearance once again the Elena Nabokova, correspondent of *Kino*, who travelled to London and Paris.

On arrival they are rapidly shepherded past blipping security cameras through electronic double-doors, along corridors with few guards (Nina has learned in the MVD that the more guards the less security – she had been put through a course on Assassinations from Julius Caesar to Mahatma Gandhi). Stalin's private secretary, Poskrebyshev, a hollowed-out ghost man of impeccable discretion, greets Chaplin in his outer office. Nina is reminded of Picasso's gaunt secretary Sabartés, the same ingrained suspicion, except that Poskrebyshev's power is such that he could eat the Spaniard for breakfast.

'Mr Chaplin, you are most welcome. Comrade Bolsharova will accompany you as interpreter.'

Chaplin smiles knowingly. 'No need, my friend Gelovani understands English.'

Poskrebyshev recoils as if slapped. He addresses Nina. 'Now translate accurately, every word. The traitor Gelovani was arrested last night. We apologise for any inconvenience his brazen impostures, clearly designed to promote Zionist-cosmopolitan treachery, may have caused Maestro Chaplin.'

Nina translates. Chaplin shrugs: 'I'm sure Mikheil is innocent.'

Nina does not translate. Poskrebyshev understands.

'The traitor Gelovani has been exposed as a running dog of the

Czechoslovak traitors in alliance with the fascist Tito.'

Chaplin sighs. 'Poor Mikheil, I liked him.'[†]

'Comrade Stalin will now receive you.' Poskrebyshev opens the door of the inner sanctum after knocking twice – pause – and one more time. 'Please enter, Mr Chaplin.'

For a moment Chaplin can see no sign of any human presence in the deeply shadowed room with soundproofed padded walls. Is that Lenin's death mask propped up on the desk? No, it's Hitler's skull (or Konstantin Savelyev's, he didn't dare meet my eye in the screening room). A discreet but eloquent motion of Poskrebyshev's hand – it reminds Chaplin of Arturo Toscannini on the rostrum of the Los Angeles Shrine Auditorium – indicates the dim outline of a head and shoulders sunk in a deep leather armchair. The man has his back turned to them and keeps it turned.

Chaplin is invited to sit behind him. Nina remains standing.

'*Gospodin* Maestro Chaplin,' Poskrebyshev announces. No greeting comes back. No sound at all except for laboured breathing and a faint rattle in the lungs. The voice, when it comes, is like the crushing of gravel. Nina trembles but finds that her translation is rapid and adroit:

'Your film *Limelight* will please Soviet audiences, Maestro. It is the only one we can show. Everything else is liable to misinterpretation. Having brought you to Moscow, I wanted to deliver my decision to you face to face.'

Face to face! How about back to back! (Nina reads Chaplin's thoughts.) And he's doodling on a pad – wolves!

'Maestro Chaplin, in *Limelight* you play an ageing clown. He is a disappointed man growing old, yet gallant, decent. I wanted the young ballerina to marry him but Calvero cannot convince himself that a beautiful young woman could truly love him – but she does! *Da!*'

Is this Chaplin's cue to speak? Poskrebyshev nods to him.

'How interesting, Generalissimo. Of course the young

---

† Gelovani was never arrested, though he had got himself into trouble. After Stalin's death he was denied film roles but continued to act in the theatre. He died in 1956.

composer, Neville, is devilishly handsome, charming, and she –'

Stalin cuts in as if he understands English. Or (Chaplin wonders) does a lifetime's service develop a sixth sense?

'The young ballerina doesn't love the young man like she loves Calvero – from the heart. But the old man lacks confidence. For an old man to lack confidence is a crime. And never say die.' *Another wolf on the pad.*

'I'm afraid my Calvero does die.' Chaplin offers his famous apologetic smile to the back of Stalin's head.

'*Da.* Never say die, Maestro Chaplin. How many times have you shared a bed with our young Soviet *devushka* here?'

Nina has to translate. She hangs her head in mute appeal to the maestro.

'What an idea, Generalissimo –' Chaplin begins.

'*Da,* but how many times?'

'I am a happily married man, Your Excellency.'

'*Da da,* but how many times?'

Nina decides to answer. 'Four-and-a-half times, Comrade Stalin.'

'Tell me about the half, girl.'

'I was in the role of Paulette Goddard, Comrade Stalin.'

'Tell me, girl, is he circumcised, no foreskin?'

'I'm not sure, Generalissimo,' Nina whispers.

'I hear you are a Jew,' he tells Chaplin. *Another wolf.*

'Me? No. Well, I admit I have never wanted not to be a Jew.'

'Never wanted not to be? Did the girl translate that correctly, Poskrebyshev?'

'Yes, Comrade Stalin, double negative.'

Relaxed, Chaplin embarks on a short family history: 'To be candid, I have never been certain that my father was Charles Chaplin Sr because my mother had a string of attachments. I think I might have Jewish blood. In Nazi Germany a volume called *Juden Sehen Dich* included a photo of Chaplin, "the little Jewish tumbler, as disgusting as he is boring".'

Poskrebyshev understands enough to groan audibly: 'Hush.'

Nina is not sure whether to translate hush.

'Let us be frank,' Stalin says slowly. 'You have come to the Soviet Union ostensibly as an honoured guest, a great artist, but in reality as an agent of the Zionist conspiracy. The British division. Yes or no?'

Chaplin nods cheerfully. 'More or less yes, more or less no.'

'Let me tell you this: if war comes England will be smashed, finished. France too. That is why it is inevitable that Britain and France will break with the USA.'

'As a matter of fact, Prime Minister Churchill has requested me to negotiate a Korean armistice with Your Excellency. Do you have time now?' *Another wolf.*

'An honest man at last. It is the guilty who deny everything. They always insist on their innocence. That has been the burden of my time as leader – the people claiming its innocence.'

Chaplin is puzzled. 'You mean the entire Soviet people?'

'I can count the loyal ones on my fingers.' *Two wolves.*

'But why should a loyal citizen plead guilty, Generalissimo?'

'To serve the Revolution. As proof of his loyalty. You should read Koestler's *Darkness at Noon*, it's all in there. Have you read it?'

'It's on my reading list – but one has so little time.'

'We had a translation made, ten copies printed, restricted circulation. I tried it but got bogged down. Too much theorising. They tell me you are acquainted with Greta Garbo. Do you know any way I can lay hands on her?' *This time a swan.*

'Greta? Oh certainly, I mean no.'

'Ninotchka, what's she like? They say shy. Why no more films from her? Not a thing for ten years!'

'She used to make you laugh, I'm told.'

'*Da. Larf.*' He adds something lengthy but almost unintelligible. Nina translates it as 'Yes to *Limelight*, no to *Modern Times* and *The Fascist Beast*. Enjoy the rest of your visit, Maestro, Poskrebyshev will see you out.'

Poskrebyshev ushers them out to the anteroom where he emits

an awkward snigger before ceremoniously presenting Chaplin with a charming old leather suitcase covered in exotic travel labels, stickers, camels meandering under palm trees.

'Gelovani wanted you to have this, Maestro Chaplin. All his Comrade Stalin outfits and moustaches. You may have to shorten the trousers. Here is the key but on no account open the case while you are still in the Soviet Union.'

Chaplin extends his hands in bafflement. 'Why?' But already they are being hustled out into the limousine, a guard carrying Gelovani's suitcase. 'Why on no account open the case?' Chaplin repeats to Nina.

'Maestro,' she smiles, 'I have not forgotten your conversation with Arkady Raikin about performing in Leningrad's Miniature Theatre. I can shorten the trousers for you.'

'Did Chaplin believe it was really Stalin?'

'I think yes and no. Perhaps mainly yes.'

'And you, Lady Stears?'

'Gelovani had been taught to iron out the Georgian accent. It was Stalin.'

38

In January 1996, I was granted one more extended session with Nina after my return from Paris. On my arrival Ivan immediately handed me an envelope which carried the printed name of Sir Henry Stears, QC. When I made as if to head for the staircase, Ivan intercepted me.

'Must rid furrst.'

'What here?'

'Heer. Now.'

Sir Henry's main purpose, it soon becomes clear, was to deter me from further dealings with Nina, though he granted 'one final visit'. She was inclined by nature to be 'rather impulsive', 'rather insecure', and invariably 'rather too anxious to please'. She had confessed to him that she had been telling me what I wanted to hear about Russia in 1952 – not a word of truth. She had a rather absurd fetish about Oxford and 'sporting oaks and all that rigmarole', and after dining with me in All Souls she had told anyone who would listen that she had shaken hands with Lord Salisbury, Lord Curzon and Colonel Lawrence of Arabia.

He could confide 'in strict confidence' that Nina's business adventures in the art market were now getting her into 'rather deep water', indeed she had 'ventured rather out of her depth'. Genuinely sincere enthusiasm had misled her to underestimate the authenticity factor in the modern art market. Several wealthy clients, supported by several major museums, were now 'rather on their horses and closing in'.

I was advised to destroy 'all notes and tape recordings' of my conversations with Nina. If I should attempt to publish anything remotely based on them, he would be obliged, as a leading barrister in the field of literary property and copyright, to intervene with an injunction. 'You and your publisher would find that onerously expensive.'

His duty done, Ivan directed me to the rococo bedroom I had first seen in my surreal dream all that time ago. Lady Stears lay in her bed, prostrate, pale and wasted. I noticed that her dogs had gone.

'Did you read Henry's letter?'

'I did.'

'Don't believe a word of it.'

'I'm sorry to hear about wealthy clients closing in on you.'

'That's bosh – Henry is inclined to panic. Shall I finish my Chaplin story?'

'I'd be grateful.' I took out my tape recorder.

She talked to me with eyes closed, a faint frown of concentration, frequently pausing for breath, about Stalin's final summons to Chaplin – but she abruptly perked up and even cavorted out of her bed when recounting the Leningrad affair with mounting excitement. (Oona was scheduled to have her fatal accident, it may be recalled.)

Back in bed, all energy spent, she asked me to sit beside her and hold her hand.

'I'm sure you'll get well soon, Nina.'

'Thank you, Oxford. You can kiss me.'

I did. Normally sweetly scented, she smelled of rebellious intestines and sour old age.

Removing my mouth from hers, I counted to five. 'Will you please give me the "Small Cowper"?'

'You can be so exasperating, Oxford! You know I don't want Olga on the cover of your book. Picasso should have painted me, he saw me often enough but never even rolled those foul, bulging eyes at me.'

I needed that picture, that fake, indeed the credibility of this entire narrative seemed to depend on taking possession of it. I might even have bid a thousand pounds I didn't have, though of course I did, I'd go to five. But this old lady, whose stick-thinness beneath the sheet shocked me, soon fell into an exhausted sleep. I thought of making a clandestine search for the picture but Ivan immediately surfaced as if reading my intention and fetched me down and out into the street, a massive boot into my backside on the last step down. My briefcase and I briefly sprawled on the pavement, enjoying a worm's eye view of Cheyne Walk.

My right hip never recovered and I never saw Nina again.

39

In January 1997, a letter postmarked MOSKVA arrived in London. Madame Lepinskaya had never written to me before. She said she felt she owed me what I had been asking for but what she could not possibly say in my presence, it would be too *'honteux'*, so she had written it down for '<u>your benefit and yours alone</u>'. Her narrative did not flinch but was oddly set out, without quotation marks for things said, and with each paragraph numbered, I'm not sure why, perhaps to convey the style of an objective report written at the scene of a crime. I have adhered to her format:

1. We were in the rue de Savoie, preparing to leave for the rue des Grands Augustins. You may remember that I was first visiting Madame Maar on the instructions of Aragon and Triolet. Madame Dora said she was no longer fertile, her periods had stopped, and was I a virgin? I said no. Had I taken precautions? I said no. Then she became confused searching in her chaotic kitchen for an old bottle of vinegar and a bowl of warm water. She said by all means take yourself to the bathroom. But I couldn't do it, it was too degrading.

2. When we reached the street, Madame Dora looked me over and announced that I was six centimetres too tall. She said Chaplin had the same phobia and his women learned to wear flat heels. Then she said, well, Pablo seemed happy with you yesterday and the day before standing behind you and gripping your waist but I'm afraid he may change his mind today.

3. Then she hailed a taxi and we drove to the rue des Grands Augustins. In the taxi she keeps repeating one thing like a mad woman, Remember you must resist.

4. Sabartés let us in silently, not a word, then he suddenly said to Dora that he was glad she had come with me. She didn't

respond to that and I followed her up the stairs I now knew well. I was carrying my shoes in my hand.

5. Picasso was waiting for us at top of stairs, naked from the waist up and just a pair of thin white cotton shorts showing his legendary *peniculus*. His genitals seemed to me huge, you can imagine my trepidation. He called me *devushka* and pinched my cheek so that it hurt. The Afghan hound Kazbek was standing with him at the head of the stairs. Pablo then said, Well, *devushka*, will you resist?

6. It was Dora who led the way into his bedroom. She whispered to me to resist but not too strongly because she herself was not strong and had lost her fight with Marie-Thérèse Walter. But when Picasso began to grope me down below, he snorted angrily, and I realised I had forgotten what Triolet told me about wearing nothing underneath my short dress. It was Maar who pulled off the small impeding garment down my legs and over my feet. I could have kicked out but didn't want to hurt her.

7. Pablo came down on top of me, smelling of garlic, wine, cloves, not unpleasant. I struggled a bit, not a lot, just enough to pleasure him. My mind was really focused on a succession of people saying to me Obligation, Duty, You alone can do it. You must go through with this for the Motherland. To me that meant the two people who didn't want me to do it, my mother and Pyotr (I have not expressed this well).

8. He was breathing heavily and urging me to resist. I think I brought my legs together and pushed up at his heaving chest, it was then that Maar tried to help him. Her odious presence was really the worst part of it but Pablo insisted. His face did not come near mine, he did not kiss me then or later, I mean never.

9. Well then he came inside me, huge and painful, then he groaned and I could feel his warm emission, it kept coming. I think I heard Dora running from the room weeping, then the dog Kazbek bit her in the arm and she screamed and Pablo

laughed, he was climbing off me and I could hear him chiding the dog and telling Dora to apply antiseptic to the bite. Then he came back in, lay beside me and slept a little.

10. When he woke up he stroked my face and said he wanted me to stay in Paris and live with him here in this house. I said, Maître you have said that to many women. He said, Never – not unless I mean it. I said, Well come to Moscow for your exhibition and then we'll see. Then he asked gently for a second '*démarche*'. I no longer resisted and Dora Maar could be heard weeping outside the door *comme une folle*, really I didn't understand her at all.

11. After his second '*démarche*' he became affectionate and extracted a sum of money from his legendary Hermès trunk. He took it back before he had given it to me. You will only run into trouble with the *douaniers*, he said. I will bring it to Moscow, *devushka*, as a guarantee of your devotion. I thought of what so much money would mean to my mother but then I thought how dangerous it could be for me to accept money from him and maybe it was his way, their way, of undermining my self-respect. Anyway, you asked me how I became pregnant. It was definitely in Paris not after Pablo arrived in Moscow because by then I had gone to my local doctor to be fitted, *zamok dveri konyushni posle togo, kak loshad' boltami!*[†]

12. That should make my Pablito a French citizen, *n'est-ce pas?*'

13. Not a word of this may be published or reported to anyone.

Lepinskaya.

---

† Locking the stable door after the horse has bolted.

40

To Leningrad! Charlie is determined to go. Oona spots a unique light in his eye, the one she associates with the first day of shooting a film. His mood has rotated through anger to recklessness. 'Tell Arkady Raikin we're on our way,' he commands a tremulous Ehrenburg. The two are walking and arguing in rubber overshoes up and down *ulitsa* Gorky through the snow and slush. Following the expulsion of Picasso and his contingent from the Soviet Union, the old fox is so petrified that he has taken to spending nights away from home, sheltering with those few friends he feels he can trust – but who can one trust when Beria has disappeared himself and the hands of clocks signal Stalin's retribution, his last-hour apocalypse for Jews of every stripe? Ehrenburg has at least spoken up for poor Olga but the best he has been able to achieve with Kemenev is her suspension on full pay. And now Chaplin has concocted this crazy journey to the end of the night, a suicidal running-amok with Arkady Raikin in Leningrad.

'This could mean the end of everything, Charlie.'

'And what is "everything"? Courage, Ilya. Stalin himself arranged for me to have poor Gelovani's double outfits. That means Stalin thinks I'm the bee's knees.'

Ehrenburg can scarcely believe that the man Chaplin was taken to see in the Kremlin was Stalin. 'What did he say?'

'He was against old Calvero giving up his young loved one in *Limelight*. Quite miffed about that.'

'Well, Stalin and Picasso agree about something.'

'He said that if I admitted to being a cosmopolitan British agent and a spy, and if I agreed to be a circumcised Jew, though I'm not, then he could do business with me. When I offered to negotiate a Korean peace treaty with him, he didn't refuse.'

'Perhaps at a later date?' Ehrenburg asks sardonically. The old fox shudders inwardly. He must get the Chaplins safely back to the West before he attends the Vienna conference of the World Peace Movement (if he does). The wheels of a passing bus splatter his trousers with slush. Simultaneously Chaplin elbows him in the ribs.

'The Generalissimo confided to me that the ones he most distrusts are those who constantly swear loyalty to him.'

Old Ehrenburg staggers and must lean against a building 'He didn't mention me by name?' he murmurs.

'It seems that he keeps two hundred million names in his head. If you'll take my advice, Ilya, go straight to Stalin and make a clean breast of it.'

'Of what?'

'Of your years as an agent of a foreign power, why not Britain, I'm sure Winston would provide an affidavit. Then you'll be in the clear. Joe simply adores *Limelight* did I tell you? I leave for Leningrad by the Red Arrow tonight.'

'With Oona?'

'With Oona and Nina – two for the price of one.'

'Charlie, I implore you! Don't you realise what has happened? All the early Picassos have vanished from the walls of the Pushkin Museum. Can you really believe they are going to screen your *Limelight* after that?'

'Joe said he would. That's enough for me.' Chaplin lowers his voice and takes Ehrenburg's arm. 'Strictly between ourselves, Leningrad could be the safest place for you to be right now. I'm told all these intrigues are confined to Moscow. And if you are seen attaching yourself to a world-famous maestro who has been gifted with the late Gelovani's outfits by Uncle Joe in person, call it a wink and a nod...'

Ehrenburg stops and stares at his sopping galoshes. 'You really think so?'

'My girl Nina has booked the train reservations for the four of us. You will be our guide to Leningrad, Petrograd and St Petersburg.' He chuckles. 'Three for the price of one.'

Having reached Chaplin's apartment block, Ehrenburg goes his elderly way, struggling to remain upright in the slush. Chaplin is humming as he mounts the stairs, excellent health, heart conditions are for wimps, yes that girl Nina seems really keen on Leningrad. She has even unlocked Gelovani's suitcases and shortened the Stalin trousers with a huge pair of scissors to fit Charlie. And Oona's up for it, too, though she'd rather leave Nina behind if Ilya Ehrenburg comes along to take care of the street signs, all those three-pronged forks turned upside down.

Leaving the *ulitsa* Gorky for the Leningradskaya railway station, Oona notices that Nina is carrying an extra suitcase covered in exotic labels, some of them picturing fancy hotels in far-flung destinations and even a few camels. Oona observes that Nina won't allow any other pair of hands, hotel porter, taxi driver or railway porter, to carry that suitcase. You can tell from Charlie's smug expression that he and Nina are up to something. Nina has told Oona that she should stay in Moscow because a clairvoyant she knows has predicted an unpleasant accident for 'a smartly dressed American woman' in Leningrad, so that's something to think about too. No, you don't ask Charlie what he thinks about it – not asking makes Oona feel like the child bride he married all over again.

What a nice train is the Red Arrow, luxury all the way. Oona takes the seat next to Ehrenburg, who has turned up in a terrible state of confusion and punctured disrepair with minutes to spare. She has almost grown fond of him because of his old-world courtesy and the way he speaks about her father with the respect due to a Nobel Laureate. 'I have to admit, Madame Oona my dear, that O'Neill is my idea of the genius of American literature – I find it in Hemingway and Fitzgerald, who of course I knew well, and of course in Bill Faulkner. I tried to wangle a visit to Oxford, Mississippi during my 1946 official trip to the States, but I was told that Bill was unavailable, buried in the composition of...was it *Sanctuary*?'

'Forgive me, Ilya, but I don't think anyone ever knew Faulkner as Bill.'

'Ah, my mistake. Presumably you and Charlie met him in Hollywood?'

'We met someone who said he was Faulkner.'

Seated in the first-class dining car (International) of the overnight Krasnaya Strela, the Red Arrow express – how pleasantly the hours pass as the wheels race across the firm rails – Ehrenburg informs them that in the lavatory they will find a little brass plate dating back to pre-1917 when the carriage belonged to the Compagnie Internationale des Wagons-Lits.

'That brass plate, dear Charlot and Oona, has survived war, revolution, civil war, collectivization, famine, purges, war again, the 900-day siege of Leningrad where a million people died – the Cold War.'

'Tell us about the siege, Ilya.'

'The stronger young workers from the Putilov plant would go out with sleds in mid-afternoon to help collect corpses. And sometimes they would find the dead sitting in their chairs almost indistinguishable from the huddled circle of the living.'

'And now our government is talking about another war against Russia.' She produces a bottle of vodka and four small glasses.

'The people of the world, my dear Oona, will not allow it. And shall I reveal to you something even more shocking?'

'By now we're shock-proof.'

'In one of the great ironies of the war, those who led the city of Leningrad throughout its struggle for survival were arrested as soon as the siege was lifted.'

'Wow!'

'Why?' Chaplin asks.

'Apparently they had failed to contact Moscow frequently enough during the siege to ask for guidance from...Somebody.'

Charlie and Oona brood on this in silence. Even Nina had not known this.

Ehrenburg's watery gaze floats to Chaplin. 'I have sent a message by secure channels to the Miniature Theatre on

Zhelyabov Street – still a haven of laughter and happiness due to the genius and courage of Raikin. Fly the flag for Arkadi, Charlot, his survival as my fellow-Jew is a miracle.'

Chaplin nods and says (long before it became the slogan of the genuine peace movement), 'We will overcome.'

'Shall overcome,' Oona says, refilling her glass but no one else's.

Nina corrects Oona. '"Will" conveys strong purpose. "Shall" is merely predictive – "we shall have good weather tomorrow". This can be learned in Soviet schools grade 4.'

We dare not describe Oona's expression. The remaining vodka in her glass will have a short life.

Ehrenburg's voice is barely above a whisper as he leans across: 'Since Zhdanov's death Leningrad has begun to rediscover a trace of the independence it once enjoyed when the immensely popular Kirov ran a liberal regime there.'

'Remind us who Kirov was,' Charlie says.

'Kirov was number two in the Party until his assassination in 1934.'

'Who killed him?'

'No one knows who killed him.'

Chaplin's eyebrows shoot up: 'Not even the assassin? I take it Kirov was too popular for No One Knows's taste.'

'My dear Charlot you could be a historian – if you had no care for your survival, since our professional historians enjoy a shorter lifespan than Stakhanovite coal miners working in the collapsing structures of the Donbass.'

Soon Ehrenburg is recalling how Lenin himself arrived in Petrograd, at the Finland Station, in 1917. 'A railway journey in a sealed carriage, paid for by Berlin, which changed the world.'

'You don't mean, you simply can't mean,' says a wide-eyed Oona, 'that the Germans can take the credit for the Bolshevik Revolution?' She produces a second bottle.

'Yes, dear. Isn't that terrible to know? The Huns needed a victory on the Eastern Front, to concentrate all their military energies in the West. Their highly intelligent and well informed Wilhelmstrasse, their Foreign Ministry, identified the obscure Lenin, mired up in the Zurich Public Library, as the key to the fall of the Tsar's regime.'

'Did you know that, Charlie?'

'I believe I was making *The Immigrant*, *The Cure* and *Easy Street* in 1917.'

Ehrenburg begins a remark then drops it, his sagging mouth collapsing into a ghostly smile. Nina can guess that the old fox sees no point in reminding his guests about something he has confided to her when visiting Mosfilm, namely the ongoing accusations in the English press during the First World War that young Chaplin was ducking military service. A sheet-music firm had published caustic lyrics to the tune of 'Redwing':

The moon shines bright on Charlie Chaplin/His boots are cracking,/For want of blacking,/And his little baggy trousers/They want mending/Before we send him/To the Dardanelles.

The two men and the two women eventually close their eyes for one of those sleeps so short that they are worse than none, only Oona, who is cooked, sleeps soundly. Chaplin comes to as fresh as the proverbial daisy, a lifetime's adrenalin pumping. Over an early breakfast, a timorous Ehrenburg reverts to the subject of their forthcoming visit to Raikin's Miniature Theatre.

'Charlot. I do suspect that Arkady will at some moment in the evening want to bring you on stage. I have had an inspired idea overnight, Charlie. Everyone in the audience will know "The Professor of the Fleas".'

'That was released in 1919.'

'Never mind! I spotted an update of it in the prologue to your new film *Limelight*. Calvero struts on stage: "I am an animal trainer", crack of the whip. Bring on the invisible fleas, Charlot, Raikin's audience will explode with delight. The great Chaplin here and now in our midst!' Old Ehrenburg quivers with joy. 'Nothing political,' he adds.

'Out of the question,' Chaplin says. 'I'm much too shy.'

'But, Charlot –' Ehrenburg protests. (He cannot help wondering about the vividly labelled suitcase tucked under Nina's feet.)

'You're too kind, but really, no. It's the back row of the stalls for me.'

Drawing in to Leningrad's Moskovsky Station, Oona witnesses a new sequence of conspiratorial manoeuvres with the exotic suitcase by Charlie and Nina, involving fending off imprecatory porters with fistfuls of roubles. By now Oona is wild with curiosity:

'Tell me, are you planning something crazy, Charlie? Is Ilya in on this?'

'Ilya is the only Russian I've met that I can fully distrust.'

She catches a glimpse of the exotic suitcase being smuggled into a private car which disappears, along with Chaplin and Nina, leaving her to explain to a bewildered Ehrenburg – as instructed – that Charlie can't wait to get to the Hermitage to view all the wonderful paintings.

'But it's six in the morning! The Hermitage won't open its doors for hours. We must follow him!'

'Ilya, my dear, take me to the Astoria, ok? I'd like to catch up on some beauty sleep.'

Standing outside the neo-Renaissance rail terminal, the Moskovzky Vokzal, while vainly gesturing to taxis already taken, the very tired old Ehrenburg is blind to the large Venetian windows and two storeys of Corinthian columns.

'Wow! Does this date from Tsarist times?'

'It does – and so does the famous Nevsky Prospekt,' he murmurs, exhausted by the overnight journey – he has spent too much time in the antique lavatory, unable to relieve himself, cursing his prostate, staring at the little brass plate of the Compagnie Internationale des Wagons-Lits. And, though he would never give a hint, he is equally exhausted by the ever-effervescent Mrs Chaplin.

'I had looked forward to showing Charlot the architectural

jewels of our most beautiful city,' he tells her.

'But you will, Ilya, you will – you'll show them to me!'

At this moment, just as she darts forward to collar a taxi, a ton of concrete topples from an overhead crane, lands almost at her feet, and covers her in dust.

'Wow! Do you think that was deliberate, Ilya?'

'Nothing in the Soviet Union is ever deliberate, my dear. But always remember the adage "women beware women" – Thomas Middleton.'

'Oh? Meaning?'

'My dear, little Nina wants your Charlie for herself.'

On *ulitsa* Zhelyabov the Miniature Theatre show begins at 8.30 (i.e. 8.45) and the laughter at 8.31 (8.46). Nina has made sure that the back row has been allocated to unidentified foreign guests who wish to remain anonymous but who will inevitably arouse the curiosity of the Miniature Theatre's usual scattering of secret police, dressed unconvincingly (wrong shoes) as bohemians and *stilyagi*. Following a morning rehearsal with Raikin, Chaplin had turned up with Nina at the Astoria in mid-afternoon, obviously elated, refused all questions, and fallen into one of his give-away pre-performance slumbers.

The Miniature Theatre, Leningrad. Enter ARKADY RAIKIN.
RAIKIN: Shalom! Tonight we have a full house – 190 of you bought tickets on the black market and the other ten, well, they don't need tickets, they're such devoted fans. (*Laughter.*) By the way, I've just been to get my winter wood ration from the Ministry. See this bulging sack? Think I got lucky? These are just the forms I have to fill out! (*Laughter.*) Now let's be serious for a change. I regret to inform you that tonight we may expect trouble. A few hours ago a bohemian arrived at our stage door dressed as a tramp and unable to identify himself in any known language – which as you know is Russian or Yiddish. (*Laughter.*) The stranger left behind this mysterious suitcase (*holds it aloft*) covered in travel

labels, stickers, camels meandering among palm trees. No idea what's inside it, of course. Might be fleas? (*Laughter, applause.*) Instinct tells me we have an unwelcome guest down there in the audience. (*He scans the excited audience.*) Some kind of foreigner – some kind of tramp who never made it in Hollywood. (*Laughter.*) Frankly, we don't need parasites like that in here.

Laughter and mounting applause as CHAPLIN flips and flaps his feet down the aisle and on to the stage. Massive clapping, everyone on their feet, becomes tearful emotion as he bows, skips and lifts his too-small bowler hat.

CHAPLIN (*pointing to RAIKIN*): Who's this? How did he get in here?

RAIKIN: 'Who's this?' he says! Lucky none of us understands Yiddish. Okay, let's follow proper procedures – in Russian if you don't mind. Proof of identity, please. Foreign passport, visa, internal passport, right to spend one night in Leningrad, currency certificate. No good? Nothing at all?

CHAPLIN wriggling, twitching, shrugging, smiling coyly.

CHAPLIN: Da. Nyet. (*Huge laughter.*)

RAIKIN: Are you married?

CHAPLIN smiles happily, performs a short tap-dance, and points to the back row of the audience.

RAIKIN: You're trying to tell us that such a beautiful and elegant young lady would give her hand to a filthy old tramp like you!

CHAPLIN smiles coyly, shrugs, then empties the pockets of his baggy trousers. A cascade of gold coins spills out on to the stage. Laughter. Now CHAPLIN is whispering in his ear. RAIKIN shakes his head in emphatic rejection.

RAIKIN: Comrades! This nobody from nowhere says he wants to perform for us! I ask you! We can't allow that, can we? (*Massive support for CHAPLIN from the audience.*) He doesn't even possess an actors' union card! I bet he's carrying fleas – and alien ones at that. (*CHAPLIN coyly whispers.*) He says the fleas travelled from Moscow economy class! (*Laughter.*)

OONA'S VOICE *from the back*: That's my joke, Charlie!

Everyone turns towards her. She waves, then stands up and waves some more. Massive applause, everyone smiling and the women calling 'Uona, Uona'.

RAIKIN: If that woman back there is Mrs Oona Chaplin, I'd like to know how they let her into the Soviet Union, she's not even Jewish.

CHAPLIN whispers in his ear.

RAIKIN: This tramp is telling me that he and his wife have been chased out of America by the war-mongers!

Massive applause.

CHAPLIN now opens Gelovani's suitcase and tosses out the contents, one garment after another. He climbs into one set of breeches and high boots, indicating to a bemused RAIKIN that he must do the same. Then come the tunics and medals until there can no longer be any doubt now that these are Somebody's uniforms – two of them.

When the two sets of wigs, moustaches and, finally, the peaked caps are in place, we hear the collective gasp from the audience. Then a deathly silence. Only eight years ago these people had emerged from one of the most ghastly collective sufferings in human history.

Both STALINS take up whips and begin to crack them at the dancing fleas.

But soon CHAPLIN/STALIN begins to scratch, wriggle, hop and slap while RAIKIN/STALIN glowers at him contemptuously, cracking his whip more vehemently. CHAPLIN grapples with the buttons of his tunic.

Now RAIKIN, too, begins to scratch, hop, leap. Desperately they jettison their uniforms until both are down to their underpants.

The fleas seem to have settled in their moustaches – now they are slapping their own faces and in mounting fury each other's faces. The moustaches are torn off.

RAIKIN: Comrades, it was all a mistake. I blame the Zionist fleas.

The laughter suddenly dies into silence. Many spectators are now scrambling to leave the theatre before disaster descends.

The two clowns scuttle into the wings, leaving the stage strewn with Stalin's uniforms. (Lights down.)

That night the MVD arrest Raikin and close the Miniature Theatre. Ehrenburg manages to slip away, travelling back to Moscow's Leningradsky Vokzal by the night train while Charles and Oona Chaplin are held in cells until the MVD receives instructions to transport them by road seven hundred kilometres to Moscow's Sheremetyevo airport, where they have to wait ten hours before seats can be found for them on a flight to Prague. No one sees them, they are kept out of sight.

Nina is put in detention in the Lubyanka and released only after Stalin's death. She loses a stone in weight. She has to work on the trams, trying to stop impatient youths from clinging to the roof, then shovelling snow from the tramlines in winter. Mosfilm do not reemploy her until after Khrushchev's anti-Stalin speech to the twentieth Party Congress in 1956 – but only as a translator-interpreter. Later she finds a job with the Kirov company, the Marinsky, in Leningrad.

'Then, do you know, I travelled with the company to Paris and London in 1961 and was all set to jump ship. I had made contact with a man from Paris-Match *and was planning to sell my story. In 1961, if you remember, both Chaplin and Picasso were still big-big. Very.'*

'But?'

Unfortunately for her, during that trip the star male dancer Rudolf Nureyev defects, just her luck. There is a Cold War uproar, the dancers are all hustled home by the KGB from Orly. The Marinsky almost falls apart, recriminations, sackings. Luckily she hadn't known Nureyev, just the occasional conversation in some bar, he is gay. She has to bide her time for a further thirteen years, a single woman, before she absconds in Canada with Mikhail Baryshnikov.

'And you never married all that time?'

'Frankly, no decent man would have me. I was tainted, I think the English word is "irreparably". Hundreds of thousands of political

prisoners were honourably rehabilitated but operatives of the MVD or KGB who had fallen foul of their masters – never.'

'You needed a new life, a new identity?'

'I found one, Oxford, but between ourselves too late. Too late for happiness. The only mensch who could have given me what I sought was living in Switzerland and married to Oona Chaplin. She gave birth to four more children, I to none. So: now I've done.'

'Tell me, did you arrange for that block of concrete to fall on her head?'

Lady Stears smiled, I would say mistily. All this was told to me, of course, before my final visit to Nina, when she refused me the Kolakowski fake Madonna and Ivan kicked me into the street, breaking my hip.

41

Nina had disappeared from Cheyne Walk, and could not be traced. Shutters covered the windows, no one answered the bell. At Sir Henry's chambers in the Temple, the clerk curtly advised me that the barrister had gone abroad and was 'incommunicado'. Yes, letters could be forwarded but his address could not be disclosed. When I asked the clerk of the chambers whether this also applied to Lady Stears, the man merely shrugged: 'We have no such instructions.' It was March 1997.

I had to assume the art-fake enterprise had turned viral and the couple were in flight from legal summonses. Perhaps Nina had sold one of Kolakowski's 'Titians' to a client who thought he was acquiring the real *Man with Three Heads*. I imagined heated exchanges at Ascot and Wimbledon, or over chilled Muscadet in the Royal Academy's members' room; I imagined accusations on the new cellphones and networked emails, while the pounds invested in Nina clattered into the small change tray of the art market's fruit machine. But I had to imagine. Years passed. Sir Henry's threat of an injunction stayed with me. My narrative was stymied by the premonition that if Nina evaporated then her narrative also evaporated – perhaps yet another fake.

My search for her became obsessive. I would even hang around outside the National Gallery, the Royal Academy and the Royal Opera House. I would stare into taxis to the consternation of the occupants. I harassed the Bond and Cork Street dealers. Then I thought I caught a glimpse of Nina wearing the Isadora Duncan tartan scarf in the dense, swirling crowd on the Embankment during the night of the Millennium festivities – premature by a year of course – but she vanished or it was an illusion. She would by then be seventy-two. I did not mention this apparition to my wife, clinging to my arm against the frightening eddies of packed bodies on that rather desperate night – we were almost trampled to death at the entrance to Victoria tube station.

I thought I might find Nina at the art deco exhibition held at the V & A in the spring of 2003. Wherever she was living (if she was), how could she resist the journey to the heartland of her desire? – but I failed to find her and again the following year when the RA devoted a show to her idol, Lempicka. *The Times*'s excellent art critic damned Nina's favourite artist as 'a glossy queen of the shallow' whose current show would leave 'a bitter taste of ashes'. I suspected that Nina had sought refuge in Russia along with her precious 'Small Cowper' and Ivan of the gangster face.

And young Alisa – do you remember her? – I had not seen her again, not until several years had passed and I was at the Royal Academy in search of Nina. I spotted Alisa through the crowd – it surely must be her, Sergei's daughter whom I had so disgracefully fancied, she who had set her heart on working in London, now dressed by Jigsaw and gazing with obvious fascination at the vulgar icons of the Tamara de Lempicka retrospective. She was with Abe Kahnleiter, unmistakable in the wheelchair, a new neatly cut Ivy League minder in attendance.

When I crossed the crowded room to greet them, Abe displayed no surprise while Alisa, obviously shaken to encounter me, dropped her gaze and did not take my hand. Never shy about the ladders of life, Kahnleiter lost no time in informing me he was now working as foreign policy consultant to Condoleezza Rice in the George W. Bush administration. He was on the Russia desk 'feathering up Putin', but only part-time, still teaching at Harvard. Yes, he laughed, an obligatory retirement age is unconstitutional in the United States. The invasion of Iraq was taking place as we spoke, I had joined a march of a million against. I asked after his CAP. For a moment he seemed at a loss to identify the acronym until Ivy League bent to murmur in his ear, then Abe told me he had handed over publishing responsibilities to younger men.

'I've moved on. Pity you refused to sign up.'

I looked again at Alisa but she kept her eyes averted, taking small steps backward into the fashionable crowd. She wore beige Russell & Bromley shoes with a button-strap across the ankle, fetching beneath the black stockings and reminiscent (to me) of Nina.

'We're still waiting for that famous book of yours,' Kahnleiter said. 'I assume you discovered you were sailing up a creek straight on to the rocks.'

'Quite so.'

He hesitated a fraction. 'In that case perhaps you would be good enough to advise me where I can find a woman you have known well, Lady Stears, aka Nina Bolsharova. She's gone from Cheyne Walk since I last spoke to her, no trace.'

'Why do you want to find her?'

'OK, I'll be frank: to discover what she told you. She wouldn't say. We believe she's on the run and probably in need of false passports and visas. Uncle Sam can help, we can even grant her temporary asylum. You see, John, to be frank again, I don't believe for one minute that you have buried that project of yours...'

'I have.'

'We know about the late Lepinskaya – did she manage to tell you everything before she died? We also know about your visits to Paris to see her son, "the heirloom apparent" as we in the Agency call him.'

'Is he a candidate for rendition?'

'For what? We still reckon you're judging the moment to come up with something big which may not be to the advantage of the Vladimir Putin regime. Right now, with this war in Iraq, we'd like to have Vladimir onside – or at least not on the other side. That means doing him a few favours.'

'Like?'

'Like giving the Soviets, hell I mean the Russians, advance warning if you're about to expose their unscrupulous 1952 operation, *Operatsiya Dvoinik*. It may have been long ago but it still could hurt.'

'So you'd like to persuade Lady Stears to disown me, a long

quote for the Kremlin news agency – at the price of a few false passports and visas?'

Kahnleiter nodded. 'Something like that. You should have worked for MI6. Perhaps you do.'

'I'm still waiting for their first pay cheque.'

I was looking across at Alisa. She had drifted away from our exchange to study the paintings. She didn't want to talk to me. I asked Abe what she was doing nowadays.

Kahnleiter called to her through the crowd: 'Alisa, darling, come and talk to the man.'

42

So that might be the end of our story but not quite. I confess that my last meeting with Olga had been almost too painful to repeat. Now that she had reached her late seventies and was navigating her small sitting room by holding on to furniture (her stick usually hiding from her), almost everything she said to me was resentful or hostile. It was during this last visit that she declared that I was a *pécheur*, a sinner; she had always seen right through Monsieur, and for that reason she had wisely concocted some 'tall stories' on which I could 'hang yourself'. I did not inflame her further with denials. Closing her door behind me and walking away from Sivashskaya 12, kv. 10, Moscow 113149, I had felt wretched.

It was by way of an email from Svetlana that I learned of Olga's death on 3 August 1999, at the age of seventy-five. This message was not sent until after the cremation, nevertheless Svetlana contrived to denigrate 'the exposed character of a man who did not even bother to attend the last rites of a woman to whom he owed so much'. And she went on: 'Your visits pushed poor Olga into terminal depression. You made false promises to her. We all think you were too insistent, shall I say too greedy? But weep for yourself not for Olga. My Mitya says that the travails our country has experienced have been manna from heaven for our academic "friends" from the West. Mitya and I warn you that anything you choose to publish about Olga, your victim, we shall publicly denounce and disprove.'

So that made two potential injunctions.

When I flew again to Moscow in a vain search for Nina, my journey took me to Olga's little urn of ashes at the Andronikov monastery where the snow lay so thick that one could not believe it would ever thaw. Svetlana refused to receive me. According to Mishkin, the only other survivor from the old circle of curators,

Olga had turned to Christ at the end, who else was there? The cyrillic inscription said simply 'Olga Maksimovna Lepinskaya 1925-2002. Beloved wife of Pyotr Vladimorovich Davidov. Mother of Pablito Pablovich Picasso.'[†]

I could never shake off the suspicion that I had been the victim of a concerted disinformation campaign designed by ex-Soviet curators and archivists to discredit the Western researchers whose triumphant exposures and scoops had been celebrated in the foreign media with whoops and hoorays. Commerce and scholarship are now close kinsmen; stilettos and pistols lurk behind every corner of the market in fabricated history. Probably we get what we deserve. One cannot disguise the fact that great artists such as Picasso and Chaplin magnetize our attention for reasons far from creditable or simon-pure. Fame itself is both an aphrodisiac and a commodity – especially if it entails bringing the famous down to earth by revealing their vanity, their excesses or misfortunes in the bedroom, their ignoble jealousy of rivals, their cavalier attitude to repaying favours and debts. And the lies they tell.

~

Late in 2001, I received a letter from Pablito, a litany of complaints. For many years he had worked as a travelling salesman for a small firm selling Chantilly lace to Spain, where there was a large market for it – one thinks of the flourishing lace fans of flamenco dancers. He complained how badly remunerated he was, too much competition and the Spanish market becoming of late 'extremely difficult'.

His mother's estate had naturally bequeathed to him the Maar photographs from 1952 and of course Picasso's portrait of Olga. But Mamochka had 'for no good reason' appointed his old childhood friend Yuri Tairov as executor and Yuri had failed to send him the portrait. Yuri made excuses, Yuri cited export regulations. Pablito did not trust him or his mother Svetlana.

[†] Pablovich is of course the patronymic. It indicates 'son of Pablo'.

'How can I trust such people, Monsieur?' he wrote heavily underlined.

Yet, I reflected, Pablito had not even flown back to attend his own mother's funeral – something that Yuri had tactfully mentioned to me without comment. If Pablito had returned it would have been twenty-five years since he had last seen his mother's face, now lying in the open coffin as is the Russian custom. I asked myself what kind of a man he was with his large, luminous, strikingly unRussian eyes and his unhappy stomach around which the belt was never quite secure? Once a childhood chum of Yuri Tairov, Pablito made a rather depressing contrast to the stopwatch extrovert bustling into the big money via a succession of high-rise spectaculars from Frankfurt to Hong Kong. Pablito exuded a sort of perky lethargy. He was the man who runs for the bus only at the last moment, not when it turns the corner and first comes into view.

I could anticipate where this letter of his would lead. It would lead to my failure to produce an affidavit on his behalf. Without that, he would insist, his claim to the Picasso estate would remain hopeless.

'Of course I wrote to all his other children some time ago, very nice letters, *très sympathiques*, explaining who I am, my situation. A shared father after all.'

But his approaches had gone unanswered, apart from the occasional threatening reply from an *avocat du Tribunal*. So (he went on) Monsieur must do his moral duty to his mother and compose a detailed affidavit in pursuit of his inheritance.

'You know more than anyone, sir, [he used the English word] and forgive me for having looked up a few reference books, but your academic credentials are most impressive. You have been translated by Gallimard, Hachette and Laffont, you are respected in France, my mother told me so in one of her letters. My mother promised you would help me! She said you were a scholar of integrity.'

And further exhortations. I thought of replying but really did not want to put anything in writing. I had other things to do in Paris so I flew there and took Pablito to dinner at the Brasserie Lipp (he liked to dine in his father's old haunts, including the Catalan, if I was paying the bill). It was our first meeting since Olga's death.

Of course, if only for Olga's sake, though she was gone, I would have liked Pablito and his family to inherit a fortune. And justice, too, would have been served. But my book would not. Gradually, across the months, I had developed an answer and now, across the table, I more or less repeated it: 'Dear Pablito, imagine the Picasso estate hires the best *avocat* in town. Imagine him cross-examining me before the Tribunal. I know nothing other than what your mother told me – and she was what the law calls an "interested party", like you. And therefore I can tell the court nothing but "hearsay", as we call it in England. The *avocat* would no doubt imply that you and I have been in cahoots, *c'est-à-dire de mêche.*'

He was horribly disappointed, gulped more wine.

'Monsieur Pablito, *tu es surune fausse piste.* You're barking up the wrong tree. Listen again to our imagined *avocat* representing the Picasso estate: "The late Madame Maar," he points out, "is named as an intimate witness but where is her affidavit? In 1952 Olga Lepinskaya was already in a relationship with the artist Pyotr Davidov, was she not? She later married M. Davidov before the child was born, did she not? The boy was registered in Moscow as M. Davidov's son, was he not? There is no attested, independent evidence that the deceased Pablo Ruiz Picasso ever met Lepinskaya, am I not correct? No biography or newspaper report has ever mentioned such a meeting."'

Pablito nodded, chastened. 'So what tree should I "bark up", Monsieur?'

I saw more clearly than ever that I had to deter Pablito from the legal route to claim his inheritance. Any full and accurate affidavit I produced for the eyes of Picasso's children or grandchildren would soon be leaked – along with the fruits of my research – to *Le Figaro*, *L'Express*, the *Daily Telegraph* and the *New York Times*, though Harrison Salisbury had died in 1993 before I knew how important a witness he had been.[†] My eventual book would become stale news, hardly worth a publisher's penny.

So I reached into my briefcase and laid on the table a document I hoped he would find intimidating. 'If you go for the inheritance, Pablito, these are the hurdles you will have to surmount.'

HEIRS OF PABLO PICASSO (1881-1973)

Paulo Picasso (1921-1975), his son by his wife Olga Khokhlova (1891-1955) and the only legitimate child

Maya Widmaier-Picasso (1935-), his daughter by Marie Thérèse Walter

Claude Picasso (1947-), his son by Françoise Gilot

Paloma Picasso (1949-), his daughter by Gilot

Pablito Picasso (1949-1973), his grandson, son of Paulo

Marina Picasso (1950-), his granddaughter, daughter of Paulo

Bernard Ruiz-Picasso (1959-), his grandson, son of Paulo's second marriage

Pablito stared at the list, those large eyes drifting down it and up it again despondently. 'Some of these people I have never heard of,' he murmured.

I then brought up the subject of the thirteen Maar photographs – could I purchase copies from him for my book? After all, Yuri must have had passed them on to him (I didn't know).

His business eye sprang to life. 'How much would you pay, Sir?'

'How much are you asking?'

---

† And before I could ask Salisbury why his day-by-day memoirs of his Moscow assignment contained not a whisper of the Picasso-Chaplin escapade. The only viable explanation I had was Olga's – namely that his contrition about Pyotr was deepened when she was suspended from the Pushkin Museum and (maybe) when Nina vanished into the Lubyanka. Salisbury's memoirs came out at the end of the fifties, when Olga and Nina remained highly vulnerable to an American's memoir, and that honourable man knew it.

'I am not asking, Sir, you are asking.'

'I am only requesting copies, not the originals.'

'I am not a fool, Monsieur.' (Monsieur was evidently a step down from sir.) 'A first-class Xerox photocopy from a print is as good as a new print from the negative, which in any case we don't have. Xerox photocopies are what you require for your famous book, just as a copy of the Madonna portrait is what you want for the dust jacket.'

I was wondering just how much my eventual publisher would be prepared to contribute to the cost of these illustrations. In recent years publishers were increasingly expecting the author to shoulder the burden of 'permissions'.

'I fear, Monsieur Pablito, that whatever price I might offer, you will ask for more.'

'I fear, Monsieur, that whatever price you might be prepared to pay, you will offer less.'

This time he had seen the bus coming as it turned the corner. As I painfully signed the credit card slip for the dinner at the Brasserie Lipp, way beyond my means, I could have pushed him under the bus.

43

We have previously encountered Yuri Tairov, the son of Svetlana and Mitya, schoolfriend of Pablito, and a witness to the moment when Picasso's paternity (plus Mitya's Facts of Life demonstration) was revealed to Pablito. Now a successful architect, Tairov was coming to London for talks with Eric Fisher about a huge project, a proposed expansion and modernisation of the Pushkin Museum of Fine Arts at an estimated cost of 670 million dollars.[†] In the early summer of 2002, Yuri gave me a call from Moscow asking whether I remembered him, I did indeed, and he suggested I join him as local guide on a day-trip to one or two architectural gems in the counties within reach of London. Did I have a car and was I happy to be his chauffeur? And where did I suggest? Did I think Hatfield and Audley End could both be encompassed within one day? I said, 'Only if you're visiting, setting foot, not if you're really looking.'

'But which would you choose between them?'

I said Hatfield for grandeur and the old palace where Elizabeth was brought up in solitude, no father, no mother, no siblings. But perhaps Audley End for sheer beauty and intricate craftsmanship.

'Who was Elizabeth?'

So I picked him up from the Connaught in Carlos Place, Mayfair, at nine in the morning and we headed up the A1, reaching Audley End by 10.30. To stay at the Connaught you had to be rich. Yuri's English was more colloquial than his late father's, with hints of America, and his energy, success (and income) were in a different league from Mitya's. Yuri brought with him a huge camera bag, traces of Svetlana's unfavoured nose, and several layers of corpulence, probably fifteen stone and not obviously healthy. But he was an educated man of

---

† Fisher and Partners (pseudonym) later pulled out after long delays and disputes between Russian officials and conservationists.

conspicuous civility. On the way he talked a while about the Pushkin Museum extension project but then he brought his broad face across from the landscape and said he had important things to tell me – 'Important to me, important to you'. I pricked up my ears as they say.

'By the way, do you mind if I smoke a cheroot in the car?'

'Not at all.' (Is nicotine addiction inherited?)

'I expect you've bankrupted yourself dining Pablito in Picasso's favourite haunts,' Yuri said. 'Pablito wrote to my mother, Svetlana, complaining that you had refused to write him an affidavit to pursue his inheritance claims. I was sorry to hear that but of course you have your reasons.'

'I do.'

'The position is this. Pablito is the sole beneficiary of Auntie Olga's will. I am the executor – she asked me a year before she died and I agreed. My mother was ruled out by her age and in any case there was bad blood between them because of. Well...'

'Your father's pursuit of Olga?'

'If you know, you know. I was really Olga's obvious choice, a relative, still young, and a reliable figure.' Yuri laughed. 'My wife doesn't think so.' I advised Auntie Olga that her most valuable possession was the Picasso portrait and I might encounter obstacles to obtaining an Export License. In that case Pablito would have to sell it on the Russian market. I would certainly act on his behalf if he so wished. Olga put her hands on my shoulders and made me promise to help Pablito.

'"He may never come back to Russia," she whispered.'

'I promised.' Yuri told me.

I said hold on, I had to concentrate at the junction coming up. We were avoiding Saffron Walden and looking for Audley End.

'OK, got it. By the way, we are now in Essex.'

'Is that a big deal?'

'In modern terms a typical slice of middle England. But in yonder times a county of great houses beyond the reach of the London mob.'

I was slowing down, regardless of impatient traffic behind, the journeymen of Essex hurrying about their business.

'By the way, this was a Roman road. Now look over to your right.'

'My God, that's something!' His camera came out like a submarine raising its conning tower from the depths. We both gazed in awe across the parkland to the enchanting symmetry of the great white house, Audley End. I drove through the gate, reaching for my wallet, but Yuri scrambled to hurl £20 notes at me. 'Is that enough?' I handed him the change. Having paid, he felt he could take us back to his story.

'As soon as Olga died and the portrait came into my possession, I consulted Mishkin and contacted someone who works in the Musée Picasso.'

'Brigitte Arnoul?'

'The same. I sent her a return air ticket, promised to cover all expenses, and begged her to fly to Moscow to inspect "the newly discovered Picasso". She knew Mishkin and I got him to give her a call. Anyway, she came, she looked, she ran delicate, gloved fingers over the patina, and she asked me loads of questions. When and where had the portrait been painted? I showed her the Dora Maar photographs of the young Olga with Picasso in Moscow. Madame Arnoul could barely disguise her amazement, her professional excitement. She kept saying *"oui"*, *"d'accord"*, *"incroyable"*, *"je suis bouleversée"* – and all of that. Authentic? Yes – but she would need second and third opinions from experts in Paris. Value? No idea at all – ten to twenty million dollars.

'"But Picasso was never in Russia!" she exclaimed.

'My mother, who was imposingly present throughout the inspection, then told Arnoul she was quite right, the portrait had been done in Paris. Arnoul asked why St Basil's Cathedral was visible in the background. Svetlana said that proved nothing, it was probably purely symbolic – Russian girl, Russian setting.

'Then I risked my mother's displeasure by mentioning that the political history of the portrait was, well, rather complicated and

I was not at liberty to divulge much of it.'

We had found the car park now but for the moment Jacobean architecture seemed irrelevant.

'What was Brigitte Arnoul's response to that?'

'She said "*C'est toujours la question avec la Russie – s'agit-il de la Russie neuve ou de la Russie nouvelle?*" How would you translate that, professor?'

'In short, have things ever really changed in Russia?'

'For that I owe you dinner tonight. Well, now the story becomes for me even more difficult to tell. My mother Svetlana made it clear to me that the portrait must on no account leave Russia. Likewise the Dora Maar photographs, Olga's diaries and her correspondence. Svetlana remains adamant about that. Her logic is simple: if Pablito's inheritance ever reached France, then you would get hold of it. Yes, you. She claims that the book you intend to publish must be a fabrication. You had allowed your imagination to concoct a sensational story which wasn't true.'

'What we historians call a "counter-factual"?'

'Well, I don't suppose my mother had ever heard that term, though I think I have seen it out of the corner of my eye. We have quasi-fakes in architecture like that glass pyramid outside the Louvre, but not "counter-factuals". What does it mean?'

'You imagine a situation which did not take place. For example, if Kaiser William had died in July 1914 on the eve of the First World War. You then ask what would have happened, would the war have been avoided, if not why not?'

We sat in the car. I could not help looking out at the magnificence – this was what had so fascinated Mitya, the struggle against the classical.

Yuri wasn't looking out, not exactly. 'I understand about your "counter-factual". Svetlana was adamant that in 1952 Olga had travelled to France, hoping to bring Picasso back to Moscow for an exhibition of his work at the Pushkin Museum. Olga had not only met Picasso but become pregnant by him – but he never made the journey, partly because of his distrust of Kemenev, partly because of Kemenev's vacillations, partly because of Picasso's fear of flying. Svetlana insists that consequently the invitation to Chaplin was cancelled.'

'I don't believe that.'

'Svetlana is convinced that having met Olga, and heard her story, you began to say to yourself, "What if Picasso had come to Moscow, what if Chaplin had come, what would have happened after that?" So you set your "unscrupulous imagination" to work...on what you call a counter-factual.'

'But that is not what Olga told me across the years I was interviewing her. Nor is it what Nina Bolsharova has been telling me in London about Chaplin. Shall I quote to you what Pablito remembers your father telling him?'

'I'd be interested.'

'Something like this: "Picasso came here to Russia and your mother organised an exhibition of his paintings. She saw him every day and some nights and they had *seks* because he loved her as well. She was very beautiful, Pablito. Then he went back to France and she never heard from him again."'

Yuri pondered this. 'Don't take offence on Pablito's behalf, but doesn't he have a vested interest in that version?'

'Not particularly. If he was conceived in France by Picasso, as I am now certain was the case, his claim would still stand.'

'Sure – but harder to make stick.'

'Both Chaplin and Picasso did travel to Moscow.'

'I happen to agree! Don't mistake me.'

'Would I have kept coming back to these witnesses, Lepinskaya and Bolsharova, month after month, year after year, if they had no story to tell, merely to listen to my own imagination?'

Yuri looked out at the great palace but his gaze remained distracted.

'Before I get swept away by Flemish craftsmen and ogee turrets, let me just add this: I have more than once put precisely that point you make to Svetlana: why did the man keep coming back? "Oh," she says, "poor, lonely Olga with no one in her life

414

but Mitya who she despised, so she began to enjoy the Englishman's visits, she was flattered by his continued attention and his little bunches of flowers, such an intelligent man with so many books to his credit."'

'But you haven't answered my question, Yuri: what induced "the Englishman" to keep coming back if Olga had no story to tell beyond her abortive visit to Paris?

'Because – and I am only quoting my very old mother – because Olga enjoyed your visits so much that she began to make things up, she learned how to tell you what you wanted to hear.'

'Really? Prodigious powers of invention. Presumably the same bizarre miracle happened with Nina Bolsharova?'

'My mother won't talk about that.'

We were now walking up from the car park, passing loads of toddlers in prams and on skates, scooters and skateboards, others triumphantly perched up on Daddy's shoulders, all taking no notice of the bulky Russian wrestling with his cameras and lenses, zooming in, zooming out. I wandered back to him:

'Perhaps the main point about these prodigy homes of the late Elizabethans and the Jacobeans –'

Yuri cut in. 'I looked up Elizabeth by the way, brought up at Hatfield in isolation, as you said, until one fine day they came running to her in the Great Hall you mentioned, fell on their knees, and hailed her as the Protestant Queen.' He smiled. 'What's my score out of ten?'

'Nine. Elizabeth and Ivan *grozny* exchanged gifts. She sent him the gilded carriage your father must have taken you to see in the Kremlin Armoury Museum.'

'Aha, nine will do. When was this house built and what did it cost?'

'It was originally a Benedictine monastery dissolved by Henry VIII during the English Reformation and gifted to the Lord Chancellor, Sir Thomas Audley, in 1538. But at the beginning of the seventeenth century Thomas Howard Earl of Suffolk pulled it down and built a palace to receive his king and queen. You are looking at two grand entrances, one for the king, one for the queen, each having their own suite of rooms. But the king visited only once and in 1619 arrested Howard, his Lord Treasurer, for embezzlement of royal funds.'

'Do we know how much this pile cost?'

'They say £200,000 to build.'

'How much is that in modern money?'

'Today? Perhaps thirty million. But I think the main point is that the English aristocracy was no longer building fortified castles. The King's Peace had come to stay.'

'But you had your civil war soon after this house was built.'

'True but during the civil war the battlefields were no longer fortified castles. Feudalism had gone. When Cromwell ordered the partial destruction of the old castles it was symbolic.'

'Do we know the architect of Audley End?'

'Robert Lyminge. They were still called surveyors at that time. As a recognised profession, architecture got into its stride with Wren, Hawksmoor and Vanbrugh. Here you see the Flemings supplanting the Italians.' We entered the house through the king's door. Nice English Heritage staff pointed the way. We were in the hall, I was indicating the Flemish carvings on the great screen. Yuri took photographs then led me away from the crowd.

'But the point I am coming to is that while I was grinding through my duties as Olga's executor, writing scores of letters to Customs and the bloody Interdepartmental Council for Export and Import of Cultural Valuables, my mother was busy sabotaging my efforts by convincing her highly placed connections in the museum world that a valuable, previously unknown work by Picasso, painted in Russia and worth millions of dollars, must not be allowed to leave the sacred soil.'

'So – painted in Russia?'

'You've got it.'

As we mounted the great staircase I said that in my opinion what we were up against was Svetlana's protracted war with Olga, even unto death. 'It's all about your father's passion for

Olga.'

Yuri murmured that I might be right.

'By the way, this suite of rooms was designed by Robert Adam in the 1770s, much admired but not by me, all this classical affectation was completely alien to England, a sort Spanish flu.'

Having completed the tour, we were now taking a break in the café, always the main attraction in Heritage houses. Yuri sat, sighed, not interested in the cakes, longing for a smoke. He drained his coffee, wiped his mouth and asked the young waitress whether 'the restaurant' (as he called it) provided 'a space' for smoking a cigar. She said very sorry, only outside, sir, and hastened away.

'The whole European Union,' Yuri almost shouted, 'is now a prisoner of these lunatic laws. Where can one go? Not even to a pub!'

I led him outside, found a bench, and he lit up a huge Partagas, snipping off the end. You could feel his anger coming down like mercury in a thermometer.

'But I must tell you,' he sighed, 'that we are not going to get that export license.' He produced from his coat pocket a print-out of the Export regulations, the salient sections marked in the margin. The first page was headed: Customs information. Таможенная информация. Import and export of cultural valuables.[†]

'I expect the Pushkin Museum would be keen to buy the painting from Pablito for a derisory sum,' I said. 'After all,' I added with a touch of acidity, 'you yourself are involved in the Museum's large-scale expansion plans.'

'Think what you like, John, that painting would be too hot to handle – at least to display to the public. No one in Russia is ready to come clean about the events of 1952. You may be right about

---

[†] The existing procedure was established by the Russian Federation Law, 'Export and Import of Cultural Valuables' dated 15 April 1993. The list of cultural valuables subject to the Law is detailed in the Russia Ministry of Culture Order 844 Annex 1 dated 07 July 2001.

Svetlana's animosity towards Olga, but the operative truth as I see it is that both my parents turned against you when you sat in our living room – I was there, you may remember – and ridiculed Soviet curators for their pusillanimous and cowardly equivocations, their failure to bring the modernists up from the cellars. My parents thought you were urinating on them. They were livid and remained so.'

Dusk was descending as we drove back to London. I was dipping my headlights for oncoming traffic. A quiet had settled between us as happens when ageing men are physically weary and tired of argument. But then Yuri touched my knee: 'Perhaps I can tell you something which may comfort you.'

'May?'

'This is all about me but I assure you it's not an ego-trip. I was born in October 1951, a bit older than Pablito. We were never in the same class in school but became friends through our parents. I remember as a boy of maybe five being taken by my mother and father to the Picasso exhibition staged at the Pushkin Museum in 1956. I can still visualise the huge crowds and my fear of getting separated from my parents. Picasso had been invited to Moscow but he didn't come. I heard my parents talking about "Hungary" but I didn't understand. What I half-understood was my father Mitya saying Picasso hadn't come because of what he had suffered during his previous visit.'

We had reached the A1 and a swirl of traffic. 'Hold on,' I said. Perhaps Yuri thought I was a version of Lyndon Johnson's quip about Gerald Ford – can't walk and chew gum at the same time. But he talked on.

'During the years of my childhood Olga and Pyotr often visited us for supper, bringing Pablito. I was getting old enough to understand the conversation. My father would always say that the reason the Picasso-Chaplin visit of 1952 ended in disaster was...and off Mitya went into politics, factions, intrigue. I also remember Olga – how beautiful she was – recounting to my parents her fable-like visit with Pablo to the legendary garden of

Stalin's dacha, and how it turned out to be the actor Gelovani. I can remember Pyotr Davidov, who was never very coherent but who gave me paints and crayons and taught me quite a lot about colour, I remember him describing the scene in Cheremushki when Picasso and Dora Maar visited the dissident artists, and I remember my friend Pablito saying, "Papa, not that story again!", at which Olga laughed affectionately though Pyotr was always very solemn and intense.'

We had reached the dual carriageway, the northern outskirts of London, the younger drivers weaving their cars like Formula I Ferraris – those brats should have to take a test every year.

'It's a pity,' I said, 'that you were only a year old when Olga brought Picasso to visit Svetlana and Mitya. Picasso probably picked you up in his arms and made a funny face, and you probably cried out in terror.'

Yuri stared at me, astonished. 'Who told you that?'

'Nobody. It's just one of my "counter-factuals".' (And it was – Olga had never even hinted to me that she had brought Picasso to visit the Tairovs.)

'But it's true!' Yuri exclaimed. 'Your uncanny intuition! When I was small and wouldn't go to bed on time, or go to sleep, Svetlana would threaten me with "Ugly Uncle Picasso": "He'll come here again and pick you up and shake you and make rude faces at you".' Yuri laughed heartily. 'One day when I was in my early teens and fooling around with Pablito at his place, I made a hideous face and said I was Ugly Uncle Picasso. Auntie Olga placed both her hands on my face, she was quite tall for a Russian woman of that era, and she told me that when "Ugly Uncle Picasso" had picked me up in my infant cot and made faces at me, I had laughed with pleasure and shouted out "More! *Boleye!*" She said, "You cried, Yuri, only when the lovely funny Uncle Pablo was led away". She said that she had cried, too, when he was taken away from her.'

'Can I quote you on that? It's incomparable evidence.'

'Not while my mother is alive – sorry.'

419

'Yuri, what I most need is a good photographic colour print of the Madonna portrait, the perfect cover for my book.'

'With or without Pablito's permission?'

'You as executor of the estate could grant it.'

'No, I couldn't.'

'Did you not give a colour print of the portrait to Brigitte Arnoul?'

'No – even though she asked for one. It was a bad moment.'

'I also badly need copies of the thirteen Maar photographs.'

'I'm afraid we're back to Pablito. They are now in his possession.'

～

Having slept off a gargantuan dinner with Yuri, I rang Paris and spoke to Brigitte Arnoul of the Picasso Museum. I had known her since she and I took part in a discussion on France-Culture about Picasso's relationship to the French Communist Party, in particular his strangely formalised, indeed artificial painting, *Massacre in Korea* (oil on plywood), which depicts a group of naked women being shot down by a phalanx of semi-medieval robotic janissaries. The debt to Goya's *3rd May* is obvious but not much else. The painting had been acquired by the Musée Picasso and Brigitte (or so I felt) had been at the France-Culture microphone to defend it.

I brought our conversation round to the Madonna portrait.

'Say no more!' she responded, 'I have seen it! The executor of Madame Lepinskaya's estate, a Monsieur Tairov, flew me to Moscow at his own expense. He and his mother showed me the portrait in the Moscow bank where it is held. *'C'est parfait, Pablo amoureux d'une jeune femme russe, une belle demoiselle séduisante, Pablo à la manière de Raphael à la manière de Pablo, une oeuvre géniale.'*

'Authentic?'

'I think so! Mind you, not typical of his output in the early fifties – and I would have to consult colleagues if only we can bring the painting to France.'

'Value?'

'Who can say? I would guess five to ten million dollars on the open market.' Had she been given a photographic print of the portrait?

'Well of course I made that request but I haven't received it. Somewhat to my annoyance, they wouldn't let me organize my own print in Moscow. Monsieur Tairov indicated that there were political difficulties, indeed machinations, but he was reluctant to go into details.'

'Monsieur Tairov also possesses thirteen photographs taken by Dora Maar, shots of Picasso with the beautiful young Olga Lepinskaya.'

'Taken where?'

'In Moscow.'

'Impossible! Pablo never set foot in Russia! He almost went in 1956 but, you know, the Hungarian affair...'

'So where do you imagine he painted his "Raphael" of Lepinskaya?'

'Oh, without doubt here in Paris. Madame Svetlana Tairova told me in strict confidence how the young Russian curator visited the studio in the rue des Grands Augustins and how Pablo fell for her. It was explained to me that the Pushkin Museum had hoped he would visit Moscow but for various reasons it didn't come off and he never met the girl again.'

'Tell me, if the Musée Picasso made an offer for the portrait to its legal owner Pablito Davidov, would that help to expedite Russian permission for the export of the painting?'

'But we can't do that until it's properly authenticated. Frankly, I rather suspect that the Pushkin Museum people would like to acquire it for themselves. Tell me, please, do you believe Picasso was the father of this Monsieur Pablito Davidov?'

'Beyond doubt.'

'Am I being *l'imbécile*, would not this make your friend a potential heir to the Picasso estate?'

'It might.'

'And if a settlement was made, I mean a grant from the estate to Monsieur Davidov, might that not include some of the works now held here in the Musée Picasso?'

I had not thought of that – the Musée did not want more heirs.

'Brigitte, I think you should meet Pablito himself. Perhaps I can arrange a dinner.'

She had cooled into an ebb-tide. 'You probably know that this museum is closing soon for renovation, it may take years and it will cost more money than we have. All donations are welcome. I wish you luck.'

44

One day in the summer of 2006, when the world had dissolved into the Internet, a letter arrived carrying the usual smudged impress M* sk* a (reminding me of the illuminated sign at Sheremetyevo which had greeted Picasso and Chaplin). Written by hand in Russian on mauve notepaper but with no indication of the sender's address, the letter caused my heart to thump. I felt like a despairing fiancé in the trenches receiving a long overdue letter from his beloved – then, as he tore at the envelope with a mud-caked hand, coiling into himself as he braced for an impending confession about some other man whose hands were not coated in slime.

Nina was now seventy-eight. Her letter was exuberantly littered with English phrases, real or imagined. Why had I suspected that she could neither read nor write?

My poor, dear Oxford, (it began) do you remember me? So sad and sorry your Nina is to have deserted you. Believe me or not – and did you ever truly-truly-truly believe me about anything? – I had no choice but to vanish. It is time to tell you that Henry's letter to you all those years ago was my idea, undertaken by Henry most reluctantly. 'It goes against the grain,' he said, but I was insistent and you know how I always have my way with men. I fled to Canada, then to Tokyo where I met up with Kolakowski (who had been cheating me all along can you believe it!) and finally I settled in Moscow, the only city where I feel truly at home, truly myself. We now have so many wealthy people here, the new billionaires with huge mansions to decorate with Imagined Art. But enough of that. I am approaching eighty now but still on my feet. I am tempted to enclose a recent photograph of myself in conversation with President Putin at a reception in the Manezh, but I fear your disapproval, you were always so censorious but I was rather fond of you and can you believe this I rather enjoyed shocking you. Mr Putin is by the way very nice unless he thinks you want his job. Should I 'have a go, Joe'? Who should I meet at Putin's gaudy reception but a man in a wheelchair who said he had been searching for me all over the world. He said he worked for the US State Department in his spare time and very much – very, very – needed to know what I had told you about *Operatsiya Dvoinik*. You might gather that the entire future of the world depended on it. I said well go and ask John. Wheelchair said you wouldn't divulge anything without my permission. So I said I wouldn't divulge without yours. I'm afraid I cannot invite you to come and see me, dear Oxford, because I find that I must now close the door on an episode which turned into more of a nightmare than a sheltered Oxford man could ever imagine. (Oh those dreaming towers or is it spires.) Perhaps you know that dear Olga 'passed away' a few years ago. Svetlana Tairova told me Olga was at the end suffering from dementia and could not remember anything. Svetlana says you met Olga's son in Paris and refused to support his claims to his huge inheritance. Is that true? I cannot believe it of you, but I'm afraid you have to regard Svetlana as an enemy, I'm not sure why. I think little Pablito could claim a fortune in France if he got hold of the right lawyer. In case you wonder what became of Sir Henry, I can tell you that he is currently managing a game reserve in Zimbabwe where he extracts a percentage from the poachers supplying the trade in elephant tusks and rhino horns. The Chinese highly value them as an aphrodisiac but does China really need more erections? Is it too much to hope that you still remember me fondly, dear Oxford? I shall never forget our dinner in All Souls. Of course you are now an elderly gentleman yourself but friends tell me that you continue to publish GREAT WORKS. Give my greetings to your wife, I regret never having met her and never having accepted your invitation to watch the Boat Race from the Hammersmith towpath. Don't Wait for Me, dear Oxford. Ever your fond friend Nina Bolsharova

P.S. You may wonder about my man Ivan, who you clearly

liked no more than he favoured you. He likes to remember how he booted you out into Cheyne Walk after our last goodbye, I'm sorry about that, I hope no lasting damage except to your very considerable self-esteem. Ivan is still with me, but now confined to a wheelchair following a bad shoot-out with some evil mafiosi demanding protection money on our trade in home-grown ersatz Mercedes, a good car, good price, very art deco, very popular. Ivan has been a true Russian husband to me, the only one since poor Sergei.

P.P.S. I forgot! How is your book coming along? I'm sorry the Kolakowski fake of Picasso's Olga Madonna had to be sold. That awful American Kahnleiter paid me above the market price, don't be cross, I do mean a lot of dollars. Shall I speak my mind? I thought it frankly unforgiveable that you planned to put Olga on the cover of your book, though you never asked for even a photograph of myself. If you had been minimally switched on, do I mean compos mentis, you would have kept that horrid little secret to yourself. By the way, at death's door (when the truth does come tumbling out, doesn't it?), Olga confessed to Svetlana that her 'little? small?' Cowper was done by the gifted Pyotr Davidov as a wedding present.

∿

I did not see Pablito – should I say poor Pablito? – again although I received another letter complaining that he was now without employment (he said he had been falsely accused of embezzlement), with a family to support, and entreating me to change my mind and provide him with a full affidavit. He also offered to sell me copies of the Maar photos for ten thousand dollars – but he would make a gift of them if I provided a comprehensive affidavit of 5,000 words to prove his right of inheritance.

Some months later I received from Pablito's wife a black-rimmed card surmounted by a crucifix: Pablito had died of a heart attack and was now resting in peace. The funeral had been at the Paroisse St Jean-Baptiste, 1 rue de l'Église, Neuilly-sur-Seine. The widow took the occasion to write on the back of the card that it had been Pablito's last wish that 'the picture should remain in the family', likewise 'the other things'.

And that was more or less the end of it. I heard that Ivan died during a shoot-out in Hong Kong, Nina herself within an hour of hearing the news, at the age of eighty. I had to wait three more years, until 2011, to receive the happy news from Yuri that the supreme liar of recent times, his mother Svetlana Tairova, died in considerable pain after breaking her hip in a fall. Or let's say I lay in wait in the garden of her nursing home at Yaroslavl and kicked her crutches from under her, then rolled her screaming into a waterlogged ditch where she would not be found until Russian foxes had made free meal of her decomposing body. So I am at last free to publish without risk of harassment. The witnesses of 1952 have all gone – regrettably Yuri too, felled in 2013 by the heart attack I had seen coming during the immense meal (four-courses, three bottles and several vodkas) he ate in the Connaught after our long-ago trip to Audley End. With him went his precious childhood memories of Ugly Uncle Picasso. Myself approaching eighty now, I shall no doubt follow soon enough and now feel free, indeed compelled, to disburden this story before I do.

What happened to the Picasso Madonna? And the thirteen Maar photos? Who knows? But I believe the reader has by now enough evidence to judge the credibility of this narrative – history, after all, is not fiction unless it is.

As I turn out the bedside light, I often find myself standing outside Sivashskaya 12, kv. 10, Moscow 113149. I wait devotedly, perhaps devoutly, holding in one hand my briefcase and in the other a small spray of flowers from the local market – but the elderly lady no longer comes to the door before I fall asleep. At my age, of course, sleep may attract the attention of death.

Author's Note

I would like to mention a few books that the reader interested in this passage of history may find particularly illuminating:

Faubion Bowers, *Entertainment in Russia* (1959)

Mary Ann Caws, *Dora Maar. With and Without Picasso: a biography* (2000)

Lydia Chukovskaya, *The Deserted House*, trans. by Alison B. Werth (1967); *Going Under*, trans. by Peter M. Weston (1972)

Françoise Gilot (with Carleton Lake), *Life with Picasso* (1965)

Boris Pasternak, *Doctor Zhivago*, trans. by Max Hayward & Manya Harari, (1959)

Harrison E. Salisbury, *Stalin's Russia and After* (1955); US edition, *An American in Russia* (1955)

Michael Scammell, *Solzhenitsyn: a biography* (1984)

Dmitry Shostakovich, *Testimony: Memoirs as Related to Solomon Volkov* (1979)

Aleksandr (Alexander) Solzhenitysn, *The First Circle*, trans. by Henry Carlisle and Olga Carlisle (1986); *The Oak and the Calf*, trans. by Harry Willets (1975)

Gertje R. Utley, *Picasso: the Communist Years* (2000)